MIRAGE

MIRAGE

An Anonymous Novel

Translated by Patrick Hanan

THE CHINESE UNIVERSITY OF HONG KONG PRESS

NEW YORK REVIEW BOOKS

Calligrams
Series editor: Eliot Weinberger
Series designer: Leslie Miller

Mirage
An Anonymous Novel
Translated by Patrick Hanan

Library of Congress Cataloging-in-Publication Data

Yulinglaoren, active 18th century author.
    [Shen lou zhi quan zhuan. English]
    Mirage : an anonymous novel / translated by Patrick Hanan.
        pages cm. -- (Calligrams)
    ISBN 978-9629966621 (pbk.) -- ISBN 978-9629968410 (ebook)
    I. Hanan, Patrick, translator. II. Title.
    PL2735.L55S4513 2016
    895.13'48--dc23
                            2015024014

Published by:

The Chinese University Press
The Chinese University of Hong Kong
Sha Tin, N.T., Hong Kong
www.chineseupress.com

New York Review Books
435 Hudson Street, New York, NY 10014, U.S.A.
www.nyrb.com

Printed in Hong Kong
10 9 8 7 6 5 4 3 2 1

Contents

Introduction   vii

I.   Riches arouse the superintendent's interest
Connections lead to the traders' release   1

II.   Li Jiangshan intercedes in a difficult dispute
Su Wankui withdraws at the height of his career   22

III.   Suxin bemoans her fate as a beauty
Jishi searches for sex in the night   40

IV.   In Break-Cassia Studio a pair of lovers open accounts
At the Double Ninth festival the class visits Mt. Yuexiu   59

V.   Matchmaking causes two birds to lose their feathers
Flirtation leads to one sister's falling in love   80

VI.   Heh Zhifu installs mistresses in a separate wing
Li Jiangshan comes upon a hero in Qujiang county   98

VII.   An ambitious river police chief plays along
A humiliated customs official hangs himself   119

VIII.   Shen Jin is restored to office by imperial grace
Su Wankui dies on hearing of a robbery   138

IX.   In burning old deeds a son carries out his father's wishes
By faking a prayer a priest engages in a lascivious act   161

X.   Lü Youkui forms an alliance at an inn
Yao Huowu is thrown into jail in Haifeng   179

XI.   Feng Gang catches a tiger on Goat's Foot Ridge
Ho Wu Kills an ox at Phoenix Tail River   200

XII.   Hearing of his brother's death, a prisoner breaks
out of jail
Taking advantage of a visit, an abbot gains a gem   218

XIII.   Emerging from reclusion, he reviews commanders
         A bandit for the present, he is awarded high rank   237

XIV.   Faced with a cruel husband, she bites her tongue and
           endures her shame
         Meeting an artful woman, he hopes for sex but gets
           feces instead   258

XV.   Three scoundrels set a trap
         Four beauties disappear   277

XVI.   Reunion, as Qiao rejoins her lord
         Justice, as Shangguan punishes scoundrels   297

XVII.   Wu Biyuan lays his complaint before the censor
         Su Jishi flees to Qingyuan to escape danger   320

XVIII.   Vice-president Yuan impounds Heh's possessions
         Governor-general Hu withdraws to Huizhou   342

XIX.   A girl suffers a tragic fate at New Year's
         An in-law embarks on a literary career   362

XX.   Yao Huowu rebuffs Mola
         Wen Chuncai outdoes Bian Ruyu   380

XXI.   A friend's letter leads a hero to submit
         A year's leave allows a censor to marry   398

XXII.   After receiving high office, a civil official joins the army
         While taking defensive measures, a demon
           practices magic   417

XXIII.   Commander Yao triumphs in a single night
         Iron Mouth Lei reads faces and predicts lives   432

XXIV.   His womenfolk compose beautiful lines
         His brothers sing a song of court delight   449

Notes   463

Introduction

The Story of the Stone (Shitou ji 石頭記), also known as *The Dream of the Red Chamber* (Honglou meng 紅樓夢), was the first novel to open up the subject of adolescence for the Chinese reader. In 1804, twelve years after the first edition of *The Stone*, a novel called *Mirage* (Shenlou zhi 屬樓志) appeared and set about exploring that subject in a somewhat different direction.

Mirage is set not in the capital but in the southeastern province of Guangdong, and largely in the city of Guangzhou itself—in fact, it is a regional novel. Its hero is not the scion of a great official family with imperial connections; instead, he is the son of one of those men, known as Hong merchants, who were licensed to deal with foreign traders in the port of Guangzhou (Canton). (*Mirage* is the earliest novel by far to treat the subject of the China trade; it was written several decades before the Opium Wars and well before opium was even a factor in the trade.) The hero's father is the long-time head of the Hong merchants' association, and he is extremely wealthy, partly from his trading, but also from his landholding and money-lending interests. When the novel opens, the hero, Su Jishi 蘇吉士 , is thirteen, attending class at a neighbor's house, and obsessed with amorous, and particularly sexual, desire. He is still only fourteen when his father dies and he has to take over the vast family properties. He follows the classic examples of philanthropy—forgiving the debts of hard-pressed tenants and distributing his grain reserves at a modest price in a time of drought—but he continues to philander, ending up at the age of seventeen with four concubines in addition to his wife.[1] He escapes, if only narrowly, certain of the dangers that beset the rich but naïve young man, and he learns how to conduct himself prudently in the adult world. Largely by good fortune, he is instrumental in ending a local rebellion, and gains thereby a measure of fame. In the course of the novel he has a number of mentors, notably Li Jiangshan 李匠山, his tutor at the school he attends. At seventeen, having somewhat tamed his libido, Jishi settles down to a private life with his family in Guangzhou. He is actually only one out of a number of youths who appear in the novel, several of whom succeed in different ways, but he is by far the most important. *Mirage* is principally a *bildungsroman*, the story of a youth's growing up and making his way in the world.

For reasons of prudence, perhaps, the novel is set in the Ming dynasty, but it is actually closely tied to two crises that took place just before the time of writing, in the years from 1799 to 1802. One was the two-year tenure (1799–1801) as Customs superintendent in Guangzhou of a Manchu named Jishan 佶山; the other was a series of rebellions that broke out in 1802 in the neighboring prefecture of Huizhou, rebellions that at one point threatened even the security of Guangzhou itself. The novel juxtaposes two worlds, the realistic social and political world of Guangzhou and the highly romanticized world of the Huizhou rebellion.

The position of licensed trader was potentially lucrative but frequently ruinous. The trader had to contend with a Customs superintendent whose objective was to make as much money for his masters in Beijing—and himself—as he could. In the eighteenth and early nineteenth centuries there is ample evidence in the records of the East India Company of a more or less constant conflict between the superintendents and the traders.[2] It was not an equal conflict; the superintendents had the traders in their power, for traders needed their permission even to resign. In this novel's brilliant opening Su Jishi's father suffers the ultimate indignity at the hands of the superintendent, but still manages by an ingenious ploy to withdraw from his appointment.

As scholars have long recognized, Superintendent Jishan appears in the novel as the corrupt and lascivious Heh Guangda 赫廣大 . But although readers of the novel were clearly meant to make that connection, the portrait of Heh Guangda has been put together from various sources, including, presumably, the author's imagination. A similar partial connection exists between Pan Youdu 潘有度 (1755–1820), the actual head of the merchants' association at the time, and Jishi's father. I believe that a further connection can be drawn between the governor-general, a Manchu named Jiqing 吉慶 , and Qing Xi 慶喜 , the governor-general in the novel. Both men, the historical and the fictional, were opposed to the way the Customs superintendent dealt with the traders. Like his fictional counterpart, Jiqing was an experienced provincial administrator who advocated a dual approach to rebels, offering them a negotiated surrender while at the same time threatening them with liquidation.[3] Qing Xi is introduced with uncharacteristic praise in the novel as "a true bulwark of the nation, a living Buddha to the common man, one who combined wisdom with gallantry and possessed all the civil and military talents." It is he who sets up the system of paying local braves (xiangyong 鄉勇) to serve as militiamen and defend their villages against the pirate raiders afflicting the south coast. But whereas the fictional governor-general triumphs, Jiqing, the historical figure, ended as a tragic failure, committing suicide when blamed for his handling of the rebellions in Huizhou prefecture.[4] A contemporary local reader of the novel would surely have seen its idealistic portrait of Qing Xi as an attempt to repair Jiqing's reputation, just as he would have drawn the other connections I have mentioned (and possibly more).

Parallel to the main thread of the novel runs the story of the rebellion in Huizhou prefecture. It is led by Yao Huowu 姚霍武, whose brother, an army officer, has been unjustly executed, and it is staffed by former militiamen who have been cheated out of their dues by corrupt officials.[5] The connection between the two plots, which alternate like the scenes of a southern play, is that Yao Huowu, when desperately poor, has been given generous help by both Jishi's father and his tutor, Li Jiangshan. If the story of Jishi in Guangzhou owes something to *The Story of the Stone*, that of Yao Huowu and his band in Huizhou prefecture owes more to the novel *Shuihu zhuan* 水滸傳 (*The Outlaws of the Marsh*).[6] Yao's band are the traditional physical heroes of Chinese fiction, men distinguished by their prodigious strength, their gargantuan appetites for meat and spirits, their lack of interest in sex, and their fierce loyalty and unsparing vengefulness.

The historical rebellions in Huizhou prefecture, which were led by the Tiandihui 天地會, a secret society,[7] were quite different from the rebellion in the novel. But there are some telling correspondences between their locations; for example, one rebel lair, Army Gate Ridge 軍門嶺, appears in both the novel and historical accounts, while another, Goat's Foot Ridge 羊蹄嶺, recalls the Goat Dung Ridge 羊屎嶺 of the historical rebellion. In each case the governor-general negotiates the surrender of the rebels, but whereas Qing Xi received high praise for the achievement, Jiqing was harshly criticized for being either too severe or too lenient.

Mirage is a strikingly original work, but its connections to *The Stone* and *The Outlaws of the Marsh* are many and varied. As an example of the subtler kind in *The Stone*, let me note the drinking party in chapter 14, in which Wu Daiyun 烏岱雲 seems to play the part of the oafish Xue Pan 薛蟠 in chapter 28 of *The Stone*. We might dismiss this as a mere generic likeness—until we look at the songs that Xue Pan and Wu Daiyun are forcing their young girl singers to sing: one song is actually a development of the other. Although Su Jishi remains a landlord and moneylender, his heart is not in the world of business. Already by the age of thirteen he has begun to question his father's devotion to making money. Like his father, he seeks to ally the family through marriage with scholars, not scholars from powerful and wealthy families, but supremely gifted youths likely to succeed in the civil service. Toward the end of the book, Jishi reflects that if he had the talent for it he would have become a scholar (and official) himself. But he then decides that if he could live a contented family life and enjoy himself drinking wine and writing poetry with his womenfolk each day, he would not change places with the highest in the land.[8] The dominant values in the novel are those articulated by the scholar and teacher Li Jiangshan, whose broadly Confucian values exert a great influence on Su Jishi's father as well as on Yao Huowu, the leader of the rebellion. Perpetually unsuccessful in the civil service examinations, constantly "sewing garments for other people's weddings," Li Jiangshan composes two key poems, both of them elegiac, that are given in chapter 4; the first poem describes the view over the rooftops and walls of Guangzhou to the foreign ships lying at anchor, while the second retraces the early history of the region as an independent kingdom. Since the book contains a good deal of classroom material, it is not surprising that scholars have suggested that there is something of the author himself in the figure of Li Jiangshan the teacher.

The author is known only by his pseudonym, Yuling Laoren 庾嶺勞人, the Heavy-Hearted Man of Yuling (Yuling is on the Guangdong–Jiangxi border). The editing is credited to Yushan Laoren 禺山老人, the Old Man of Mount Yu (possibly Guangzhou).[9] The fact that we do not know the author's name is hardly surprising.

Unless Chinese authors were presenting their novels as history, they generally published under pseudonyms, and in many cases their real names have never been discovered.

Although Mirage is set entirely in Guangdong province, it was first published in Changshu, Jiangsu. Furthermore, the Mandarin in which it is written contains a number of Wu-dialect expressions, enough to support the assumption that the author was from Jiangsu or Zhejiang.[10] On the other hand, the preface, by the Layman of Mount Luofu 羅浮居士 (in Guangdong), asserts that the author "was born and brought up in Guangdong" and hence had a detailed knowledge of the local scene, while the author's own pseudonym refers to Yuling, which is on the Guangdong border. We can only assume that, if the author was a native of Guangdong, he must have spent a good deal of his life outside the province.

The word "mirage" in a novel's title is usually a claim that the work is fiction or fantasy. Perhaps it is intended here as a superficial denial of the close connection between the novel and contemporary history.

My translation is based on the 1804 edition. I have used the Shanghai guji chubanshe edition of 1996, which is based on that edition, and also the 1804 edition itself in the possession of the Peking University Library. (Note that most of the available modern editions tend to amplify the erotic description here and there with lubricious clichés. The original work uses relatively plain language for sexual description, occasionally embellished with comic images drawn from the classics.) My translation omits the poems introducing chapters 2 to 23 because they do little more than expound the meaning of the chapter headings. The other two poems, those introducing chapters 1 and 24, are about the author and his work.

I have used the pinyin system of transliteration except in the case of certain surnames. There happen to be two different surnames (何, 赫) in the novel that would appear as "He" in pinyin, and three more (施, 時, 史) that would appear as "Shi." To differentiate, I have turned to other romanization systems as well as to pinyin, resulting in the names Heh and Ho; Shy, Shr, and Shi.

     ★   ★   ★

I am grateful to the friends and relatives who offered to help with the manuscript of my translation during a period in the spring and summer when I suffered an incapacitating illness. I am also indebted, as ever, to the staff of the Harvard-Yenching Library, particularly to the Librarian, Mr. James Cheng, and the Librarian for the Chinese Collection, Mr. Xiaohe Ma, for helping me obtain copies of rare texts. My greatest debt of gratitude is to my editor, Dr. Yanni Yang of The Chinese University Press. She kindly took the trouble to recheck my manuscript against the original. Thanks to her knowledge and perceptiveness, this translation is significantly more accurate than it would otherwise have been.

Patrick Hanan
Cambridge, Mass.
November 24, 2013

Chapter I

Riches arouse the superintendent's interest
Connections lead to the traders' release

◦≋◦

Out at elbows am I, my spirits low;
I'm like some pheasant wandering lake and plain
Whose pride insists it has the strength to stay
When on tired wings it should fly back again.

Spring's at its ebb, the western sun departs—
An endless stretch of cloud, the waters still.
I'll take this brilliant, luckless brush of mine
And shatter the desires that bind our will.

The frog at the bottom of the well sees nothing of the heavens, just as the mayfly in the height of summer cannot conceive of winter's ice—those with limited vision will always suffer from their lack of knowledge. The naked tribes deride our silken garments as gaudy, just as the ugly neighbor once scorned the classic beauty for her artful smile[1]—those with shame in their hearts will always display envy in their faces. The world is so vast and the span of history so huge that all manner of weird and wonderful things must either exist or have once existed. In the case of the sexual relations that are carried on night and day in the privacy of people's homes, they number in the untold billions, but our self-styled moralists have routinely fulminated against them. The centuries from Han through Song teem with cases of wrongdoing, but those who seek to cover up such things have regularly deleted all mention of them. Think of the exchanges of gifts in the "Airs of the States" section of the *Poetry Classic*—what harm did such little gnats ever do to the rule of the sage kings? Why, then, have the moralists kept their lips sealed, gaining a reputation as men of virtue while depriving later generations of reliable knowledge?

The foreign trade of Guangdong province is carried on outside the Taiping Gate of the city of Guangzhou. The goods are brought there in the foreign devils' ships and then, after the customs duties have been declared by the Chinese traders, they are sold to merchants from all over the country. For central Guangdong it is big business. A certain Su Wankui, style Zhancun, was a smooth-talking businessman of exceptional ability who headed the traders' association—and made himself extremely rich. His wife, Mistress Mao, had no children of her own; his only son, Su Fang, style Jishi, childhood name Xiaoguan, who was now thirteen years old, was born of a concubine, Mistress Hua, while his two daughters, Pearl and Belle, neither of whom was yet engaged, were the children of a second concubine, Mistress Hu. Su Wankui himself, now in his fifties, had bought himself an official rank at the fifth level. Whole rooms in his house were stacked high with silver dollars, and when it became necessary to spend money, it would be carried out by the sackful.

However, Su Wankui was also a shrewd operator whose business transactions were planned with great finesse. He would offer heavily discounted loans at 30 percent interest over a five-month period, insisting on real estate or commercial goods as collateral. As a result, although many brokers held him in warm, fraternal regard, there were a goodly number of local people who cursed his very name. The gentleman himself, however, had enjoyed a thirty-year run of luck and was not in the least perturbed.

He was doing business one day in the association headquarters when a notice was handed to him by Wu Fu, one of his servants. He studied it carefully:

> Proclamation by Order of Superintendent Heh of the Guangdong Customs[2]
>
> With regard to the trade passing through Customs, merchants from the interior flock to this port and foreign ships arrive here in great numbers. The trade was established, firstly, to raise taxes for the nation and, secondly, to enhance the people's livelihood. How is it, then, that Su Wankui and other traders are depriving the nation in order to enrich themselves, deceiving the officials and engaging in corrupt practices? They manipulate the price of commodities by exploiting the fact that no one understands the foreign devils' language. Calculating that merchants from the interior do not stay here very long, they deliberately raise difficulties for them in doing business. In addition, they underreport the duties they owe and depreciate our money against the foreign currency, with the entire surplus going into their own pockets. Now that the Customs Department has confirmed these charges, you traders will find it hard to escape the consequences of your crimes. But to punish you without prior warning would, I fear, violate the principle of cherishing life. If you can see your way to reforming yourselves, I hope that you will begin the process of redemption forthwith. Let each of you have a change of heart. Just see that you do not leave it until it is too late.
>
> By Special Order

Staggered by the proclamation, Su Wankui at first thought he should try offering a bribe. However, the superintendent quickly followed up his proclamation by sending Zheng Zhong and Li Xin from his staff to arrest the traders and detain them in the orderly room of the Customs offices. They had now been held there for two whole days.

All of them were men of some standing in the community. When greeting high provincial officials, they were accustomed merely to drop to one knee and then stand with their hands at their sides. On crucial occasions, the great men might even invite them to stay for tea or dinner. Local officials such as prefects, subprefects, deputy prefects, district magistrates and the like, treated them with the utmost courtesy for the sake of their dollars. On this occasion, however, the traders found themselves detained in the orderly room. While their plight could hardly be compared to that of common criminals, they were nonetheless being treated like officials accused of a crime.

Looks passed between them as they wondered what the superintendent might have in store for them. "The fact that His Honor has had us detained certainly does not bode well," opined a certain Sheng Boshi.

"That notice was awfully harsh," volunteered another trader named Li Hanchen. "We'll need to ask someone to do us a tremendous favor."

"I have a relative who prepares memorials in the governor's office," put in Pock-marked Pan. "What if we got him to plead with the governor to intercede?"

Everyone was in favor of this idea except Su Wankui. "This Superintendent Heh has only just arrived here and hasn't yet established any sort of rapport with the governor," he said, "so the latter could hardly ask him for a favor. In my humble opinion Master Heh will surely be open to a bribe, and we ought to go straight to the money without making any detours."

"What makes you think he'll take a bribe?" asked the others.

"That proclamation the other day spoke about 'beginning the process of redemption.' What that means is that we shall need to spend some money in order to redeem ourselves."

"How very perceptive of you! But if we do need to offer a bribe, I imagine it will run into the tens of thousands. What's more, we'll have to find some suitable person to handle the deal."

"I understand that he spent money to wangle this superintendent's position. I doubt very much that even tens of thousands will be enough to settle the matter."

"Well, at least we have the General Fund,"[3] said other merchants. "Don't forget that."

Let us now turn to Superintendent Heh Guangda, style Zhifu. He was about thirty years old and six feet tall, with a great love of money and an equal appetite for wine and women. His wife, Mistress Huang, was the second daughter of Ming Zong, vice-president of the Board of Works. In addition, he had a dozen concubines, who had provided him so far with eight daughters but no sons. Attracted by the wealth and splendor of Guangdong, he had actively sought out the post of Customs superintendent and then brought his family south with him. On this occasion he had detained the traders in the expectation that they would try to curry favor with him, but when the third day came and they had still made no approach, he called in his chief of staff, Bao Jincai.

"You know what I have in mind, I presume," he said.

"I do indeed, but these merchants have been so pampered by previous superintendents that they've become a little confused. Let's drop a hint or two. If they don't see reason, we'll just have to resort to tougher measures."

"Yes, do that."

Bao withdrew to the porters' lodge, where he called his page, Du Chong, to his side: "Get over to the orderly room and announce that those traders are going to be tried at the evening session today, then see what they have to say." Du Chong went off to carry out his instructions.

In the main hall a number of runners asked Du Chong where he was going. He surprised them by saying "I don't need an escort. I'm going somewhere on my own."

In the orderly room the traders were bemoaning their fate when a good-looking youth wearing a gown with narrow lapels and short sleeves walked in from the Customs offices. As one man they rose to welcome him. "What directions do you have for us, young master?" they asked.

But Du Chong completely ignored them and addressed himself to the orderlies: "His Honor wants you to bring the traders over to stand trial this evening. You'll have to see to it that they're there on time." The men acknowledged the order. Du Chong was turning slowly around when a man wearing an official's cap came forward and took his hand.

"Would you care to step outside for a little talk, my good man?" he asked.

Du Chong glanced at him. "And who might you be, sir?" he asked. "I need to report back to His Honor so that he can get on with his breakfast. I don't have time to sit and chat."

From his manner of speaking, Su Wankui gathered that he was a page. Taking out the foreign pocket watch that he was wearing, he consulted it and said, "As I understand it, His Honor doesn't breakfast until nine. There's still plenty of time."

At sight of the watch, Du Chong remarked, "May I take a look at that?" When Su Wankui handed it to him, he fondled it lovingly.

> Shaped like a goose's egg,
> Divided inside into a dozen figures,
> Covered outside with fine glass,
> Suited to all the year's seasons,

Exquisitely edged with a jade border,
Charmingly linked to a gold chain—
An exquisite Western product
Sure to make a young fellow drool.

Now, people from the capital have a common failing—they talk a great game, but their interests are really very narrowly focused. At sight of this article, Du Chong couldn't stop praising it. "It keeps good time," said Su Wankui promptly. "If you won't be offended, I'd like to make you a present of it."

Du Chong shot him a sidelong glance. "May I ask your name, sir?" he asked with a smile.

"My surname is Su. But you've still not favored me with your name."

"My name is Du. But Master Su, this is only the first time we've met. It wouldn't be right to receive such a favor from you."

"This? This is *nothing!* My colleagues and I will be depending on you in so many ways. Let me invite you outside for a little chat." This time Du Chong went with him, to a vacant room in the shrine of the God of Wealth, where both men sat down.

"The other day when His Honor arrived to take up office, everything was done according to precedent," said Su Wankui, "but for some reason that I still don't understand we've offended him, and now he's keeping us locked up in the orderly room. I wish you'd tell us why. Your compensation won't be neglected, I can assure you of that."

"I'm none too clear myself," said Du Chong. "Yesterday His Honor came out from his residence and told several gentlemen that he had spent too much money getting this position. Now every creditor has a man sitting on his doorstep demanding repayment, and he has to find some way to raise the money. By the look of things, this move must have been designed to raise some funds."

"The foreign trade is not what it was," remarked Su Wankui. "Could you tell Master Bao that we'll contribute a full fifty thousand, not including the compensation for yourself and him?" He bowed.

Du Chong grasped his hand. "You're such a good man, Master Su. No one is more concerned to help than I am, but that sum just won't do, I'm afraid. I'll report back to you after I've seen him." He bowed and left.

Returning to the orderly room, Su Wankui addressed the other traders, "It looks as if this affair shouldn't be too hard to settle. We'll be rather hard pressed to find the money, though."

"We're indebted to you for seeing this opening. But if a good deal of money is required, we'd better get ourselves a draft without delay."

"Let's wait for their reply first. There'll be time enough afterward to get a draft." He sent Ye Xing over to the pawnbroker's in front of the Customs compound to borrow fifty silver dollars.

As Du Chong stepped inside, he found Bao Jincai playing cards with the runners. At a sign from the youth, Bao strolled over to a side room and stood there. "I went to the orderly room and relayed your message, sir," reported Du Chong. "Those traders were well and truly scared. There was a man named Su who pleaded with me again and again, saying he was willing to offer money. When I asked him how much, he said fifty thousand, excluding your compensation."

"Tell him to stop daydreaming," said Bao. "When this case goes to trial, every last one of them will get a beating as well as a sentence of exile. *Fifty thousand!* How naïve can they get? Take no notice of them." He went off to the inner quarters.

Du Chong hurried back to the orderly room, where he whispered to Su Wankui, "It didn't work. My master says that you're all going to be found guilty and sentenced to exile as well as a beating, and that the fifty thousand wouldn't even be enough for him, let alone for His Honor. And now I'd better say goodbye."

Su Wankui quickly took thirty dollars from his sleeve and handed them to him. "This is a mere trifle. Use it to buy yourself some fruit. But do continue to help us!"

"But I haven't done anything for you! Why do I deserve a reward?"

"When it's all settled, we'll reward you further."

Du Chong pocketed the money, musing as he walked away: No wonder people want to work for the superintendent! I've made a small fortune right out of the blue. The only trouble is that I'll need to do something for Master Su. With these thoughts running through his mind, he arrived in the anteroom.

Bao Jincai was sitting on a couch, and Du Chong came in and bowed. "I have a request I'd like to make, sir: that you tell these traders to increase their offer and then do your best to get the detention order rescinded."

Bai Jincai looked him in the eye. "His Honor's really furious. You'd better go and find out if he's free."

Du Chong walked quietly over to a side room off the great hall and then turned into the western library, where he found some runners lounging about outside the door. "Is His Honor in the library?" he asked with a chuckle. Du Chong was an extremely attractive youth, sixteen or seventeen years old, who was Bao Jincai's pretty boy, and since no one else had ever defiled him, these men had dubbed him One Cock Du.

When he asked about the superintendent, a runner named Bu Liang sidled up to him and gave him a hug. "One Cock, my boy, His Honor was calling for you just now."

"His Honor never *calls* for me."

"Ren Ding's at work in the library, but he's been at it for ages, and he still hasn't managed to bring him off, so His Honor wants you to take over."

Du Chong laughed. "Stop the kidding. When they're done in there, let me know, will you, so that I can tell Master Bao?"

Bu Liang was about to go on harassing him when the others intervened. "Better not mess with him, or you'll make old Bao jealous." Du Chong slipped away.

Let us turn to the superintendent, who that afternoon had drunk some liquor and sampled some fresh lichees in his concubine Pinwa's room. Stimulated by the wine, he had indulged himself with her before strolling over to the western library, where Ren Ding came up and offered him tea. The superintendent noted that the boy was from Hangzhou and just thirteen years of age, and that he was rather good-looking. He told him to shut the library door, then climb onto the couch and massage his legs. Ren Ding took up the massage mallet and, squatting on the couch, began tapping his master's legs with blows alternately soft and hard. The superintendent's passions were still inflamed by the liquor, and all of a sudden his member reared up. He told the boy to strip off his clothes. Ren Ding knew well enough what was expected of him, but he wished to please his master. "Oh, I couldn't do *that*," he simpered, covering his mouth with his hand.

"You'll be all right." The superintendent pulled down the boy's silken trousers and told him to turn over. Ren Ding gritted his teeth and let his master have his way with him, but afterward, as he got down from the couch, he gave a cry of dismay and almost fell over. "I'm all torn inside, and it hurts terribly," he cried in a pathetic tone.

"Never mind," said the superintendent. "You'll be all right in no time."

Ren Ding stood up by supporting himself on the table, then managed to open the door, and taking the imported gold-plated brass basin with him, walked along the portico. The men outside all made faces at him. Flushed and swaying unsteadily, he walked out and called on the waiter to bring some hot water for him to deliver to the superintendent. He also brought in an imported cloth towel from the railing.

After washing his hands, the superintendent took a seat on the couch, and Bu Liang called Bao Jincai in to give his report. "Well, how did it go?" he asked.

"Those traders are truly naïve," replied Bao. "They're offering *fifty thousand* for their release! To clear up the debt, I think we need to give those people from the capital between three and four hundred thousand. Anyway, the traders get their money from swindling the foreign devils, and it would not be going too far to demand that they pay a bit more. But we'll need to give them a good scare before they'll be ready to deal."

"Quite right. I'll hold the trial this evening." Bao Jincai bowed and withdrew.

Du Chong had positioned himself outside the window and had heard the entire conversation. He quickly pulled out the brush and paper that he carried with him and wrote a private message that he gave someone to deliver. Before long Bao arrived in the anteroom, and Du Chong helped him off with his outer clothes. Taking a seat, Bao summoned the head orderly on duty and told him, "His Honor will try the traders this evening." The orderly went off to transmit the order.

Meanwhile Su Wankui and the other traders had received Du

Chong's message and were at a complete loss as to what to do. "The General Fund comes to only a little over a hundred thousand. From what they say, we gather they want two or three times that amount. How are we going to raise it?"

At this point Zheng Zhong and Li Xin came in and announced, "The trial is set for this evening."

"I'm afraid we'll have to take another loss," said Su Wankui. "We're relying on good friends like you two to look out for us."

"With us here, you can set your mind at rest," said Zheng Zhong.

Su Wankui heaved a sigh. "In all the years that superintendents have been dealing with us, this is the most humiliating thing we've ever had to face!"

"I expect you'll have to spend a little more time on your knees, but you definitely won't be ill-treated," said Li Xin.

As they spoke, they heard the sound of bugles and drums, and a number of men swarmed into the room. The traders nervously straightened their clothes and followed the men into the vestibule of the courtroom, where they stood waiting. How can one describe the grandeur of that courtroom?

> Twin flagpoles with the words "Guangdong Customs" on
>   banners that float aloft;
> Between decorated halberds sit a pair of lions formed of
>   white jade;
> On the railings hang notices: "Silence in the Court,"
> "Unauthorized Persons Subject to Arrest."
> On the main door are signs: "Apprehend Tax Evaders,"
> "Punish Late Payment of Taxes."
> The great hall towers up, surrounded by lofty chambers
>   like floating clouds;

In a heated chamber, hidden deep, a red silk streamer flies;
Three times the booming cannon sounds,
As from the darkness the superintendent is carried forth.

To the accompaniment of a chorus of shouts from his attendants, Heh ascended the tribunal and ordered the traders to be led in, at which point a messenger entered with a visiting card and announced, "His Honor Shen of the Guangzhou Grain Bureau has come to visit you, sir. His chair had already passed through the outer gate."

The superintendent glanced at the card. "I see my teacher's come to visit me," he said. He told his servants to take Master Shen aside and open up the gate to his private quarters. By the time the superintendent had made his way slowly down from his heated chamber, Shen had stepped out of his sedan chair at the inner gate. The superintendent stood just outside the residence, while Shen hurried forward and bowed. Returning the bow, the superintendent said, "So kind of you to come and see me again!"

"I should have paid my respects to you the day before yesterday. I hope you'll excuse the delay."

"I'm still very much a novice, you know." As they spoke, they walked into the western library. It was a good two hours before the superintendent showed Shen out again and extended an invitation for the following day. Shen accepted, then stepped into his sedan chair just outside the main hall, and departed.

Readers, let us explain. Heh held a hereditary rank, and although the head of the Guangzhou Grain Bureau was not a subordinate of his, their two offices differed vastly in prestige. Moreover, the superintendent had an overbearing nature and thought all the provincial officials beneath his notice. Why, then, was he so modest in speaking to Shen? Because Shen, whose full name was Shen Jin, style Xiangxuan, and who came from Songjiang in Jiangnan, had been a teacher in the capital, and for three years Heh had studied with him. Shen had later succeeded in the metropolitan examination and been selected for the Hanlin Academy. Meanwhile, by means of his hereditary privilege, Heh was appointed to the Imperial Bodyguard and continued to treat his teacher with the utmost deference. Shen fell out of favor with the premier and in the next official review was ordered to a position in the provinces. He was sent first to a hardship post in malaria-ridden Si'en prefecture in Guangxi province, then promoted to be military intendant of Shanzhou and Ruzhou in Henan province. Later, because of a mistake he made, he was demoted by the board. By rights he ought to have been demoted merely to sub-prefect, but once more the premier lodged an accusation with his department, and instead of serving in a high official post, he was appointed an assistant sub-prefect. On this occasion he was paying a visit to the superintendent as an old friend encountered far from home.

After seeing off his guest, the superintendent returned to the courtroom and ordered the traders brought in. To the accompaniment of a shout of compliance from the guards, the traders answered their names and knelt down. In the past, when meeting superintendents, they had always knelt down and kowtowed three times before standing up again. On this occasion, as suspected criminals, they kowtowed three times and then remained on their knees, not daring to get up.

"How many of you are there in this business?" asked the superintendent.

"There are thirteen of us altogether," said Su Wankui. "My name is Su, and I'm the head of the association."

"I find that you have all been evading taxes and abusing merchants. Are you telling me that those charges are false?"

"Taxes are assessed and paid according to the established rule on all imports, which are then sold off wholesale at set prices. We traders would never dare to permit the slightest irregularity."

The superintendent gave a cynical smile. "I'm well aware of your enormous personal wealth. If it doesn't come from playing the foreigners for fools, from swindling the merchants, or from evading taxes, where does it come from?"

"I've been handling foreign imports for seventeen years now, and all my transactions have been entered in printed ledgers, which are available for your inspection. I certainly don't possess enormous wealth. I would request that Your Honor be gracious enough to examine the ledgers."

The superintendent rapped with his gavel. "A smooth-talking rogue, if ever there was one! Those findings of the Customs are irrefutable, and yet you want to contest them? Strike his face!"

The guards on either side shouted their assent, and four or five of them stepped forward and prepared to start. A frantic Su Wankui cried out, "I hold official rank! I beg Your Honor to grant me a favor."

"What do I care about your rank?" roared the superintendent. "Come on, hit him in earnest!" The guards set to work from each side, dutifully presenting him with twenty blows to the face, while Su Wankui's colleagues pleaded for mercy.

"I'm punishing him alone, as head of your association. But if you people are too foolish, I'll take harsh action against *all* of you!" He gave orders that they be taken as a group to the Nanhai county prison and dealt with severely. He also cursed Zheng Zhong and Li Xin, "These suspects ought to have been put in chains. You two scoundrels have been bought off—that's unconscionable." He threw down three tallies, and the two men were each rewarded with fifteen strokes of the number 1 rod. Before withdrawing, he ordered two other men, Ru Hu and Bi Jia, to escort the traders.

The traders were taken out and brought back to the orderly room, where they were greeted by their sons and nephews. For his part, Su Wankui felt too humiliated to say anything. Ru Hu and Bi Jia came in with a number of chains. "Gentlemen," they said, "we don't want to insult you, but you heard what His Honor said. We have no choice but to offend you. One day we'll call on you and offer our humble apologies." The traders were terrified.

Before long Song Renyuan from Heh's library and Lü Dexin, one of his messengers, came in and said to the guards, "We underlings weren't fooled by His Honor's order. Why would you want to bring all this trouble on yourselves?"

"What happened to Zheng and Li was a warning to us," said Ru Hu. "If the leadership ever got to hear of it, do you suppose for one moment that we'd escape a beating with the number 1 rod?" Much as Song and Lü tried to dissuade them, it was only after the traders had parted with three hundred dollars that the guards finally took responsibility for ignoring the chains.

"We can't let Zheng and Li suffer unjustly on our account," said Su Wankui. "Let's send someone over with a couple of hundred to cheer them up."

"There's something else we have to consider," said the other traders. "Surely we're not going to let him send us to Nanhai jail?"

"This show he's putting on is designed solely to get more money out of us," said Su Wankui. "The only problem is that he wants too much."

"Together with the General Fund our houses could put up two hundred thousand. If you were to add something to that, could the matter be settled, do you think?"

"I'm going to go bankrupt, anyway," said Su Wankui. "And once this is over I'm getting out of the business for good. If you gentlemen will put up two hundred thousand, I'll make up the difference. The only problem is that so far no one has come out to talk to us. Do you have anything to suggest, my good man?" he asked, turning to Song Renyuan.

"Whatever goes on in there, Master Bao's the one in charge. Let me take a message. I feel obliged to try and do something for you. How much should I offer?"

"I don't think there's any point in offering too little. We're thinking in terms of three hundred thousand, excluding staff gratuities and a present for yourself."

"Let's not talk about a present for me," said Song as he left.

Let us turn now to Su Wankui's son Jishi,⁴ a strikingly handsome youth with a gentle disposition. At the age of twelve, on the strength of his father's standing as a trader, he had entered the official school, but his father, fearing that the boy might embarrass himself in the annual examination, had engaged a private tutor. In the residence of the salt merchant Wen on Provincial Administrative Commission Rear Street, Jishi had been studying together with three other boys: Yinzhi, the son of Shen Jin, head of the Guangzhou Grain Bureau, Daiyun, the son of Wu Biyuan, head of the River Police, and Wen Chuncai, the salt merchant's own son.

Su Wankui now called Jishi to his side. "I'm going to lose money over this, but I don't think it's anything too serious. Go back now and get on with your studies."

The son whispered in his father's ear. "Wait until Song comes out again and then promise him the money, no matter how much it is. I only hope this doesn't come to anything." His father nodded. Some of the traders asked the boy what texts he had been studying, while others asked whether he was engaged or not.

It was almost dusk. "Go back to school now," said his father. "I'm afraid the gates will be closing soon."

"It doesn't matter about the gates. I'm quite happy spending the night here."

As they were talking, Song Renyuan came up.

"How did things go?" asked the traders.

"I went in and told Master Bao all about it. 'To be frank,' he said, 'we need five hundred thousand for the leadership plus a hundred thousand for the rest of us. Anything that falls even slightly short of that won't do. Tell them to go and think it over in Nanhai jail.' He was so firm about it that there was nothing I could do."

This information left his audience stunned. Jishi broke in: "Father, promise them the five hundred thousand! I'll think of some way of raising it. Your life is the important thing."

"Don't talk such rubbish!" snapped Sun Wankui. "You surely don't think we'll be *killed* if we're taken to Nanhai?" Jishi didn't dare say another word. Song Renyuan left the room.

"Now that things have come to this stage, Brother Su," said the other traders, "we can only trust to fate."

Then Du Chong arrived and pulled Su Wankui aside. "Could I have a word with you?" he asked. Su Wankui took him to a small room on the western side of the building. "Sir, I've received some very generous gifts from you and not managed to do anything in return, so I seized this chance to sneak over here," he said. "The leadership has never had a definite figure in mind—it's Master Bao who's behind all of this. I've thought of someone who could get through to the leadership, but I don't know whether you'd be able to work with him."

"Who's that?" Su Wankui asked eagerly.

"That grain director Shen who was here today. He's the master's teacher, and the master is very close to him and will do anything he says. If you can find someone to plead your case with Master Shen, three hundred thousand should definitely be enough to settle. Master Shen will be coming back for a drinking party tomorrow, and he has only to mention the sum for my master to agree. Give Master Bao a thousand or more, and that'll be the end of it."

"I'm *most* grateful to you for the advice. I'll certainly do as you suggest."

"In that case, the sooner, the better," said Du as he left.

As Su Wankui emerged from the room, the other merchants asked, "What did he have to say this time?"

"He has our interests at heart, and he's been thinking what he can do for us. It looks to me as if the case can very likely be settled, but at this point I don't want to reveal what I have in mind." Calling Jishi to his side, he whispered, "Hurry back to your school and ask the teacher if he'd go out to the grain bureau the first thing tomorrow morning and appeal to Master Shen to take this on. After you've done that, return home and get a draft for three hundred thousand, then go with your teacher and hand it to Master Shen and ask him to deliver it. I'll personally see that he's well rewarded for his help." Jishi promised to do so.

Jishi's teacher was Li Guodong, style Jiangshan, a distinguished scholar from Jiangsu province. Because he greatly enjoyed the natural scenery of the south, he had extended his travels as far as Guangdong, where his reputation so impressed Wen, the salt merchant, that he invited him to teach his son, Chuncai. Then, when Jiangshan's uncle, Shen Jin, was demoted and sent to Guangzhou to direct the grain bureau, he wanted to have his son taught, too. Jiangshan couldn't bear to spurn the salt merchant's kind invitation, so he agreed to teach Shen's son as well as Chuncai in the Wen family school. Master Wen treated the teacher with fully as much respect as did Su Wankui, and Jiangshan had remained in Guangzhou for three years.

After Jishi had left the city to visit his father, Jiangshan initiated a free-ranging discussion by lamplight with his students about the character of various historical figures. With Wu Daiyun the discussion went in one ear and out the other, and as for Wen Chuncai, he was already fast asleep. Shen Yinzhi was the only one who kept nodding his head as he absorbed the teacher's information. Jiangshan came to the anecdote about Chen Wannian of the Former Han dynasty, who fell ill and then, after calling in his son, Chen Xian, proceeded to teach him at his bedside. He went on talking until midnight, by which time the boy had dropped off to sleep. When his head fell back and hit the screen, his father was on the point of giving him a beating: "You fell asleep while your father was trying to teach you something!" he cried. The son kowtowed and replied, "I know everything you said. The gist of it was that you want me to flatter the people in power." Jiangshan's comment on the anecdote was, "Chen Wannian was ill, and it was nighttime, but he was indeed faulted by Bing Ji for being too much of a flatterer. On the other hand, the son, Chen Xian, himself came to grief in the end because of his stubbornness. For officials serving at court the hardest thing is to steer a middle course. At the same time they mustn't try to follow Hu Guang's 'middle way'!"[5]

In the midst of his comments Wen Chuncai suddenly cried out, "*Oh, no!* Sis caught a butterfly this morning, and I tied it to the screen, but just now I saw it fly away."

"Nonsense!" said Jiangshan. "Go off to bed." He also told Wu Daiyun to go to bed. To Shen Yinzhi he remarked, "Young Wen really did dream of a butterfly, which goes to show that that story in the *Zhuang Zi* wasn't just fable, after all." They both laughed.

Suddenly the classroom page called out, "Master Su is back." Jishi came in and bowed.

"Why did you come back so late?" asked Jiangshan.

"My father has a favor to ask of you, sir, and he told me to come back tonight." Asked what the favor was, he replied, "Master Shen is Master Heh's teacher. We were told by someone from inside the Customs that the only sure way to settle the matter would be to have Master Shen talk to the superintendent. If I may be so bold, sir, let me beg you to go and see Master Shen early tomorrow morning. My father will provide you with a generous reward." After finishing his plea, he dropped to his knees.

"Now tell me the whole story from beginning to end," said Jiangshan, pulling the boy to his feet. Jishi told in detail how the superintendent needed money, how his father had been punished, and how someone in the Customs had given them information.

"You're perfectly right. Your father *has* suffered an injustice, and for his sake of course I shall go there in the morning. Now, off to bed with you."

If you are wondering what approach Jiangshan will take in trying to persuade Master Shen, please turn to the next chapter.

Chapter II
Li Jiangshan intercedes in a difficult dispute
Su Wankui withdraws at the height of his career

The Guangzhou Grain Bureau was situated outside Guide Gate beside the governor-general's yamen. Although Shen had been demoted from the rank of intendant, he was not one to neglect his duties, being assiduous about such official matters as bandit suppression, salt supervision, maritime defense, and water conservation. In his spare time he relaxed with wine and poetry. His residence was always full of distinguished friends, and the meetings of the poetry society were regularly held there, meetings that Jiangshan frequently attended.

On this particular morning Shen left his office early, and after visiting the offices of the governor-general, the governor, the lieutenant-governor, and the judicial commissioner, arrived at the office of the salt comptroller, with whom he discussed arms manufacture and shipbuilding. By the time he got back to his own office, it was about nine, and Jiangshan and his companions had already been waiting there for some time.

Shen came to the rear quarters, where Jiangshan brought forward Shen's son Yinzhi as well as Su Jishi to greet him.

"You're all here together, and so early, too!" exclaimed Shen.

"We needed to ask a favor of you, Uncle, and that meant we had to come early," said Jiangshan.

"But you *never* ask favors of anyone!"

"Ah, but this time I'm merely sewing the garments for someone else's wedding."[1]

Shen laughed. "Are you playing the advocate for an official or for a private individual?"

Jiangshan laughed. "In my case, it's for a private individual, but what we are asking you to do is play the advocate with an official." Pointing at Jishi, he added, "You're acquainted with Su Wankui, this boy's father. From the time of Superintendent Heh's arrival here, he's been insisting that Master Su and his fellow traders pay for the loans that he took out in the capital, and yesterday he insulted them. As a gesture of good faith, the traders are now willing to offer him three hundred thousand taels, and since you're an old friend of Master Heh's, I've been requested to ask you to intercede for them. It occurs to me that mediating disputes is also one of the obligations of a gentleman."

As he finished speaking, Jishi dropped to his knees and began kowtowing. "My father's in danger, sir, and I hope you'll save him. We'd be eternally grateful."

Shen pulled him to his feet. "Do sit down. Since your father's in difficulty, of course I'll do my best to help. But neither your teacher nor I are the sort of people who look for any reward. The millions of dollars the traders possess don't mean a thing to us."

"As a man of integrity, Uncle, of course you would never touch a penny of anyone else's money," said Jiangshan. "Personally, however, I intend to ask him for a bottle of imported liquor to banish the autumn blues."

"In that case, I deserve to share in the bounty."

Jiangshan told Jishi to hand over the draft for three hundred thousand. "He's invited me to dinner today," said Shen, "and I'll bring this up with him." Again Jishi kowtowed in gratitude. Jiangshan then told Jishi to go back, while he and Yinzhi went in to greet Shen's wife. Afterwards he spent some time chatting with Shen's aides.

On leaving the grain bureau, Jishi told the bearers to take him to the Customs compound, where he confided the news to his father before going on into the city. Along the way he began to reflect: My father never gives a thought to his own happiness, he just devotes himself to this foreign trade in order to make money. He lost over a hundred thousand today—I can't imagine how painful that must have been! The truth is, he puts far too much emphasis on money. Outside of the business itself there are many people who are against him. But what ought he to do, I wonder? Then Jishi's thoughts took a different turn: I shouldn't worry too much about any of this. I think I'll make the most of my teacher's absence by going over to the women's quarters and having a bit of fun with Miss Wen. It'll be a relief after all this stress.

With these thoughts running through his mind, he arrived at the gate, where he left the sedan chair and went to the schoolroom. Wen Chuncai and Wu Daiyun were away on a trip to Mt. Yuexiu, and Jishi said to his servant, Su Bang, "Go over to the Customs compound and find out how the master's getting on, then report back to me." He also sent his page, Aqing, home to tell the womenfolk not to worry. Having dispatched them both, he took off his jacket and cap and put on a jade-green, pearl-studded gown of fine silk and, leaving the schoolroom by the back door, passed by the West Studio and entered the garden.

It was early in the fifth month. There was green foliage overhead and red pomegranate flowers that dazzled the eye, but he paid no attention to the scene around him and went straight to Pity-the-Flowers Lodge, where he noticed a young maid with a few jasmine flowers in her hands. "Master Su," she called out, "did you bring those pearls the young mistress asked you to have strung?"

"Is she inside?"

"The elder one's downstairs. The younger one is playing cards in Third Lady's room."

Let us explain that Merchant Wen, whose given name was Zhongweng, came from Shaoxing in Zhejiang province. His wife, Mistress Shi, had borne a son, Chuncai, while his first concubine, Mistress Xiao, and his second concubine, Mistress Ren, had borne daughters named Suxin and Huiruo, respectively. Pity-the-Flowers Lodge, with three rooms, was where the girls slept, and from the age of ten or eleven Jishi had been accustomed to visiting them there. Master Wen and his wife meant to betroth their second daughter to Jishi, but because she was still very young they had not yet arranged the betrothal and hence had not placed the lodge off limits to him.

Suxin was fourteen and well educated. She admired Jishi's looks, and hearing that her parents intended to betroth her sister to him, she felt rather envious and would often flirt with him herself. Young as he was, Jishi was well acquainted with sexual desire, but his teacher kept such strict discipline that he was unable to visit her very often for a tête-à-tête.

Arriving at the lodge on this occasion, he found Suxin sprawled across her dressing table half asleep. After motioning to her maid, he sneaked up behind Suxin and, twiddling a thread that he had plucked from a towel, tickled her nose with it. She sneezed, gave a yawn, and stretched her slender form backward, which brought her left hand into contact with his face. "Stop playing games, Sis," she said. "Let me get some sleep."

Jishi brought his head forward. "This is your brother here, not your sister."

She blushed. "When did you come in?"

"Oh, a long time ago."

"He's only just arrived," said the maid.

Suxin invited him to take a seat. "How is it you have time to come over here today?"

"I went out of town with the teacher and came back before him. I felt awfully thirsty, so I've called in for some tea."

"You mean to say you couldn't find tea anywhere else and you just had to come over here for it?"

"I like the tea better here."

She told the maid to make him some. "It's all the same tea. What's the difference?" she asked with a smile.

"Everything of yours is better. Let me drink this half cup while I wait."

"But I've already drunk from it!"

She shot out a hand to snatch the cup from him, but Jishi had already gulped the tea down. "You may have drunk from it, but it has a slight taste of lipstick."

"Oh, you're just too naughty for words! Are you going to keep on saying these things when you grow up?"

"When I grow up, that's when I can *really* play around!"

"The other day I heard that your father was arranging a marriage for you. Do you still want to play around with us?"

"Oh, I don't hold with that at all. I only want to marry someone like you."

"Don't talk such nonsense, or I'll smack you!"

Jishi came closer to her and put his cheek against hers. "Come on, you can smack me anywhere you like!"

"I don't think your face could stand it. I shall let you off."

He clutched her hand and held it against his face. "I don't mind. I actually *want* you to smack me with hands that are as white as lotus stems and as soft as cotton floss." He stretched out his left hand and slipped it inside her right sleeve. In the hot summer weather she was wearing nothing but a wide-sleeved silk gown, and his hand had no sooner entered the sleeve than it began to fondle a smooth, firm little breast.

She shrank from his touch. "That's so childish! You're more of a pest than ever!"

He dropped his hand, but put his arm around her shoulders. "Dearest girl," he said, "let's play around over there!"

"Stop the joking. Someone's coming."

He set his cheek against hers and was about to slip his tongue into her mouth when the maid came in with the tea. Suxin hastily pushed him upright and asked the maid, "What took you so long?"

"Everyone's in Third Lady's room playing cards. This tea is freshly made."

"Didn't Madam ask any questions?" asked Suxin.

"She asked who the tea was for, and I told her Master Su had come in from the garden and wanted some. She said, 'That boy is playing truant over here again instead of getting on with his studies. Tell him to come up and sit with us. There's something I want to ask him about.'"

"You can come back again after you've seen her," Suxin said to Jishi.

"I don't want to go. Once she gets me to sit down, I'll be stuck there all day." To the maid he said, "Go back, and when you see that Madam has finished playing cards, I'll go up there myself." The maid went off.

Jishi approached Suxin again. "My dear girl, 'blossoms grow from that clever tongue of yours.' Let me taste them where they're sweetest." He made as if to put his body alongside hers.

Much as Suxin loved him, she was afraid someone might come in and catch them. "You can't do that, I'm afraid." Taking his hand, she cried, "I'll go up there with you. If your teacher's still not back, perhaps we could meet again this evening for a little chat."

He pleaded with her again and again, wanting to kiss her, and she did allow him to hold her tongue in his mouth and try sucking it. He also put his hand on her breasts and fondled them tenderly for some time. If granted his own foolish desire, he would even have extended his hand down below her navel, but there was no way she would let him do that. Up they went to the main house, hand in hand.

Now that he's stolen a taste of her tea,
He would scorn the elixir of life.

Let us turn to Mistress Ren, Merchant Wen's second concubine, who was Huiruo's mother. The women were all in her room playing cards.

Mistress Shi had lost several silver dollars, and she was just about to be dealt a new hand when she saw Jishi coming in with Suxin. Greeting her as "Aunt," he bowed. "Young master," Mistress Shi said, "there's no need for that sort of formality with us. Come over here and bring me a change of luck." The two concubines both welcomed him, but Mistress Shi pulled him over to sit beside Mistress Xiao.

At this point Huiruo rose to her feet and begged to be excused: "I'm feeling rather tired and don't want to play anymore." Mistress Shi told Suxin to take her place. "I'm sorry I can't stay," said Huiruo, making a graceful exit.

"I heard your father had been wrongfully accused of something," Mistress Shi said to Jishi. "How did that turn out?"

"I've just spent half the day with our teacher seeing to it. It's ninety percent settled now, but thank you for your concern."

The three women then began their game, with Mistress Shi watching from the side. After a while she called out, "Don't play an old card, draw a new one! You're about to lose, my girl." A moment later she cried, "Mistress Xiao, you never challenge anyone. Do you have your wits about you?" Then a little later still she began praising Jishi. "Oh, what a happy match! You're playing a very clever game, young master!"

At this point Mistress Xiao turned aside and looked at him out of the corner of her eye. "I suspect that the clever game the young master's playing corresponds to what it says in the manual, 'Lust after flowers, and you'll not see thirty.'"[2] Jishi had to cover his mouth to hide a smile, while Suxin pressed his foot under the table. Fascinating!

> They gamble and gamble—
> Among the girls it's rife.
> Well dressed, well fed they are,
> But not yet paired for life.
> Boys and girls together;
> What evil won't they try?
> Whatever rank they hold,
> They'll fondle on the sly.
> However pure they were,
> Hairpins askew, in simple slippers.
> Take heed, you boys and girls;
> It's a thin screen hiding you.

Let us turn back to Superintendent Heh, who every day since taking up office had been busy calling on people and receiving guests. He had entertained the governor-general, the governor, and the other high provincial officials, all of whom had reciprocated by inviting him back. Today was reserved for officials in charge of prefectures, agencies, and counties. He arose early and in his eight-man sedan chair, fitted out with all his regalia, went to the number 1 dock to welcome his guests. On the way he called in on Shen Jin, but found that he was out. After the superintendent had returned to his yamen, Magistrate Ma of Panyu county excused himself on the grounds that he had a case he needed to investigate that afternoon. The superintendent had sent separate invitations to Prefect Mu of Guangzhou, Sub-prefect Bu of Foshan, Sub-prefect Deng of Macao, Assistant Sub-prefect Shen of the Guangzhou Grain Bureau, Magistrate Qian of Nanhai, as well as three officials from outlying districts, Prefect Shangguan Yiyuan of Zhaoqing, Prefect Jiang Shiren of Chaozhou, and Magistrate Shr Buqi of Jiaying—eight guests in all. Four were seated on each side of the table, with the superintendent in the host's position at the end. Two acting troupes had been engaged.

Shen Jin was the first to arrive that afternoon, and the superintendent took him into his private quarters. "I called on you this morning, but you weren't back from the salt comptroller's. That just shows how many appointments you have and how lucky I am to have this chance to talk to you."

"It was very kind of you to visit, and I'm only sorry I wasn't there to welcome you. But as for all these mundane affairs and petty officials, I must say I find them extremely wearing."

"The other day I was in such a hurry that I didn't ask you about your present situation. How old is your son now?"

"My situation can be summed up in two words: virtuous poverty. Yinzhi is fifteen and studying with a teacher."

"That position you lost can quite possibly be restored in the future. If I see any opportunity, you may be sure that I'll do my best for you."

"The official life is full of ups and downs, and it doesn't concern me anymore. The main thing is that I don't lose the pleasure I get from drinking and composing poetry with my friends. Today, however, there's a certain mundane matter that I need to take up with you."

"What is it you'd like me to do for you?"

"The son of that trader Su Wankui is one of my son's classmates, and yesterday the boy came and pleaded with me again and again, saying that his father had acknowledged his culpability and was willing to pay the set fine of 300,000. All things considered, it would seem like an act of compassion on your part to accept the offer, but I wonder how you see it?"

The superintendent was quick to respond. "I had no idea he was a friend of yours. He treated me with such contempt that I gave him a mild reprimand. But I would never ignore an order from you, sir. I'll tell them to set him free." He issued an order to release the traders.

Shen also handed over the money draft, for which the superintendent thanked him, tucking it away in a small purse of fireproof material that he wore next to his skin. At this point a servant announced that the prefects of Guangzhou and Zhaoqing had arrived, and he went out to receive them. Before long all of the guests had come, and soon song and dance brought the breath of spring to the beautiful scene. Not until the second watch was nearly over did the guests disperse.

The superintendent invited Shen alone to stay the night, taking him into the library, where they had more wine. Heh called in his singing girls to pour their wine and sing for them.

> The wine lover's weak, already infirm,
> But the girls insist on another toast.

With song and dance in great halls long ago
He's more than willing to regale his host.

To return to the traders, who had now been released from the orderly room. They gave Du Chong fifty dollars and Bao Jincai a thousand taels of the finest silver. Bao realized that the case was now settled and was quite content to accept his share.

Taking leave of the other traders, Su Wankui went by sedan chair into the city. He first expressed his thanks to Jiangshan, who by this time had returned to the schoolroom. The students were all in their seats when Su Wankui walked in and thanked their teacher profusely. "If you hadn't shown such deep concern, I wouldn't be here today."

"It was my obligation as a friend—there's no need to thank me. The settlement came about entirely through your money and my uncle's influence. I don't deserve any credit for it."

"I won't go on about your nobility of character, except to say that it's im-printed on my mind. But there's one other thing I'd like to discuss with you."

"That case was the exception, you know—it won't occur again. You should use your own judgment in these matters."

"I've run my foreign-trade business and worked with the other traders, and by now I've acquired more than enough of the ne-cessities of life. It's not worth my while to go on slaving away for others. What's more, good and bad fortune always follow each other, and if I don't look to my own security, I'm afraid that my life may be in danger."

Jiangshan burst out laughing. "How did you acquire such insight, my friend? Superintendent Heh seems to have been the perfect teacher! But what was it that you wanted to discuss?"

"I was thinking, foolishly perhaps, of begging you to solicit Master Shen's help in allowing me to withdraw from my position as trader. If the superintendent should object, I'm quite prepared to part with a little more money. What do you think?"

"To quit at the height of your career—that's a crucial move in the world of fame and fortune. But you can hardly ask my uncle to negotiate your resignation for you. Even though you fully intend to withdraw, you will still need some sort of pretext, so that it doesn't look as if you're just trying to evade your duties."

"Please tell me what I should do."

Jiangshan thought for a moment before replying. "You were prepared to give up some money, anyway, so why not use the occasion of the earthquake in Gansu to contribute an appropriate sum for immediate use in rebuilding the Great Wall. As an official of the fifth rank, if you spent ten thousand, you could obtain a post. The trouble is that someone who buys an official post is no better off than a trader—his superior will still cheat him. However, once you've been selected for a post, you're free to accept it or not. Let me think, now. The first thing to do would be to dispatch someone to the capital with your contribution. After that, you should apply to withdraw from your position. The superintendent will have no grounds for stopping you from serving as an official and forcing you to remain as a trader. Wouldn't that be the most honorable thing to do—as well as the safest?"

Su Wankui was beside himself with joy at hearing this suggestion. "You've really opened my eyes! I shall certainly do my best."

As they were talking, Merchant Wen came home. He made a point of coming over to see Wankui and commiserate with him, ordering wine to be served to help Wankui get over the shock. A round table of red sandalwood was set up, and the three men took their places at it. Wankui mentioned his plan to leave the foreign trade and make a contribution to the earthquake fund.

"That's all very well," said Master Wen, "but if you have the honor to receive an official post, it means that we shall be seeing less of you."

"But I wouldn't *really* become an official, you know; I'd merely be using that as a pretext for getting out of the foreign trade."

Wen Chuncai broke in. "Uncle Su, don't be an official!"

Jiangshan smiled. "Chuncai, what makes you think it's not a good thing to be an official?"

"The other day the salt comptroller was going past our door, and at the sight of all those fierce-looking runners and villainous-looking executioners I was a little afraid. If you're an official, don't you have to look at those ferocious people every day?"

"That's nonsense!" exclaimed his father.

"Not necessarily," said Jiangshan. "Men who use their master's power to extort money from others are indeed frightening."

"I don't mean to be either an official or a trader," said Wankui. "Instead I shall find myself a quiet place in the country and return to farming for the rest of my days."

"Happiness of that sort is something we rarely attain in life," commented Jiangshan. "Just see that you don't enjoy it *too* much." They drank heartily, with much talk and laughter, before Wankui got up to go.

The next day he prepared some presents to show his gratitude to Shen, but the latter would accept only the foreign liquor, the baked goods, and the ten lengths of Dutch camlets, and returned all the other presents. Su Wankui was mortified. He had a heated couch specially made of glass and a large sedan chair and told Jishi to deliver them. After much pleading, Shen was finally induced to accept the presents.

Su Wankui sent one of his men to deliver his contribution to the capital. He also bought land in the Huatian district and began building.

Money does indeed work wonders. Within days his man had made the contribution in the capital and, traveling by long-distance horses provided by the Salt Administration, had brought back the donor's certificate from the board. Once Su Wankui had read it, he wrote out a petition and personally delivered it to the Customs offices.

Bao Jincai brought the petition in and showed it to the superintendent.

> The petitioner, the trader Su Wankui, requests your gracious permission to withdraw from the foreign trade.
>
> In the second month of the third year of Jiajing I began my service as a broker in the foreign trade.[3] In the eighth month of the fifth year, I followed the practice established at the time of the Taiqing Temple sacrifice and bought the position of salt inspector.[4] Now, because of the earthquake in Gansu, all military and civilian personnel are permitted to contribute funds for immediate use in rebuilding the Great Wall. I have long cherished a sincere desire to see the splendid sights of the empire. I have sent a man to the capital to contribute for immediate use the amount appropriate to my station, and I have received a certificate from the board to that effect. I feel that a functionary is someone who attends to business, while an official is one who devotes his life to a cause. As a trader, how could I ever repay the debt that I owe the nation? I humbly beseech you to graciously review my case, removing my name from the list of foreign-trade brokers and appointing another in my place, so that I may be evaluated by the board for appointment. I would be forever grateful to you as my benefactor, and would handsomely repay the favor. In a related matter, my son, Su Fang, is now thirteen and a supplementary student in Panyu

county of Guangzhou prefecture. By established precedent, he ought not to become my replacement. I am combining both petitions and presenting them as one.

The superintendent, who had a forthright nature, had no sooner read the petition than he picked up his brush and wrote, "Let him be removed from office and replaced."

"You shouldn't approve this, sir," said Bao Jincai. "This man took a loss the other day, and now he's intent on evading his duties. We could squeeze some more money out of him."

"I don't care what he's intent on doing. These trader appointments are next to impossible to get. If he doesn't want his, that's that; no one's going to force it on him. Besides, repairing the Great Wall is an urgent priority for the court, and when there's a rich merchant eager to help, who are we to stand in his way?" He ordered the document issued without change.

Wankui's heart was in his mouth as he waited outside. When he read the order, he was jubilant and hurried home.

> I'm free to wander far afield;
> Where can the hunter catch me now?[5]

When the other traders found that Su Wankui had resigned, several of them followed suit and also handed in their resignations. In seeking replacements, the superintendent, at Bao Jincai's urging, demanded a great deal of money, and so no candidates dared to come forward. Someone wrote the following on the wall inside the gate of the Customs compound:

> Heh's our new superintendent,
> With money and sex on the brain.

While the money all goes to the whores,
Only half of the traders remain.

After Wankui had taken leave of his friends outside the compound gate, he walked as far as Provincial Administrative Commission Rear Street, where he called for a sedan chair to carry him back to the Wen household. There in the schoolroom he told Jiangshan what had happened, adding, "I've found myself a little place in Huatian. I'll be moving in soon, but my boy will continue to study with you."

"So you really *are* going to withdraw? I must certainly see you to your new home."

"When the time comes, of course I'll ask you to honor my humble abode with your presence." He bowed and took his leave, then walked back accompanied by two of his servants.

As he crossed the road at the Warehouse Street intersection, he found a knot of people yelling at one other. One man was shouting, "What are you doing? You owe us money, and yet you want to beat us up!"

"I don't have any money on hand just now," said another, "and yet you bring all these people here to beat *me* up! You surely don't think you can beat the money out of me, do you?"

"He's still denying it! Come on, lads, let's get him!" The group of hooligans surged forward.

The other man roared with laughter. "Now, don't you start playing games with me! You Cantonese may be capable enough on the water, but on land you're hopeless!"

"That northern bastard is accusing us of being pirates! Come on, let's beat him to death!" The crowd pressed forward.

"Don't come any closer," said the man in a calm voice. Then he lashed out with both arms, and the hooligans fell to right and left, some with cracked heads, others with broken hands. Some of them maintained that their own men had run into them, others that they had slipped on the stones and fallen down. All in all, a pretty sight!

In the past Wankui had never paid much attention to people in distress, but after his recent bitter experience he was now more concerned about justice and humanity than fame and fortune. Parting the crowd, he pushed his way to the front. "Now, what's all this quarreling about?" he asked.

A young man replied, "I run a little lodging house at the top of the lane. That man has been staying with us from the third of the third month. Through yesterday, that's over four months! I explained to him that the rent was two qian a day. Altogether he owes twenty-four taels six qian, but so far I've only received a little over four taels of silver of doubtful quality, a set of bedding worth three taels two qian, plus a few old items of clothing and a chest worth six taels nine qian together. That makes a total of fourteen taels one qian. Even if you ignore the quality of the silver, he still owes me ten taels five qian. Day after day I ask him to pay up, but he always says he hasn't got the money and threatens to beat *me*! I ask you, is that fair!"

His lodger then came forward and explained his position. "My name is Yao Huowu, from Laizhou in Shandong. I came here to join a relative of mine, but I couldn't find him and was left stranded at the lodging house. It's true that I owe him a few taels, but he has brought along a whole lot of men to beat me up. As you saw just now, sir, it's not worth my while to beat them."

The young man began cursing him: "You Shandong bandit, you! If these men can't beat you, we'll take you before the magistrate of Panyu county." The crowd pressed forward and seized hold of him.

Wankui interceded. "There's no need for that!" He took five ingots of ten taels each from a bag that a servant was carrying and handed them to the lodger. "Here, you can use this ingot to clear up your debt and the others to pay for your travel back home. You shouldn't try to hang on here in poverty."

The lodger bowed low before him. "We've met entirely by chance, sir. How can I accept such generosity from you? May I ask you your name?"

The crowd broke in, "He's Master Su Wankui, the trader."

"Your name will be forever engraved on my heart," said the man. "I only hope that we will meet again." Raising his hand in a salute, he departed.

Never before had the bystanders seen such behavior from a trader.

Please turn to the next chapter.

Chapter III

Suxin bemoans her fate as a beauty
Jishi searches for sex in the night

༄

Let us turn from Su Wankui befriending a heroic figure to Wen Suxin lingering among the flowers by moonlight. As the sage once said, "Seductive looks are an inducement to lust."[1] This clearly means that it's not that the boy sets out to seduce the girl but that the girl induces him do so. For if a girl is somewhat attractive, she will look in the mirror and start pitying herself, feeling that she simply has to marry a paragon. To do so, she will seize any possible chance and stoop to any number of unseemly actions. The responsibility in such cases rests entirely with her parents, who must be especially careful to keep outsiders away from their daughter and enforce a strict segregation of the sexes, so that there is no lust there to be induced. As it says in the *Classic of Rites*, "At nine, boys should go out to study with a teacher, living and sleeping away from the inner quarters; they should share neither the same mats as the girls, nor the same clothes trees, nor the same towels or combs"—a truly comprehensive list of precautions! But parents nowadays tend to dote on their children and let the sexes mingle, which frequently leads to clandestine meetings and shameful acts as they are overcome by their desires. Meanwhile the parents continue to dream away, constantly reassuring themselves, "After all, what do they know at their age?" How wrong they are!

Clandestine love, all of them know it;
Nobody has to teach them how.

Suxin in her boudoir was not yet engaged, but she had eye-brows to rival the new moon and a face that would drive the spring breeze to distraction. However, she also had a wanton nature cou-pled with a liquid, sidelong glance as well as a romantic tempera-ment paired with a lissome, graceful figure. Ever since her flirta-tion with Jishi downstairs, her passions had been stirred, and every day she made herself up seductively and longed for him to come over and dally with her.

One day she had played a couple of games of checkers in her birth mother's room and was still there at nightfall when her father came in chuckling to himself. "Suxin is grown up and I still haven't chosen a husband for her," he said to her mother, "but it looks as if Huiruo will be engaged to that Su boy, whose family is moving to Huatian. We'll probably be receiving the betrothal gifts next spring." He added to Suxin, "Now, don't you go telling your sister about this, lest she feels she has to avoid him." Suxin assented and left the room.

She was assailed in rapid succession by both sadness and joy—sadness, because her sister would be marrying Jishi and she would definitely have no chance herself, but also joy, because her father had not told them to avoid Jishi, which meant that she could still carry on with him if the occasion presented itself. She walked over to Pity-the-Flowers Lodge where, because the weather was turning chilly, both girls had been moved upstairs to sleep. As she climbed the staircase, she was greeted by Huiruo, who asked, "Where've you been all this time?"

"I've been playing a couple of games of checkers—that's why I'm late. But what are you doing in my room?"

"I felt tired after embroidering a pillow slip, so I came to your room and noticed *The West Chamber* on your table. I read half of the 'Fulfilling the billet-doux' scene and then couldn't bring myself to read any more.² Send someone straight to Hell, for writing that kind of thing! If you have anything good, Sis, do lend it to me."

"I don't have anything else. Even this play is not something we girls are supposed to be reading. Don't tell them up in front."

"I know. Let's have supper now."

"I don't want any."

Huiruo went to her room, finished her supper, and sat for a while before going to bed.

Suxin had learned to read as a little girl, and Jishi had brought her this erotic literature in order to arouse her passions. It was not just *The West Chamber* that she possessed, but also *The Story of Jiao and Hong*, *The Lantern Festival Destiny*, *A Captivating Tale*, *The Merry Tale*, and the like.³ She treasured the books, and would take them out and browse through them when she was alone. Because Huiruo had sneaked a look at the "Fulfilling the billet-doux" scene, she picked up the play and read its account of the clandestine love between Yingying and Zhang. Then by lamplight she read in *The Lantern Festival Destiny* the story of Zhen Liancheng's romantic encounters at various places. By the time she went to bed her heart was pounding and her face flushed. Jishi can't lack all feeling, she thought, because those loving sentiments of his make you just *die* of longing! And he can't be too young, either, because to judge from that brazen approach of his he must have had some experience with girls. Moreover, when we tangled with each other the other day, I seemed to touch that thing of his and it gave me quite a jolt. But why haven't I seen any sign of him in all this time? Then another thought struck her. When my sister marries him, she'll be able to enjoy him all her life, but if I were to make love to him first, it's possible he might tell his father, who just might choose me over her. But then she had another thought: how could he possibly tell his father about an illicit affair? Moreover, my sister is just as pretty and clever as I am. So having an affair probably wouldn't make any difference at all.

Her thoughts were in such a whirl that she found it impossible to close her eyes. Instead she threw on some clothes, got up, trimmed the lamp, added some incense to the burner, and sat down at her dressing table. Then, taking out a brush, she wrote the following:

> A bright moon at autumn's start—
> I spy a man beneath my window.
> It's hard to describe what troubles my heart!
> As I put my slippers on my lotus feet,
> The silver lamp bursts into sparks,
> And I take up my brush and write:
> "Willowy form a mere wisp."[4]
> Since he's in love with me,
> How can I not love him too?
> Cold is this coverlet,
> Hot my waiting heart.
> I call him by his childhood name,
> And mutter my curses over and over.
> I curse my handsome love;
> With whom is he chatting now?
> My frail and delicate self
> Is withering on the vine.
> I'd like to bind our feet with red,
> And if he won't play me false,
> Dare I be false to him?

After writing these lines, she murmured them to herself a few times, shedding streams of impassioned tears. Then she heard the tower sounding the fourth watch, and she lay down on her bed again and drifted off to sleep. She saw Jishi approach and say, "You're so sleepy! Your bridal chair is at the door."

She gave a faint smile. "I was asleep in my bed! Weren't you afraid someone would see you coming in here?"

He sat on the bed and said nothing, just stretched his hand inside the bedclothes and gently fondled her. Gradually he extended his hand down as far as the edge of her seat of passion. She made as if to push him away, protesting, "You can't touch me *there!*"

At once he withdrew his hand. "I wouldn't dare," he said. "But what a pity it is that this body of yours, of purest jade, is going to be enjoyed by someone other than me!"

"Dear one, when I said you couldn't touch me there, I was only teasing. You can do whatever you like. But who would dare to enjoy me?"

"You were engaged long ago to Wu Jiangxi. The girl I enjoy will be your sister. You and I will have to part."

"How fickle you are!" she snapped.

"I shall always be your loyal friend, but your bridal chair is waiting outside for you outside! How can I ever hope for anything more from you?"

At this remark she cast all modesty aside and sat up, naked as she was, clutching at his hand and weeping: "My dear, I love you, and I definitely want to marry you. If you marry my sister, I'm willing to be your concubine."

"But you've slept with young Wu, and you were willing enough to marry *him.* How can you now talk of loving me?" As he pushed her hand away, she suddenly awoke.

A few drops of rain had fallen outside her window, and the sunlight was streaming through the silken curtains. Her face was still wet with tears, and the place on her body where he had meant to touch her was damp. What a strange dream, she thought. My sister is going to be betrothed to Jishi, my father said. How could someone called Wu Jiangxi have slept with me and now be about to marry me? Oh, if I don't sleep with Jishi, there's no hope for me! Why would I seek out someone called "Young Wu"? Then she had another thought. Every day Jishi goes into the garden and relieves himself beside the roseleaf raspberry trellis. I'll go there today and hope for a meeting.

Soon the sun was high in the sky. She got up and dressed in her most exquisite style.

> Powdered and rouged,
> Like a lotus open on a pond.
> Raven hair dangling to one side,
> Like a peony half shrouded in mist.
> Golden phoenixes set in roseate horn;
> Blue-green hairpins athwart her jeweled chignon.
> Brows superbly arched,
> Like the moon's first phase.
> Ears hung with rings
> Bound with bright pearls.
> Trousers of red silk
> And a jet-black skirt below.
> Dress of white crepe
> And a royal blue jacket above.
> Truly—
> On tiny feet she trips along, like gentle rain;
> Her side-curls brushed aslant, like a sheet of cloud.

After dressing, she studied herself once more in the mirror. Her maid brought in some tea, of which she took a few sips and said, "Wait for me downstairs. I'm going to take a look at the cassia flowers in the garden." Tripping along on her tiny feet, she entered the garden gate, walked past Welcome Spring Dell and Play-with-Flowers Pavilion until by a roundabout route she came to Break-Cassia Studio. He'll have to pass by here, she thought, when he goes from the schoolroom over to the raspberry trellis. I'll just sit here and watch for him. She made her way slowly inside.

Although Master Wen was not a cultivated man himself, his garden and its pavilions were laid out in excellent taste. In the middle of Break-Cassia Studio was a carved side table of red sandalwood and a small hexagonal table with six hexagonal easy chairs and six hexagonal stools. Along each side of the room was a rosewood couch with sheets of imported cloth, imported rattan mats and rush cushions, pillows, and bedside tables of betel palm. On one side was a musical stone made of emerald, on the other side a chiming clock. At the eastern end was a horizontal scroll entitled "Gazing in Wonder at the Ocean," and at the western end a vertical scroll entitled "Wu Gang Cutting Down the Cassia Tree."[5] At the sides and at one end were tall windows, the end one of glass, the others of fresh green cicada-wing silk glued along both sides. Outside the windows was a low ghost wall, beyond which grew a dozen scattered orange osmanthus plants.

Suxin sat there musing: I wonder if Jishi has had his breakfast yet. It's a good thing I got here early. If I'd left it any later, and my mother and the maids had appeared, I'd have really got myself into trouble! She fingered the half-opened cassia buds and let out a sigh. I'm just like you buds, she thought, the only difference being that you'll flower soon and give off your scent and bear your seeds, whereas I have no idea when I'll be able do the same! Preoccupied with such thoughts, she suddenly noticed someone standing among the flowers. Assuming it was Jishi, she was on the point of calling out when she noticed that he had a swarthy complexion and was also a good deal taller than Jishi, and so she remained inside and watched him through the silk window. He lifted up his underwear and, holding a massive object in his hand, began to relieve himself. Her heart pounding violently, she thought, whoever he is, it's a lucky thing he didn't see me, or I'd have really been made a fool of! At this thought she blushed scarlet and gulped nervously. Meanwhile the stranger finished up and left the scene.

She waited, dejectedly, a little longer—she was furious with Jishi for his heartless behavior—and then decided that she might as well return. Readers, let us explain something: Suxin's fury was completely misplaced. Since Jishi had never arranged to meet her there, and since she had never sent him word that she would be waiting for him, how on earth was he going to guess what she had in mind—unless he was some sort of internal parasite of hers? It was only because her emotions were in such turmoil that these wild thoughts possessed her mind.

However, their ill fate was about to bring the pair together, for she had gone only a few steps when she heard someone calling her from behind, "What are you doing here all on your own?" Shocked, she leapt to the conclusion that it was the man she had just seen, and so she walked on with her head down, not daring to say a word. But then there came another call, "My dear, why are you ignoring me like this?" By now the speaker was right behind her, and when she turned her head to look, she saw that it was Jishi.

"I've been admiring the cassia flowers and now I'm going in," she said. "Why did you call?"

"My dear, there's something I want to tell you. There's no one in the pavilion now. Let's sit down in there for a moment." Taking her by the hand, he led her inside.

"I don't mind if you ignore me, but why drag me in here?" she asked.

"My dear girl, just now you were the one who ignored me. I'd never dare do any such thing."

"But this morning..." As soon as she uttered the words, she stopped. She had been back in the world of her dreams.

"But I didn't do *anything* this morning!"

"Then tell me this: Why didn't you come into the garden for a walk this morning? I suppose you're blaming me for something?"

Her suggestion so agitated Jishi that he rattled off an oath: "If I ever blame you for anything, let me be turned into a pig or a dog!"

She interrupted him with a smile. "You can't stand the slightest comment without coming out with some kind of oath, can you? It's so unnecessary!"

"I tell you, it's a curse having to study with that teacher of mine. I get up at the crack of dawn and study all day without a break. I'm never allowed out of that classroom."

"Now, don't upset yourself. Anyway, studying is good for you. One day you'll pass the examinations and become an official!"

"I don't want to pass, and I don't want to be an official. I want to spend the whole of my life with you." He came forward and sat beside her on the couch. Putting his left arm around her neck, he gradually brought his face against hers. "You're dressed even more gorgeously today. Let me breathe in some of your fragrance."

As his right hand inserted itself inside her lapel, she put up only a half-hearted resistance. Placing a hand on his shoulder, she said, "Stop playing around. Someone might see us, and it wouldn't look at all nice."

"No one comes along here at this hour." As he said these words, his hand darted about like quicksilver, fondling both breasts—like a baby sucking on one breast who can't bear to give up the other. Gently he fingered her small breasts with their nipples, then inserted a finger into that magical spot below her midriff. She shrank back frantically, but Jishi, who was now at the height of his ecstasy, held her in a firm embrace with his other arm. As for Suxin, she, too, had entered the realm of bliss and did not try very hard to defend herself. Eager to make love, he was just about to pull down her trousers when a young maid happened to come along to fetch her for breakfast, calling out as she came.

Hearing her from a distance, Suxin hastily pushed him away.

"The teacher will be at the grain bureau tomorrow," he said. "Let me come over at night. But don't lock the door."

She nodded and quickly left the pavilion. The maid had almost reached them. "It's only breakfast," Suxin said to her. "What's the hurry?"

"Breakfast's already served, and the young mistress told me to call you." She added, "Miss, your hair's come undone on the right side."

"Oh, I caught it on a branch just now." Smoothing her hair into place, she took the maid's arm.

> Startled by a cuckoo from a midnight dream,
> Two lovebirds are compelled to separate.

Jishi waited a little while before daring to leave the pavilion. When he reached the classroom, Jiangshan asked him, "Why were you away so long?" Jishi didn't dare say anything.

"I expect he's been catching crickets," said Chuncai.

The teacher took no notice, and proceeded to lecture Jishi: "Everyone receives his physical form from his parents, and his nature and character from heaven and man, and that is my concern.

You've been sent here to study, and the classics, histories, and essays are your concern. Everything else has to be set aside."

Jishi meekly assented and took his seat, but to himself he thought, You don't look all that old. Surely you can't be so ignorant of human feeling that you have to keep coming out with that sort of old-fashioned twaddle? I vaguely remember that in one of the classics it says something like, "Food, drink and sex, these are the objects of men's greatest desire."[6] Now, isn't that an instruction from the Sage himself? He followed up this thought with another: What a passionate girl Suxin is! If that maid hadn't called out as she came along, I'd have really gotten a taste of it. Then he had a further thought. It's lucky I was smart enough to take action ahead of time by touching that thing of hers. Tomorrow night she won't be full of excuses, and I'll thoroughly enjoy myself. However, even though the teacher's away, I'll still need to think up some scheme to get rid of my classmates.

> He devises an ingenious scheme
> To seek out the one he loves.

Let us turn to Master Qing, governor-general of Guangdong and Guangxi, whose given name was Xi. He was a true bulwark of the nation, a living Buddha to the common man, one who combined wisdom with gallantry and possessed all the civil and military virtues. He was also descended from one who had rendered great service to the state. He had been promoted from secretary of the Board of Revenue to vice-president. Later, because of his service in the collection of taxes, he was given the rank of president and appointed governor-general of Yunnan and Guizhou, then of Zhejiang and Fujian, and now of Guangdong and Guangxi, where he dealt with the pirate raiders by either negotiating their surrender or eliminating them by force, whichever was the more appropriate.

On this occasion, as he returned from a tour of inspection of the coastal regions, he reflected that, although Guangdong was a prosperous and heavily populated province, the pirate raiders did strike there from time to time—it was a situation that held the potential for disaster. The brigades commanded by the governor-general, the governor, and the provincial commander-in-chief, together with the various battalions on garrison duty were sufficient for the land defense of the cities, but the coastal battalions existed in name only; if a sudden crisis were to occur, it would be extremely difficult to cope with. Then he had a further thought: Many of the residents of the coastal counties have been forced into going to sea and becoming pirates. If they were to be treated with benevolence and inspired with high ideals, as the main support of their families they would never choose a path that led only to death. And so he had a notice printed, and posted it far and wide:

> Governor-general Qing of Guangdong and Guangxi: The Recruitment of Local Militiamen as a Precaution against Disaster.
>
> Appointed by the Emperor's grace to military command in the south after serving for years in a number of posts, I know the situation well. I expect that all of you in civil and military life will understand the need to take precautions against danger. Because the pirate raiders are on the lookout for opportunities to ignite trouble in the remote coastal areas, robbing our people and waylaying our merchants, I have severally ordered the commanders of the garrisons to join forces and apprehend the pirates, while continuing to train their own men in order to eliminate the scourge. But although the situation on the coast has suddenly quieted down, the remaining rebels have not yet been destroyed; they continue to spurn the Emperor's benevolence and thwart the people's hopes. This is cause for grave concern.

It occurs to me that many of you living along the coast have been forced into going to sea and becoming pirates. I am now pardoning you for your previous misdeeds and, if your military skills and courage are of a high order, and if you are keen to volunteer, you may go to your local prefectural or county offices and enroll. Have the official concerned report to my office, then await the process of screening and assignment. You will be paid a monthly retainer according to your abilities, enabling you to return home and cooperate with the battalion officers so as to be constantly on guard in the defense of your village. If you distinguish yourself by capturing or killing some of the enemy, we will collectively recommend you for an official position. If no incident occurs, you will be engaged in mutual defense. If some incident does occur, you will take the lead in forming a common front against the enemy, which will be of no small assistance in capturing pirates. I hereby declare that rewards will be distributed as of this date. Everyone should exert himself to the utmost and not miss this opportunity for advancement. By Special Order.

After the notice appeared, men from all the prefectures and counties volunteered in large numbers, several hundred in all. The governor-general made the selection himself, dividing the volunteers into three categories. The top category was to receive a monthly stipend of three taels, the second of two taels, and the third of one tael. All the money was to come out of his own savings from his official salary; no treasury funds were to be used. The men who volunteered were motivated by a desire to preserve their lives and protect their families. Although having volunteers defend their own districts might not in itself be able to stop the raiders, the number of those who became raiders did shrink considerably. The measure came close to being a radical reform.

On the third of the eighth month, Qing Xi received an imperial order to take up the governor-generalship of Sichuan and

Shaanxi. His duties as governor-general were to be temporarily turned over to the governor of Guangdong, Qu Qiang. As Qing Xi was preparing to hand over his office, the thought occurred to him that, so far as the militiamen were concerned, his successor might not be ready to give up his parsimonious habits for the good of the nation. And so together with the other high provincial officials he met to consider setting up a common fund that would provide a long-term solution. He also wished to erect a stele to commemorate the occasion. He knew that Director Shen of the Guangzhou Grain Bureau enjoyed a considerable reputation in literary circles and asked him to compose the text. Shen had long respected Qing Xi. In a poem congratulating him on his birthday, he had written the lines "I seek no advancement, only friendship / With your governing principles, it's talent that you love," and so he accepted the commission without demur. But he was tired of preparing official documents and preferred for the present to divert himself with poetry. The ancient style required for the stele demanded serious concentration, which was something he was in no mood to provide, and so he decided to invite Jiangshan to compose the text in his stead, arranging that they meet in his office that evening. Jiangshan took Shen's son Yinzhi with him.

Readers, let us explain that before Jiangshan left, Jishi had already worked out in his mind a number of schemes, and that after his teacher's departure he was like a prisoner at a time of general amnesty. He was just about to make a suggestion when Chuncai leapt up out from his seat and exclaimed, "What a blackguard that man is! He *would* have to go off at night instead of in the daytime! Well, let's stay up and spend half the night gambling."

"I'm going back home for a little fun," said Wu Daiyun. "Sorry."

Jishi, intent on his own desires, affected a self-righteous attitude. "Now, let's not get too carried away, old man; a classroom is hardly the place for gambling, you know. I'm not going home, but I'm not going to gamble, either. I'd rather catch up on my sleep and give my mind a bit of a rest."

"Today you sound just like the teacher! Well, I don't care about you two. I'd rather go in and challenge my sister to a cricket fight."

"That's even worse," said Jishi. "I'll tell the teacher."

Chuncai took no notice of him, just skipped off into the house, leaving Jishi to curse his luck under his breath. This only means more delay, he thought, as he longed gloomily for the sun to set.

It was soon time to light the lamps. After supper he sent his pages off, then went to the West Studio and flung himself across the couch. After an hour or two everything was quiet, and he walked slowly out of the door to the garden gate, which was fastened from the inside. Gently he raised the latch. There was a full moon overhead and a constant thrum of insects around him. The shadows of the trees formed a jagged silhouette, and the flowers gave off a heady fragrance. A faint sound could be heard from among the trees in the distance. Jishi felt alarmed, but since people are blinded by their sexual desires, he took his courage in his hands and walked on, searching as he went. Soon he came to Pity-the-Flowers Lodge. There was no sound of voices inside, and the vermilion door was shut. He tried pushing it, but it wouldn't budge. He lent an ear; there was a faint sound of people talking, but he couldn't make out whose voices they were. Surely she can't have forgotten, he thought. Then he corrected himself: That's absurd. In the studio yesterday her tender, loving response was *so* intense! As we parted, I reminded her, and she nodded in agreement—she'd never break her word. I expect she's still up ahead, unless Chuncai has started a quarrel. Oh, Chuncai! What grudge do you hold against me that you keep me from my moment of bliss? Soon the moonlight will be gone, and it's bound to rain. What am I going to do?

He waited there for a good two hours before he heard the drum sounding midnight. He was filled with bitter remorse. To make matters worse, a thin drizzle began to fall, and he had to make his way back through the rain. The path was wet, and he slipped. Scrambling to his feet, he felt angry and miserable. He rushed inside the garden gate, all the way to his own room, where he collapsed on his bed with his clothes still on. When he had had time to collect his thoughts, he began to reflect—and took a more tolerant view of Suxin. She's not as heartless as all that, he thought; there must be some reason for her behavior. The trouble is that I've been through so much torment waiting for this one chance, and when will I ever get another? He began to calculate: at the mid-autumn festival, the teacher will certainly dismiss the class. I'll go a little slower in my work and tell the teacher that I'll catch up over the festival. Naturally he'll approve. He won't be able to get back early tomorrow, so I'll run in and find out what happened and then arrange with Suxin to meet at a later date. Having decided on a course of action, he undressed and went to bed.

Not yet upon the Tiantai road,[7]
He can but meet her in his dreams.

Meanwhile Suxin had been in a state of anticipation just like Jishi—she could hardly wait until evening. But that afternoon one of Third Lady's nieces, a girl of the Shy family, came to visit her aunt. Suxin made the excuse that she was feeling unwell and didn't join them, but they came to see her in her room instead, and because Suxin had always gotten on well with her cousin, she had to chat for a while before seeing them off again. At long last it was evening, but then Chuncai came bounding upstairs, chortling to himself and calling out to a servant to bring a number of cricket cages. "Great news!" he shouted. "Our teacher's gone off and won't be back till morning. Sis, bring out your Crabshell Blue and let him go up against my Golden Wing."

"I'm not going to fight you. The other day we got a scolding from Mother."

"Oh, I'm not afraid of *her*. If she scolds me again, I'll just kill myself. Doesn't she have a knife in her room? Is there a cover on top of that well? I'll kill myself, and then she can go and get herself a better son."

"What nonsense you talk! You're such a dog."

"I'd only be pretending, and of course she'd plead with me to stop. You don't think I'd really do it, do you? You must think I'm perverse or something."

"Look, I don't have the patience today. Go and play with Sis."

"She's outside having a drink with our cousin. If you need cheering up, I'll go and get young Su in, and the three of us will play all night long."

He went about to go and call Jishi, but Suxin pulled him back. "Don't make such a fuss. I don't like him."

"You always used to like him. Why don't you now? I expect it's because he's acting like such a prig these days, and that's what's offended you. Let me apologize on his behalf." He bowed.

Amused despite her anger, Suxin had no choice but to match her cricket against his. Chuncai's cricket, however, showed no desire for victory and lost a dozen times in a row. Even then Chuncai was unwilling to stop, and Suxin had to make him a present of her Crabshell Blue before he went happily on his way.

My cousin is visiting, she thought, and I expect she'll come back here to sleep. It would certainly be dangerous if Jishi were to show up. I'll have to wait for him in the garden and warn him. She was about to go downstairs when her mother, Mistress Xiao, came up with the cousin, Xia, as well as Huiruo and several maids, chattering and laughing together. Suxin had to go forward and greet them.

"Since you're feeling unwell," said Xia, "why not have an early night instead of going on with your needlework?"

"It's nothing too serious, just a chill."

"I expect you caught a cold," said her mother. "Xia wanted to come and see you, and I came with her. But since you're not well and she's so young, I'll take her back to my room before long."

Suxin ceased worrying, but her visitors continued their chatter, reluctant to leave. Then, with Suxin showing no inclination to entertain them, Xia said, "We mustn't bother her anymore. Let's go to Huiruo's room and play checkers." They moved to the other room.

Suxin continued to lie on her bed fully dressed, not daring to go downstairs and unlock the door. It wasn't until after the shower ended that she heard the visitors departing. Only a few maids were left with her upstairs, but they had been in attendance half the night and were dead to the world as soon as their heads touched the pillow. When she was sure they were all asleep, Suxin got down from her bed, picked up the lantern and quietly opened her door, then went downstairs and gingerly opened the door in the west corner of the lodge. There was no sign of anyone there. He must have come, she thought. With the aid of the lantern she looked carefully about and found a couple of dry footprints on the steps. She sighed. I kept him waiting half the night! He's gone now, and

I can't *imagine* how he must hate me! Oh, Master Su! You think I deliberately broke my promise, but I couldn't help it! Then she went upstairs to sleep without locking the outside door again.

Chapter IV

In Break-Cassia Studio a pair of lovers open accounts
At the Double Ninth festival the class visits Mt. Yuexiu

⤳

It was broad daylight when Jishi awoke, but no one was up, and he hurriedly dressed himself and headed for the garden, racing all the way to the lodge lest the teacher return in the meantime. The door was unlocked, and hearing no sound from above, he stole up the stairs and pushed open Suxin's door.

She was already up. She meant to use the time while no one else was about to tell Jishi, the moment he arrived, all that had happened during the previous evening. With a crimson padded cotton jacket around her shoulders but otherwise undressed, she was sitting on the edge of her bed putting on her slippers when she heard a sound at the door, and there he was. Without a word, he fell into her arms, the tears streaming down his cheeks.

She put one arm around him, at the same time drying his tears with her handkerchief. "Dear one," she whispered, "don't be upset. You were very badly treated last night." She told him what had happened, adding, "You mustn't think I'm heartless."

"Oh, I'd *never* think that!" he protested, stopping his crying. "I blame it on my own ill fate. How I longed for the day when that teacher would leave! And then when finally he did leave, *this* had to happen!" He inserted a hand inside her clothes and began fondling her breasts. "What a pity! You have such gifts, and I shall never have the good fortune to enjoy them!"

"Don't talk as if you were saying a final farewell! We should take our time and try to find a solution."

"Come to think of it, isn't it the seventh today? In four or five days' time, the teacher's bound to dismiss the class. I'll just tell him I want to stay on here and study. Then I'll be able to come over and see you."

"That problem we had yesterday has set me thinking, too. Sis's room is right next to mine, and young though she is, it would be very awkward for us to meet here. It might be better to settle on a date and then meet at the Break-Cassia. What do you think?"

"That's fine, except that you'll have to put up with all the cold."

"You had to endure all that rain last night," she said with a smile. "Surely I can put up with the cold?"

"My dear, my soul belongs to you," he said, extending his hand further down. "Our next meeting is such a long way off. Do let me have a taste of it now."

"Not now! The maids will be getting up."

He kept on pestering her. "Look, can't you hear the floor-boards creaking?" she said. "Let me see you to the garden." She stood up, fastened her skirt, pulled up her hair, and taking his hand, led him out of the room. As she did so, she made a show of giving orders to the maids. "Aren't you up yet?" she demanded.

"We're just getting dressed," they replied.

She went downstairs with Jishi and into the garden as far as Welcome Spring Dell. "Off you go," she said. "I won't see you any further."

"Let's sit in here for a little while."

"But they'll come looking for me!" she said. Ignoring her protests, he pulled her inside, clasped her in both arms, and pushed her down on the couch. "You mustn't!" she cried. He said nothing in reply, just tore off her skirt and trousers, then his own trousers, and brought out his three-inch pocket giant,[1] like a young champion riding forth to do battle. She fended him off with both hands.

"My dear, it's not that I'm absolutely against it, but in the first place I'm worried that one of the maids will come looking for me, and secondly, I'm afraid that your teacher will return and someone will be sent to look for you. There'd be such a scandal we'd never be able to show our faces anywhere again. Let's stick to our plan."

Jishi was a timid youth, after all, and on hearing the word "teacher," he simply froze. Moreover, it was quite late, just the time when the teacher might well return. He loosened his grip, and she stood up and put on her skirt and trousers. Then she noticed that Jishi still wasn't dressed. "Just look at you!" she cried. "Get dressed!"

He seized her hand. "You dress me. Look at this thing of mine. Isn't it pathetic?"

She pressed her fingers against his cheek and shook her head: "Not necessarily." Then she whipped her hand away and fled.

Jishi hastily pulled on his trousers and chased after her, calling out, "Don't forget our arrangement!"

She turned her head. "I know."

Jishi rushed back to the schoolroom, arriving just at the same time as the teacher, who proceeded to set out the curriculum.

"Sir, I caught a chill, and I've been having continual stomach cramps," said Jishi. "I ask leave to cut back on my work now and then make it up over the mid-autumn holiday."

"It's perfectly all right to make up your lessons over the holiday instead of merely amusing yourself. But when we get near that time, you're not to come up with some other excuse."

"If I'm studying here on my own in peace and quiet, I'll naturally be devoting all my energies to my work. I'd never dare to be remiss."

If study brings you a beautiful girl,
It matters not that no teacher is there.

On the fourteenth of the eighth month Jiangshan dismissed the class, and he and Shen Yinzhi left for the grain bureau, arranging to return on the twenty-fourth. Before leaving, he gave Jishi some additional instructions: "Concentrate on your studies here until the eighteenth, when I'll come back and go with you to see your father to his new house." Jishi assented and then, after seeing the teacher out of the classroom, returned and told Su Bang, "Go home and tell my father that I'm behind with my schoolwork and will be staying on here to catch up. I won't be able to get home for the holidays. You should remain there and await further orders. I'll have Aqing to attend on me."

In the house they won't know that the class has been dismissed, thought Jishi. If things are to go smoothly tonight, I'll have to go over there and break the news to them. He accompanied Chuncai through the parlor to the main room and paid his respects to Mistress Shi, explaining why he would continue to impose on them. She was genuinely pleased, and said to Chuncai, "Since Master Su will be studying here, you should do your revising together."

"My name is not Revise.[2] Oh, do be quiet, Mother!" And with a skip and a jump he was off.

Mistress Shi sighed. "When will that boy ever change?"

"He's not behind in his work the way I am, and the teacher didn't have any instructions for him," said Jishi with a laugh. "You shouldn't keep him on too tight a rein, Aunt. But I still need to call on the other ladies."

Mistress Shi took his hand and led him to see Mistresses Xiao and Ren. Jishi was a personable youth, and he ingratiated himself with both of them before going on to the lodge at the rear. Because

Chuncai had already been there, Suxin knew that the class had been dismissed, and as soon as she saw her mother bringing Jishi upstairs, she came forward with a welcoming smile. "Master Su, this is good news, but why didn't you go home?"

Mistress Shi explained why and added to Jishi, "You're still young, Master Su, and I'm afraid that with your teacher away it'll be lonely for you out there. Why not bring your bedding over here and sleep in one of our outer rooms?"

Jishi's heart skipped a beat. "I may be young," he hastened to reply, "but I'm not easily scared. What's more, I'll have our servants there with me. There's nothing to be afraid of."

"In that case, I won't press you. But you must come over in the evenings and join us in the inner quarters for a little entertainment. You shouldn't spend every minute of the day studying."

"I understand." He sat with them for a long time without being able to exchange a single word in private with Suxin. All he could do was make gestures whenever Mistress Shi's back was turned, gestures to which Suxin would respond with a nod of her head.

Then he left and returned to the schoolroom, where he forced himself to do a little studying. It was late when Aqing and the others finally went to bed, but there was a harvest moon that night; it was a time for "hunting for incense in the palace of the moon."

> A dazzling moonlight floods the rail
> And forms a world of autumn hue.
> But now the watchmen sound the hour,
> And drums beat out a brief tattoo.
> Unbridled passions delight the mind;
> (To whom can I express that I feel?)

I'll head toward the flowers' heart,
And there we'll turn to butterflies.

With a bundle of soft bedding under his arm, Jishi sneaked out of the garden gate and made his way to the studio. Fortunately the moonlight shone through the silk windowpanes and turned the studio as bright as snow. He arranged the bedding neatly on the couch and waited there for some time. Then, although greatly emboldened by sexual desire, he began to feel lonely. Leaving the studio, he walked over toward the Play-with-Lotus Pavilion in order to meet Suxin on the way. In the distance he could make out a human form and called out but received no reply. Then when he went up and took a closer look, he was surprised to find that it was only the shadow of a weeping willow beside Fragrance-seeping Bridge. He was walking slowly past Welcome Spring Dell as she arrived, and he clutched at her as if she were some precious jewel that he had just discovered. "Dear girl, I've put you to so much trouble!" he exclaimed.

"Shh! Keep your voice down," she whispered. Hand in hand they went into the studio, where he took her in his arms and pressed his face against hers. "Your cheeks are cold," he said. As he took off her jacket and skirt, the moonlight struck her bare flesh and turned it a glistening white. Gently he fondled and stroked her, and then said, "Everyone talks about beautiful girls beneath the moon. They don't know about that marvelous spot beneath the girls." He went to take off her trousers, but she pushed his hand away and wriggled inside the bedclothes. Quickly stripping off his own clothes, he parted the bedding and also entered, clasping her in both arms. She was truly like jade, only soft, like incense, only warm, with a thousand coy and bashful protestations. Carefully he removed her underwear and reared himself above her, while she knitted her brows and, trembling, received him.

> Silent and dark the studio, by moonlight shafted.
> So handsome and brilliant you are, you made me fall in
>   love!
> My bud is about to open,
> My body is about to bloom;
> How can I stand this wanton bee
> That gnaws at the flower's heart?
> I love him, and
> I hate him, too.
> "We've a world of time before us, dear;
> Let's take things easy tonight."

This was Jishi's first entry into the realm of bliss, and he inevitably lacked stamina; before long "the jade mountain toppled." They wiped up the blood and clung to each other. "Why aren't you saying anything?" said Jishi. "I'm not dreaming all of this, am I?"

"What do you want me to say?"

"Well, did you enjoy it?"

"It was awfully painful. There was nothing enjoyable about it."

He touched her down below. "Putting this in there—of course it hurts. It'll be better next time, though."

She squeezed his hand. "Don't move. Let's have a little nap before we go back." She drifted off to sleep, awakening after awhile to find Jishi eager for more. At first she was unwilling, but after he had implored her again and again, she had to consent. This time it was a familiar route that he traveled, and she received him joyfully. Jishi was indefatigable. Twice he spent, and by the second time the moon had gone down, and they hastily got up and dressed. He took her arm and saw her back, urging her to meet him the following night. "There's something I have to tell you," she added, agreeing to his request. "When you come over during the day, see that you act respectfully toward me. If you say anything frivolous, they'll know there's something going on."

"I understand."

> In his conduct, for fear of jealousy,
> She'll not allow familiarity.

They held their trysts for two or three nights in a row, and it is impossible to do justice to the closeness of their relationship.

Let us turn to Su Wankui as he built his new compound at Huatian. Altogether it consisted of thirteen courtyards with over one hundred forty rooms and a small flower garden in the center. It was surrounded by a brick wall twenty feet high, the kind of wall that rich people built to repel pirate raiders. When the whole compound had been finished inside and out, Wankui set the eighteenth of the eighth month as the date for moving in. Two days before that he sent in the furniture and other items that they had been using. His money and valuables he would take there himself on the day of the move.

Scores of friends and relatives living in the city, including Jiangshan, Merchant Wen, and Jishi, came to see him off. At the number 1 dock they hired pleasure boats and prepared feasts on board. Wankui arranged everything to his satisfaction and told Su Xing and Su Bang to look after the old house on Haoxian Street and also to attend on Jishi. He then had his other men and women servants and maids escort his family and go on ahead, while he took a sedan chair and visited people's houses to say goodbye. At each house he was handed invitation cards and gifts and told that their masters were already at the dock waiting to see him off. Highly embarrassed, he promptly visited each of the boats at the dock to express his thanks, apologizing for his lateness on the grounds that he had been visiting their houses. They raised their cups and urged him to drink, and it was not until dusk that he was able to take his leave. They even wanted to escort him to his new compound, but he firmly declined and instead gave them a special invitation for the following day, one that they all accepted. He also held Jiangshan's hand and repeatedly urged him to come, then embarked on his boat accompanied by Jishi.

Less than two hours later they were moored at their destination. Huatian was one of the most famous scenic resorts in the province, and in the spring young ladies and gentlemen would flock there, the high-minded gentlemen to drink wine and compose poetry, the rich and powerful ones to visit courtesans, but it was mid-autumn now and visitors were few. Wankui's residence was also several hundred yards from Huatian itself, and after telling his servants to bring the money, he and Jishi set off for the compound on foot.

After taking a roundabout route past fields and inlets, they found before them a village plunged in darkness, a village of towering walls and a main gate with gaily decorated pavilions on each side. When people saw that the father and son had arrived, they came forward at once to welcome them with pipes and drums. Three cannon shots were fired. There were fifty or sixty members of the staff lining each side of the road. Jishi and his father entered the main gate and passed by a spacious building, which was the main hall, with reception rooms on each side of it, all splendidly appointed and quite magnificent. Wankui's servant Wu Jing had seen to the decoration, copying the style used in the old house in the city. Above the door hung a gilded name tablet, "The Recluse is Pure of Heart and Blest with Luck," by the hand of Qu Qiang, the governor of Guangdong. On the right was a tablet by the hand of Grain Bureau Director Shen, "The People Said,"³ and on the left a tablet presented by Prefect Mu of Guangzhou, "The Hermit's Abode." In the center was a pair of parallel hanging scrolls: "Virtue Can Be Passed Down to Posterity with the True Flavor of Plain Living" and "Even If He Did Not Withdraw from the World, He Would Still Surpass the Likes of Tao Zhu and Yi Dun."⁴ The scrolls were signed "Li Guodong of Suzhou." Many other tablets were mere flattery, and there is no need to give the details here.

As you entered, you came to the women's residence as well as a two-story building behind which was the nine-span main room. Of the three courtyards, the middle one was Jishi's mother's apartment, the one on the right his birth mother's, and the one on the left that of the two concubines. Further to the left a small three-room lodge with its own courtyard was for his two sisters. Jishi said to his mother, "You people all have your own bedrooms, but they've forgotten to build one for me."

"What's that over there, then, inside that courtyard to the right of your birth mother's, with a courtyard opening to the east? Isn't that yours? I told Wuyun and Youyan to get it ready for you." Jishi turned and went into Mistress Hua's rooms. To one side of the courtyard was an ornamental rock. If you went through, you found a small round door that led to a scene of lush vegetation and tall, graceful bamboos. Directly to the south was a one-story, three-room building with a corridor all around it. Facing it was another three-room building, but only one of the rooms had windows, which were of fine workmanship and painted black, white, and red. After looking over his quarters, Jishi said to a maid, "Put my bedding in the front room on the right," and walked out again.

Wankui gave orders that a banquet for the whole family should be set out in the main hall, and that the theatrical performances celebrating the occasion be held in the courtyard. He also ordered his staff to prepare ten or more feasts in the two halls on each side, and accompanied his neighbors and tenants in a hearty drinking session. He got little, if any, sleep that night.

The following day he sent his servants into town with an invitation for each of the guests, a card that read "Your Gracious Presence Is Requested at Noontime to Drink a Cup in Celebration." He hired three medium-sized pleasure boats to stand ready for them and also, in an extraordinary measure, hired a troupe of actors. By afternoon all the guests had arrived, an opera was being performed, wine was being drunk, and literary and guessing games were underway. But—ominous thought!

> Where once there was music and dance,
> One night you'll hear the ravens caw.

After spending three days at home, Jishi explained that he urgently needed to get on with his schoolwork and hurried back to the city. From the schoolroom he went first to see Madam Shi and thanked her on behalf of his mother for the handsome presents she had sent, adding that his mother would certainly come and invite her to visit them in the country. That done, he went to the back to see the girls. Loving glances passed between him and Suxin—their few days apart had seemed like an eternity—and before leaving he covertly arranged to meet her that evening.

When nightfall came at last and all was quiet, he did as he had done before; he took his bedding and a tinderbox and made his way to the studio, then went in and waited for her. Before long she came, fully made up, and stepped forward and took his hand. Jishi put an arm around her shoulders and laid his cheek against hers, studying her minutely. "Don't be so childish," she said. "What happened about that matter I mentioned the other day?"

"I did tell my mother," said Jishi, "and she said that my father spoke the other day of his intention to betroth me to your sister. 'If you want to marry the elder one,' she said, 'I expect it's because you think she's prettier. Well, it's all the same to me. Let me take it up with your father.' So it looks as if we have a fair chance of success."

She gave him a hug. "My dear, even if your father doesn't agree and you do marry my sister, I would still want to do as Ehuang did."[5]

"So long as you and I remain firm, I have no doubt it will work out. Moreover, my mother's particularly fond of me, and my father listens to her more than to anyone else." They undressed and made passionate love.

"I'm still young," said Jishi. "When I grow up, it'll be much better."

"Let's not talk about the future. Rather than waiting until you're grown up, what concerns me is that once your teacher is back you won't dare come over anymore."

"Meet me here in the daytime, please do. If you can't come, I'll die of longing!"

"It's just not convenient during the day. We'll have to set a time. Once every three or four days would be fine."

"That's not so difficult. If we meet every other day and set the hour for the next meeting, and if each of us keeps an eye on the clock, we can't go wrong." He began another passionate onslaught.

"It's the fourth watch already," she said. "Aren't you going to try and get some sleep?"

"I do feel drowsy, but this little priest of mine won't let me sleep. He's looking for more trouble." Suxin gave him a smack, but then took pains to accommodate him.

> In making love, who wins, who loses?
> Do kindred spirits feel as one?

Later, when the teacher resumed his classes, the pair did meet every other day. They couldn't really let themselves go, but they were fortunate that no one found out about them.

The days flew by, and soon it was the Double Ninth. Mt. Yuexiu in Guangzhou was the site of the tomb of Zhao Tuo, king of Southern Yue during the Han dynasty. In those days Mt. Pan and Mt. Yu formed a single hill inside Little North Gate, and looking south from the summit you saw before you a panorama of the city and its environs. One day Jiangshan said to his students, "All the hills and rivers of the country serve to stimulate the writer's imagination. The Grand Historian was the first to praise this place, and he was followed in due course by Su Zhe. We're now in the middle of the Hill-climbing Festival, and we simply have to visit Mt. Yuexiu. But we won't be able to travel up there by sedan chair, or we'll be cursed by the mountain spirits."

The teacher and his four students, accompanied by the school pages, strolled out of the school. When they came to the Dragon Palace, they paused briefly before beginning their climb. Then, after admiring the scene, they visited a monk's cell to rest. From the window of the cell the multitude of houses, as well as the hustle and bustle at the city's center, were truly beyond the powers of any artist to depict. On the water they saw the pleasure boats and rice transports shuttling back and forth. Inspired by the scene, Jiangshan picked up a brush and wrote as follows:

On Climbing Mt. Yuexiu

An autumn breeze picks up on the Royal Terrace.[6]
On impulse I climb—to a sight for weary eyes:
Rows of jagged rooftops in steamy ocean air;
Great walls and parapets embracing hills and dales;
Splendid mansions towering up to distant skies;
Hosts of treasure-laden ships as from a painting.[7]
Why should this old peasant be so downcast over it?
An age-old palace reduced to a wilderness.

A Lament over the King of Zhao's Tomb

He served in Longchuan, and there his ascent began;[8]
His Five Mountains area was distinct from China;[9]
Ren Xiao had a strategy and vanquished the foe—[10]
How could Lu Jia mock him as a toad in a well?[11]
The Emperor repaired the king's ancestral tombs;[12]
Yue would share a natural border with Changsha.[13]
The rise and fall of nations is by fate decreed;
Why do they have to deride Prime Minister Jia?[14]

When he had finished, he stood up again, and an elderly priest came forward. "Would you be so kind, sir, as to honor my humble shrine by presenting me with those poems of yours?" he asked.

"You're a poet yourself, I assume? In that case, I'd be displaying my poor skills before a true master of the art."

"Although I don't know anything about poetry, many famous and gifted visitors have written poems on this place, most of whom spent too long on their deliberations. But such facility as yours, sir, is rare indeed. I would definitely treasure your poems and take them out again and again and fondly remind myself of this occasion." With a laugh Jiangshan took his leave.

The group then wound its way down the mountain. "We've got poetry but no wine," said Yinzhi, "which is bound to make the mountain spirits laugh at us. Sir, why don't you send a servant home to bring us some wine and food, and then we'll have a drink when we're halfway down?"

"You're perfectly right, but you're still young, and it wouldn't look good if you were making merry up here. It would be better if we went back and celebrated the chrysanthemums we have there."

Returning to the schoolroom, they set out wine for a party on the porch and drank together in front of a few dozen pots of chrysanthemums. "After coming back from the hills in high spirits," said Jiangshan, "we mustn't just sit here and glumly drink our wine. I'll set the rules for a drinking game. We'll each choose five lines from the *Poetry Classic*, the first with four level tones, the second with four rising tones, the third with four falling tones, the fourth with four entering tones, and the fifth with all four tones in order. For every word you get wrong, you'll be fined one cup of wine. I shall drink the master's cup and take my turn: *Yun ru zhi he; Wo you zhi jiu; Xin zhe dan dan; Wo su chu bu; Qi zi zao ji.*"[15]

He passed the cup to Daiyun, who thought for a moment and then came out with: "*Guan guan ju jiu; Yao tiao shu nü.*"[16]

"Wrong! The word *shu* is entering tone. One cup!"

"I'm not familiar with the *Poetry Classic*. I'd rather drink a few more cups."

"I can't allow that. Drink up, then think how you're going to go on."

Left with no choice, Daiyun said, "*Zheng shi guo ren; Wei ye mo mo; Qi zi hao he.*"[17]

"*Guo* is entering tone, while *ren* is level tone—two cups. *Wei* is level tone—another cup. Three cups in all."

Daiyun was indeed unfamiliar with the *Poetry Classic*, but he had a good capacity for wine, and he downed the three cups in quick succession.

Then the cup was passed to Yinzhi, who said, *"Yi qi jia ren; Fei si fei hu; Shang di shen dao; Le yuan le yuan; Xiong di ji xi."*[18]

"The word *ti* is in the rising tone in its derived sense,[19] but in its basic sense it's in the falling tone. In this line it is used in its basic sense. For mistaking a falling for a rising tone, drink one cup and find another line."

Yinzhi drank the cup and said, *"Yu ru bei su,"*[20] then handed on the cup.

It should have been Chuncai's turn, but Jiangshan passed the cup to Jishi, who rose to his feet and said, "Brother Wen should go first."

"It's all the same," said Jiangshan. "You go ahead, then pass it on to him."

Jishi said, *"Wu hu ai zai."*[21]

Jiangshan's face dropped. "There are a great many lines with four level tones. Why did you have to pick that one?[22] Drink half a cup and find another line."

Flushed with embarrassment, Jishi drank the half cup and said, *"Ren zhi duo yan; You gu you gu; Shi lei shi ma; Lü zhu ruo ze; Tong zi pei she."*[23]

"You've read the word *ru* as *ruo*. The line makes sense, but you've misquoted it. You'll have to drink two cups." After he had drunk them, Jiangshan continued, "Chuncai, you don't need to try. Just drink three cups of wine as a penalty."

"I don't agree with that at all," said Chuncai. "I'd like to try. My first line is *'Shi yun Zhou sui.'*[24] Surely that's four level tones?"

"You don't understand the principle of the game, and that is my fault. Quickly, drink your three cups, and we'll choose a game for all levels." Chuncai drank up. "And now," said Jiangshan, "we'll all play Things I'm Afraid to Hear, Things I'm Afraid to See, Things I Love to Hear, and Things I Love to See. Each one should rhyme.[25] Let me drink the master's cup." He began,

"Things I'm afraid to hear: people affecting a Mandarin accent to intimidate the locals; a stepmother screaming at her stepchildren and a wife being mean to a concubine; and silly women chanting Buddhist phrases along with the priest.

"Things I'm afraid to see: corrupt officials holding court and a prostitute washing her face; a rich man putting on airs and a priest's buttocks; and an old man suddenly coming upon a coffin shop.

"Things I love to hear: clever pupils reciting their texts; beautiful birds in spring singing their songs of triumph; sitting on a white rock beside a clear stream and playing the lute.

"Things I love to see: an eminent man remembering a lowly childhood friend; an official exhorting the peasants in green fields at the height of spring; the implacable face of justice as a censor impeaches a prince."

"We won't go according to age," he added. "Whoever is ready first should speak up."

Yinzhi began, "Things I'm afraid to hear: local guards beating a thief behind closed doors; people in the marketplace chanting poetry and discussing morality; boys making fun of old men.

"Things I'm afraid to see: officials rapidly changing their friends; sycophantic aides and phony recluses; people who put on an act in order to claim friendship.

"Things I love to hear: runners keeping their voices down as they clear the road for an official; swallows warbling in late spring and flutes at midnight; the morning bell after a long night.

"Things I love to see: the examination results being announced at the palace; coming upon someone from home in a distant region; a groom watching his bride reveal her face."

Jishi followed with a spontaneous list:

"Things I'm afraid to hear: rain pattering down from the eaves on a spring day; a pretty maid being beaten for no reason; neighbors at night grieving over the loss of a young son.

"Things I'm afraid to see: vicious servants and malicious clerks; a petite beauty being subjected to judicial torture; the fierce looks of the runners from the Guangzhou Customs.

"Things I love to hear: a parrot in the corridor calling me for tea; a new opera being performed at a banquet; the song of love-birds in the garden at midnight.

"Things I love to see: a weary girl throwing aside her needle and thread after a long day's work; a swing flying up into the clouds; coming upon a girl in the moonlight, her face half-covered."

Daiyun then said, "I shall give just one item in each. I'm perfectly willing to drink a few more cups."

"Go ahead," said Jiangshan.

"A thing I'm afraid to hear: someone who has just died in the house next door."

"You've copied Jishi's idea," said Jiangshan.

"I thought of it first," said Daiyun. He continued,

"A thing I'd be afraid to see: The face of Yama in the Tenth Hell.

"A thing I love to hear: the *pipa* and strings and the *moyu* sound.[26]

"A thing I love to see: The faces of my sister and mother."

"That's far too trite. What's more, 'Moyu song' is the name

of a Guangdong tune. You can't leave out the word 'song' and say 'sound' instead."

Chuncai said, "I shall say just one of each, too:

"A thing I'm afraid to hear: A crow cawing in the eaves in front of the door."

"Trust you!" said Jiangshan.

Chuncai then pointed at Jiangshan and continued,

"A thing I'm afraid to see: Our teacher's face in the school-room."

The students burst out laughing. Jiangshan joined in, adding, "You never spoke a truer word." Chuncai went on,

"A thing I love to hear: a servant coming to call me for wonton soup.

"A thing I love to see: the first winter plum blossom."

"That last line was quite good," said Jiangshan. "But tell me; what do you love about it?"

"When the first winter plum blossoms appear, sir, you're about to dismiss us for the holidays, so of course I like to see them!" His audience erupted in laughter.

Jiangshan then offered his critique. "Chuncai's and Daiyun's contributions aren't worthy of comment. Yinzhi's desire for success is as little too pronounced, but it's still authentic. His line about the bridegroom at his wedding, although fine and delicate, is also a pleasure only a young man would feel. Jishi's sexual desires are too pronounced, which is something a young man should guard against. Moreover, what's so enjoyable about the cry of lovebirds at midnight? Only the line about Customs officials shows true local color as well as feeling. And now let's all drink a toast to conclude the game."

Just as they were beginning to feel the effects of the wine, the schoolroom page came and announced, "Master Shen has sent someone to see you, sir." Jiangshan ordered the man to be shown in.

"My master told me to ask you and the young master to pay him a visit," he said. "A letter from home arrived today."

Jiangshan was delighted. "You go back," he said to the messenger. "We'll be along soon." He hired a sedan chair, and when he had finished his meal, he and Yinzhi left the city together.

At the offices of the grain bureau, Shen welcomed them and then handed Jiangshan the letter. He opened and read it:

> From his father to his son Guodong: My son, you have been visiting Guangdong for three years now, and during that time I have received five letters from you. I have recently learned that your uncle Xiangxuan [Shen] has taken you under his wing, which is a source of great comfort to me. But in my old age I find myself with a son who has traveled far afield, which causes your mother to anxiously await your return and greatly saddens me. In a festive season like this, how can we help feeling depressed? Next autumn is the time for the provincial examinations, and you must pack up and head north again. This spring, my grandson Yuan passed the entrance examination to the prefectural school, and your elderly parents rejoiced at the news. Next year, if both father and son should take the provincials together with each trying his utmost, who knows which one will play the part of Wu Gang's axe?[27]

Jiangshan passed the letter to Shen, who read it and said, "In his letter to me your father also told me to urge you to go back. I wonder what you intend to do?"

"My luckless wanderings started out as nothing more than youthful high spirits," said Jiangshan with tears in his eyes. "Due to the affection you have shown me, Uncle, as well as the friendship of the other gentlemen, I've extended my stay here to three years, which has caused my parents a great deal of grief. I must certainly go back in the spring to relieve their anxiety."

"Quite right. In Yinzhi's case, I've followed the established practice: I'll have him go back with you and sit the provincial examination at the same time you do. Your son is to be congratulated on his success. How old is he?"

"Thirteen. It was just luck on his part."

"'The young should be looked on with awe!'[28] This shows the profound effect his father's teaching has had on him." He ordered that wine be set out to celebrate the achievement.

As they drank, Shen confided in Jiangshan. "Ever since Governor-general Qing left here, Governor-general Hu has not known what action to take, while Governor Qu is simply pigheaded. The pirate raids are increasing by the day. I have few duties in this post, but I'm afraid I won't be able to stay here much longer. Moreover, Heh Zhifu has recently become more arrogant than ever, and he's bound to cause further trouble in the future. The other day I read him quite a lecture, but he only pretended to agree. Nephew, do stay with me for a few days and cheer me up."

Jiangshan agreed and sent a servant into the city to tell everyone.

The next chapter takes up another thread of the story.

Chapter V

Matchmaking causes two birds to lose their feathers
Flirtation leads to one sister's falling in love

꧁

Once their teacher had left, Jishi and his classmates set out the wine cups again and had more food and drink brought in. Wu Daiyun, who combined a strong capacity for wine with a cunning and devious nature, had a suggestion: "We've been suppressed for some time now. Let's take turns playing guess-fingers and drinking as much as we like before he comes back again." He proceeded to play a series of furious games with Chuncai who, after losing half a dozen times, became more than a little drunk.

"Better to have three bearers to a sedan chair than two people playing guess-fingers," said Jishi, who proceeded to collude with Daiyun. After Chuncai had drunk a dozen cups in succession he couldn't help throwing himself about and creating a ruckus. At that point a servant who had left with the teacher returned with a message. When Daiyun heard that the teacher would be away for several days, he got to his feet and announced: "Since he won't be back anytime soon, I'm off home."

"You don't have a wife, so what's the hurry?" asked Jishi.

"I'm feeling the effects of the wine," said Daiyun, "and I'm going to take a trip downriver. If you're in the mood for a little fun, you're welcome to come along. Yangzhou girls, Chaozhou girls, Silver Vermilion Street, Pearl Light Alley, the Shamian flower boats, large and small—they all come under my father's jurisdiction, and when the whores see me coming, they don't dare not to make up to me. I can have as many of them as I like."

Listening to Daiyun, Jishi grew quite excited, but he was in love with Suxin and had been hoping to take advantage of the teacher's absence to sleep with her again that night. "No, I'm not going," he said. "I'd be too afraid that our teacher would find out."

"Those places? In his wildest dreams he couldn't imagine what they're like! Your trouble is that you're too young. If you can't keep your mouth shut, you shouldn't go whoring." He excused himself and left.

"What did he mean by that?" asked Chuncai. Jishi explained in detail.

"But where's the fun in being with *strangers*? Let's go in and have some fun with my sisters. Wouldn't that be better?"

Jishi almost choked with laughter. "That sort of fun is *quite* different," he said.

"I don't agree with you. Today I insist that you come in with me and have some fun." He seized hold of Jishi and pulled him along. Someone as drunk as Chuncai is incapable of reason, and Jishi had no choice but to go along. Once in the main room, Chuncai bawled out, "Mother!"

When Mistress Shi came up and saw him reeling from side to side while keeping a firm grip on Jishi, she cried out, "Let go of him at once! Look, the young master's jacket is all creased."

"He wouldn't come and play, so I pulled him in here. If I let go, he'll slip off somewhere."

"The young master's a perfect gentleman, and this place is a second home to you, Master Su. Chuncai, why are you holding him like that? Let go of him at once. You're drunk."

"I am *not* drunk! I want to drag him to the back and have fun. Quick, bring us some wine. We'll have some fun with the girls." Mistress Shi actually did tell the maids to prepare wine for them.

"Take no notice of him, Aunt," said Jishi. "He can't drink anymore." But even as he spoke, Chuncai was dragging him off.

Mistress Shi ordered the wine and food sent to the rear building. They're such good friends, she thought, just like brothers-in-law. I think I'll let the four of them have a party.

> Little did she know a bad boy is a snake in the grass,
> And a certain fiancé had been "riding the dragon."[1]

Chuncai pulled Jishi straight upstairs, where the sisters were having their supper. "Bring us some wine and food," he bawled, "and be quick about it. We're going to eat, drink and be merry the whole night long. Old Su here refused to come, and I nearly killed myself dragging him over here. Quick, shut the door in case he tries to get away!" The sisters asked them both to sit down.

"It's a long time since we last met," Suxin said to Jishi. "Why don't you have anything to say for yourself?"

"He's trying to behave like a gentleman, but I'm not going to let him get away with it," said Chuncai. "Bring on the wine!"

The sisters could make neither head nor tail of the situation, but just then a maid brought in some wine and food, saying, "Madam says the young master is drunk already and the elder miss should be the host and encourage Master Su to drink a cup or two. We won't send his supper over to the school." Turning to Chuncai, she continued, "Madam says you should have very little to drink. It won't look nice if you throw up."

"Anyone who throws up is no better than a dog!" said Chuncai. Now that Suxin knew that these were orders from her mother, she told the maids to wipe the table and set out the dishes.

Jishi took his place, and Suxin and Chuncai sat down one after the other. "I can't drink," said Huiruo. "I hope Brother Su will excuse me."

Chuncai sprang to his feet. "Whether you're too young or you're just being sly, you've broken my rules. You can't drink, you say? I've *seen* you drink! I'm fining you a large cup straight off!" He pulled her down into her seat, poured out the wine, and was about to force her to drink when Huiruo, who saw how violent he had become, hurriedly acquiesced. "Don't force me, Brother. I'll drink."

"Everyone has to down a large cup for openers and then obey my orders." They drank up.

"I learned a brand-new game today, and you'll have to listen while I tell you the rules." They listened. However, no matter how Chuncai racked his brains, he couldn't remember the rules. Then he suddenly glanced at his sisters and said, "Now I remember! You're both girls, aren't you?" They burst out laughing.

"Quiet! Everyone has to come up with one line about things girls are afraid of and a second line about things girls like, and the lines have to rhyme. I'll be the master of the game, and I want old Su here to start us off."

Jishi began. "Things girls are afraid of: Their tiny feet suddenly slipping on a swing. Things girls like: Looking in the mirror in the morning and watching their hair being done."

"That's none too clear. One cup!" Jishi drank.

Suxin was next. "Things girls are afraid of: Two rows of wedding candles, with hairpins and jewels stripped away. Things girls like: Stopping their sewing when they're tired of embroidery and watching the swallows."

"Wedding candles, that's the happiest time, and yet you say girls are afraid of them? That makes no sense at all. You need to drink a cup, too."

In looks and talent Huiruo was not at all inferior to Suxin, but she had a calmer, gentler nature than her sister, who was quite uninhibited. Ever since her betrothal to Jishi, Huiruo's parents had kept the fact from her, but she had an inkling of it and often tried to avoid him. When in the course of this game she noticed how coquettishly her sister was behaving, she flushed with embarrassment. "I don't understand the 'rules,'" she said. "I'd rather drink a large cup."

"You're *always* writing poetry and practicing calligraphy, so why can't you play this game?" demanded Chuncai. "If you won't even try, you'll have to drink ten large cups!" He poured one out for her.

Huiruo was afraid he might use force and felt she had to drink. She said, "Things girls are afraid of: A friend telling a ghost story at midnight. Things girls like: Reading from the classics and histories at the dressing table."

"That second line is *disgusting*! Drink another cup, and then listen to me!" She drank the second cup, and he went on. "Things girls are afraid of: Getting pregnant before marriage with a belly the size of a hamper." He pointed at Jishi. "Things girls like: Marrying a husband like you."

Huiruo was so embarrassed that she hung her head and said nothing. Suxin nudged Jishi with her foot under the table. "That doesn't make any sense," said Jishi. "Why say 'like me'? Why not 'like you'? I'm fining *you* a cup, too!"

"My honorable face doesn't look as nice as yours—it doesn't appeal to people. If you don't believe me, just ask these two which one of us they love better."

"Don't talk such rot!" said Suxin. "Drink up your wine."

Huiruo had a very small capacity for wine, and after being forced to drink several cups in quick succession, she began to fidget. She was about to excuse herself when Chuncai pulled her back. He then played guess-fingers with her, and she had to drink another three or four cups. By that time she could stand it no longer and fled to her room, where she flopped down on her bed fully clothed.

Chuncai was now completely drunk. "She's too young to have any fun with," he said. "Let's go on without her." Suxin and Jishi, however, had a plan in mind and managed in less than an hour to render Chuncai utterly helpless. If his younger sister was a Chen Tuan, he was a Chen Bian.[2] He collapsed onto the platform bed and was soon lost in the world of dreams.

Jishi pretended to be drunk himself, sprawling face down on the table.

"Has Madam gone to bed yet?" Suxin asked one of the maids.

"A long time ago. It's nearly the end of the third watch."

"You two help Master Su onto the platform bed and then you can go," said Suxin as she went to her room. The maids helped Jishi onto the bed, which he shared with Chuncai. After fetching a blanket and covering them both up, the maids went off to sleep.

Jishi may have had wine in his belly, but his mind was full of other things. When he knew that the household was asleep, he pushed and pinched Chuncai a few times without getting any response. Then, ever so gently, he rose and felt his way to Suxin's room, where she had trimmed the lamp and was sitting up waiting for him. Feverishly they embraced, stripped off their clothes, and went to bed, taking their full pleasure in each other. With her arms wrapped around him, Suxin said, "What we need for our lovemaking is some really sound arrangement."

"Let's go on meeting in the studio while the teacher's away," said Jishi.

"But it's so cold now. The studio's only good in the daytime, not at night."

"The only other place is here, but I wouldn't dare come in."

"There's nothing to be afraid of. Even if my sister's quite sharp, the maids have no idea. I have thought of one thing, though. I wonder if you'd be willing to try it."

"Of course I would."

"After all, my sister and I are both going to be married to you. And young as she is, she does have some notion of what's going on. She's drunk now, so take this chance to go in and join her. If it's feasible to do it, go ahead. If not, all you need do is lie beside her for a while. After that we won't have anything to fear from her."

"I'd never dare do any such thing!"

"How are you going to catch a tiger cub if you won't go into the tiger's den?³ Oh, don't be so timid! I'll go and take a look at her first. If she's awake, I'll explain everything to her. If she's still drunk, I'll strip off her clothes so that you can have your way with her." She threw on some clothes.

Jishi tried to stop her. "Please don't go! I'm afraid she's too young."

"You're not even engaged, and already you're springing to her defense. Do you think *I* didn't suffer the other day?" Off she went to her sister's room.

Readers, let us explain. Once a girl in involved in a love affair, once she has gone astray, she will become utterly shameless and often resort to all kinds of seductive wiles solely in order to tempt her lover. However, this ploy of Suxin's was simply too ruthless.

Picking up the lantern, she went straight to her sister's room. The door was open and the lamp still alight. She pulled aside the bed curtain and found Huiruo lying with her back to the wall sound asleep, looking like a *haitang* flower after a shower of rain.

Gently Suxin helped her to sit up and removed all of her clothes. Huiruo was so heavily intoxicated that she had no idea what was happening to her. Suxin then helped her to lie down and studied her minutely for some time before covering her up again. Back in her own room, she pulled Jishi to his feet. "She's all ready for you. It's up to you now."

He was still afraid. "Oh, don't be so useless!" she said. "I'm here, in case she cries out."

Step by faltering step, Jishi made his way slowly to Huiruo's room. He hung up the curtain hook, lifted aside the embroidered coverlet, and wriggled inside her bedclothes without mishap. Then, putting one arm around her neck, he used the other to feel all over her body. He found tender breasts sprouting, darling buds about to open, dainty and soft, enough to ravish a man's soul. Then, very gently, he began to explore her nether parts with his little finger. Drunk as she was, Huiruo felt a faint twinge and turned over. At once Jishi tried to withdraw his hand, but it was now pinned beneath her, and when he tried to pull it out, she awoke. In her shock at finding herself in someone's arms, she called out to her sister for help and struggled to get up, but found herself still too weak to move.

Jishi was afraid that her cries would be overheard by Chuncai, so he hastily let her go, sat up, and said, "My dear, this is all my fault, but I wouldn't dream of offending you."

Realizing it was Jishi, she said, "You're an educated person! How could you behave in such a crazy fashion? My mother and my brother invited you here to a party—how could you use that to take advantage of me?"

When Jishi saw that she had stopped crying out, he felt somewhat relieved. "I admire your beauty so much, and I had no way of expressing myself. Since I've been granted this heaven-sent opportunity, I dearly hope you'll let me do so."

"Our marriage has already been agreed to by my parents. Once we're married, of course I'll serve you in the women's quarters. That's why at the party yesterday I didn't try to avoid your company. But as for an illicit affair, I'd rather lose my life! If people ever learned about it, I'd die of shame."

Jishi noticed how her tone had softened. "I wouldn't dare to have any such wild ideas, either. But I'm freezing out here. Please let me have a corner of the blanket so that I can warm up a bit before I leave." With that, he tried to wriggle inside her bedding again.

Huiruo cared deeply for Jishi and now, seeing him scared to death, stark naked, and piteously pleading, she felt she had to let him in. But she shrank back against the wall, where she felt about for her underclothes, put them on, and fastened them tightly. Meanwhile Jishi, having gained the advantage that he sought, began to edge slowly closer. He took her in his arms, felt her breasts and kissed her on the lips, then pulled down her drawers again. She was so alarmed that her heart pounded, but she didn't like to cry out again and had to resort to pleading: "My dear, once we are husband and wife, I will never dare to disobey you. But I'm still very young. I was asleep before, which allowed you to play a trick on me. But now that I'm aware of it, if you still insist on doing this, doesn't it mean you want me to die of pain? Please, I beg of you, wait another year or two!"

"You're right. I do love you, and I would never hurt you. My dear, let go of my hand, pull up your drawers and let me play around a little."

She had no choice but to agree. They fondled each other for a while, after which she urged him to leave. "I'm afraid my sister will find out."

Jishi explained what had happened, adding, "It was her idea that I come here tonight."

"No wonder she kicked you under the table when we were playing those drinking games last night! Well, so much the better. Hurry up and go back to her. Why do you have to keep bothering me? As for my brother, it doesn't look as if he's going to wake up before morning."

Jishi did as she said and went back to Suxin's room. Fearing that Jishi would be too rash and that her sister would raise the alarm, Suxin had sat waiting on the edge of her bed with her clothes draped around her shoulders. She heard her sister cry out, followed by silence, and concluded that her scheme had probably succeeded. She meant to undress and go to bed, but she couldn't help feeling a touch of jealousy. It was at this point that Jishi returned and told her what had happened, adding, "Your sister begged me to come back, so it's partly for her sake and partly out of gratitude to the matchmaker that I have to do this once more." They had sex again and were even more loving than before.

"This is a nice place to visit, but it's no place to stay," said Suxin.[4] "You need to go and lie down on the platform bed lest someone see you in here in the morning." She helped him on with his clothes.

When he arrived in the middle room, he found Chuncai still snoring thunderously and mumbling in his sleep. Having fought hard all night, Jishi was now exhausted in body and spirit, and he fell asleep as soon as his head hit the pillow. Suxin closed both doors and settled down to sleep herself.

Mistress Shi was a singularly crass woman. When the young people held their party the previous evening, her one concern was that they might start quarreling afterward. She listened for a while from downstairs, and then when she heard them enjoying themselves over their wine, she cheered up and went to bed, telling the maids to see to the youngsters' needs. Next morning she got up early and visited the lodge to see how things stood. The maids were still in bed, so she went upstairs herself and found the table strewn with cups and dishes. Jishi lay fully dressed on the platform bed in the center of the room, while Chuncai's head was pillowed on Jishi's legs and all of the bedding was piled on one side. She quickly ordered the maids to get up and tidy the room, while she covered the two youths with the bedclothes. When she came to Suxin's room, she found it locked. Suxin heard her mother's footsteps and threw on some clothes and opened the door. "You're up early, Mother!"

"Not all that early. How long did the party go on last night?"

"Oh, until almost the fourth watch. We girls went to bed first, while the boys continued a while longer."

"Your sister's still very young, but you ought to know better. Why didn't you girls share one room and let them have the other? Sleeping on that cold platform bed may give them both a chill. It's one thing if it's your own brother, but with someone else's child we need to take special care."

"I had too much to drink. It didn't occur to me."

"It was very thoughtless of you." She went downstairs and told the servants to prepare a broth to cure their hangovers.

Suxin chuckled to herself as she washed and combed.

It was not long before the two youths awoke, and by that time Huiruo had also finished dressing. Her awkward embarrassment when she met the others was even more touching than the night before.

"We had a high old time drinking last night," said Chuncai. "Let's do the same thing tonight."

"If we keep on like that every night, you'll drink some of us to death," said Suxin. "Mother was here just now. You'd better go and see her."

"She was? I had no idea. Let's go down together."

Thanks to his brother-in-law, the thief was welcomed in;
Thanks to his mother-in-law, he played a madman's role.

Jishi followed this pattern of wild behavior for a full five days, while his teacher remained at the grain bureau. He made a secret arrangement with Suxin that when the teacher did return they would go back to holding their meetings in the studio at noon.

On the day the teacher came back, it was time for "the birds to return to the cage, the horses to the stable," as the students pulled themselves together and began concentrating on their texts once more. However, now that Jishi's animal passions had been unleashed, he found it impossible to rein them in, and his mind was in turmoil all day long. Moreover, he had exhausted his energy for several nights in a row, and now he caught a chill. How could that delicate frame of his withstand all the wear and tear it had been subjected to? Before he knew it, he had developed a raging fever and suffered aches and pains throughout his body.

Jiangshan sent Su Bang to report on Jishi's illness to Su Wankui, while he himself hurried into town to find a doctor. He invited a Doctor Wang to come and check Jishi's pulse. After the examination the doctor asked a few questions about the origin of the illness and then went on to the schoolroom, where Jiangshan offered him a seat. "Your young gentleman's illness is due to a chill, as well as to the enervating effects of study," the doctor said. "As a result, the exogenous factors have impaired his internal organs.

Fortunately, however, the root of the trouble is still quite superficial, and he is also young, so it should not be difficult to cure. Moreover, this illness is not at its most virulent in the autumn. If I first dispel the wind and heat from his body, and then, once the external evil influences have been removed, fortify his spleen and kidneys, he should be fine."

"We shall follow your advice to the letter," said Jiangshan. The doctor then wrote out a prescription as follows:

> Radix noto-pterygii, 1½ qian; radix ledebouriellae, 1 qian; radix rehmanniae 1 qian; rhizoma ligustici, 1 qian; rhizoma atractylodis, 1½ qian; radix scutellariae, 1 qian; radix angelicae dahuriae, 1 qian; radix glycyrrhizae, 8 fen; herba asari, 5 fen; to all of which add one large piece of ginger and four large dates.

He handed the prescription to Jiangshan, who remarked, "Chonghe broth is essential medicine for a chill in all seasons. Your opinion is undoubtedly the correct one."

"Kindly consider the matter and make your decision, sir. I shall take my leave now."

Jiangshan saw him out. After Jishi began taking the medicine, he broke out in a sweat, and his illness receded a good deal. On the third day Doctor Wang returned to check his pulse and wrote a report on the patient's condition:

Exogenous factors gradually being eliminated. Pulse shallow and weak. For treatment, a tonic medicine is indicated, as follows:

> Ginseng, 3 qian; radix angelicae sinensis, 3 qian; radix astralagi, 3 qian; fried rhizoma rehmanniae, 3 qian; rhizoma ligustici, 1 qian; radix bupleuri, 3 qian; pericarpium citri reticulatae, 40 grains; rhizoma atractylodis (Taiwan), 2 qian, earth-baked; psoralea corylifolia, 3 qian; poria cum ligno hospite, 3 qian; zhicao, 25 grains; herba asari, 25 grains; add two large dates and seven lotus seeds. To be taken in five doses.

Let us now turn to Suxin. When she made love with Jishi night after night, her passions had been fully engaged, and she now found it impossible to restrain her libido. After the teacher returned, she made four or five visits to the garden without seeing any sign of Jishi. Not even Chuncai came, so she spent her days in idle conversation with Huiruo and had trouble getting to sleep at night. She would trim the lamp and sit there in silence, going over in her mind all that had happened, and when her thoughts turned to a particular incident of tender love-making, she would gulp with excitement. On the other hand, when she thought of her present lonely plight, the tears would cascade down her cheeks, and she would toss and turn, bored to distraction. The only way to pass the time was to pick up some trifling novel or play. The novel she happened to pick up was *The Merry Tale of Passionate Love*, which she read carefully from the beginning. She read of the first meeting between Sextus and Meiniang, and of how the empress suddenly made Aocao her favorite, and she thought, nothing as strange as that has ever happened in the real world. How could any man possess such an extraordinary instrument? That first time with Jishi I found the pain terribly hard to bear, and with an object like Aocao's I can't imagine how I could have coped. That sort of thing has been made up by the novelists; you just can't believe everything they say. Although her thoughts ran along these lines, the flames of her desire soared up, irrepressible. But in the depths of the women's quarters there was nothing she could do except resolve to go to the garden the next day and wait there for Jishi in order to plan some more lovemaking.

There's none to tell her secret to;
Only she can know her heart.

Speaking of Wu Daiyun's father, Biyuan, he came from Linjiang prefecture in Jiangxi and now lived in the township of Camphor Tree. Initially, he had had no trade or profession, but he passed himself off as a broker and, by relying on his native cunning, cheated and oppressed the ordinary people and lorded it over the merchants. In this way he managed to acquire a considerable stake. He then took a post as a clerk in Qingjiang county. As a minor official he went to the capital to seek preferment and was given an unranked title and assigned to Guangdong. After spending several hundred more dollars, he obtained the position of director of the River Police of Panyu county, supervising several dozen courtesan boats and collecting taxes on the money that they earned. However, the river swarmed with local, unlicensed prostitutes whose few brass hairpins could no more pay for the cases he might bring than their few pairs of smelly foot-bindings could pay for the tips he needed for the gatekeepers. Director Wu was a man greatly to be pitied, but although the job brought in very little money, if he needed a few prostitutes to serve him, they were there at his beck and call.

His wife, Mistress Gui, had borne him two children, a boy and a girl, and she was now in her forties, so Biyuan ordered one of the madams to select four young prostitutes who would be periodically rotated, nominally to attend on his wife and daughter but actually to serve his own pleasure. In this splendid situation he could drink hard liquor and consort with beautiful women, engaging with them every night. The better ones would be kept on a little longer than their normal term. Among them was one named Aqian, just fifteen years old, exceptionally beautiful and accomplished and skilled in many bedchamber arts, and Biyuan was particularly pleased with her. However, there is a limit to the sexual stamina of any man in his forties. Although Aqian instructed him in her erotic secrets, the medicinal tonics, which are helpful to the strong but not to the weak, proved rather ineffective in his case. What's more, Aqian's well-tempered furnace was capable of melting gold, let alone a waxen spearhead trying to pass itself off as silver,[5] and as time wore on Biyuan failed to rise to the occasion. As luck would have it, however, where the father failed, the son excelled. The passage from the *Analects* that runs "When there is work to be done, the young take up the burdens of their elders"[6] was one that Daiyun was well acquainted with, and the affair that developed between him and Aqian was burning hot and sticky sweet. One day Biyuan caught them at it and in a fit of jealousy gave each of them a hiding and drove Aqian out and replaced her with another girl. But then it occurred to him that with his son at home the situation would never be satisfactory, and because he was on good terms with Merchant Wen, he sent Daiyun away to study in the Wen family school. Daiyun, however, was always eager to return home. Although Aqian had been driven out, but her successors may have been equally successful, under Aqian's tutelage Daiyun had developed a very fine turtle, and the girls were all enamored of such a champion.

One day Daiyun was studying in the family school when Wankui came by to visit the teacher and check on his ailing son. Merchant Wen was at home at the time, and he invited them both in for a drink. Daiyun went out into the garden to relieve himself and found the chrysanthemums still in bloom beside Break-Cassia Studio. Stopping to admire them, he heard someone inside sighing ever so faintly. This leads to the women's quarters, he thought; no one but family would ever come here. I've long heard that Chuncai had a sister about the same age as he. I did think of asking for her in marriage, but I was afraid she might look like Chuncai, so I never opened my mouth. This just might be her—I'll go and see.

He walked around to the front of the studio, where he had a faint vision of a beautiful girl sitting on the couch, her head cast down as if deep in thought. Overwhelmed by the sight, he marveled that the world should contain so gorgeous a creature. Heaven is offering me this chance today, he thought, and I mustn't let it slip. He rushed toward her.

Suxin was sitting there quietly waiting for Jishi, her mind full of amorous thoughts. She heard someone come rushing in and assumed it was Jishi, but when she looked up, she received a shock. Daiyun, nothing if not crude, uttered a cry of "Miss" and then rushed forward and threw his arms about her.

"You brute! How dare you take such liberties!" she cried, her heart in her mouth.

"My name is Wu, and I study every day in your family school. It must be my destiny, meeting you today. No one ever comes along here, so it's no use crying out." As he said these words, he pinned her down on the couch, planted his mouth against her cherry-red lips, and inserted his tongue between them like a thirsty dragon in search of water. Suxin's mouth ran with saliva and her body went limp. With his free hand Daiyun tore at the sash that held her skirt. Since Suxin had been making love to Jishi, she wore only a sash, not a belt, and with one tug, both skirt and trousers came down. He had meant to make a frontal attack, but she would not let him. However, she could not free herself from his tight embrace, and, after stealing a glance at his instrument, she became even more scared. I'm dead, she thought, wriggling frantically from side to side, her tiny feet thrashing about in a wild dance.

"Dear Master Wu, have mercy on me!" she pleaded.

"Don't worry. I know what I'm doing."

Readers, you should understand that Suxin had a wanton, lascivious streak in her, and she let go of him and allowed him to try. For some time she bore the pain, but then it turned to plea-sure, and she felt a thrill unlike anything she had ever experienced with Jishi. Gradually, she brought her hands closer and clutched at him. Daiyun had reached the height of ecstasy, and the flood-gates opened. He was under the impression that he had taken her vir-ginity, whereas he had actually been following in Jishi's footsteps. Eventually he would come to have a latecomer's remorse.

He helped her up and dressed her, but she couldn't move her limbs, and he took her gently into his arms and sat her on his lap and showed her a tender affection. He then suggested a second meeting, and she naturally consented. After that he left, but she stayed there for some time before slowly making her way back to her room. Utterly exhausted in spirit, she lay on her bed as if paralyzed, thinking, such bliss does exist, after all! He may not be Master Su's equal in looks, but if I were married to him, my life would be all I could wish for. Moreover, this very thing came up in that dream I had the other day. I'll take advantage of the fact that Master Su is still in the dark and get this man to propose first. My sister will marry Master Su, and no one will be able to accuse me of breaking my word. With this sudden change of mind, she cast aside the love she had felt for Jishi.

The next day Daiyun returned to the garden. This time Suxin was able to receive him, and he spared no effort in his lovemak-ing. Each was as ardent as the other, and they swore eternal vows over and over again. Daiyun asked leave from the teacher to return home, where he told his father. Biyuan, who was an avid social climber, had high hopes of a dowry from marriage to a rich man's daughter, and he promptly entrusted the matchmaking to a certain Master Lü of the Salt Administration. Merchant Wen readily ac-cepted the proposal, and the dispatching of the betrothal presents was set for the eighteenth of the tenth month.

More of this in the next chapter.

Chapter VI

Heh Zhifu installs mistresses in a separate wing
Li Jiangshan comes upon a hero in Qujiang county

After Jishi began taking the tonic medicine, his illness showed a steady improvement, and then, after he had taken ten doses of the great all-purpose restorative broth, he fully regained his normal vitality. However, because the teacher had forbidden him to leave his room, he had to stay there for over a month before he could do as he wanted. Then, with his mind focused on Suxin, he took a walk in the garden. It was the middle of the tenth month, and the weather was turning cold. He wore a satin brocade gown with a down lining and a formal jacket of leather studded with pearls. He intended to walk around the garden as far as Pity-the-Flowers Lodge and then on to the main room for a little diversion, but when he came to Break-Cassia Studio, the memory of what had occurred there came back to him and he lingered awhile, reluctant to leave. Just at that moment Suxin herself happened to come in with her light tread. Bursting into a smile, Jishi rushed forward and exclaimed, "My dear, I never expected to meet you here!"

Suxin had not even realized that he had been ill; it was to see Daiyun that she had come. But these words of Jishi's touched on the cause of her own undoing, and she gave a lukewarm reply: "What do you mean? I only came out to look at the hibiscus and stopped by just for a moment."

"That just shows that you and I are destined for each other!" Taking her by the hand, he led her into the studio, intent on trying out his energies on the couch after a month or more away.

But Suxin was unwilling. "Things are not the way they were. People come here all the time, and if someone were to see us, we'd never be able to hold our heads up again."

Jishi continued to pester her, and she had to let him dally with her for awhile. He had the impression that her flesh was softer and looser than it had been. Fearing that Daiyun would suddenly come upon them, she made a perfunctory effort to respond, and Jishi, weakened by his illness, promptly discharged like Zhong Zi.[1] She quickly got up to leave, trying to think of some way to break off her relationship with Jishi. She would have to meet Daiyun in the evenings, she decided.

After that Jishi never saw her again when he visited the garden. And if he went into the house to see her, she treated him with the same studied indifference. He was still puzzling over the reason when it came time for the betrothal ceremony.

On that day the Wen house resounded with the music of drums and pipes, and there was a lively gathering of friends and relatives, including both Jiangshan and Wankui. The students at the school were also invited, but Jishi declined and sat brooding in his room. I never expected her to be so faithless as actually to accept the proposal of the Wus, he thought; no wonder she was so cold to me a few days ago. Then another thought struck him. She's a girl, and she has no control over such matters. Her parents must have agreed to the match, leaving her with no choice. The only pity is that I was sick at the time and had no idea of what was going on. I don't know whether she somehow blames me, but I can hardly blame her! But if she really was unwilling, why didn't she give me any hint of it? It's so hard to be sure. Then another thought occurred to him: when we met the other day in the studio not only was she less loving than before, even that thing of hers was not as tight as it used to be. Don't say Wu succeeded with her while I was on my sickbed! If that's the case, he and I are mortal enemies. But then his thoughts took another turn. When she formally becomes his wife, I shall have a guilty conscience and will hardly be able to set myself against old Wu. I'll just congratulate him and then go in and see her and find out the truth.

He made a long detour through the building to the main hall, where he found Madam Shi feverishly at work with a number of female relatives. Bowing, he congratulated her.

"Master Su, why aren't you up front celebrating?"

"Thank you, but I'm still recovering from my illness, and I can't eat anything too rich. But I do need to go and see Suxin and offer her my congratulations."

"She's very bashful and is hiding out in her room. I don't have time to go myself, but I'll get one of the maids to take you."

Jishi went to the lodge and climbed the stairs, only to find Suxin's door shut tight. He rapped on it and said, "My dear, there's someone here to congratulate you." No sound came from inside. After standing there for some time, he grew bored; there was nothing for it but to go despondently downstairs again. Huiruo was just coming up at the time, and Jishi stopped and told her why he had come.

"I never expected her to change like this," Huiruo confided in a whisper. "When I heard the news the other day, I asked her about it time and again, but all she would say was that Father and Mother had made the decision and it couldn't be changed. However, I looked into it and found there was another reason as well, and I would urge you to give up all hope of her. But you and I are bound to each other by our lovemaking in a lifelong commitment, and you must make your decision as soon as possible. If anything should go amiss, I shall take my own life. From now on it will be hard for us to meet. Look after yourself." As she said these words, the tears began streaming down her cheeks. Afraid that someone might see, she began slowly climbing the stairs, at the same time motioning to him to leave.

Jishi did not go out on the street again, but walked back through the garden. He was full of hatred for Suxin but full of love for Huiruo. What she had said was so impassioned and yet so prudent, but he couldn't for the life of him think what she meant by "another reason" and "hard for us to meet." (Readers, Huiruo had discovered Suxin's guilty secret. Fearing that Daiyun would extend his attentions to her, she had found a pretext to get her mother to approach her father and see if the garden gate could be locked. Her father had agreed.)

Jishi spent the night in a state of dazed melancholy. Next morning he rose, took some tonic, and pondered two courses of action: to find out what Daiyun had done, and to go home and beg his mother to complete his own betrothal arrangements as soon as possible. Toward evening, he saw Daiyun heading into the garden and slowly followed him. When he came to the studio, Jishi heard voices inside and slipped around to the back to eavesdrop. All he could hear was, "Don't be so violent. You were too rough last time, and I ached for half the night. It felt burning hot down there, and I needed two days to recover." Then he heard another voice saying, "But what pleasure will we get if I don't put some effort into it? Next year, when we're married, I shall have a lot of wonderful techniques to show you."

So that was the reason! thought Jishi. Then he took a cautious look through a crack in the window and saw Suxin lying on the side of the platform bed and Daiyun standing there beside it, thrusting hard. After glimpsing Daiyun's laundry beater of an instrument, Jishi felt ashamed of his own inadequacy. No wonder she gave me the cold shoulder, he thought. But since they're engaged, why do I need to concern myself with them anymore? I'll just keep to my Huiruo and not run the risk of losing one thing by pursuing another. He promptly returned to the school and applied to the teacher for permission to go home on urgent business.

The flowers wither, fade, and fall to earth—
Let bees, butterflies, and winds do their worst.

Let us turn back to Master Heh, who had schemed to be the superintendent of the Guangdong Customs for the sole purpose of getting rich and indulging in sex. After he received that sum of money from Su Wankui, thousands and tens of thousands kept pouring in. He issued an order changing the personnel in the various customs posts in the Chaozhou and Huizhou prefectures, and then dispatched a number of able assistants to occupy the central customs post and levy an extra twenty percent, labeled "expenses," on top of the regular taxes. Goods hitherto exempt from tax such as clothes, cases, packages, and miscellaneous utensils were also subjected to a special tax called a "candlelight levy." All of these ideas emanated from Bao Jincai.

From keeping company all the time with the same group of girls, Heh found the domestic fare too humdrum and began to long for a taste of the exotic flavors of Guangdong. He consulted his servant Ma Bole on the matter, and Ma replied, "That's no problem at all! The Guangdong pleasure boats come under the river police of Panyu county. All I need do is have a word with Wu Biyuan and tell him to select a few dozen girls and send them over for you to choose from. If they serve you particularly well, you just give them a few dollars."

"Yes, go ahead and do that, by all means! But see you look

them over carefully." Bole assented and took a sedan chair to the river police headquarters.

On hearing that Customs had sent someone to see him, Wu Biyuan naturally wanted to make a special fuss of the messenger, and he hurried out to the inner gate to receive him. "I wasn't expecting a visit from you, sir," he said, as he brought his visitor inside. "Let me apologize for not receiving you in the proper manner."

"Oh, not at all. I wouldn't be so presumptuous as to call on you, except that my master has ordered me to consult you about something."

Startled, Wu Biyuan thought to himself, surely Customs isn't going to start supervising tax collection from the women? "What orders does His Honor have for me?" he asked.

"When he came here, he brought his family with him, but he has a very small staff. He wants you to select several dozen girls from the river and send them along. After he's received them, there'll naturally be a reward for you."

"Of course I'll do as directed, but can you tell me whether he wants them young or rather older?"

Ma Bole laughed. "You're not a scholar—how can you be so daft? Young or old—what do you think these servant girls are for? So long as they're between the ages of thirteen and seventeen, they'll do."

"Of course," said Biyuan. As he prepared wine to serve to his guest, he issued a summons to the madams and runners.

Bole was still afraid that the prostitutes would get wind of his mission and flee, so he accompanied Wu along the river, selecting from the Yangzhou girls as he went. The river people were reluctant to comply, but when they saw their own director there, backed by the power of the Customs, they had to permit the selection to take place and allow the names of the chosen girls to be entered in a register. The whole process took almost two days. After Bole had chosen forty-four girls, he hired sedan chairs for them and sent them to the Customs. Wu Biyuan escorted them himself.

Heh read the report submitted to him and then told Wu to wait outside while the girls went into the western reception room to await selection. Heh himself had his concubines examine them from every angle before selecting four who were both beautiful and gifted—Qinyun, Aitao, Aqian, and Sihui—and four others of flawless beauty who were still virgins—Youjia, Huanfei, Ke'er, and Meizi. The rest he sent back to the river, paying out a thousand taels. The eight girls selected he assigned to live in four separate compounds, each with maids and women servants to attend on them. He also detailed his concubines Pinxing and Pinting to instruct them in etiquette, and Pinwa, supervisor of his domestic cashier's office, to pay each of them four taels a month. He himself took his time appreciating their various charms, taking them one after the other.

> He's a butterfly among the flowers;
> No salt is needed to attract his cart.[2]

After catching Suxin having sex with Daiyun in the garden, Jishi abandoned his love for her and went home to recuperate for a few days and also to urge his mother to arrange the match with Huiruo. She spoke to his father, who sent a matchmaker to the Wens with the proposal. Merchant Wen had a lively appreciation of the wealth of the Sus, and in addition to that, Jishi was a handsome young licentiate; he had long had this match in mind and readily accepted the proposal. Only after the betrothal gifts had been delivered did Jishi finally go back to school. Now that the marriage had been arranged, Mistress Shi and the others treated him more affectionately than ever, but the two sisters avoided him completely. Since his daughters were now grown up, Merchant Wen had workmen block up the side entrance to Pity-the-Flowers Lodge, so that even Wu Daiyun could only face the wall and sigh in frustration. With a pair of wings, he'd have still found it hard to get in.

Time slipped by, and soon the chill north wind was blowing and the winter plum was blossoming on the slopes. Jiangshan gathered his employers together and told them that he was about to close the school and would be returning home in the first month of the new year—he could stay no longer. Before anyone else could reply, Wankui said, "With regard to your desire to ease your filial concerns by returning home, we never expected such a swift steed could be held to a mere walk. However, my son has been receiving instruction from you for some time, and I too have often benefited from your guidance. When can I show you how grateful I am? I shall never forget what I owe you."

"For the three years that I have tarried here, I can perhaps escape the reproach of 'eating the food of idleness,' but the boys have remarkable natural talents, and I do deserve the criticism that they have surpassed their teacher. I feel truly ashamed about that."

"Let me avail myself of the presence of Kinsmen Wen and Wu. I have a heartfelt request that I hope you will agree to."

"May I ask what instructions you have for me?"

"I understand that your son is thirteen, which is the same age as my daughter Pearl. If I may be so bold as to ask Brother Wen to act as matchmaker, my daughter would gladly serve your son as his wife."

Jiangshan burst out laughing. "But that's simply too absurd! I live in an out-of-the-way place, and we have always been poor, frugal people, the men farming and the women weaving as we dabble in the classics. Such a marriage would not only be demeaning for your daughter, who is a young lady, but also for a man of your stature. I fear that our humble dwelling would only bring disgrace upon you. The whole idea is *most* unsuitable."

"Under your guidance I've come to realize that wealth is not something that can be depended on and that poverty is perfectly acceptable. However, your latest views on poverty and wealth contrast sharply with what you taught me before. No matter how far it is to your home, so long as you send me an invitation, I shall personally escort my daughter there. My mind is made up; I hope you won't refuse my request." So saying, he took from his pocket a red satin betrothal card containing a gold hairpin adorned with two phoenixes holding pearls in their mouths and gave it to Wen, who passed it on to Jiangshan. He had no choice but to accept it, and he produced an emerald paperweight himself as a makeshift betrothal present. The two men bowed to each other before proceeding to enjoy the feast. Afterward, Jishi accompanied his father home. Of course people made the inevitable jokes about a rich man allying himself in marriage with a poor scholar, but the fact that Wankui actually took pleasure in the union was truly exceptional.

As winter gave way to spring, Jiangshan set the date for his departure and went about saying his farewells but not accepting any of the parting gifts that he was offered. After taking leave of Shen, who gave him some advice, he hired a boat and together with Yinzhi and three servants set off for home. Merchant Wen and Chuncai gave him a farewell feast on the dock. Wu Daiyun was also present as well as several others whom Jiangshan knew. Only

Wankui and Jishi were absent. Although Jiangshan did not mind in the least, the others were distinctly surprised.

Having said his farewells, he had sailed as far as Huatian when he saw in the distance a pleasure boat with many people in the bow, including Wankui and his son. As the boats came closer, they greeted each other. "Kinsman," said Wankui, "your leaving is like the yellow stork ascending to heaven; I shall not be able to welcome you again. I deeply regret the rash behavior of my youth, when I willfully persisted in my actions. I wonder if you have any words of advice for me on parting. How does one bring a dead man back to life and put flesh on his bones? I hope you will teach me how to live out the rest of my life."

"You're a naturally perceptive man, and you've awakened extremely early from illusion. The love of charity—that's the one thing worth devoting your life to. My only caveat is that you mustn't pray for any of the rewards that come from charity."

He turned to Jishi: "You're still very young. You should concentrate on the classics and the histories. The sage's Three Prohibitions are something you should ponder over and over again."[3] Jishi undertook to do so.

"Your instructions will be engraved on our foolish hearts," said Wankui. "The other day I received a letter from the capital saying that my son would be promoted to senior licentiate in time for the provincials in Beijing. If both teacher and student should be at the examination together, I beg you to take good care of him."

"Of course I will."

"I've prepared a box of embroidered clothing and a set of bedding that will help protect you a little from the spring cold along the way. I hope you will accept."

"That's such a generous gesture, I wouldn't think of refusing. But fortunately I'm not begging for food like Zixu, and you don't need to offer me a silk gown like Fan Sui."[4]

"The clothes and bedding are merely for use on a long journey. If you were to decline them, wouldn't it seem a trifle... affected?"

"I accept your generosity. I wouldn't dare decline."

They drank heartily before parting. "You must make a careful note of what your teacher said," Wankui said to his son afterward. "I'll take this boat into town and offer my New Year's greetings to people. I'll probably be away two or three days. You go on home."

Jishi did so, accompanied by several servants. At the inner gate, a maid took his clothes bag from him, and in his mother's room he took off his coat and lay down on the bed. "I've drunk several cups of wine and walked ever so far," he said. "My feet are awfully sore."

"Your face is still bright red," said his mother. "I expect you're tired out from all that walking." She told Wuyun to massage his feet. Jishi was a lad with girls constantly on his mind. Ever since he broke up with Suxin, he had genuinely toiled at his studies, while looking forward eagerly to satisfying his desires with the maids once school was out. Unfortunately, his father had become stricter than ever and would let him stay only in the outer study. During the day he came in only if he was needed, and at night he slept in the study. As a result he was a hero without a battlefield on which to display his prowess. On this occasion, as Wuyun massaged his legs, he seized the chance when his mother's back was turned to start fondling the girl's hands and feet. She did not dare say anything, just gave him a faint smile.

"Father won't be back for a few days," he told his mother, "and it's so lonely out there. What if I were to sleep in one of the inner rooms?"

"Well, the rooms *are* empty on that side. I've told your father several times that you ought to be sleeping in an inner room, but he would never agree. He says that you can only move in after you are married. But he's not here just now, so why don't you move in for a few days? I'll have the maids get a room ready. There'll be two young maids and two women servants there. If you think you'll be lonely, let me get a few more older ones to keep you company."

"My dear mother, I don't care for those vulgar creatures. Just tell Wuyun to get the room ready." His mother smiled and told Wuyun and Chuyao to make up the bed, hang up the bed curtain, and warm and scent the bedclothes.

After Jishi had had supper with his sisters, he got very drunk. Mistress Mao had Wuyun and Xiayun support him, while she herself saw him to his room and safely into bed. She then told Chuyao and Xiuyan to bed down beside the couch as company for him. "If the young master calls for anything during the night, see that you don't shirk," she told them. Before returning to her own room, she also told two young maids and two women servants to sleep in the passageway outside and look after him.

Jishi was drunk but not hopelessly so, and when he heard his mother leaving, he turned over and called to Wuyun to bring him some tea. Of all the maids Wuyun was the prettiest, and Jishi had long had his eye on her. However, because she was older than Jishi, Mistress Mao had been afraid she might seduce him and did not assign her to him as a companion. The two girls she did assign were both of only middling attractiveness. When Xiuyan heard Jishi calling for tea, she gave Chuyao a push to get her up. "He called for Wuyun, not me," Chuyao said. Jishi called out twice more, and Xiuyan had to go and pour the tea herself.

"Where's Wuyun?" he asked, as she handed him the tea.

"Why are you so anxious to have her especially?" asked Xiuyan. "She's with the mistress, not here. Are you saying we aren't capable of attending on you?"

"That's not what I meant at all. Are you the only one here? Is there anybody else?"

"Chuyao's here with me. The four outside have always looked after the place."

"We don't need a whole lot of people. Chuyao, you sleep in the anteroom. Let's set up a rotation, with one of you attending on me each night." Chuyao left the room.

When Xiuyan shut the door and came to take his teacup. Jishi caught her hand. "Don't make up a pallet for yourself. Let's share the bed together."

"I'm not so blessed—I've not slept with anyone. Wouldn't it be better to call Wuyun in to keep you company?" She pulled her hand away, and with a smile on her face began to spread out her bedclothes on the floor. Jishi, who was naked, jumped down from the bed, seized her, and stripped off her clothes, after which they got into bed together.

"How old are you?"

"Thirteen."

"Silly girl! Thirteen, and you still don't know what's what? Let's try. I'm not a virgin myself. You'll just have to be a stand-in for Wuyun." All Xiuyan could do was grit her teeth and endure the pain. The following night Chuyao was unable to avoid the same fate. These incidents must be counted among the sins of Jishi's youth.

The three of them continued in this fashion for four or five nights, until Wankui returned and Jishi moved out again.

"Your future parents-in-law miss you a great deal," Wankui told Jishi. "You'd better take a trip into town tomorrow. But you're not to do any wild carousing on the night of the Lantern Festival." Jishi, who felt bored at home, leapt at the chance. The next day he went into the city, taking Su Bang and Aqing with him, and at the

Wen compound greeted the master and mistress and the two concubines. Merchant Wen had to go out on business, but Mistress Shi
arranged a dinner for him. Jishi wanted to see Suxin. She refused to
come out of her room, but Mistress Shi pressed her, and she finally
had to come out and meet him. Jishi had been hoping that she
would drink a cup of wine with them, but she gave a single curtsey
and returned to her room.

"What you don't realize, young master, is that she's going to
be married in the third month," said Mistress Shi.

"So the date has been set? Well, I'll offer her my congratulations some other time." Mistress Shi and Chuncai accompanied
Jishi in his drinking, and he stayed in their house that night, then
next day took his leave and went about town offering New Year's
greetings. He delivered an invitation at the grain bureau and
called in at all of the traders' houses. On his return, he visited Wu
Biyuan's yamen, where Biyuan treated him lavishly. Jishi asked to
greet Mistress Gui, and Biyuan took him to the rear. Jishi stepped
forward and gave a deep bow.

Space at the river police yamen was highly restricted; Mistress
Gui and her daughter lived in three rooms, the middle one being a
tiny sitting room. Jishi had entered before the daughter, Qiao, had
had time to leave the room, and he was struck by her extraordinary beauty. So old Wu has a daughter like this, he marveled. She
couldn't be more different than her brother! Mistress Gui invited
him to sit down, and a maid served tea. Qiao slowly withdrew to
her room, where she hung up a door curtain that allowed her to
watch him as much as she liked. She was greatly taken by what she
saw.

Before long Jishi said goodbye to Mistress Gui. Because Daiyun
was not at home, he meant to leave, but Biyuan wouldn't hear of
it. "A visit from you is a great occasion. My son has gone to Zhong-

tang Township for the celebrations,⁵ but he'll certainly be back tomorrow. You must stay with us for a few days. We have all kinds of amusements. The only drawback is our lack of space, which is demeaning for someone like you." He told his servants to treat Jishi's servants to a meal, and at the same time prepared a feast for Jishi. Because the latter was a rich man's son with good prospects, the reception was solicitous and the hospitality lavish. After dinner, Biyuan personally escorted Jishi to an inner room to sleep, telling him, "This is my son's bedroom, where I'd like you to stay. Don't laugh, small though it is. There's a modest garden at the back, if you care to amuse yourself there. And now I'm afraid you'll have to excuse me; there's some business I need to see to."

Jishi, who was beginning to feel the effects of the wine, sprawled out across the couch and took a brief rest. Then Su Bang came in and reported, "I need to go down to Great New Street to buy a few odds and ends. Aqing would like to go with me."

"Off you go, then. Come back soon, and see you don't get into any fights."

Jishi lay down but couldn't sleep. He sat up, chose some of Daiyun's books, and started leafing through them. A servant brought in some tea, and he dismissed her. As he drank the tea, he continued leafing through the books. Tucked between the pages of one book were a few exotic prescriptions, which he pored over, thinking, no wonder old Wu has such a marvelous instrument on him! He's been taking medicine in order to cultivate it! Snatching up a brush, he copied out the prescriptions. Then he stood up and looked around. The back door was open. Old Wu mentioned something about a garden, he recalled; I wonder what it's like. Outside he found trees of various sizes and a vegetable garden, but no pavilions or terraces. Strolling along a brick path, he saw in the distance a few withered plum trees and beside them a tall pavilion. He walked toward it. It was furnished with tables, chairs and couches. Above the doorway was a tablet that bore the name Plum-tree Vista, and at the head of the pavilion was a statue of Guanyin the White-robed. It was wonderfully quiet and tranquil. He enjoyed the scene for awhile, then turned and came out, only to be confronted by the sight of Qiao heading directly toward him, parting the flowers and willow fronds as she came. He was so delighted that he bowed and said, "I didn't realize you were coming here. I should have kept away."

She blushed and giggled as she curtsied. "It's all my fault. I'm the one who should have kept away." Jishi was about to say something, but she had already walked slowly off.

He gazed after her. "What a beautiful, clever girl!" he exclaimed in admiration. "Even better than the Wen girls! It must be fate that I met her today." He returned slowly to his room.

> He glimpsed a goddess come down from Heaven,
> With grace and beauty fair, a nubile maid,
> He painted eyebrows with the governor's skill,[6]
> The strokes with heavy sadness overlaid.

Let us turn to Li Jiangshan. After parting from Wankui, he had hoisted sail and set off, passing by Foshan. Along the way he heard the boatmen discussing a recent increase in the number of pirates and mentioning places where merchants had been robbed and their boats burned. This journey, however, was quite uneventful, except that travel by night was impossible. The boatmen also said that fully half of the embankment guards were in league with the robbers. Jiangshan listened to all of this talk but paid it scant attention, whereas Shen Yinzhi was distinctly worried. Fortunately, Heaven favors the good, and within ten days they had reached Shaoguan. Since the river was too shallow for their boat to proceed to Nanxiong, they had to change to another boat, and while their belongings were being transferred, all five of them, masters and servants, put up at an inn. Magistrate Yuan of Qujiang county, in which Shaoguan was situated, had taken the examinations in the same year as Master Shen, and when Yinzhi sent in his visiting card, the magistrate invited him to stay for dinner. By dusk he had still not returned, and Jiangshan told his servants to open up the cases of bedding and clothes that Wankui had given them. They found six sets of bedclothes, four lined and two unlined, plus imported blankets and sheets, all of the finest quality, for which Jiangshan was profoundly grateful. The clothing cases were full of embroidered lined garments of down and wool, as well as a package of foreign cloth that felt extremely heavy. When they opened it, they found a small gilded box containing six large ingots of silver, six ingots of gold, and a letter, which read as follows:

> Every day I received instruction from a man of lofty aspirations and uncompromising integrity, and to my shame I failed to realize it. By good fortune a marriage has been arranged between our children, and I can therefore attach myself to you. But now that you have suddenly left us and are far away, how can I dispel the concern that I feel? I have respectfully prepared three hundred taels of silver and two catties of gold to help in a small way with the expenses of your long journey. My thoughts go with you as you travel. Words cannot adequately express what I feel.

After reading the letter, Jiangshan heaved a sigh: "What concern he has for us! We can't possibly go back and return the money, so we'll have to try to find some good use for it." He locked the box, picked up a candle, and began to read. Then he heard someone in the next room beating his chest and sighing deeply, and he thought: That fellow who's sighing with grief must surely be some stranger in despair. I wonder if he could be a literary man or a scholar. Then he heard, very faintly, the words, "What am I to do?" and could restrain himself no longer. He gave orders to his servant Li Xiang: "Go over and ask that gentleman why he's sighing like that so late at night."

Li Xiang found that the man's room was pitch dark, with no lamp. "My young master would like to know what you're doing all this sighing for in the middle of the night," he said.

"And just what does your young master propose to do about it, if he won't let a man sigh?" the other demanded. "I suppose if he was an old man instead of a young one, he wouldn't even let anybody speak! Who does he think he is, throwing his weight about in this inn? Go and tell him to mind his own business!"

"Someone asks you a question with the best of intentions, and you go crazy!"

"Who's crazy?" said the man furiously. "You're trying to push me around, but I'm not afraid of you."

Li Xiang was about to reply when the innkeeper came in with a lantern. "Look here, don't you start making any trouble," he said to the man. "These two gentlemen are from Guangzhou, and they're related to the local magistrate. Now, no more trouble, do you hear!"

This made the man even more furious. "Even if they are related to the magistrate, they can't fucking well tell me what to do!" he shouted.

Jiangshan heard the uproar, and chided himself for interfering in other people's affairs. He promptly went out and shouted at Li Xiang to leave, then bowed to the man and said with a smile, "Don't be angry, worthy brother. You gave a deep sigh, so I sent him around to ask you what the matter was. Unfortunately he was rude and offended you, but I hope that for my sake you'll overlook it."

Jiangshan was so respectful and expressed himself so humbly that the other man raised his hand. "I was the one who was offensive," he said.

Jiangshan saw that, although somewhat rough and coarse, this fellow cut a noble, heroic figure, and he added, "If there's something bothering you, perhaps you might care to step over to my room and discuss it?"

"That's most kind of you, sir, but I wouldn't want to bother you."

"We're staying here in the same in, on equal terms." They moved to the other room.

Jiangshan told the innkeeper to prepare some wine, and the other man expressed his thanks, bowed, and sat down. "May I be so bold as to ask your name and what brings you here?" said Jiangshan.

"I'm Yao Huowu, from Shandong. Because my brother, Weiwu, was a commander in the governor's brigade, I came here to visit him, but when I got to Guangzhou I found that he'd been promoted to a post in Fujian. I had no one to turn to, and so I was stranded there in Guangzhou at the mercy of some very mean-spirited people. Luckily, I met up with a trader, Master Su Wankui, who gave me fifty taels of silver. I paid off my debt at the inn, reclaimed my baggage from the pawnbroker, and arranged to return home. However, when I got here in the tenth month of last year, I heard that my brother had been transferred once more, this time to be a colonel at Jieshi. I was thinking of turning back and seeking him out, when—talk about troubles coming in pairs!—I got ill and needed over two months to recover. By now all of my money is gone, and I still owe the innkeeper a few taels for food. I can't leave this place and I can't stay here, either—that's why I gave that sigh."

"So your brother was a commander in the governor's brigade?"

"That's right. May I be so bold as to ask your name?"

Jiangshan told him, adding that he was a relative and good friend of Su Wankui. Yao was delighted to hear it. When the food arrived, he wolfed it down without any polite protestations. Jiangshan saw how much he was enjoying the food, and he kept ordering more, at the same time asking, "What did you have in mind in going to join your brother?"

"I'm a rough-and-ready sort of fellow. I don't have any other talents, but I can lift a couple of thousand catties, and I'm an expert archer and horseman. I thought I'd capture a few pirates along the coast in order to serve the court and win honors for my family. I've had plenty to eat and drink, so I'll take my leave now."

Jiangshan was attracted by his blunt, direct manner. "You're the real hero type," he said. "I have a little money on me that I'd like to share with you, to help you on your way."

"But how can I accept such a favor from you?" asked Yao Huowu. Jiangshan told one of his servants to open the box and take out the three hundred taels that Wankui had given him. "These were a present from my relative, Su Wankui, and I'd like to pass them on to you."

"But twenty or thirty taels would be enough to get me to Huizhou! What do I need with all of this?"

"There'll come a time when you need it. I have more than enough for my journey. Now don't be too modest."

"You're so generous, I wouldn't dare refuse. But before I accept there's one favor I'd like to ask."

"What is that?"

"If you don't think me too crude and hot-headed, I beg you

to accept me as a sworn brother. Could you lower yourself to do that?"

"When a request comes from the heart, it's granted in a flash."

Huowu made a resounding kowtow, but Jiangshan pulled him to his feet. They exchanged bows and addressed each other as brother.

When Shen Yinzhi returned, he greeted Huowu and suggested that they ask the magistrate to hire them a boat. "But the pirates are running wild around here," objected Huowu, "and they have no fear of officials. As for the Meiling road, it's swarming with bandits. Let me escort you as far as Nan'an and then come back here."

"Even better!" said Jiangshan. "I was reluctant to part with you so soon, anyway."

The next day they embarked together. Along the way Jiangshan had numerous opportunities to instruct and encourage Huowu, and the latter gratefully accepted his advice. Only after escorting them as far as Meiling did he disembark, parting from Jiangshan in tears.

Chapter VII

An ambitious river police chief plays along
A humiliated customs official hangs himself

⤳

Wu Biyuan had arranged his son's wedding for the third of the third month, and on that day a banquet was prepared and his yamen decorated with bunting and lanterns. Merchant Wen did likewise, and also invited a group of female guests to escort the dowry. Two days before he had invited the women of the Shy, Wen, and Su families to come over and see it. After they had arrived and greeted each other, Mistress Shi told Huiruo to pay her respects to her future mother-in-law. The four girls of the two families were extremely polite and cordial with one another and went over to the lodge together. Pearl and Belle still felt like strangers, but Xia welcomed them warmly. She was a gifted talker and had a free and easy manner with many quips and jests at her disposal. Suxin affected a certain bashfulness and made some small talk with the others, but when she saw the two Su girls, her thoughts inevitably turned to Jishi, and it was fortunate that he was not there.

He had been staying for some time at the Wu house. When the dowry was delivered, he had no desire to go and see it. Instead, he joined a group of Daiyun's friends in their eagerness to eat, drink, banter, and play practical jokes. Who were these friends, you ask. One was Shr Bangchen, a minor official from Suzhou who had retired and made his home in Guangzhou, where he ran a fashionable curio shop. He could sing a few song suites and was a good lute player. Another was Shy Yannian, whose father was the clerk in charge of a customs post; Yannian himself, however, was a drifter and debauchee. There were also two brothers, Zhu Zhonghuang and Zhu Lihuang, whose father used to be the deputy magistrate of Lingtang township. After it came to light that he had been taking bribes, he wasted away in prison, and his sons, without the money to get home, made a living in Guangzhou as hangers-on. Another was Qu Guanglang, from Hangzhou, who could not read a word and posed as an educated man. He had lost his tutoring position many years before. These five were all idlers and scroungers who attached themselves to the gambling world and the prostitutes. At sight of Jishi, they concluded that he was a regular young toff and employed all of their skills in flattering him, while Jishi, for his part, thought of them as amusing companions. On this occasion the banter continued until evening, when they broke up. Daiyun invited all of them to his wedding, insisting that they come, and they respectfully agreed.

Jishi was about to take his leave, too, when Biyuan and his son urged him to stay longer, insisting that he not go back until after the bride's return home on the third day. Biyuan personally took Jishi into the inner quarters to rest and then, after dismissing his servants, called in the prostitute on duty to serve tea. After Jishi had sent his own servants home, Biyuan grasped his hand and said in a low voice, "There's a favor I'd like to ask of you. I don't know if you'd be amenable."

"Just tell me what I can do for you."

"This wretched job of mine has recently gotten even worse. There are countless expenses, and the income simply doesn't match the outgoings. Lately I've spent a lot on my son's wedding, and I'm finding it next to impossible to cope. Could I ask you to be so kind as to lend me three hundred taels, to be paid back this winter?"

"That's no problem at all. Since you need the money, I'll have it brought around tomorrow."

Biyuan bowed as he thanked him, then added, "Do stay on a few nights in this cramped little place of mine. That maid Yeyun is really quite smart; I'll have her look after you."

"As you wish, but I do feel a little awkward about it."

"We're relatives, after all; there's no need to be so formal." With that Biyuan took his leave.

Yeyun came forward, pulled off Jishi's boots and socks, and helped him undress. He was under the impression that she was one of the maids and didn't like to flirt with her, but simply lay down on the bed. To his astonishment, after covering him up, she shut the door, and then undressed and slipped under the bedclothes beside him. Before he had even made a move, she put one arm around his neck and felt him down below with the other. He had by now fully recovered from his illness and was also somewhat older. In addition, he had taken a good deal of the medicine and could well be described as "presenting an entirely different aspect after a brief absence." Their lovemaking was easy and enjoyable. Yeyun had superlative seductive techniques, something Jishi had never before experienced. "Where are you from?" he asked. "How long have you been here? And who do you attend on in the family?"

"I'm from Xiangshan county, and I came to Guangzhou last year. I used to be on the boats, but in the first month of this year I came to serve in this household and attend on the young mistress."

It was only then that Jishi realized she was a prostitute. "How old is the young mistress?" he asked. "And what is she like?"

"She's thirteen, with a very sweet nature. She gives the impression of being a little simple."

Jishi put his cheek against hers and said, "If you can arrange a meeting, I'll give you a hundred in silver."

"That's no problem. She saw you before and seemed to be quite impressed. I'll bring her to the garden tomorrow. Wait for us at the Guanyin Pavilion. They're so busy around here that no one goes to the back, and she'll hardly be able to fly away."

"How very thoughtful of you!" said Jishi delightedly. He then had another erection and paid court to her in earnest before falling asleep.

Next morning he called Su Bang in and sent him to the money shop to withdraw four hundred taels. Before long Su Bang was back with the money, and while the members of the Wu family were busy entertaining the guests and matchmakers, Jishi asked Wu Biyuan to come in and handed him three hundred taels, "There's a request I'd like to make," he added. "You were kind enough to invite me to stay for a few days, and I couldn't very well refuse. However, there are many guests outside and a great deal of activity, and I really dread these social occasions. Would you mind if I didn't join in?"

"I'm so sorry we've bothered you. Since that's what you'd prefer, of course we'll honor your wishes and have your food brought in here."

"There's no need to go to all *that* trouble." Pocketing the money, Wu Biyuan left the room.

Yeyun brought in his soup, and Jishi handed her a hundred taels. She kowtowed her thanks and said, "I made this soup in her room, and she asked me who I was making it for. When I told her, she said it was no wonder you didn't attend last night. I'll bring her to the garden sometime after noon."

"I must make the most of the opportunity. Whatever you do, don't give her any hint of what I have in mind."

"No need to remind me."

Wu Biyuan's daughter Qiao, although physically beautiful, had a peculiar nature. She would play about all day, but to an observer's eye she seemed somewhat simple-minded. Her feelings were inevitably stirred by the licentious behavior of her father and brother, but she herself was most particular about whom she would associate with. Ever since that time at New Year's when she had first laid eyes on Jishi, she had been full of admiration for him. Now her brother was getting married, and her mother considered Qiao too young to help with the preparations, and so she was musing alone in her room when Yeyun came in and said, "You've not had your lunch, miss. I'll get it for you. Afterward we can go and enjoy ourselves in the garden. Why are you just sitting there staring into space?"

"Have you had your lunch?"

"Yes, I had it with Master Su."

"Why should he favor *you* like that?"

"Oh, he looks so dashing, and he has the most agreeable nature! He must be just about the finest man in the entire world!" Then, with her hand over her mouth, she continued, "There's something else you don't know about him—he's even more adorable than we are!"

Qiao blushed. "Silly girl, you must be out of your mind!" With a broad smile on her face, Yeyun brought in her lunch. After eating one bowl of it, Xiaoqiao patted her hair into place in the mirror, then took Yeyun's hand and went out into the back garden.

As they made their way slowly to the pavilion, Yeyun said, "You take a seat inside, miss. I've lost one of my hairpins, and I want to go back and look for it." Qiao nodded. With one hand on the plum tree to steady herself, she tried to reach some of the tiny plums with the other.

The branch was pulled down beside the pavilion, as Jishi had already noticed. At once he came out and said, "Don't prick your hand, Miss Wu. Let me get some for you."

Hearing a sudden voice behind her, Qiao was startled. She turned and saw it was Jishi, and then was all smiles as she said, "So you're here, Master Su." She was about to turn away, when he pulled her into the pavilion. She made no sound, just smiled ingenuously. Jishi took her in his arms and brought her inside, then sat her on his knee. She was charmingly petite, "too frail to bear the weight of her clothes." Jishi took her to the couch, where matters followed their usual course. At first Qiao maintained her ingenuous smile, but then she began to knit her brows—she had no idea that the experience would be so painful. For his part Jishi expressed his pity for her and, after showering her with tenderness, brought matters to a hasty conclusion. At that precise moment Yeyun came in, and Jishi told her to help Qiao back to her room, while he left the garden. That evening he arranged with Yeyun that she would secretly leave the back gate open, so that at night, when all was quiet, he could go to Qiao's room and all three of them could enjoy themselves together.

The next day was the wedding itself, and the hangers-on arrived and rousted Jishi from his room. That evening the bridal sedan arrived at the gate, and the young couple prayed to the gods and worshipped the groom's ancestors. Then the guests threw coins and fruit at the newly married pair and the groom removed his bride's veil. The festivities went on until midnight, when the guests finally dispersed. Then, while in one room a couple of newlyweds brought forth two well-acquainted objects, in another four beautiful arms were wrapped around a single male lover. The river police yamen was a lively place that night.

But joy never lasts for long—parting comes apace. After the third day, Suxin left her room and went to pay her respects to her parents-in-law. Because Jishi was due to marry into the Wen family, Wu Biyuan invited him to meet Suxin. He did so willingly enough, but Suxin's embarrassment was such that all the waters of the West River could not have washed it away. Wu Daiyun attributed her reaction to a typical bride's attitudes and had no idea that anything else lay behind it. Just as the two of them were exchanging greetings, a servant reported, "Master Ma of His Honor Heh's yamen would like to see you, sir."

Wu Biyuan went out for a while and then came back and said to his wife, "Cousin Su is not an outsider, so there's no reason why we shouldn't discuss this in front of him. Just now Master Ma came here to congratulate me. He brought a thousand taels and told me that the Customs superintendent has heard of our Qiao's beauty and wants her as his concubine. When it's all settled, he also promises to appoint me to the concurrent position of treasurer. I gave him a non-committal reply. You're the one who'll have to decide."

"There's nothing wrong with it, except that she *is* rather young."

In his astonishment at the news Jishi broke in. "But my cousin is still not engaged! Surely there'll be no shortage of proposals from prominent families? The superintendent would only make her a concubine, which just seems wrong to me! Moreover, a thousand taels is hardly a big consideration. Do give this some more thought!"

"I wasn't in favor at first, but this superintendent is adamant about this, so I felt I had to agree," said Wu Biyuan. Jishi realized he was getting nowhere and had to take his leave. Secretly he passed the word to Yeyun that she bring Qiao to meet him in the garden that evening to talk things over.

But Yeyun had not been gone long when Qiao herself came in from the back door of the study, her cheeks streaked with tears, and fell into his arms. "I may be a foolish creature, but I did receive your love," she sobbed. "What happened the other day was not you forcing yourself on me—it was something that I longed for myself. I'd be happy even to be a concubine or a maid in your house. But now the superintendent is using his power to force the issue, and my father is going to sell his daughter for a profit! I tell you, I'd rather die than live with that sort of disgrace! I only hope that you'll think of some way to save me."

Jishi was moved to tears himself. "We share a secret love, you and I, but what can I do about it? This has all happened so suddenly that it will be almost impossible to undo. I did speak up, but your father was adamant. I would only ask you to be flexible for the moment. Meanwhile let's arrange another meeting."

She flew into a rage. "To take a girl's honor and then abandon her—that's not the way a gentleman behaves! What's worse, we've only just made love, and you come out with that sort of heartless remark! Oh, how I regret that I was ever so blind! Aren't you ashamed of yourself? And now I shall die for the mistake I made in loving you!" Slipping out of his embrace, she went to ram her head against a pillar.

Jishi quickly caught and held her, begging her again and again for forgiveness and trying to calm her. "With me here, you don't need to worry," he said. "By tonight I'll certainly have worked out a plan."

Yeyun was terrified lest someone come along and see them, and she managed by one means or another to pull Qiao out the back door. Jishi was utterly distraught—he felt as if a swarm of wasps were drilling into his brain.

Before long Wu Biyuan came in. "With regard to that matter we were talking about," he told Jishi, "I really had no choice, you know—I had to agree. We've set the tenth of the month for the betrothal gifts. In this wretched job of mine, I can never really hope for a change of fortune, but in the future, as treasurer, I'll be able to repay that loan of yours."

Jishi realized it was impossible to get him to reverse his decision. "The money's not important," he said. "There's no need to mention it. I'll be leaving you tomorrow and returning home. I just thought I'd let you know."

"Stay a few days longer, why don't you, until my daughter's married."

"I've been here a long time already. I definitely need to get home tomorrow."

After Wu Biyuan had left, Jishi waited dejectedly for nighttime, when Yeyun came and said, "There's no need for you to go in there tonight; she's coming here. It looks to me as if she'll definitely refuse to go to Customs. You'll just have to keep on at her until she changes her mind. If she makes a scene, I expect that all of us will suffer. I never dreamt she'd be such a firebrand. Had I known, I would never have dared to play matchmaker."

Toward midnight Qiao arrived looking the picture of grief, her evening toilette not complete, her hair disheveled, and her powdered face streaked with tears. Jishi wiped away the tears, clasped her to his chest, and tried to calm her. "My dear, you know from your own reading how many cases there are throughout history of lovers being reunited! You just need to be patient for the present and give me time to come up with some way of getting you out of this. Whatever you do, don't be too inflexible."

"I don't have the luck to be another Princess Lechang.[1] Those great mansions are like the ocean—once I'm in there, how can I ever hope to get out? I know there's really nothing you can do, and I would never dream of calling you faithless, but after our meeting tonight my soul will always be with you."

"But you mustn't do any such thing! It wouldn't be an act of love—you'd be destroying me!"

"What do you mean? How could my death destroy you?"

"The superintendent has power—everyone knows that. If you take your life for my sake, do you suppose for one moment that he won't find out why? Yeyun won't be able to stand the torture, and if she tells him what really happened, it will be a case of adultery leading to suicide, and I'll lose my life over it. And I'm an only son! My dear, you've got to take pity on me!"

Yeyun added tearfully, "I've served you, miss, and I would never dare to offend you, but do spare my life, I beg of you!"

On and on they went, one after the other, pleading with her until she began to change her mind. "Well, if for your sake I do force myself to put up with the disgrace, what brilliant plan do you have in mind to bring us together again?"

"There are plenty of men like the Slave of Kunlun, and GuYaya.² I'll put up tens of thousands of taels and throw money around to hire myself a knight-errant, and perhaps there'll be some opportunity.... But that's just a pipe dream. I'm afraid you'll have to put up with it for two or three years."

"Two or three years is not such a long time if we really can meet again. I'm only afraid that with my ill fate I'll never be able to serve you. We should pray to Heaven."

They prayed together, and afterwards Jishi took a jade disk from his belt, held it in his hand, and uttered this further prayer, "If Qiao and I are to be reunited one day, may this disk break in two when I throw it down. If we are not fated to be reunited, let it shatter into tiny fragments. I beseech thee to give us a sign." With that, he flung down the disk, which actually did break into two pieces. He was elated, and tied one half to his own belt and gave the other to her, saying, "This is our mirror.[3] Please take good care of it." He turned to Yeyun. "If your mistress does go into the Customs yamen, you must go with her, to attend on her and encourage her to persevere. If you do that, I'll single you out for special favor in the future."

She knelt down. "Having received your affection, I shall naturally do what little I can, in the hope that one day you'll make me your concubine."

"Of course I will," he said, helping her to her feet. Then they undressed and went to bed, where their joy was outweighed by their sorrow.

> This is the time to say farewell;
> Their hearts are filled with grief and pain.
> On Mount Wu, where the clouds are stilled,
> When will she see the king again?[4]

Let us put this question to you: Superintendent Heh may have been arrogant and lascivious, but how did he even know that the Wus had a daughter? There is an explanation. The prostitute Aqian had been full of resentment after being beaten by Wu Biyuan, and so when she entered the Customs and Heh asked her for the names of the most beautiful girls in the area, she praised Miss Wu to the skies. Heh had never heard of the principle that daughters of officials ought not to serve as concubines, and he consulted Ma Bole, who fell in with his master's evil desire and strove to carry it out. If Wu Biyuan could have given a righteous response accompanied by a stern lecture, Heh could not have done anything to him. Surely Wu was not afraid that Heh would dismiss him from office and cut off his head? But the fact is that even if the superintendent had not asked for his daughter, this ambitious little social climber would have been only too eager to give her to him, and now that someone had come forward to propose the match, he naturally offered her up with both hands. From that point of view, this is not a case of the author's adding an extra twist to the plot; it arose partly from Wu Daiyun's karmic retribution and partly from his father's own shamelessness.

Heh prepared several rooms and on the appointed day sent a small sedan chair for Qiao that was fitted out with four lanterns decorated with his official insignia. Already half drunk at the time, he saw her though a vinous haze:

> Eyebrows like new moons,
> Eyes abrim with tears,
> A face like peach blossom;
> Cheeks aglow with dewdrops,
> Waist like a willow wand,
> Light as a jewel in the palm;
> Feet like lotus flowers,
> Graceful as if tripping among clouds.
> Can it be that from Mount Wu
> The beauty has come at last?
> Pity the lotus rising from the pond
> With mud besmearing its head!
> You may find her tear-stained beauty sad,
> But her seductive charm shines through.

"She really is exceptional," exclaimed Heh. His women ushered her into the chamber, but Yeyun stuck close behind and whispered in her ear, "Miss, you've already lost your virginity, and you'll have to be very careful as to how you treat him any moment now. You mustn't let him find out." But Qiao was someone who had tried to kill herself—she was only prolonging her life because of Jishi—and she paid not the slightest attention to what Yeyun was saying.

Soon Heh came in, and his women left. Yeyun stepped forward and kowtowed. "You've been attending on my new concubine, I take it," said Heh.

"Yes. Master Wu chose me just now to attend on her."

"That Master Wu certainly knows how to make himself agreeable. Well, you'd better leave us alone now." Yeyun pulled the door to as she left.

Heh raised the curtain to find Qiao lying on the bed with her clothes still on, and he pulled her up. She knew that she could not escape what was in store for her, and she had to undress. She then lay down again, her face to the wall. Stimulated by the wine he had drunk, Heh pulled her around to face him and mounted a bold attack. She felt the coarseness of his skin but paid it scant attention, for with his jade pestle suddenly thrusting, her vagina seemed about to split, and she tried desperately with both her hands to fend him off. But he didn't care whether she lived or died and plunged wildly ahead, stopping only when he had reduced her to a pitiful state. The sun was full on the window before he got up, and the maids and concubines in attendance had already come in. Heh told them to look after Qiao carefully and to call her New Lady, with a rank below that of Pinxing.

He then strolled off to the library, where an attendant handed him a report. He tore it open and read it:

Dong Cai, clerk of the Shanwei[5] Customs post, begs leave
to report to pour Honor: From the tenth month of Jiajing
12 until the eleventh month of last year I served as clerk of
the Shawei Customs post, after which I handed over my responsibilities to my successor. Altogether I was due to remit
taxes in the amount of 135,243 taels, three qian, one fen. In
successive payments I have remitted over 124,942 taels. The
sum remaining to be remitted is 10,310 taels, three qian, one
fen, and I recently received an order from you urging me to
remit that amount. On the twenty-eighth of the second month
of this year I collected it and on the twenty-ninth in Lufeng
county I gathered it all together and set off to deliver it. On
the fourth of the third month when I came near Goat's Foot
Ridge in Haifeng county, I was suddenly confronted with over
fifty pirate raiders, who came swarming forward, armed with
swords and firearms, and seized the money and baggage. The
additional personnel appointed by Lufeng county as well as the
servants all fled in terror, and I sustained a sword wound on my
left arm. I think that when pirates loot and plunder so freely
that merchants are too afraid to travel, the customs taxes will
always be in deficit, and when the raiders are brazen enough to
run riot in the interior and seize consignments of taxes, their
crimes have already reached the limit! I entreat Your Honor to
communicate with the governor and commander-in-chief and
urge them to call up their forces to stamp out the pirates so
that we can complete the collection of taxes and reassure the
merchants and the general public. In addition to proceeding to
Haifeng county to report on the need to arrest the robbers, it is
my duty that I report these facts truthfully to you.

After rereading the report, Heh hesitated, then asked the man
at the door. Bao Jincai had been waiting there for some time when
Heh handed him the report. "What do I do about this?" he asked.

"As I see it," said Bao, "we don't yet know if it's true. Last year
when we were changing the personnel at the posts, this same Dong

Cai offered us two thousand taels in hopes of keeping his position, but Your Honor did not agree and we made the change. These ten thousand odd are the sum total of his deficit, and even if his story about the robbery is true, we must still get him to make good the shortfall. He can only be reimbursed after we've caught the pirates. There's no case for an exemption."

Heh gave a nod, picked up his brush, and wrote his decision:

> In the eleventh month of last year you left your position with taxes still unpaid. How is it that you waited until the second month of this year before trying to deliver them? This is clearly an attempt to cover up fraud!
>
> The deficit in the prescribed amount of taxes must first be made good by him. In addition to informing the governor so that he may summon troops to apprehend the raiders, have Candidate for Sub-prefect Hu of Jieshi investigate to see if there is any fraud in the payment of taxes and bring Dong Cai in chains to the yamen, where a strict time-limit will be set for repayment.

He handed the decision to Bao to send out, and also gave orders that Wu Biyuan be installed in the joint post of treasurer.

The eight customs posts in Huizhou prefecture were Wudun, Jiazi, Shawei, Shenquan, Jieshi, Jinghai, Qian'ao, and Duntou. Each was headed by a clerk who collected the duties. Dong Cai, clerk of the Shawei post, was originally surnamed Shy. He was the father of Shy Yannian and the brother-in-law of Merchant Wen, and he came originally from Shaoxing in Zhejiang province. At first he was a port merchant in Guangzhou, but after he married, because of a deficit in the accounts, he was sent back to Shaoxing under guard by the salt comptroller. However, because he continued to hanker after Guangdong, he resorted to a little deception and managed by changing his name to wangle another position there. Clerkships were customarily held for a term of one year, and payment was required each time they were granted. The Shawei clerkship had always cost three thousand silver dollars, but Bao Jincai had changed the amount to four thousand, and it was snapped up by someone quicker off the mark than Shy Cai.[6] He was thoroughly depressed already, and now this additional trouble had come upon him out of the blue.

He was taken to Guangzhou in chains that day by the Huizhou sub-prefect's men. Again and again he begged them to take him first to his own house, where he would wine and dine them. He knew that the tax deficit would have to be paid, but over the years he had sent home between ten thousand and twenty thousand taels, and he was not too concerned; he merely regretted the years of hard work that had gone to waste. It was only when he suggested to his son, Yannian, that they pay the deficit off in installments that he learned to his horror that Yannian, blessed with a father who earned good money, had squandered it day after day on whoring, gambling, and wining and dining, leaving virtually nothing in the house—a mere a thousand or two. Shocked, Shy Cai gave his son a tongue-lashing and ordered him to do his utmost to scrape some money together. He was then led away to the yamen to plead his case and await the outcome.

Before long Heh mounted his tribunal. At the outset he ordered Shy to be given thirty strokes with the heavy bamboo for gross neglect. "From what Sub-prefect Hu has said in your defense," declared Heh, "there was no fraud involved, so I shall spare you the death penalty for now. But the payment of the prescribed amount of taxes cannot be delayed. I shall allow you just ten days to eliminate the deficit, with a check on your progress every third day."

Shy Cai kowtowed, thanked the superintendent, and left the court. On the third day he took in the three thousand that he had gathered together at home and avoided a beating by handing it over in part payment. In the second three-day period, Yannian obtained a mere one thousand three hundred taels by pawning his mother's and sister's jewelry and clothes as well as several cases of his own belongings. Since six days had passed and the payments had not yet reached halfway, Shy Cai was given another thirty severe strokes. Emerging from the beating, he bitterly castigated his son, but there was nothing Yannian could do except go back and ask all of his relatives and friends for help.

Readers, let us point out that in times of distress friends and relatives are nowhere to be found. Moreover, Yannian and his father had never associated with decent folk, so those who came to their aid were far outnumbered by those who chose to mock the family. It was a good thing that the people of Guangdong were rough and straightforward rather than smooth and devious like the inhabitants of Jiangsu and Zhejiang! After racing about for an entire day, Yannian managed to obtain two hundred taels from Merchant Wen. He was forced to sell the house and rent a tiny cottage instead, and also to sell their three maids and their furniture. When the time limit expired, he had obtained a full two thousand taels, which he gave to his father, explaining the circumstances and adding, "There's nothing else we can hope to get. Father, you've got to think of some way to petition for an exemption. After all, it's not as if we had *embezzled* the money."

At the end of the ten-day period, Shy Cai had paid up over six thousand taels. At that point Heh actually showed some humanity and extended the time limit for another ten days, but Bao Jincai, since his own attempt at extortion had failed, maliciously stirred up trouble for Shy Cai and gave him several more strokes of the rod.

Although given to debauchery, Shy Cai had always led a comfortable life and had certainly never experienced any judicial torture. In the meantime his son had disappeared, and Shy Cai begged someone to take a letter and go and find him. His womenfolk, having run out of food, also begged someone to go in search of the son. With a heavy sigh, Shy Cai said to the messenger, "Please tell my wife and daughter to try and survive as best they can. I can't take care of them anymore."

Fortunately, Customs did not have much of a prison. Although Shy Cai wore a chain around his neck, he was still able to move his hands and feet freely, and at night, after a spell of bitter weeping, he undid his belt and hanged himself. Next morning his death was reported to the superintendent, who had the men on guard duty beaten and then ordered that the body be released to the relatives for the laying-in. As to the remainder of the deficit, it was to be entered in the records under the heading "Location Unknown" with the appended note "To be settled once the robbers are caught."

When Yannian heard the news, he rushed in and made a scene, shouting that he was going to the governor-general's office to protest the injustice. But what did a young and inexperienced person like Yannian know about such things? When people came forward and tried to dissuade him, he got the idea of extorting money from them, and then, while the dispute was still raging, along came the Nanhai magistrate, Qian Lao, who carried out an examination of the corpse. The superintendent's men reported that the dead man had hanged himself while overwrought because of a tax deficit. The magistrate then called Yannian before him and accused him of using the corpse for the purpose of blackmail and gave him twenty savage strokes of the rod. He also threatened, falsely, to have Yannian make good the deficit himself, which gave the latter such a fright that he kowtowed and began pleading for mercy. Only then did the magistrate order him to provide an affidavit and remove the body.

It was Bao Jincai who had sent for Magistrate Qian. Naturally, Bao later thanked him for his services. We need not go into the details.

Yannian took his father's body home, and his mother and sister wept bitterly over it. They were desperately poor—not only did they lack a coffin or any funeral garments, they had also run out of food. To make matters worse, Yannian had welts on both of his legs from the beating he had received, and he moaned with pain even while sitting down. Xia had to take off a jeweled hairpin of hers just to pay the men who brought in the corpse. When the family looked at the dead body covered with injuries, they felt they had suffered an injustice, but it was not one that they could ever protest. They thought of borrowing money, but what happened the last time they tried to borrow any was still vivid in their minds. Yannian's mother told him to go back to the Wen household and make a private appeal to her sister. "But they didn't owe you anything before," Yannian objected, "and out of the goodness of their hearts they gave you two hundred taels. Asking them again would be putting the squeeze on the most decent people. Frankly, I wouldn't have the nerve!" They thought and thought, but there was only one way out, because in the heat of the fifth month, the injured corpse had begun to swell up: to get the money for the laying in, they would have to sell Xia.

Turn to the next chapter and read on.

Chapter VIII

Shen Jin is restored to office by imperial grace
Su Wankui dies on hearing of a robbery

⤳

Jishi had had no peace of mind since parting from Qiao, but his father was very strict and would not let him return to the city, and he had to get the servants to make discreet inquiries for him. When he learned that Qiao had joined the Heh household, he naturally felt heartbroken, but he was also relieved that the superintendent had fortunately not discovered her secret. At the festival he sent men into town to deliver presents to various people, and they brought back the message that the teacher was holding his monthly test on the thirteenth and that Jishi's presence was required. He reported this to his father, who said, "Certainly you should attend. And isn't it Director Shen's birthday on the eighteenth? In that case you'll need to prepare some presents and go and offer him our congratulations. You should also ask your teacher if he has had any news. Come back on the nineteenth. But you mustn't go bothering your friends and relatives; stay at our house instead. And check the accounts that Su Xing has been keeping. You're not a child anymore; next year we'll be holding your wedding, and then the house will be your concern. I'm too busy to see to it."

Early on the thirteenth Jishi set off for the city, and after he had finished the test, he paid a visit to the Wens and stayed there the night. Mistress Shi told him about the Shy family, and he felt a keen sympathy and resolved to help, although he didn't say so at the time. After breakfast the following day he took a chair back to the old house on Haoxian Street. On alighting, he heard a piteous sobbing from across the way and asked the person at the gate, "There never used to be anyone living there. Why all this sobbing?"

The youth at the gate, Awang, replied, "It's the Shy family, who've just moved in. The head of the family used to be a Customs clerk, but he was driven to take his life by the superintendent. There's no coffin in the house, so they have to sell their daughter. At the moment there's no one to buy her, and mother and daughter have been sobbing for a long time. Do a good deed and help them out, sir!"

"You don't understand—they're relatives of ours. Go over and tell them I'm coming to pay them a visit."

The youth left, and Jishi strolled over. The house was narrow and probably had no more than three rooms in all—a wretched little place. Shy Yannian soon came out to welcome him, and Jishi took his hand and expressed his sympathies, then asked if he could pay his respects to Yannian's mother. He expressed his feelings to her as a relative, and both mother and son told him of their ordeal. Jishi then ordered Aqing to go and ask Su Xing for three hundred taels. He was also to find a coffin of good quality and bring it to the house as quickly as possible. Mistress Shi then drew her son and daughter together and they kowtowed in gratitude. As Jishi helped them to their feet one after the other, he couldn't hold back his tears. He noticed that although Xia's face was drawn and stained with tears, it was quite touching in its poignant beauty. However, in the midst of the intense grief that he felt for Qiao he paid it scant attention. Before long the money arrived, and he handed it to Yannian, who thanked him. Jishi then asked Su Bang to buy all the things that they needed. "Last night at my father-in-law's they hadn't heard the sad news," he said. "I must send them a message."

He told Su Bang to have some servants come over and attend on the family, then took his leave. Inevitably, the thought of the superintendent's vicious behavior made him feel sick at heart.

Before long Chuncai arrived. His mother had received Jishi's message and sent him with some servants to visit the Shy family and ask how they were. She had also sent two loads of rice as well as ten taels. "That place they're in isn't fit for human beings," Chuncai said to Jishi when they met. "It's such a pity that Cousin Xia will have to live in such a hovel. Why don't you get her to move over here?"

"It's no time for joking around when there's a funeral in the family."

"Look, there's a question I've been meaning to ask you. You and I are school-mates, and we're also related. I need you to teach me about something."

"Teach you what?"

"I heard my mother say she was going to find me a wife next year. I thought that marrying a stranger wouldn't be any fun at all, so I was most reluctant, but they've gone ahead and arranged a marriage, anyway. What approach do I use on the first day?"

"No approach. You just have to sleep with her, that's all."

"You're not willing to teach me, are you? Else why talk such rot? How do people get babies?"

"When you're sleeping with her, she'll naturally be able to teach you. You won't need instructions from anyone else."

"So the wife is a teacher, too? But my sister Suxin has been married for over two months, and she hasn't had a baby. Could it be that she doesn't know how to teach?"

"Even I don't know the answer to that one," said Jishi with a smile.

In the midst of their discussion, Su Bang came in to report. "Everything has been settled over there, but Master Shy says he has nowhere to put the coffin and would like you to tell him where it should go."

"The Finger-at-the-Moon Temple outside the city is our family shrine," said Jishi. "Send someone to tell them in advance and then put it in there for the time being." He also called Su Xing in and gave him orders: "The eighteenth is Master Shen's birthday. As you know, he doesn't want anything really elaborate done for him. You need to keep that in mind when you're getting the presents ready."

Jishi invited Chuncai to stay with him that night and the next day went back to the Shy house. The laying in had been completed, and the whole family was in mourning dress. Jishi and Chuncai performed the mourning ritual, then knelt down and offered sacrifices. Ridiculous though it might seem, of Shy Cai's many friends only two came to grieve and offer sacrifices on this first day of the mourning period; the rest of those present were neighbors who had come to help eat up the food. The family made a hasty trip outside the city to deposit the coffin, and by the time they returned, Chuncai had left. Jishi went over once more and consoled them. When he saw how tiny their apartment was, he called in the landlord and told him to give them another two rooms, ordering Su Xing to pay the rent. Jishi also gave them two hundred taels for their living costs. The gratitude of the three family members is not hard to imagine.

On the evening of the seventeenth Yannian prepared a dinner for Jishi so that the family could offer their thanks. Mistress Shi kowtowed before him,[1] followed by Yannian and Xia, which so embarrassed Jishi that he promptly knelt down and kowtowed himself. At dinner Mistress Shi asked Jishi to occupy the place of honor, with Yannian beside him, while she herself took the host's place and Xia poured the wine and urged Jishi to drink. After they had drunk three cups, Mistress Shi said, "While my husband was alive, he had a good many friends, but when disaster struck, no one responded except Brother-in-Law Wen, who lent us two hundred taels. After my husband took his life, we had no way of providing for the funeral, and we would have had to sell my daughter in order to bury her father. Because of your extraordinary kindness, sir, both the deceased and the living are indebted to you, and I would like to give you this girl as a maid or concubine to repay you for your great generosity. I hope you will deign to accept her."

"Aunt, I'm afraid you're going much too far! You're relatives of mine, and it was my duty to look after you, but even if we'd been complete strangers, I'd still have wanted to help out on seeing such a tragic case as yours. The unfortunate thing is that I got back to the city a few days too late, which cost Uncle his life. I feel ashamed enough about that, as it is—how can I possibly think of myself as generous? My cousin is a noted beauty from a distinguished family; how could she lower herself to become a mere concubine? I wouldn't dream of accepting your offer."

"The suggestion comes from the heart. She may be a plain-looking girl, but she can read a little, and if you tell her what to do, she may not actually spill the ink."

"I've led a dissolute life," said Yannian, "and it's only in situations like this that you see what people's hearts are really like. If my sister were to enter your household, she would naturally have someone to depend on for the rest of her life. If you are determined to refuse her, all three of us will surely die of starvation."

"You can set your mind at rest on that point," said Jishi. "Although I can't be sure what the future will bring, of course I shall look after you from now on. However, on this marriage question I find it impossible to do as you ask." He got up to leave, but the three of them kept trying to persuade him to stay. Xia, blushing, poured out a cup of wine and handed it to him. He had to drink it and then another three cups before he could leave. He told his servants to take them quantities of rice, fuel, and food.

Readers, let us explain something. Jishi was young and romantically inclined; how could he fail to be attracted by Xia? However, the support he gave the family was the product of a compassion unmixed with selfish motives, and so he couldn't bring himself to accept her. Moreover, his love for Qiao was still strong. All of this stood to his credit, but Mistress Shi and her son were not about to let him get away, and Xia, for her part, was familiar with his wife Huiruo's temperament and perfectly willing to join her.

The next day Jishi went to the grain bureau and offered birthday congratulations. Since Jishi was a classmate of his son's and a relative of Jiangshan's, and also because he was an inoffensive young man, Director Shen treated him handsomely. After accepting all the presents Jishi brought, he gave him in return ten boxes of Huzhou writing brushes, a hundred sheets of Songjiang letter paper, ten boxes of Huizhou ink, and a volume of poetry. He also said, "Jiangshan has had a safe journey. I've had a letter from him at Nanchang with good wishes for your father. I expect he will be home by now. If your father has time, ask him to pay me a visit when it's convenient. I've had a letter from the capital recently that indicates I probably won't be in this office very much longer, and in the future we won't have many opportunities to meet." After assuring him that he would pass on the message, Jishi took his leave.

With nothing more to detain him, he went straight home, where he handed the presents to his father and reported what Master Shen had said. He also mentioned what had happened to the Shy family. "I saw that they were suffering, just as we did, so I gave them some help. They wanted me to accept their daughter in return, but I refused."

"And here was I thinking you were too young to know about such things!" said Wankui approvingly. "You've handled all of this very well. If you stick to Master Li's teaching and fulfill the hopes I have for you, you'll benefit your whole life long."

> Reform gets harder the later it's tried;
> Consider the flux in the human state.
> Why must you scheme for a transient glory?
> The Lord of Heaven will decide your fate.

Let us turn to Director Shen, who had been sent down to the provinces from the Hanlin Academy and demoted to the position of intendant. The court official who was at odds with him was one Chong Yi, who as a lowly functionary had so ingratiated himself that within two years he had risen to become grand secretary of the Pole Star Palace. After receiving such an honor by the emperor's grace, he ought to have striven to repay the favor by excelling in his work, but once he had obtained a grip on power, he promoted and demoted people quite arbitrarily, avenging even so slight a thing as an unfriendly glance. He was also avid for bribes and utterly corrupt, failing the court and committing countless offences. The high officials said not a word about all of this, but left everything to the emperor, who flew into a rage, seized Chong's property, allowed him to commit suicide, and banished his family to the frontier.[2] In our humble view, the sudden eclipse of Chong Yi, who lost his life and property after a lifetime of seizing other people's possessions, is an example of precise retribution according to the Principle of Heaven and the laws of the land. In a laughable development, the nation's censors, who had previously shown a complete lack of backbone, picked up their papier-mâché cross-bows and their candlewick arrows now that Chong Yi had been allowed to commit suicide and, as if cradling a baby under one arm and holding Mount Tai with the other, began shooting wildly at the dead tiger. They charged that there were lesser demons of some sort who had clung to Chong's coattails as well as remnants of his faction who were lying low and biding their time, and earnestly begged that they be executed to make justice apparent to all. Fortunately, His Majesty showed the extent of his magnanimity and consigned the petitions—fawning, begging for pity, offering gifts and money—to the fire, which caused all of these greater and lesser officials in the capital and the provinces to feel shame in their hearts even if it failed to appear in their faces. The emperor's purpose was nothing less than to get them to reform their ways and strive to repay the faith that he had placed in them.

Among the officials was one Gao Feng, a supervising censor of the Huguang circuit, who had previously accused Chong Yi. At this point he alone was unwilling to make any wild accusations. Instead, he submitted a memorial that differed from all of the others:

> Gao Feng, supervising censor of the Huguang circuit, memorializes as follows:
>
> I understand that when rewards and punishments are made clear, the world will be eager to be virtuous,[3] that when good is shown to be distinct from evil, justice will become apparent. This is the reason that the five punishments and their five applications, the five degrees of garments, and the five classes of emblems are listed together in the Book of Yu.[4] I have observed Your Majesty's single-handed exercise of authority. Your anger calmed the populace; you dismissed Chong Yi and allowed him to commit suicide; you confiscated his

property and banished his family; you permitted the worst of his adherents to leave office; and you censured his lesser followers and ordered them to reform. Your Majesty's orders were decisive and authoritative, and it may be expected that no further punishment will be necessary. As a censor, I am absolutely delighted. The one thing that grieves me is that while Chong Yi has acknowledged his guilt, those who incurred his anger and were removed from office, as well as those who disobeyed his orders and were demoted, have not yet been restored to their positions by your benevolence. Now, so long as there is a single victim who has not been restored to office, I fear that it will mar the clear perception of your enlightened rule. Moreover, the praise of the populace will fast accrue if you act. It would be advisable to issue a statute of commendation. I entreat Your Majesty to instruct the boards to carry out an investigation and request that the measure be put into effect.

Imperial rescript: What the censor memorializes about is correct: Let the boards concerned investigate and report back in all such cases. The deceased should be accorded posthumous honors, while those still alive who lost their offices or were demoted should be restored to their former positions.

Once the order went out, Shen Jin, assistant sub-prefect in charge of the Guangzhou Grain Bureau, was appointed intendant in charge of military defenses in Jinqu in Zhejiang. As soon as the proclamation reached Guangdong, all the officials came to the bureau to congratulate him.

It was early in the eighth month, and Jishi had gone into the city to wait for the provincial examinations. On receiving the news about Shen, he rushed over to congratulate him. Shen offered him tea and then said, "I still have some things here that I need to attend to, and it will probably be the tenth month before I can set off. When the time comes, I shall call on you and let you know." Jishi thanked him and left.

The examinations were soon over, and the Wen family gave a dinner in celebration. Yannian also invited Jishi for supper that same evening. The reason for the invitation was that Yannian's mother felt under a heavy obligation because of Jishi's generosity and wanted very much to give Xia to him. She spoke to Yannian about it. "I've often noticed him stealing glances at our Xia," said Yannian, "so I don't think he'd be unwilling. He's reluctant because he's afraid of being criticized over our relationship. Let's use his visit to get him drunk and then have Sister work on him. I'm not sure she'd agree, though."

"It's a question of your marriage," Mistress Shi said to her daughter, "and you will have to make up your own mind. I'm not asking you to do anything shameful; I merely want you to repay his kindness. Moreover, if you do, Yannian and I will have someone to depend on in the future."

"I'd be far too embarrassed to do any such thing!" said Xia. "If he rejected me, I'd never marry as long as I lived."

"That's not what I meant at all. I don't want you to *do* anything, I'm just telling you to attend on him."

"Well, it's my duty to do that much."

Now that her mind was made up, they bought some of the finest Shaoxing wine, prepared some exquisite hors d'oeuvres, and waited for his arrival that evening.

Jishi had been drinking at his future in-laws' and was already more than a little inebriated. After he arrived, Yannian and his mother, who had been waiting respectfully a long time, hustled him inside. In a room at the back, outside Xia's bedroom, they had lit candles and censers, and with great deference they invited him to sit down. "You understood, sir, that we lesser folk could not provide the best wine and food, so you went first to those good people over the way. But what we do have here, although it comes from you, is most sincerely offered."

"How can you say that? I mean to drink to my heart's content. But where has Sister gone?"

"We don't have anyone to do the cooking, just one young maid to help out, so I told my daughter to do it. We won't have much in the way of dishes, but at least the food will have been properly washed."

"But that won't do at all! Give me a day or two and I'll send someone out to find a capable woman to cook for you." She thanked him, and then she and her son busied themselves offering him wine. She also helped him off with his coat.

Soon the dishes were brought out, and Xia, wearing a white dress, her face and hair appearing freshly powdered and pomaded, came in. Jishi went to get up, but Madam Shi held him down. "The young master was praising your skills just now," she said to Xia. "Come and offer him a cup of wine."

"The dishes I've cooked certainly won't taste very good, sir, but you mustn't make fun of me. This is your home, as it were, so you will have to drink several cups."

"Why are you calling me 'sir'?"

"It's a case of 'each one saying what he wishes.'"[5] She poured out a large cup and offered it to him with both hands.

"I can't possibly drink this. You'll have to change the way you address me before I do as you say."

Xia flashed him a glance and whispered the word "brother," after which he drank up happily enough and presented her with a large cup in return.

"I've a very small capacity where wine's concerned. Let me keep you company with a little cup." By this time Yannian had fled the scene, and now Mistress Shi also took herself off, saying that she had to see to things in the kitchen. Jishi was three-quarters drunk, and raising a large cup, he urged Xia to drink. She had to drain it. Then she picked up some steamed duckling with her chopsticks and offered it to him, and also poured him another cup of wine. They sat side by side, their bodies touching, as they pressed each other to drink. Jishi was no puritan at heart, and with this flower-like creature beside him how could he help but be attracted? He held her slender wrists, rubbed one foot against her tiny feet, gradually brought his cheek against hers, and then fondled her breasts and ran his fingers over her flesh. Finally, he abandoned his wine altogether and went into the bedroom to lie down. In their lovemaking that night, he was the only one who enjoyed it; she had to endure a good deal of pain.

The following morning he arose and thanked Mistress Shi. "I am greatly indebted to you for your kindness, Aunt, and I shall do my best to repay it. However, Xia will have to stay here for the time being. After I've married Miss Wen next spring, I shall let my parents know and then come and welcome Xia into the family." Mistress Shi approved of the arrangement. Jishi also told one of his servants to buy two maids and a serving woman to attend on them. He stayed four or five nights there before returning home.

When the results of the examination were announced, he went back into the city and stayed the night. His name was not on the list of those who passed, which was no more than he had expected. He simply drank a few more cups of wine to cheer himself up.

By the beginning of the tenth month, Master Shen had set the date for his departure. Wankui was waiting to receive him at home, and he told Jishi to go into the city to say farewell and hand him the invitation. After Jishi had attended on him for two days, Shen set off. At the dock the officials and salt merchants, among others, had set up a shared pavilion in which they entertained Shen to a farewell meal, while the governor-general's and governor's runners and servants brought invitations to a farewell party. The Customs superintendent set up his own pavilion and personally provided a farewell meal. At each pavilion Master Shen expressed his appreciation, and in Heh's case he took his hand and plied him with advice. It was getting toward evening when the drum sounded for his departure.

With Jishi accompanying him, Shen sailed as far as Huatian, where he disembarked. The shore was lined with lanterns, torches, sedan chairs and horses. When they reached the Su house, Wankui was waiting for them at the gate dressed in his official robes. He welcomed them into the hall, which was bright with gaily decorated lanterns. Master Shen asked Wankui to change out of his official robes and make himself comfortable. "I have often been favored with your magnificent generosity," he said, "but although I was eager to come to your house and extend my thanks, I was always prevented by my official duties. Now that I am no longer an official in these parts, I can enjoy your company as much as I wish, but unfortunately the imperial deadline is pressing, and I shall not be able to repay your great kindness."

"I've received extraordinary generosity from you, sir," said Wankui, "and I've not been able to repay one ten-thousandth part of it. I expect I shall have to repay you in my next existence, while ordering my son to show his gratitude all his life."

"That's going much too far—we're linked by marriage, after all. Your son has a sincere and generous nature; he is a gentle, mild-mannered young man, and a great future can be predicted for him. Your son-in-law has succeeded impressively in the examinations. Congratulations! The only unfortunate thing is that Jiangshan, a superior person who has never received his due, has failed again. That's a huge disappointment."

"I haven't had a word from him since he left, and I've been constantly worried. Do you have a letter from him, then?"

"No, not yet, but yesterday I saw the list of new graduates from the governor-general's office, and I noticed that his son was number twelve. To win such laurels as his age—there's no telling what the future might hold for him!"

The servants brought out all kinds of gourmet food, and Master Shen got up to take his leave. Once more he urged Jishi to come and visit him. Wankui and Jishi then saw him out of the main gate, where his servants gathered around him and escorted him on his way.

Wankui was privately delighted to learn of his son-in-law's success.

He decided to hold Jishi's wedding in the first month of the new year and confirmed the date with the girl's family. At year's end he received a letter from Jiangsu saying, "Having succeeded in the examination, my son decided to accompany me to the capital this winter. Once he has taken the metropolitan examination, he should go to Guangzhou to deliver the betrothal gifts and complete the marriage." Needless to say, the whole family was delighted at the news.

Wankui prepared New Year's presents for the various families, and told Jishi to go into the city to settle accounts and convey New Year compliments. Once more Jishi stayed at the Shy house. Returning after a long absence, he thought that Xia looked particularly fetching. "Take this opportunity to tell your father about us," she urged him. "Then marry me and take me back with you. Next year, when you marry Huiruo, I'll naturally become your concubine. But you mustn't forget the first one in your passion for the second and leave me to grow old alone." Jishi reassured her, and each day went around presenting New Year compliments and settling the family's accounts. He handed the interest that he collected to Su Xing for safekeeping.

One day he was returning from settling accounts with the traders when he happened to pass by the Customs, which brought to mind certain concerns of his. I've heard Yannian say, he reflected, that a strange priest has recently come to the Tianfei Temple inside Jinghai Gate. I wonder what he's like. Now that I'm in the vicinity I think I'll pay a call on him. He told the bearers to stop where they were, then got out and walked over to the temple with Aqing. He found a crowd of people surrounding a priest who was sitting cross-legged on the ground:

> Hair hanging over his ears,
> Bodhisattva-like, with lowered head;
> A soaring nose covering his lips,
> Like an angry guardian god.
> Empty hands pressed together,
> Their hard bones fully exposed;
> His hairy legs all bare,
> The purple veins in bold relief;
> His basket holding bizarre prescriptions,
> His gourd filled with untested medicines.
> Resembling a monk from the Western lands—
> And also a desperado from the isles.

Jishi pushed his way through the crowd and shouted at the top of his voice, "Priest! As you sit there, are you seeking the truth through meditation or are you appealing for alms?"

Opening his eyes, the priest replied, "I am not seeking the truth, but I do understand an infinite number of concerns. Nor am I appealing for alms, although I am converting a few outstanding people who have the gift of spiritual perception."

Noting the cryptic reply, Jishi continued, "Despite my vulgar perception, I wonder if I could have a talk with you in your cell?" The priest took a slip of paper from his basket and, letting no one see, wrote a few words on it, then passed it to Jishi to take home and read. He then resumed his seat, leaving Jishi with nothing to do but return. In the sedan chair he opened the message: "Layman Su should proceed this evening to the entrance of the Five-story Building and wait there to discuss his concerns." Jishi was astonished. How did that priest know my name, he asked himself. There's something very strange about that man; I mustn't let this opportunity slip.

At dusk he went out again with Aqing. His servants assumed that he was going to spend the night in the house opposite and didn't try to dissuade him, but when he got to the Shy house, he told them, "You needn't wait for me. I have some other business that will take a little time." With Aqing in attendance, he left Granary Street and headed north. Aqing had no idea of his master's purpose, but he followed with the lantern. As they passed the intersection, Jishi told him to stop there: "I won't be long."

"But you mustn't do that, sir! Where are you going on your own so late at night? Let me go with you. If it's some lover you want to visit, I won't tell any tales, no matter what."

"Rubbish! What do *you* know about such things? All you need to do is wait here for me. I'll be back between the first and second watches." Aqing had to let him have his way.

As he approached the side of the Five-story Building, Jishi found the priest sitting on the ground waiting for him. At once he prostrated himself and said, "I had no idea that a living Buddha had come down to earth. I ought to have withdrawn."

The priest helped him to his feet. "I am from Tibet," he said, "and I came here to make a favorable connection. I'm no living Buddha."

"If you're not a living Buddha, how did you know my name or that I have certain concerns?"

"It was just a lucky guess on my part. But if you do have any concerns, perhaps I might be able to help you with them."

"In the presence of an arhat I can speak nothing but the truth. My father was punished for no fault of his own—that's the first of my regrets. I'm young, but I'm no good at sex, and I lost a wife—that's the second. A virtuous concubine was seized by a local tyrant—that's the third. If you really can find some way to help me, I shall do homage to you for the rest of my life."

"Your second point presents no difficulty at all. Results will become apparent in a very short period of time. In the third case, who is your adversary?"

"Compassion is your watchword, Master; I doubt very much that you'd ever be willing to harm a soul. The man who sets my teeth on edge is Heh Guangda, superintendent of Customs."

"So he's the one! I was hoping to get a very large contribution from him. But if you want satisfaction, you will have to follow my plan."

"I can provide all the alms you want, but what plan do you have in mind?"

"Nothing very grand. When you go back, all you need do is spread the word that there's a foreign priest in town who's an expert at praying for sons. In no time at all the rumor will come to the superintendent's attention and I'll be able to say 'mission accomplished.'"

Jishi promised to do as he was asked. The priest took three pills from his bag and said, "Take one of these, and you'll not only be a champion of the boudoir, you'll also be able to escape disease and preserve your youthful complexion. You'll need to tell me your favorite's name, and from now on we shan't have to meet again." Jishi bowed as he accepted the pills from the priest and gave him Qiao's name. The priest then waved him on his way.

It was the third watch when Jishi returned, and the streets were deserted. Aqing was at the crossroads, sobbing miserably. Jishi shouted at him to stop, and they went off together. At the Shy house, Jishi knocked at the door and went in, only to find Xia still sitting by the lamp. Jishi was about to tell the maids to go and warm up some wine, when she said, "There's no need for that. I have some here, ready for you. But where've you been all this time?"

"Oh, just settling accounts."

She brought out several dishes, and the two of them sat beside each other and drank their wine. Without letting her see, Jishi popped one of the pills into his mouth. He felt a sudden rush of exhilaration, followed by a surge of heat that traveled from his throat to his pelvis and then all the way to his tailbone, causing his legs to feel strangely different. He gave Xia a hug and told her to fondle him. As she did so, she received a shock. On opening his trousers to take a look, she found the object to be twice its normal size and questioned him closely. He told her everything, but urged her not to reveal his secret. Then they drank a few hasty cups of wine, undressed, and went to bed. When a mighty sword is brought forth from its scabbard, its point can well be imagined, but Jishi proceeded slowly until they both reached a state of ecstasy. From this time on Jishi became a man of infinite capacity, and Xia regarded him as a rare and wonderful creature and enjoyed herself with him night after night.

The accounts had now all been settled. In rough numbers, the traders, money shops, and salt merchants together owed more than three hundred thousand taels, while the tenant farmers' debts coupled with odd loans throughout the city amounted to over two hundred thousand more. Jishi collected between fifty and sixty thousand in interest and told Su Xing to store the money away. He also paid a thousand to Xia for the New Year festivities, then hurried home and distributed the things he had bought in the city to his mother, sisters, his father's concubines, and others, as well as to servants, maids, and serving women. When Wankui saw how methodically Jishi had gone about the task, he was vastly relieved.

Spring returned, and the wedding date drew near. Wankui ordered the study where Jishi slept to be converted into the bridal quarters, moving Mistress Hua to another location. This courtyard became a separate establishment with six more maids and four more serving women. All the furnishings had by now been satisfactorily completed. The Wens' dowry, stored a mile or so away, was exceptionally handsome, in fact dazzling. The Su family engaged several acting troupes as well as dozens of musicians, and their servants were all outfitted with new clothes and hats, while the serving women were fully made up. Each room was hung with gaily decorated lanterns and spread with carpets—truly a festive scene.

On the day itself the bridal chair was decorated with brightly-colored lanterns that looked even more brilliant. In the evening the bride entered the house to the applause of relatives and friends and the strains of music and song, which made Jishi feel as if he were walking on air. The wedding rituals were duly performed, and when the celebrating was over and the guests had departed, he entered the bridal chamber and, after dismissing the maids, personally removed Huiruo's makeup. "My dear," he said, "it's been such a long time since we last saw each other, and you're prettier than ever!" While jesting with her, he helped her out of her clothes and got into bed with her. But after her silken undergarments had been removed, it proved difficult to penetrate her defenses, and she begged him to go slowly. Jishi took pity on her and moderated his approach. However, in the end the Little Pilgrim's gold-hooped rod was no match for the Ageless Dame's fire tongs, and the few drops of crimson turned into a shower of snow.[6]

At midmorning they arose. Their new maids and serving women came in and kowtowed, and Jishi rewarded each of them. After the third day the couple paid their respects to the groom's parents. Since his son was newly married, Wankui couldn't bear to have him leave the compound, and at New Year's, because no one had been into the city to offer the family's compliments of the season, Wankui had to go himself.

Riches, when carelessly stored, attract the robber—so goes the proverb. Wankui's vast wealth had long been common knowledge, but he ought not to have been so ostentatious in the way he held the wedding, for in that area there were many people of limited perspective who had never seen such nuptials. One particular group of scoundrels, made up of men who had owed money for rent or loans and had suffered losses at Wankui's hands, joined up with soldiers from the guard posts and fishermen along the embankment who were in league with robbers. They waited until Wankui had left, and then forty or more of them headed for the compound holding torches and clutching weapons. Arriving at the compound, some climbed up on the roof, while others set fires, and still others split open the gates, then surged inside uttering menacing cries. The servants, awakening from their slumber with no idea of how many men were attacking, promptly fled. The robbers did not realize that the treasury was managed by servants and situated outside the inner gate, and swarmed straight into the main rooms, where they killed two maids, Mistress Mao having hidden herself behind the bed. They then stripped the place bare as they hunted for the newlyweds' chamber.

Jishi was just pleasuring himself with Huiruo at the time, and they were wrapped in each other's arms. Hearing the uproar, he realized that it meant trouble. He jumped out of bed and looked out at the courtyard, where he saw flames soaring up into the night sky and heard a thunderous shouting. He was about to go out when Huiruo, stark naked, pulled him back in: "When bandits set fires, they're out for loot, not murder. If you go out there, you're bound to run straight into a sword. Hurry up and hide."

"We can hide in that wainscot over there. But if they start a fire, won't we be burnt alive!"

"They're starting fires outside, but that's only to scare us. Once they're inside, they won't start any because they'll be too concerned about their own safety."

As they spoke, they heard raucous voices outside their door and were so panic-stricken that they had no time to dress. Jishi hastily pulled out a fur jacket of his and threw it around her shoulders and they proceeded to hide in the wall. There was no time to worry about the maids and the serving women.

Before long the robbers broke down the door and swarmed in, ransacking all the chests and boxes, and not leaving until the fifth watch. The young couple, trembling with fear, didn't dare emerge even at daybreak, when the servants, who had all been in hiding, came in to inspect the damage. The servants went first to the main room, calling out as they came, and Mistress Mao wriggled out from under the bed. Everything in the room had been taken. Then they rushed into Jishi's room, only to find that all the chests and boxes had been cleaned out. The maids' room had not been touched, and the maids now scrambled out one after the other. But the young master and mistress were nowhere to be seen, and although the servants turned the bed and all the furniture upside down, they were unable to find them. Jishi was well aware that it was his own servants who were looking for them, but Huiruo had nothing on except his fur jacket around her shoulders, the lower part of her body being stark naked, while he himself had no trousers, and so he didn't dare say anything. The servants cried out in alarm, "*Oh, no!* The young master and mistress have been seized by the robbers!" Some of them began to tidy up, while others went into the city to report on what had happened. They were all rushed off their feet.

Meanwhile Wankui was living in the old house in the city. He had risen early in the morning and was washing himself when Su Xing rushed in gasping for breath and said, "Master, something terrible has happened! The Huatian compound has been attacked by robbers and the main gate and the great hall have been burned down."

Wankui was deeply shocked. "Was anyone hurt?" he was quick to ask.

"They killed Uncle Su and two maids whose names we don't yet know."

Just as Wankui was grieving over these deaths, another servant, Dong Mao, came rushing in and cried, "Terrible news! All the rooms have been stripped bare, and the young master and mistress have been kidnapped!"

On hearing this, Wankui sagged to the floor, unconscious. His servants rushed to help him onto his bed and proceeded to pour ginger broth down his throat. He returned to semiconsciousness twice, cried out "Enough!" and died.

The next chapter will explain.

Chapter IX

In burning old deeds a son carries out his father's wishes
By faking a prayer a priest engages in a lascivious act

⁓

Fortunately Su Xing retained a measure of loyalty and integrity after Su Wankui's death from shock. He told some men to watch over the body and sent others to the country compound to report the news, then waited for his mistress to come and decide what should be done. By the time the messenger reached the compound, however, Jishi had already emerged and taken charge of the situation, sending a servant to report the case to the authorities and have them come and examine the corpses. Luckily the robbers had merely looted two rooms, and neither the treasury nor the contents of the other rooms had been touched. Although no accurate assessment of the losses could be made, the gold and silver, jewelry, and clothes alone that had been stolen came to somewhere between forty and fifty thousand. In addition, three lives had been taken and two entrance halls burned. Jishi was about to go into town to consult his father when the report reached him of his father's death. He began wailing, and the whole household joined him in a prolonged expression of grief. After ordering Dong Mao locked up until the magistrate could come and deal with the case, Jishi took his womenfolk with him into the city. He and his mother, wife, and sisters went on ahead, while his father's two concubines stayed behind and began the process of careful tidying up. Jishi also detailed several older servants and serving women to watch over the property.

Arriving in the city soon afterward, they stroked the corpse and wailed over it. Su Xing now realized that the report of Jishi's death had been false, but fortunately he had done nothing to reproach himself with, and he came forward and kowtowed. "You're a sensible fellow," said Jishi. "You and Su Bang take charge of the funeral arrangements, each of you making himself responsible for some of the duties—draw up a list and give it to me. As for the mourning hall, go and ask Masters Wen, Pan, and Shy (from over the way) if they would make themselves collectively responsible. For the inner quarters, ask Mistresses Shy and Wen to take charge. It looks as if we won't be able to go on living at the Huatian property, so have some experienced men go over there and bring the money and goods back from the treasury as well as all the articles from the young ladies' and the concubines' rooms."

Su Xing and Su Bang withdrew, bought a coffin for the laying in, and also sent out the funeral notices. Jishi told his mother about Xia and invited her to come over and mourn with everyone else. The funeral rites extended over five days. The first day was for the local gentry, officeholders, and assistants with whom the deceased had associated; the second day was for colleagues and friends from the various trading houses; the third day was for all the relatives by marriage; the fourth day was for female relatives; and the fifth day was for his own clan. Only after the coffin had remained there for five consecutive seven-day periods did the funeral procession leave. With more than twenty families of friends and relatives offering sacrifices along the route, the procession went directly out through the Great East Gate and laid the coffin in the ancestral tomb.

While Jishi was in mourning at home, he developed a roster of household duties. He promoted Su Xing to be manager in Su Yuan's place, with concurrent responsibility for the treasury and the warehouses. Su Bang would manage the granary and all the rural loans and rents; Su Yu would take responsibility for the urban loans; Wu Fu would be in charge of the main gate and Ye Xing of purchasing. Four ledgers were to be set up, one for each man, and Su Xing was to check income and expenditure each month and see that every item was entered. Jishi himself would examine the ledgers once a year. He also established rules for the household: males over the age of eleven were not allowed through the inner gate without permission, and females were not allowed to go out to the main hall without permission. Room was left outside the inner gate for signal clappers, and eight boys in shifts would await orders and transmit messages, while inside the gate eight women servants in shifts would run errands and deliver articles. At night the women would rest in the annex and keep watch. Jishi renovated two studies for himself, an outer study on the west side of the main hall where Aqing would serve and have charge of six assistants, and an inner one to the east of the women's quarters where four maids who had some education would take turns on duty. He gave the five-room two-story building to his mother and sisters to live in, and the five-room building to the two concubines. Huiruo would occupy the bungalow opposite the six-room eastern court, while Xia would live in the six-room western court. Each of the apartments was assigned maids and women servants as before. Any girls born to the staff would go into service in the household at ten years of age and at eighteen would be sent out to marry. The same principle would apply to boys born to the staff, except that those wishing to remain in the household would be allowed to do so. As for dispensing money in the inner quarters, the manager deputed Xia, Wuyun, and Xiuyan to help him. He put Ye Xing's wife in charge of the kitchen in the inner quarters. He also directed Su Xing's wife, Su Bang's wife, and Wu Fu's wife to supervise the inner quarters on a ten-day rotation. When one of the serving women or maids did something wrong, so long as it was a minor infraction, the three women would investigate and mete out the punishment themselves; if it was a major offense, it was to be reported and the culprit expelled. The garden in the rear would be kept in order by servants from the two apartments in turn.

Altogether over one hundred fifty male and female servants were to be paid a monthly wage ranging from five qian up to two or three taels according to their responsibilities. Su Xing in the outer quarters and Xia in the inner quarters were to pay out the wages each month. The system worked smoothly, and everyone was happy with it. In addition, there were the three sons and two daughters of former servant Su Yuan. The eldest son was permitted to leave the household and go back to his ancestral place, while the others were raised in the household with substantial monthly stipends. At the same time the new compound at Huatian was sold, and men were sent to the Panyu county yamen to request that the robbers be pursued and arrested.

Magistrate Ma of Panyu county had already conducted his examination and was pressing the search for the culprits. He gave Dong Mao a beating and sent him back to the compound, from which he was driven out. Later the constables arrested two local men, Bai Aguang and Lai Deda, both of whom owed money to Su Wankui. They testified as follows: "Because we were in debt and faced with ruin, we had the idea of seizing some money by force. We joined a band of forty-six men. They all fled, but because we had obtained a double share of the goods and couldn't divide it evenly, we delayed and were captured." The magistrate confined both of them to jail and issued orders to apprehend the rest of the gang.

A servant came back and reported all of this to Jishi. Now that he knew what lay behind the robbery, he reflected that his father had been plagued by money the whole of his life. The thought troubled him deeply, and tears streamed down his face. Calling Su Bang in, he asked him, "I know you haven't been in charge very long, but tell me this: what is the sum total of all our rural loans and longstanding rental debts?"

"The original capital for the rural loans was less than 30,000; combined with interest, it now comes to over 70,000. The leased land is in three places: In Hua county it's over 3,200 mu, handled by manager Wang Fu; altogether the tenants owe over 5,800 piculs of grain. In Dongguan county it totals 2,700 mu, handled by manager Zheng Sheng; the tenants owe over 1,200 piculs of grain. In Panyu it totals over 6,700 mu, handled by manger Bao Fu; the tenants owe over 19,500 piculs of grain. The three managers came and kowtowed the other day, and I went over the figures with them and told them to press for prompt repayment. They undertook to collect twenty percent of the amount due."

"Well, get the loan contracts and the articles used as collateral and also the title deeds, check them, and seal them up. Then call the debtors together at the Huatian compound on the third of the third month. There's something I want to tell them." Su Bang left to carry out his orders.

Jishi was plunged in gloom when Shy Yannian happened to pay a visit, and the two men relaxed over wine. Yannian was only too eager to produce a few exotic items of gossip for Jishi, but the latter suddenly cut him short: "Last winter I came into town and saw that priest at the Tianfei Temple. He has nothing to offer except the fact that he excels at praying for sons. For his sake you ought to spread the news around—you'll also be doing a good deed. But you mustn't let on that it comes from either of us."

"That's simple enough. You may not realize how many good friends I have. This one tells two others, who will each tell three more, and in a few days' time it'll be all over town." He lowered his voice: "You're in mourning and so you're sleeping in the outer quarters, but it's so lonely out here—I don't know how you can stand it. The fact is, there's no need to be *overly* strict about these things. Why not go and spend the night in the inner quarters?"

"I'm merely observing the mourning period, staying outside for a hundred days. Then I'll go in and out as before, don't you worry. But you must find yourself a wife without delay so that she can serve your mother. If you need any money, naturally I'll provide it." Yannian thanked him and left.

On the third day of the third month, Jishi took a sedan chair with the curtain lowered and early in the morning went out into the countryside. When he arrived at Huatian, the men keeping watch over the property came forward and kowtowed, and Jishi told them to form up on both sides of the room. Su Bang then led in a large number of villagers, who came forward one by one. This is how they looked:

> Gaunt,
> Undernourished,
> Bent over, crook-backed;
> Howling like wolves,
> Crouching like tigers,
> Rubbing their fists together.
> Tattered coats covering bony, fleshless bodies;
> Blackened shoulders;
> Straw sandals without sides or lining, showing their mud-
>   caked heels.
> Pushing and shoving
> Like starving peasants lectured by some impoverished

director of schools;
    Hesitant, hanging back
    Like reluctant troops forced into battle by some bellicose
        commander.

Jishi called on several of the older, more experienced men to come forward. They all excused themselves, but eventually seven or eight men did come up and bow before him. They were about to kneel when Jishi told his servants to help them up. "All of you men owe me money. Is that so?"

"That's right!" they said. "It's not that we deliberately didn't pay; the truth is, we can't. Young master, we beg you, do us a favor and allow us to pay you in the winter after the harvest is in."

"I'm not expecting any payment from you at all. From the poverty-stricken look of you, I doubt that you could pay your debts, so I'm going to suggest a plan for you. Let each village choose a few people who can read and write to come up in front." He told his servants to bring out all the articles that had been used as collateral. Altogether thirty-odd villagers stepped forward.

"Village neighbors," Jishi began, "this money was lent to you at a high rate of interest. Before, while my father was alive, our expenditures were heavy, and so he was dependant on the interest from your loans. But now we are cutting back in all respects and can do without it. Those of you who are in real trouble need not pay back either principal or interest. Those who have a little over should pay the principal only; there's no need for any interest. As for these articles used as collateral, let me trouble you to go from door to door returning them to their owners. All the loan contracts will be burned. That was my father's dying command. But you must all act in accordance with your consciences and without any dishonesty."

The villagers were jubilant. "We are so grateful to you for your generosity in canceling the interest," they said, "but the principal must be paid, no matter whether we're rich or poor. We'll leave it to our village heads to arrange."

"There's no need to bother about that, gentlemen. Just see that you return the collateral items carefully to their rightful owners, and we'll rely on people's consciences." He proceeded to burn a large quantity of loan contracts. The debtors clapped their hands in appreciation and gave thunderous cheers as they left the room.

Jishi felt exhilarated himself. As he took the boat back to the city, he told Su Bang, "You mustn't spread this around. Go back at once and write out an order in triplicate and send one copy to each of the managers, telling him to cancel all the old rents that are owed and to reduce any new rents by ten percent. If any of those debtors I spoke to should bring the principal into the city and hand it in, see that you reimburse them liberally for their travel."

Jishi returned home and told Su Xing to cancel the accounts, while he himself went before his father's tomb and tearfully reported what he had done. He then continued his mourning at home, which is where we shall leave him.

Let us turn to the priest whom Jishi had encountered in front of the Tianfei temple. He came from Shenmu county in Sichuan, his lay name was Dayong, and he was a surviving adherent of a White Lotus sect. Because he had taken six lives with his evil powers, he had fled for safety to Tibet. Crafty by nature and superlatively skilled in hand-to-hand fighting, he regarded such feats as leaping onto roofs or over high walls as mere child's play. After stealing a Lama Buddhist's ordination certificate, he dressed up as a foreign priest, changed his name to Mola, and slipped back into China. In Si'an prefecture of Guangxi he killed a man and then escaped to sea, where he joined a large band of pirate raiders and set up camp on Mount Fuyuan in the middle of the ocean. Because of his enormous physical strength and the fact that he knew how to cast a few spells, they elected him chief, and he gathered over four thousand men, seized over a hundred ships, and made a career of pillaging. Recently, because pirate raiders were running rampant everywhere, merchants had become too afraid to travel, and food shortages had gradually developed. It occurred to Mola that Guangdong was a rich area, and he ordered his chieftains to guard the camp, while he himself with a hundred or two braves set sail for Guangzhou. After hiding the ship at some distance, he took a handful of spies with him into the city. There he heard that Superintendant Heh was amply supplied with wealth and beautiful women, and he licked his lips at the thought. From someone or other he also learned that Heh was devoutly praying for a son, so he kept saying to everyone he met that he could chant mantras to the White-robed Goddess, which was a most effective way of obtaining a son. A day or two previously he had noticed Jishi coming toward him and had dropped a few hints that impressed Jishi, who failed to realize that his worries were apparent in his face and that the lantern Aqing was carrying bore the name "Su" on it. It was fortunate that he didn't invite the priest to offer sacrifices at his house; in that respect the man's focus on the superintendant was a stroke of luck. But Jishi should never have given him Qiao's name in the hope that he might turn out to be a sort of Kunlun Slave and rescue her—that was pure fantasy on his part.

The talk about the priest's ability to obtain a son did come to the superintendant's ear. At this time Heh was delighted with Wu Biyuan's sycophantic attentions and entrusted him with such matters as making money through influence peddling. Biyuan also became a sworn brother of Bao Jincai, and the two men cemented their friendship. The one thing that bothered him was the woeful look on his daughter's face. For a whole year now she had not been seen to smile, and Heh was none too pleased with her. Several times he had urged Biyuan to speak to her, but she took not the slightest notice. Biyuan was greatly put out by this and reported back to Heh, who had her placed in solitary confinement, with only Yeyun in attendance, in order to bend her to his will. However, Qiao, having achieved her objective, was well content with the quiet life she could now lead.

One day when Biyuan came in to pay his respects, Heh mentioned how eager he was to have a son, and Biyuan strongly recommended this priest. Heh at once summoned the man, who gave an extravagant priestly greeting and then sat down with his legs crossed and his face upturned. "Where are you from, priest?" asked Heh. "Where did you join the order? Do you have an ordination certificate? And on what virtues and talents do you base those boasts that you've been making?"

"I come from Tibet. I served the Patriarch Dale Hundu, and my name in religion is Mola. I have no virtues or talents, except that I am good at chanting mantras that free people from their worldly concerns. Following the orders of the Patriarch, I pray to bring people blessings and avert disasters. Yes, I do have an ordination certificate. I wonder if it's genuine?" He took it out of his sleeve and handed it to Heh.

Heh looked at it. All he saw was a charm printed in red and black that used the ancient seal script, and he assumed that it was some sort of treasure of Lama Buddhism. He quickly rose from his seat and gave it back to the priest with both hands, saying, "I was too blind to see the truth in front of my eyes. I beg you to take pity on me and forgive me." He invited the priest into his private quarters and asked him to sit down while he knelt before him. Early every morning from then on he and his wife, Mistress Hu, prostrated themselves devoutly before the priest.

Five or six days later Heh wanted to spy on what the priest was doing, and so he stole along outside the priest's room and peered through a crack in the window. He found the priest amusing himself by turning somersaults, chanting something as he did so. He was wearing a monk's robe but no trousers, and as he turned upside down, the area between his legs appeared to be flat and smooth with nothing protruding. Heh was amazed, and he walked into the room and bowed. Mola took a seat, and Heh asked him, "Master, what were those devotions you were performing just now? Is it something that could be taught to a mere mortal like me?"

"Those weren't devotions. I was merely divining to see if you're going to have a son."

Heh was delighted. "Master, how can I show my gratitude for all the trouble you have taken? But I happened to notice your outward form, and you looked just like a woman. Why is that?"

"I used that object up. I used it for over twenty years of religious practice before I could cut off the root of passion once and for all. If I didn't have some good conduct to my credit, my patriarch would never have allowed me to mingle in society."

Heh believed all of this implicitly, and actually held sacrifices in the inner courtyard from which the concubines were not excluded. Pinwa, Pinjiao, Pinxing, Pinting, and others of Heh's dozen northern girls all addressed the priest as Living Buddha and prostrated themselves before him morning and evening, competing with each other to have a son and so win special favor. Unfortunately, although Heh was not yet forty, his semen had dried up as a result of overindulgence in drink and sex, and he was dependant on central

Guangdong pills made with a few ounces of Beijing medicine. In the daytime he still wanted to play about with boys, and at night he longed for the company of his young girls like Ke'er and Meizi. This month he had visited his concubines on a couple of nights only. And so there was much sighing and moaning among the women in the west courtyard. Although they prayed every day for a son, their unseeded fields were unlikely to produce much of a harvest.

Mola learned that Pinwa was the one who handled the money, and he thought he would overcome her first. One morning, after the women had prostrated themselves before him, he announced, "You may withdraw now. I'll just keep Pinwa behind and teach her a mantra." He whispered something in her ear. After she emerged from the room, the others asked her what he had said.

"If you were presented with an opportunity, you wouldn't dare reveal it to anyone else, would you? You just need to worship Buddha with faithful hearts, and you'll naturally be blessed."

She returned to her room and hastily tidied it up. That evening she sent her maid away, lit the finest incense, and sat there alone in silent meditation. Mola had told her that she was destined to bear a son, and that she should burn incense that evening and wait for him on her own; he would pass on to her a short mantra. That was why she was waiting there so devoutly.

At the second watch, when a dark shadow leapt down into the courtyard, her heart skipped a beat. By this time the Living Buddha had already entered her room and was sitting cross-legged on the bed. Kneeling down before him, Pinwa asked him in a reverent tone to teach her the mantra. When he helped her to her feet and took her in his arms, she was not in the least concerned, believing that he was a eunuch priest. "It's a pillow mantra," he said. "It's a shortcut to having a son, but I shall need to convey it to you secretly in bed. I wonder if you'd be willing to try."

"To be able to share a bed with a Living Buddha—why, that would be no small karma! Moreover, you're just like us women, Master, so what is there to be afraid of?" She helped him off with his robe and found that there really was nothing between his thighs. She also took off her own clothes and lay down. When Mola reared himself above her, she began to giggle: "Does the Living Buddha think he's another Lu Zhishen? Why are you just knocking at the temple gate?"[1]

"If I don't get inside the temple gate, how am I going to chant the scriptures and preach the faith? Behold, the treasure of Buddha!" he replied. He employed all of his techniques, and soon she felt her passions deeply stirred. There isn't time to go into detail, but she spent twice in quick succession, dying and then coming back to life. Still he didn't stop, and all she could do was clutch at him with both arms and beg him over and over to pause for just a moment.

"You have such a wonderful instrument, Master! What I don't understand is where you've been hiding it all this time."

"It's the marvelous practice known as 'Retracting the Dragon.' Lay folk know nothing about external manifestations." He pulled her hand down to feel the object in question, which both startled and enthralled her. "The first time you do it, you can't enjoy yourself to the full," he continued. "This mendicant priest of mine has still not had his fill, but that's quite a sin, isn't it? You'll need to show him more compassion."

She gave the priest a smack, but let him resume his onslaught, which continued until the fifth watch. Mola then sat cross-legged, silently cultivating his virtue, while Pinwa's body was in raptures and her limbs were trembling. She hugged him. "This encounter with you has made my life worth living. I wonder if we could arrange to meet again?"

"That's no problem, and I guarantee that you'll get pregnant and have a son. But you won't be able to serve me on your own. You'll need to get a group of women together if I'm going to employ even a few of my techniques."

"The three women who share the same compound with me are all trusted friends of mine. I'll bring them here tomorrow and you can do whatever you like with them. Will that be enough?" Mola agreed that it would be.

As she had promised, the next night Pinwa told the three women they would be receiving instruction together, and none of them was averse to trying out the novel experience. They gathered in Pinwa's room, four she-crabs about to attack a single iron rod from all sides.[2] But Mola's ability was simply too prodigious, and he forced them into a formal surrender, then bellowed with laughter as he returned in triumph to his own quarters. Pinxing was left with a sore pelvis; Pinjiao wore a deep frown; and Pinting stood up only to fall down again in a coma; all of them had experienced novel sensations, but they had also suffered unbounded misery. "He's just not born of woman," said Pinjiao. "That instrument of his—it's as if it's made of iron or brass. How could we possibly find room for it? Our compound has over twenty maids altogether. If we exclude those who are a little too young, we'll be left with fifteen or sixteen. Let's get them all together, each one of us bringing four girls, and take him on—then we'll see who comes out on top."

"Don't be silly!" said Pinwa. "If we veterans couldn't stand up to him, how do you suppose the maids are going to cope? I'm afraid they'll die with the first thrust. It's not worth it to create such dreadful karma for ourselves."

"You're right," said Pinting. "We're old hands, and still we lost. Just imagine how they would get on! I've been told there's new girl in the east court called Aqian who has some sort of technique. Why don't you call her over and ask her? She'll want to please and won't dare hold out on you. Once we've learned that, we'll be able to win a battle."

"I've also heard the master praising her," said Pinwa. "Tomorrow I'll call her over and ask her about it. But we'll need to drink a few extra bowls of ginseng broth to keep up our strength before we go charging into battle."

While the women were discussing their strategy of resistance, Qiao in her solitary confinement was the only one with no inkling of what was going on. Mola remembered her name, but fortunately he was so enamored of the others that he had no time to think of how to get her. One day, as she was chatting with Yeyun, she saw the door suddenly open and her father come in. As she got up to receive him, he noticed that her hair was askew and her face pathetically thin, and that she was living in a darkened room, and he couldn't help shedding tears. "The other day when I urged you to change your mind, you refused, and now you're suffering this misery—I feel terrible about it. Recently the master invited a Living Buddha into his household to pray for a son. His women all kneel devoutly before him and ask for a mantra. If you are prepared to ask him nicely, well, he was originally recommended by me, and I'm sure he would give you one. Then later on, when you have a son who obtains office on the strength of his forbears' service, you're sure to become a dame yourself! My dear girl, do listen to what I have to say. Keep your resentment to yourself and reveal some of your good nature, and I'll beg the master to let you out. If you go on like this, you'll spend your life cooped up in here. You're a perfect flower with only a couple of buds open. Aren't you wasting all of your youth?"

"Ever since I came here I've done his bidding in every possible way," she sobbed. "This is my natural look. What do you expect me to do?"

"You can talk and laugh well enough when you're at home. In fact, you do more laughing than talking—I'm constantly shouting at you to stop. Why is it that after you come here you never have a smile on your face? The master liked you at first, and this is the only thing about you that he doesn't like. He says that if you'd give him just one smile, he'll offer me a promotion! Think of it as doing your duty as a daughter and try to smile!"

"You can't force yourself to show emotion. And if you want to be promoted, why don't you raise a few more daughters who know how to smile and send them to the governor-general and governor? That way you might even be promoted to prefect! Wouldn't that be better than treasurer?"

He flew into a rage. "Little hussy, how dare you defy me like this? If you're won't listen to me, we don't need to see each other anymore!" He got to his feet and stormed out.

She sighed. In my opinion, you're on very thin ice, she thought, and I'm afraid that at the first clap of spring thunder that ice is going to melt. With this disgraced body of mine I naturally cannot serve Master Su, but if Heaven pities me and lets me see him just one more time, I'll die without regret!

After storming out full of rage and shame, Biyuan went to see Heh, who asked, "Well, what did she say when you tried to persuade her?"

Biyuan knelt down. "It's my own evil karma that has brought me such an unfilial daughter, but I beg Your Honor to make an exception in her case and forgive her for the present."

"She's done nothing wrong—it's just that she doesn't try to please. She's a stupid, narrow-minded girl, but I can't bear to be hard on her. I'll decide what to do with her at a later date." Biyuan thanked him and stood up again.

Heh had another question: "We ought to have collected the customs dues by now, but all the posts are showing shortfalls. When I draw up my report, how am I going to make up the loss? You'll have to find a solution for me."

"I've already discussed it with Master Bao. Your Honor should call him in so that we can go over it together."

Heh summoned Bao Jincai. "About the shortfall in the tax collection," he said, "what was it that you and Master Wu were thinking of doing?"

"I've given it careful thought. The shortfall clearly springs from the fact that there are too many pirates and too few merchants, as a result of which the taxes can't be collected; it's not because anyone has been skimming the proceeds. Governor Qu memorialized just now that the pirates had been wiped out and peace restored along the coast, and he's been promoted one grade in rank. Someone else gets the credit while we get the blame, and in the future, when we're trying to make up the arrears, don't imagine for one moment that the governor will come to our aid! I would suggest that Your Honor send in a memorial pointing out that the pirates are running rampant and that merchants are prevented from traveling. At present all the posts—at least fifty altogether—are reporting raids. Last year in the spring Dong Cai committed suicide after being robbed, and this spring Colonel Yao was impeached by the governor-general because he couldn't wipe out the pirates. These are facts, not something that we've concocted."

"Excellent idea! That Qu fellow is so headstrong and foolish.

But I have to retaliate. Have Master Hao draw up a memorial and show it to me."

He sauntered over to the inner quarters as far as the west court, where he found Pinwa and the others talking to Aqian. "What are you doing here?" he asked Aqian. "Don't tell me you want to worship the Living Buddha, too, and pray for a son? I'm afraid it's just not your turn!"

"I chose her and asked her to come over," said Pinwa. "Why are you so upset? I want to keep her here to attend on me." She turned to Aqian: "From now on you're not allowed to go over there anymore. If the master likes you, surely we're allowed to enjoy you, too?"

Pinxing added with a smile. "We're such a tightly-knit group of kindred spirits that perhaps he thinks she's too good for us."

Heh smiled. "I'm not playing favorites. I am just afraid you may be trying to stir up a little trouble for me, though. And now I'm off to talk to the Living Buddha."

Pinwa spent the whole evening on her bed with Aqian, and who knows what matters were discussed and what techniques were passed on? Later, when the four women warriors square off against Mola, will they be able to turn the tables on the villainous baldhead? The next chapter will continue the tale.

Chapter X

Lü Youkui forms an alliance at an inn
Yao Huowu is thrown into jail in Haifeng

⁓

Yao Huowu had returned to Nanxiong with the intention of going on to Jieshi. There was a track that led over the mountains, but because he didn't know the way he took passage on a boat instead, disembarking at Huizhou. With his iron staff slung over his shoulder and his bags and bedroll dangling from it, he strode off on his journey. It was late spring, and the early rice of central Guangdong had already been planted; a breeze came off the green rice paddies; and Huowu felt fresh and vigorous. The twenty or so miles to Pingshan took him less than half a day.

Entering an inn, he put down his baggage, and a hulking fellow behind the counter looked him up and down very carefully, then raised a hand and asked, "Where have you come from? Are you intending to stay the night?"

"I've come from Huizhou, and I'm on my way to Jieshi. Do you have a room for me? I want to stay the night and then set off early in the morning."

"I have plenty of rooms. You can take your pick." He leapt out from behind the counter and began to carry Huowu's baggage for him. The iron staff weighed over fifty catties, and there was the baggage as well. As he picked the articles up in both hands, the man said with a smile, "You must be fairly strong to have carried all this gear."

"Oh, it's not so heavy," said Huowu, walking into one of the rooms and taking a seat. "If you have any good liquor and meat, bring me a good amount of it. And cook me up a peck of rice as well. Put it all on my bill." He took a seat.

"We have the finest Taihe spirits, bought in the city. And we have stewed and smoked pork, salted beef, and also fish and lobsters."

"Bring me ten catties of spirits, five of smoked pork, and five of beef. That's all." The innkeeper smiled to himself and told the boy to bring out two large plates of meat, while he himself carried in a big bottle of spirits. Huowu finished all of the food and drink without pausing and then called to the innkeeper, who bustled in. "You'd like the rice now?" he asked.

"No hurry. Just cut me another five catties of beef."

The innkeeper kept his astonishment to himself as he gave orders to the boy: "Cut some more beef and bring out another five catties of spirits. I'm going to keep our guest company."

At this indication that the innkeeper was a good drinker, Huowu said, "Why didn't you tell me before that you could drink? Let's have a cup together to begin with." The innkeeper took a seat beside him and they drank together.

"With your build," said Huowu, "you had no trouble carrying my bags in just now. You must be strong. What's your name?"

"I'm Wang Dahai, from around here. I used to be a local militiaman under the command of Governor-general Qing, earning two taels a month for holding off the pirates. Later, because the governor-general left, 'militiaman' became an empty word, and if you captured any pirates, there was nowhere you could go to claim credit for them. Instead you ran afoul of the local officials, which took up all of your monthly wage. As a result my sworn brothers and I refused to be militiamen and looked for some other means of making a living. I opened up this inn, and I manage to get by that way."

"How is it you couldn't claim any credit but instead ran afoul of the local officials?"

"In the past, if we captured any pirates, the local officials used to help us transfer them to their yamens. At worst we'd get a bounty; at best we'd be given a position. In these two or three counties, six or seven out of the fifteen or sixteen of us sworn brothers received positions that way. But nowadays, if we capture any pirates, we first have to take them to the local civil official's yamen and make out a report, have the case reviewed, and then pay off the official before he will accept the accusation as genuine. If you don't pay him off, he'll declare the case fraudulent and either let the pirates go or else take them away and allow someone with money to claim credit for capturing them. People who pay for pirates in order to claim credit for catching them will put up as much as several score taels a head—which means that our band of militiamen was toiling away for the benefit of those with money! Who would work under that kind of injustice?"

"Why didn't you go and report it to the military officer?"

"He wouldn't have any authority. Even if he were to capture some pirates himself, he would still have to explain everything in detail to the prefect or magistrate, the only difference being that he would have less troublemaking to contend with. In any case, there are very few military officers with any ability. The pity is that my brothers and I have no way to be of service!"

"What about Master Yao of the Jieshi station? Is he all right?"

"He's a military graduate who arrived here last year. He takes his duties seriously, and he has great physical strength and outstanding military skills. Unfortunately, he did not get along very well with the governor-general and governor, and he's always being sent out on marine patrol, so he rarely gets back to his yamen. I can see what a capacity you have for drink, and I'd guess you're one of us. But you haven't favored me with your name yet."

"I'm Yao Huowu, from Donglai. I'm Colonel Yao's brother."

"So you're a gentleman, sir! Please forgive me. May I ask what brings you here?" Huowu explained what had happened and said he wanted to go on to Jieshi and help capture pirates.

"I don't want to dash your hopes, but you shouldn't bother about capturing any pirates. Even a man as loyal and brave as your brother would, I'm afraid, find himself ignored by the governor-general and governor."

"'When a man masters a skill, how can he not offer it to his ruler?' Your experience is just too limited."

"We have a certain amount of physical strength, but we have no one to instruct us, and our martial skills are mediocre at best. If we had an instructor, we could really be of some help."

"That's no problem! I don't wish to boast, but I do have some knowledge of the eighteen combat techniques. If you and your sworn brothers are willing to learn, you're bound to be of service."

Dahai quickly bowed before him. "If you're willing to teach us, I'll collect my brothers so that we can study together."

Huowu raised him to his feet. "Since my brother's away from his yamen, there's no point in my going there. I'll stay and give you a little instruction, but as soon as I hear that he's back, I'll have to leave." That evening the pair drank heartily together.

Next morning Huowu stayed behind, while Dahai sent men out to summon his sworn brothers. Before long three of them had arrived and seated themselves around the counter.

"I've called you here today for this purpose only: because we haven't perfected our martial skills, our physical strength is going to waste. Yesterday a certain Master Yao, who is the brother of Colonel Yao of the Jieshi station, arrived at the inn. I called you here today so that we can acknowledge him as our teacher and study combat techniques with him, techniques that we can put to good use in the future."

One of the men, Xu Zhen, asked, "But, Brother, have you actually seen his military skills?"

"No, I haven't, but I expect they're fine."

Another, Lü Youkui, said, "Brother, how can you promote someone else's ambitions at the expense of our prestige? Where is this Yao fellow, anyway? Let's call him in and have him take me on before we decide on anything."

"Not so hasty, Brother. By the look of him, we might not be a match for him even if all four of us took him on together."

"How can you say such a thing!" shouted Youkui. "Call him in at once!"

A man named You Qi said, "Brothers, there's no need to argue about this. Taking someone as your teacher is a serious matter. Let's invite him out to meet us. It would be hard to compare martial skills in a tiny place like this, but at the entrance to West River Academy there's plenty of open space. When we've eaten, let's go over there and have some fun. If he loses, we'll just have a good laugh, but if he wins, we'll take him as our teacher." His suggestion was approved.

Dahai invited Huowu to come out, and the men greeted him and introduced themselves. After they had eaten and drunk heartily, Dahai told Huowu what the men wanted to do and, as a highly competitive person, Huowu was happy to agree. They went to the entrance of the Academy, where there was indeed a broad, level area. "If we use weapons," said Huowu, "there are bound to be some injuries, even though we don't mean to cause any. Let's try unarmed combat instead. Who would like to go first?"

Lü Youkui, a singularly forthright man of immense strength, stepped forward. "I will! I will! But I want to make one thing clear—if you get hurt, I won't have the money to pay for your treatment."

Huowu laughed. "Don't you worry about that. I can treat myself."

Youkui took off his outer garments and came at Huowu's head with both fists raised. Huowu dodged to one side and seized the chance to press with two fingers against his opponent's leg. Youkui found himself sitting inexplicably on the ground. Instead of trying to scramble up, he shot out his right foot, hooking it around his opponent's calf. Huowu took a step forward and Youkui found that he had hooked nothing, while his left foot was high up in the air. In a deft move Huowu caught the foot lightly in his hand, and Youkui, lying on the ground, called out, "Don't use force! I'm willing to accept you as my teacher."

Huowu let go, and Youkui turned over and began kowtowing. "There's no need for any of that!" Huowu said, helping him up. "I treated you badly just now; I hope you won't hold it against me."

"My dear teacher, the only way I'll be happy is if you teach me for the rest of my life."

"Of course we all have to admire Master Yao's skill," said You Qi, "but there are three rocks in front of the temple, and I wonder if he'd care to try out his strength on them."

"Let's go," said Huowu.

With people swarming around—including spectators, they numbered over a hundred—the men made their way to the front of the temple, where they found three rocks of varying sizes set in a row. "My brothers and I often amuse ourselves with the small one," said You Qi. "Only Brother Lü can lift the middle-sized one. No one has ever managed to lift the large rock."

"How heavy is it?" asked Huowu. "I'll have to try, but if I can't lift it, you mustn't laugh at me." He hitched up his gown, strode forward and easily lifted the middle-sized rock, which weighed only a thousand catties. He held it in one hand, then told everyone to get out of the way and threw it with all his strength. It traveled over ten feet and buried itself in the earth. He then picked up the large rock, which was a mere five hundred catties heavier than the last one. Huowu, however, acted completely unconcerned. He brought the rock up to chest level with both hands, then held it with one hand while he took a short walk over open ground and threw it at the middle-sized rock. There was an earth-shattering noise as the latter broke into three pieces.

The onlookers were flabbergasted. "With such godlike strength, he's unmatched anywhere in the world. I wonder if he's willing to take us on as his students."

"Since you've made me welcome, let's call each other brother rather than teacher and student," said Huowu.

The men were elated and went together to the inn, where a pig and an ox were slaughtered. They exchanged bows with Huowu and held a joyous celebration.

Huowu sent a man to Jieshi to find out if Colonel Yao had returned and meanwhile devoted himself to giving lessons. Dahai also invited his brothers from all around—Chu Hu, Gu Shen, Jiang Xinyi, and the military licentiates Han Pu and Qi Guangzu—to come and study with them.

Time went swiftly by, and soon over half a year had passed. Because of his close ties to the other men, and also because his brother had still not returned to his yamen, Huowu continued to delay his departure. One day, in the depths of winter, they were competing in archery beside a highway in the countryside when they saw a post-horse come galloping toward them. Huowu stepped forward, seized the horse's bridle, and asked the rider where he had come from. At sight of Huowu's fierce appearance, the man replied, "I'm a lieutenant at the Jieshi station. My superior had some urgent business, and he's sent me to deliver a document to the commander-in-chief in Huizhou. Let go at once!"

"Is Colonel Yao back in his yamen yet?"

"Of course not! He's still at sea." As soon as Huowu released his hold on the bridle, the rider raised his whip and galloped off.

Huowu then addressed the assembled men. "Since you've made me so welcome here, I really shouldn't leave you. But my brother is facing some kind of emergency, and I need to rush off and help him."

"If you go, I'll gladly go with you," said Youkui.

"But Brother, you shouldn't be so hasty," said Dahai to Huowu. "Wait until the winter's over, and then in the spring we'll all go down there together. No matter what pirates there may be, with your awesome prowess, and with my brothers and me there to back you up, we should have no trouble capturing them!"

They returned to the inn with Huowu insisting he would leave the next day and everyone else trying to dissuade him. "That lieutenant just now said your brother was still out at sea," said You Qi. "Being at sea is very different from being on land. How will you set about finding him? If you're determined to go, you should first of all find out the facts. Jieshi is less than a hundred and forty miles from here, and once you hear that your brother has returned, you'll be able to get there in just three or four days, so what's the hurry?"

Huowu hesitated before replying. "I don't need to find out any more facts. At the beginning of spring I'm definitely going. Brothers, please be patient and wait for me. When I get the chance, I'll write to you."

Everyone acquiesced except Lü Youkui, who said, "I don't

agree! I'm going with you, Brother. I have no family, and wherever you go, I'll go too."

When spring arrived, the brothers were still reluctant to part with Huowu. At first they tried their best to dissuade him from going, and then they took turns giving him farewell feasts, which delayed his departure until the twentieth of the second month. Then, with Youkui carrying the baggage, the two men finally set off on foot. At every inn they came to they drank spirits or wine, arriving at Ebu only at the first watch. All the inns were full and their doors closed, except one on the north side whose door was ajar and its lantern alight. They went in intending to spend the night, but found no one there except an old man sitting on a bench staring into space. He stood up. "Travelers," he said, "this place isn't suitable for an overnight stay. Please go somewhere else."

"Are you trying to cheat us because we're outsiders and don't know you? Well. I come to this piffling little town four or five times a year, and yours is an old established inn. Why won't you let us stay the night?"

"There's something troubling me, and I wouldn't be able to look after my guests properly, and so I've closed down for a few days."

"There's just the two of us," said Huowu. "We don't need any looking after, and we only want to stay the one night. I hope you'll do us a favor."

"Well, if you don't mind poor service, there's no reason why you shouldn't stay." He told the boy to lock the door and himself led the way to a guest room. "May I ask your names, and where you've come from and where you are headed? I need to fill out the register."

"I know that your surname is Ho—how is it you don't know

mine is Lü?" said Youkui. "This gentleman is the brother of Colonel Yao of the Jieshi station. We've come from Pingshan and we're on our way to Jieshi."

"So you're a gentleman, sir? I'm quite familiar with Brother Lü; the only trouble is that he's gotten so much fatter and darker."

"What is it that you need to register?" asked Huowu.

"In recent years the pirate situation has become more critical. Last year, near Goat's Foot Ridge they robbed a consignment of taxes, and so the authorities issued registers to all the inns. At each inn they stop at, traveling merchants give their names, where their journey started, and where they are headed, in order to aid in any inquiry."

"But we're going there to *capture* pirates," said Youkui. "Surely we don't need to register?"

"It's just a matter of the local officials being cautious," said Huowu. "You don't need to be concerned, Brother."

"I don't suppose you've had anything to eat," said the innkeeper. "Let me cook you up something."

"We've had nothing but wine and spirits all day," said Youkui. "If you have any good meat and wine, bring it out, and then cook us up two pecks of rice."

"Brother Lü always did have a good appetite," said the innkeeper. "Let me tell someone to get it for you."

By the time the two men had set down their baggage and opened their bedrolls, the wine and food had arrived. They ate for a while, and then the innkeeper came in and said, "Is that enough meat for you? If you'd like anything more, I also have a stewed pig's head."

"By all means bring it in," said Youkui.

The innkeeper went and sliced up a large dish of piping hot

pig's head. Huowu invited him to sit down with them. "Have some yourself."

"I'm a strict vegetarian. I don't touch either wine or meat."

"Well, innkeeper, you're an old hand. Why don't you let more travelers stay here? What is it that's troubling you?"

"It's a long story," said the innkeeper. "I had two sons, Awen and Awu. Awu is just seventeen. He has a good deal of strength, and he's always out on the ridge trapping hares or hunting deer, without any concern for the work of the inn. My elder son, Awen, took a serious interest in the business, and I was completely dependent on him. In the third month of last year I arranged a marriage for him with Master Guan's daughter, a demure and virtuous girl. Unfortunately in the tenth month of last year Awen took ill and died." Before the innkeeper could finish what he was saying, tears began streaming down his face.

"Don't be so helpless," said Huowu. "The length of a man's life is predetermined—it's not something that should trouble you."

"That's as may be. Well, in the twelfth month Jail Warden Qian, who lives nearby, sent a servant over with twenty taels to buy my daughter-in-law as his concubine. Although I missed my son terribly, I was still afraid that my daughter-in-law, being so young, wouldn't be able to stand the life of a widow, and so I put it to her. But as soon as she heard of the offer, she burst out sobbing and went into her room and cut off the little finger of one hand, vowing that she would never marry again. And so I refused Qian's offer. Then on the eighth of the second month of this year, five or six men suddenly leapt over the wall during the night and seized someone in the courtyard outside my daughter-in-law's room. I was startled, and I got up and took a look at the man, but I didn't recognize him and assumed he was a thief. However, the other men claimed he'd been caught in adultery, and they broke into my daughter-in-law's room, seized her in her bed, and bound her up and took her before the authorities. At the trial Master Niu ordered the thief held and allowed my daughter-in-law to come home on bail, but he didn't declare the case closed. Today he's sent someone here to say that he'll retry it at the midday court tomorrow. I've found out that Warden Qian has given thirty taels to Deputy Magistrate Niu to declare it a case of adultery and put her up for sale. When my daughter-in-law heard this news today, she tried to hang herself, but fortunately an old servant woman rescued her in time. Now, Master Yao, wouldn't you agree that that was something that might well trouble a man?"

"Who is this Master Niu, anyway, who dares to take a bribe and force the sale of a virtuous widow?" demanded an enraged Huowu.

"You don't realize, Brother," said Youkui. "He's Niu Zao, the deputy magistrate here. When we used to capture pirates, he would let many of them go after receiving a bribe. He's the vilest, most corrupt of men."

"Don't you worry, old fellow," said Huowu to the innkeeper. "I'll go and observe that trial tomorrow. If he decides the case unjustly, I shall have something to say to him."

The innkeeper bowed in gratitude, then went in and drew several catties of wine, and also brought out some wild game such as venison and hare. Then, hearing a knocking at the door, he went out to see who it was. It turned out to be his second son, Awu, carrying a bird trap over his shoulder and holding several deer and hares in his hands. He came bursting in the door. "You're still spending all your time away," said his father. "Today your sister-in-law tried to hang herself, and you weren't here to look after her."

"Why would she do a thing like that?" Awu asked. His father explained, and his son said, "I'm going to run that scoundrel of a warden and that accursed magistrate through with a single thrust of my sword. Then Sister-in-Law won't have to hang herself."

"You're talking nonsense again!" roared his father. "Quick, come with me. We have the brother of Colonel Yao of Jieshi in the guest room. Come and meet him and talk to him about it."

Awu put down what he was carrying and followed his father inside. He did not greet either guest, but looked around until he spotted an iron staff standing in front of the bed. He seized it, swung it around once or twice, and found that he liked the grip. "Which one of you is Master Yao?" he asked. "Is this your weapon?"

"I am," said Huowu, "but that's no weapon. I just use it for carrying my baggage."

At this point Awu stepped forward and bowed. After they had introduced themselves, the men began drinking together. They got on well and did not go to bed until midnight.

The next morning, after Huowu and Youkui were up, the innkeeper invited them stay on at the inn. Awu kept them company and invited them into the central room, where they had no sooner finished their breakfast than the court bailiffs arrived. Seeing the three men seated together, the bailiffs said nothing, simply headed straight for the inner quarters. Awu sprang up and barred their way. One man dodged aside, while the other fell to the ground. "There's such a thing as private quarters in a house!" roared Awu. "What sort of pricks are you, to go barging in there like that?"

The bailiff who had fallen scrambled to his feet. He realized that Awu was too fierce a tiger to risk provoking and glanced over at the other two men, who looked equally fierce. He gave a hasty smile: "Surely you know who we are. We're carrying out official orders. We've come specially to invite your sister-in-law to attend trial."

"What's the hurry?" demanded Awu. "I'll take her there myself when I'm good and ready."

Meanwhile the old innkeeper had come out, and he invited the bailiffs to take a seat while he went to fetch his daughter-in-law:

> Hairpins of thorn, a cotton skirt—
> Dressed like a village maid;
> With oval face and rosy cheeks,
> An almost perfect belle.
> On tiny shoes she goes,
> A pair of lotus petals,
> Her hair all piled up high
> In a jet-black coiffure.
> She's like Qian, who leapt into the river;[1]
> Her purity will last.
> She's like Cao E, who cut off her nose;[2]
> Her finger oozes blood.
> Lissom like a willow in spring,
> A spirit as chill as autumn frost.

She came into the room, glanced at Huowu and Youkui, then knelt down with her head bowed. Huowu asked someone to help her up, after which the bailiffs and the innkeeper escorted her away. "You stay here and look after our things," Huowu told Youkui. "I'll go and see what happens." He walked to the yamen, where Deputy Magistrate Niu was already at his tribunal trying the case. First he questioned the man who had hidden in the courtyard; he swore it was a case of adultery. Then the magistrate questioned the men who had seized him, and they swore that they had done so in the woman's room. He then called on Mistress Guan to come forward and put this question to her: "Woman, why did you behave so immorally and bring such disgrace to your family? Come on, tell me the truth! When did you start? And how many times did you sleep with that fellow?"

"After my husband died," she said through her sobs, "I did not want to go on living without him, but because of my father-in-law's age, I decided for the time being to eke out a dishonorable existence. Last winter my father-in-law suggested I marry again, and I had to cut off one of my fingers to show him how I felt. It's absurd to suppose that I would have an affair! I hope Your Honor will examine the facts of the case."

Deputy Magistrate Niu laughed. "You were already having an affair, and *that's* why you didn't want to remarry! It helps to prove the case against you! Quick, now, tell me the truth, and I won't be too hard on you."

"But I don't even know the scoundrel! How could I have committed adultery with him? Moreover, on the night when these people seized him, the door to my room was bolted—they broke in, I tell you. My father-in-law saw them."

"The witnesses testify that they caught the man on your bed, while you say that your door was bolted—who's going to believe you? Your father-in-law's a family member, so he can't testify in your behalf. A lustful trollop like you will never admit to anything. Come on, apply the finger press!"

Three or four runners came forward and were just about to apply the press when Huowu roared out from his side of the court: "Stop! You there, magistrate! Why don't you question these scoundrels under torture instead of using a finger press on this virtuous widow?"

Startled, the deputy magistrate roared back, "Who is this man who's so out of control? You're disrupting my court!"

"I am Yao Huowu, and my brother is the colonel in Jieshi. When I saw you about to apply a harsh punishment to a virtuous widow, I tried with the best of intentions to dissuade you. What do you mean, 'disrupting your court'?"

"So you're trying to use a military man's authority to dictate to a civil official, are you? Well, your brother has been secretly collaborating with the pirates, and so he's been brought back from sea patrol and detained for questioning. It looks as if you're in league with the pirates yourself. Constables, arrest that man!" The runners on both sides of the courtroom saw how menacing Huowu looked and feared they would not be able to arrest him. A dozen of them ran up to him, intending to put him in chains, but Huowu parried their attack with both hands, and several of them fell to the ground. Deputy Magistrate Niu rose to his feet and told the archers to advance on him together. Considering Huowu's martial skills, many times that number of men could not have captured him, let alone the few dozen who now approached. However, because his conscience was clear, and also because he remembered Jiangshan's words of warning—that he not let his own strength and courage be the cause of injury to others—he feared that if he made the slightest move he might cause someone's death. It would not matter so far as he himself was concerned, but it would affect the innkeeper's fate, and so he allowed the men to put him in chains.

"Well, Magistrate Niu, what do you propose to do now that you've arrested me?" he asked, laughing uproariously.

"That wild outburst of yours shows without a doubt that you're a pirate," retorted Niu. He ordered the people in the adultery case detained while he sent runners out to pick up Huowu's baggage, which he intended to search for stolen goods.

Seven or eight runners with the innkeeper as guide hurried off to the inn. As it happened, Youkui and Awu had already left in search of an open area in which to try their martial skills. The runners swarmed into the inn and brought Huowu's packages, bedroll, and boxes back to the courtroom, where they were opened and carefully checked; they were found to contain nothing significant except the ingots of silver. On the way there Huowu and Youkui had spent one ingot, but the other five were untouched, and the deputy magistrate fastened a greedy eye on them. "Bring them here!" he ordered. "Aren't these from that Customs consignment that was robbed last year?"

"Where did you get these five ingots?" he asked Huowu.

"Why do you want to know?"

The deputy magistrate laughed. "You didn't look to me like a good man, and I was absolutely right! Let me ask you this: How many men took part in robbing Clerk Dong's Customs consignment last year? Where did you stow the rest of the loot? If you won't tell me the truth, well, we have some very harsh methods of torture, I can assure you."

"Stop your daydreaming, Niu Zao!" said Huowu in a fury. "That silver was given to me by my friend Li Jiangshan. What Customs consignment, what loot, are you talking about?"

The deputy magistrate gave a sardonic smile. "A glib defense, if ever there was one! Here am I, a civil official of the ninth grade, someone who administers an area of this country, and when people pay me for a case, it's never more than a tael at best. No one has ever given me an ingot of silver, so why on earth would anyone want to curry favor with you, the brother of a cashiered officer? Without the foot press, you bandit trash, you'll never admit to

anything! Come on, apply the press!" Huowu stood in the middle
of the runners as they made a chaotic attempt to pull him down,
and like minor imps trying to trip up a guardian god, they could
not budge him. Shooting out his left foot, he knocked over three or
four.

"Since the bandit's so violent, get some more men up here
and put him in irons, then clap him in jail," cried Niu. "Call out
the coastal defense forces. We'll take him to the county yamen for
trial."

Huowu raised no objection, but let them make a show of taking him off to prison.

Deputy Magistrate Niu, with no outlet for his anger, had Mistress Guan brought before him and the finger press applied, then
put her up for official sale. He had the old innkeeper given thirty
strokes, declaring, "You had the audacity to hide the loot and give
shelter to bandits. I won't try you just yet, but after I've returned
from the county yamen I shall conduct a thorough investigation."
He had no sooner disposed of the case than Warden Qian's men
came forward to negotiate a price. Mistress Guan took a tearful
farewell of her father-in-law and then, when no one was looking, seized the chance to throw herself into the river, where she
drowned.

> She returned her righteous spirit to Heaven and Earth;
> Henceforth her fragrant soul will cause the gods to weep.

After his daughter-in-law's death, the old innkeeper saw nothing but misfortune ahead of him, and he went home and hanged
himself. The deputy magistrate was shocked at the thought that
he had forced two people to take their lives at the same time, but
he clung to the theory that his arrest of the bandit chief had led

the man who had sheltered him to hang himself for fear of punishment. He ordered the local constable to complete the laying in. He also called up a guard of between one hundred and two hundred archers and that same day began to escort Huowu to the county yamen.

For his part, Huowu felt no anxiety whatsoever; he merely wondered why, since his baggage had been brought to court, Youkui had not appeared, too. His one fear was that if Youkui did not know the facts he would certainly cause some kind of trouble.

Their route took them through Phoenix Tail and Goat's Foot and other places on their way to Haifeng. It was the second watch before they arrived, but the men gave a shout when they came to the gate and were allowed through.

Magistrate Gongyang Sheng, hearing that the deputy magistrate had personally escorted a bandit leader to his yamen, promptly held a hearing. First, Niu Zao came forward and greeted him, then reported as follows: "Yao Huowu is the brother of Colonel Yao Weiwu, who collaborated with the pirates and has now been cashiered and is awaiting sentence. Yao Huowu disrupted my court, and I suspected that he might be one of the pirates himself. I searched his baggage, and sure enough I found five large ingots in it. The silver dollar is the common currency in the Guangdong area, and the silver in the provincial treasury is all in ten-ounce ingots. Only the traders' money and the dues from the various Customs posts use the fifty-tael ingots of the national scale. That fact was suspicious in itself, but in addition this fellow has exceptional strength; forty or fifty men could not get near him. Your Honor will need to take proper precautions."

After telling him to withdraw, the magistrate assembled all the guards and runners in the county seat as well as the deputy magistrate's archers and arranged them along both sides of the courtroom. He then lit over a hundred lanterns and torches before having Huowu brought in. Huowu did not kneel, but remained standing, and the magistrate roared at him. "You disrupted the proceedings in the deputy magistrate's yamen, and now you come before the county court and have the effrontery not to kneel!"

"It's true that I had a few things to say to Deputy Magistrate Niu when he was going to torture a virtuous widow as an adulteress. But I've not been charged with any crime, so to whom should I kneel down?"

"Your brother let the pirates get away, and the governor-general and governor impeached him for it, yet you have the audacity to presume on that relationship to behave in an unruly manner yourself! Of course the deputy magistrate would want to question you! Why don't you confess where the Customs loot is hidden?"

When Huowu had previously been told that his brother had been impeached, he had assumed that the story was a deliberate fabrication, but now, on hearing it repeated by the magistrate, he concluded that it must be true, and he knelt down and kowtowed. "I didn't know for a fact that my brother had been impeached. Let me ask Your Honor how it came about."

"I expect you escaped and came back from the sea, so you must know all about that yourself. Why ask me?"

"I genuinely don't know." He explained how the year before he had been to Guangzhou and how he had returned from Nan'an and taught martial arts at Pingshan.

"What sort of man is this Li Jiangshan that he should run into you at an inn and have all that money to give you? Clearly, last year at Pingshan you got together with some shameless scoundrels to carry out a robbery and then divide up the loot. It might have been possible to explain away your brother's actions, but now, in view of your case, I very much fear that the verdict on him will be confirmed."

Huowu kowtowed again. "I really am being unjustly accused. I beg Your Honor to send to Jiangsu for information that will vindicate my brother and me."

"Out of the question! Tell me the truth about the robbery, and as a favor to you I won't implicate your brother. Come on, now, confess!"

"But I didn't do it. How can I *confess?*"

At this point, Magistrate Gongyang called for the use of torture. Huowu let them squeeze his feet three times while pretending to be oblivious to the pain, and the magistrate had no choice but to order him held in jail until the case against the rest of the gang had been settled. The booty was to be stored in the treasury.

The next chapter will go into detail.

Chapter XI

Feng Gang catches a tiger on Goat's Foot Ridge
Ho Wu kills an ox at Phoenix Tail River[1]

⤙⤚

Let us turn to Lü Youkui and Ho Wu, one with an iron staff, the other with a steel trident, as they came out to the crossroads in search of a place to compete. "There's no open space here," said Ho Wu. "To find one, we'll need to go a mile or two further to a chain of hills leading to Goat's Foot Ridge. I go hunting there every day."

"There's no reason why we shouldn't go a bit further," said Lü Youkui. They climbed to the top of a hill from which the jagged outline of countless peaks could be seen stretching on and on, over an area some ten miles long and a mile and a half wide. There they chose some level ground where they could pit their weapons against each other. Although Ho Wu was well-endowed with strength, he had had no training and was no match for Youkui. Throwing down his trident, he flung himself on the ground and kowtowed in front of his companion.

"How I regret that I've never had a master to teach me! A little brute strength—it's just no use. I hope you'll accept me as a pupil, Brother. I'm ready to be your groom."

Youkui roared with laughter. "How could *I* be your teacher? You had your teacher right there in front of you, but you come and pester me instead of asking him!"

"What teacher do you mean?"

"Brother Yao Huowu back at the inn—he's the greatest teacher of them all! With the sort of martial arts that you and I practice, three or four of us together wouldn't be able to get near him."

Ho Wu wanted to go straight back and acknowledge Huowu as his teacher, but Youkui said, "What's the hurry? I'll put in a word for you, and I'm sure he'll take you on. But that wild game we had yesterday tasted rather good. Why don't we find some more to take back as a present for your teacher?"

This suggestion appealed strongly to Ho Wu, and he accompanied Youkui up hill and down dale in search of game.

However, a couple of hours later, after circling five or six hilltops, they had found nothing more than a few hares. "These seven or eight hares aren't nearly enough to satisfy me, let alone the two of us," said Youkui. "We need to find something bigger."

Just as they were considering what to do, a sudden gust of wind came whistling past their ears and left the trees quivering and the grasses flattened. Ho Wu sniffed the air. "That's a tiger wind, and it's bringing us tonight's dinner. Let's wait here with our weapons at the ready." The words were out hardly of his mouth when a magnificently striped tiger came bounding up and sprang at him. He was quick enough to dodge to one side, and the tiger missed its prey. Using his trident, Ho Wu thrust at the beast with all his might, but it had already sprung at Youkui, and the trident merely struck its back in a blow that it hardly felt. Youkui was about to wield his staff when he saw the tiger springing at him. He ducked, and at the same time rammed his iron staff into the animal's chest. In its pain, the tiger whirled around, lashing with its tail. Ho Wu struck at it again, but the tiger's tail hit the trident and jarred his hands so severely that he had to let his weapon drop to the ground, while the tiger's tail went limp. Taking careful aim, Youkui struck the tiger in the belly, and the injured beast raced away with the two men in hot pursuit.

Just then another man came striding down from South Mountain toward them. With his bare hands he grasped the animal around the neck, and the tiger, having exhausted every ounce of its strength, could not break free.

"Hoy, you there!" Ho Wu shouted. "We were the ones who beat that tiger. You can't go taking other people's property!"

"I chased it down here, and I was the one who caught it. How can you say it's yours?"

In his fury Ho Wu was about to go forward and give battle. The other man dropped the tiger and also came forward to fight, but then Youkui took a closer look at him and cried out, "Don't fight! Aren't you Brother Feng?"

The man looked at him and said, "So we're all kinsmen, after all! What brings you here, Brother Lü?" The three men bowed to each other, and Youkui explained how he had taken a teacher the year before and yesterday had accompanied him to Ebu.

"With the training you've had, you must have made rapid progress in the year or more since we last met. I wonder if I could enroll with that teacher of yours?"

"Of course! This Brother Ho also wants to take him as his teacher today. Let's go down together."

The man's name was Feng Gang. The descendant of a general, he had started out as a militiaman like the others. Governor-general Qing had given him the rank of lieutenant, but he had later left his post and returned home. On this day he had just happened to go up on the ridge to look around. Not only did he have great courage and strength, he was also a skilled horseman and archer and had a broad knowledge of tactics. On the far side of the mountain he had spotted the tiger, which was now dead from its injuries. With Ho Wu carrying the beast on his back, the three men made their way down the hill.

By the time they reached the inn, it was dusk, and the place was silent and deserted. Ho Wu dragged the tiger inside but had to shout for some time before an old woman servant came out, her eyes streaming with tears.

"Where's that guest of ours?" asked Ho Wu. "And where are my father and sister-in-law?"

"Your father and sister-in-law are both dead," she replied. "Their coffins are still behind the deputy magistrate's yamen. That bandit has been taken under guard to the county seat."

"What are you *talking* about?"

"I was scared to death," she replied, "and I don't know the full story. Ask the neighbors, if you want to know the details."

Ho Wu rushed out to ask what had happened and then came back and told the other two men. Youkui exploded in rage: "How could they accuse my brother of being a bandit? That Deputy Magistrate Niu is so vile! Unless I kill the scoundrel, I'll never be rid of my hatred!"

"That scoundrel has forced two people to kill themselves," said Ho Wu. "I'll never be able to rest while he and I share this same world. I hope you two brothers will help."

"Let's not be too hasty," said Feng Gang. "Human life means nothing to him, he has slandered a good man by calling him a bandit. We could go before his superior and appeal the injustice. If we actually killed him, wouldn't it simply confirm the lie that your teacher is a bandit?"

"These corrupt officials always back each other up," said Youkui. "I don't have the patience to go and talk to them. If you won't come, Brother Feng, we'll go on our own."

Feng tried to dissuade them. "From what we've just heard, Deputy Magistrate Niu isn't even at his yamen. There's no point in going there."

"If he's not at home, let's vent our anger by slaughtering his family, then kill him later," said Ho Wu.

He went to get two swords—he was determined to leave. Feng Gang could not dissuade him, and was reduced to saying, "Even if you do want to slaughter his family, it's too early in the day. But I wouldn't want to stand idly by, either. What if we have a meal first and then go there together?" Ho Wu threw down the swords and bowed in gratitude, then rushed into the inner quarters and set to work with the old servant. Before long they brought out the tiger meat. Youkui, however, was so furious that he wouldn't even drink any wine, and simply packed the meat into his bag.

Feng Gang sighed. "Brother Lü loves drink above everything else, but today he's so furious he won't touch it. There's a loyal friend for you!"

By the time they had finished their meal, it was the beginning of the third watch. Feng Gang was armed with an iron staff while the two others had swords. As they came to the yamen, Feng said, "Deputy Magistrate Niu is guilty of every crime under the sun. Brother Lü and I have both suffered from his double-dealing, and it would not be going too far to slaughter his entire household, but we'll have to go about it with great care. Let Brother Lü go in from the side and kill all the men in the outer quarters, while Brother Ho goes in from the rear and kills all the women in the inner quarters. I'll stand guard at the main entrance and stop anyone from coming to their assistance from outside. When we've finished our business, we'll meet up at the entrance." The others agreed to his plan.

Ho Wu went around to the back gate, climbed onto the roof, then leapt down into the courtyard, where not a sound was to be heard. I'll have to find someone in order to learn the layout, he thought. He cocked an ear and heard voices coming from his left. Walking over, he found it was the back wall, but he couldn't hear clearly what was being said. He climbed lightly onto the roof again, walked forward and then leapt down, to find two large south-facing doors standing ajar. Inside there was a row of six rooms with two courtyards, the side door to which was also open. He walked over to where the voices were coming from. A fire still shone brightly, and he could hear a man's voice inside whispering, "It's been such a long time since I came in to do you. You're much tighter than you used to be."

A woman's voice replied, "Thank goodness Daddy has gone off escorting some bandit or other—that's the only reason we have this chance."

The man said, "It was a little unjust, what happened today. That daughter-in-law of the Ho family—such a pretty girl!—was unfairly sentenced to be sold, but unfortunately she threw herself into the river and drowned. If our affair ever got out, you wouldn't want to be sold, would you?"

"Don't be ridiculous! She's just common folk, while I'm a lady. How could I possibly be sold? Even if Daddy found out, he'd want to save face and wouldn't be too hard on us. You don't need to worry about that." As she spoke, a series of pumping sounds could be hear from down below.

An enraged Ho Wu dashed into the room shouting, "You *animals*! It's a fine thing you're up to!" Bright lamplight shone full on the man. There came a sudden swishing sound, and his head rolled onto the floor.

Stark naked, the girl knelt down like a snow-white kid in front of Youkui and kowtowed. "I didn't want to go with him at first, but he pleaded with me ever so pitifully, time and time again, and I made the wrong decision and gave in. I'll let you do anything you wish, but please spare my life!"

Ho Wu laughed. "Well, well, so I've found myself a real case of adultery, have I? Listen, you little slut, tell me the truth. How many times did you do it? And when did you start?"

"I wouldn't dare tell you any lies. Last year in the sixth month Daddy went to Guangzhou, and I was out in the courtyard enjoying the cool air when we started. We slept together for twenty-one nights before Daddy came back and he couldn't visit me anymore. This is the first time since then."

"How many people are living in your house? Where are their rooms? Give me a clear answer, and I'll spare your life."

"There's my mother, a concubine, and my little two-year-old brother; their rooms are in the east wing. Opposite me here is my younger sister. Altogether we have three maids...." Ho Wu didn't wait for her to finish before dispatching her with a single stroke of his sword.

I won't bother about Niu's younger daughter, he thought. I'll kill the old crone first and then see what remains to be done. He went over to the east wing and into the western chamber. From the bed a voice called out, "Who is it?"

"It's your old man!" shouted Ho Wu, as he jerked aside the bed curtain and with one thrust killed both woman and child. He then went around to a room on the eastern side and kicked open the door. Having heard the racket, the concubine was already up and had called to her maid. Ho Wu struck her in the face with his sword and concluded she couldn't survive. There was a lamp burning on the table and several packets of silver beside it. "Bribes," said Ho Wu to himself. "I'll take it with me to pay for our drink." As he went out the door of the chamber, two maids started screaming, and he rewarded each of them with a thrust of his sword.

By now Youkui had fought his way in from outside. "Have you taken care of everything?" asked Ho Wu.

"There were only six or seven of them, hardly a massacre."

"I've left just one young girl. Let's spare her, so as to leave someone behind."

The two men went out together and found Feng Gang standing by the gate with his iron staff. "We've done our business," said Youkui. "Let's go."

"I didn't meet a single person," said Feng. "It was most disappointing. We don't have any vendetta against the runners, so let's climb over the wall and leave."

The three men leapt over the wall and returned to the inn. "We can't stay here long," said Feng. "You'd better come to my place for the time being."

"Brother Ho," said Youkui, "you've vented your *anger*, but unfortunately Brother Yao has been taken to Haifeng, and we don't even know if he's still alive. We'll have to find some way to rescue him. Moreover, he'll certainly be implicated in what we've just done. Brother Feng, you need to come up with a plan."

"Having begun, we need to see it through," said Feng. "We should go to Haifeng and rescue him by force, then find somewhere we can live in peace."

Youkui clapped his hands. "Bravo! Let's go tonight."

"Haifeng may be a small town, but it does have a wall and a moat, plus a couple of thousand troops. It's not at all like Ebu. Brother Lü, it's asking a lot of you, I know, but could you go to Pingshan tonight and gather all of your brethren and bring them back here? Brother Ho and I will hide out for a day, and then we'll all meet in the evening."

"Good idea!" said Youkui. "I'll leave at once and see you again at midnight tomorrow."

"You ought to have something to eat before you go," said Ho Wu.

"Our brother in jail will be watching anxiously for us," said Youkui. "This is no time for drinking, but bring me a big cup and I'll have a few before I go." He downed four or five cups in quick succession, then picked up his iron staff and raced off with giant strides.

By dawn he had reached the inn. Wang Dahai was doing some business when he saw Youkui approaching, and he came out from behind the counter to greet him. "Why are you back so soon?" he asked. "I suppose our brother drove you out?" Youkui told him the whole story.

"Our brother's in trouble, and it's our duty to rescue him," said Wang Dahai. "Fortunately the others haven't dispersed yet. Get yourself something to eat and drink while I send people out to invite them." Youkui was still eating his meal when they arrived. After hearing what he had to say, they pounded the table in fury and said, "Let's leave at once!"

"Don't be so impatient," said You Qi. "We'll be risking our lives in this operation, and we have to work everything out perfectly in advance. You mustn't get too carried away, only to regret it later."

"None of us has a fortune," the men answered, "so we have nothing to lose. So long as we rescue our brother, it would be good to have somewhere to hide. If not, we'll just go to sea. What a life that would be!"

"Since we're all agreed, the first thing you should do is bring your families to my house, and we'll ask Brother Jiang take care of them. When we've settled on where to go, we'll come back for them in secret. As for our hired hands, those who want to come should do so; those who don't should please themselves as to where they go." After the plan had been adopted, eight heroes leading twelve brave fellows—everyone except Jiang Xinyi and four or five idle characters who were looking after the families—ate a big meal and then left with their weapons hidden under their clothes.

They arrived at Ebu just at midnight. Feng Gang and Ho Wu had long been watching for them at the entrance and were delighted to see them. They went together into the hall, where they stood in a circle and bowed to each other before taking their seats. Ho Wu opened the discussion. "I'm ashamed of my own incompetence, which resulted in my father's hanging himself and Teacher Yao's being thrown into jail. Fortunately, you brave men have come to our aid, and of course we'll sweep away the dark clouds of injustice. But what plan should we adopt?"

"Brother Yao is our beloved teacher, and we ought to take an oath to live or die with him," said You Qi. "However, that would also involve Brother Feng. We should ask him to decide the issue."

"Although I received an appointment at the same time as Qin Shuming and Cao Zhiren, those two have seized Camp Gate Ridge and turned outlaw," said Feng Gang. "I am the only one who is stuck at home with no prospects. I feel as if your teacher is also my teacher and that it's my duty to go to his rescue. I've already spoken to Brother Ho about it; first we have to swear an oath of brotherhood, then make plans to go to Haifeng."

"Your suggestion is perfectly correct, Brother Feng," said the men. "Come on, set up an incense table, and we'll all bow down together."

Ho Wu had already prepared the three sacrificial offerings, the paper money and the incense candles, and Han Pu had written the petition to the gods. "Although Brother Yao isn't here, we should still add his name," said Wang Dahai. "I doubt very much that he's the sort who would back out. There's also Brother Jiang, who's looking after our families at home. We need to add his name, too."

"There's a true friend for you!" commented Feng Gang.

Han Pu had drafted a few sentences of literary prose:

Year month day

Yao Huowu, Feng Gang, You Qi, Wang Dahai, Lü Youkui, Xu Zhen, Jiang Xinyi, Chu Hu, Gu Shen, Qi Guangzu, Ho Wu, and Han Pu respectfully with scented candles and delicacies declare before the passing gods: The "Tree Chopping" song in the Odes section of the *Poetry Classic*[2] like the "Fellowship" hexagram[3] in the Changes, are about the molding of our natures by the forces of Yin and Yang; hence friendship fills a gap in the Five Relationships. Firm in our reliance on this belief, we are ashamed only that we do not share the same surname. Some of us hail from Eastern Shandong, while others come from the mountains of Guangdong, an ocean apart. Some boast descent from the gentry, while others are registered as commoners, but happily our hearts are as one. Admiring Guan Yu's and Zhang Fei's dying together, but despising Guan Zhong's sharing of his money with Bao Shu,[4] we draw our blood and form a bond; pointing to the heavens, we swear an oath. The gods are not blind; let them examine our sincerity of purpose.

They bowed down in order and then burned the petition. Each man pricked his arm and, after adding his blood to the heated wine, drank his share of the mixture. Afterward they went in to dine. Feng Gang said, "There are a good many of us, and it wouldn't be suitable to travel by day. Let's use this evening when we're drunk and well fed to divide into two groups, one traveling by land, the other by water, both of them meeting up at my house. Tomorrow night we'll go into town and take action."

"But it's nighttime, anyway," said Youkui. "Why not travel together? It would be more lively that way."

"You don't understand, Brother Lü," said Feng Gang. "The chief villain is Niu Zao of the Ebu district, and he can never be forgiven. Last night we killed thirteen members of his household.

When he gets the news today, he'll naturally come racing back, traveling through the night. If we separate into two groups, he won't be able to escape us."

"Brother, you think of everything!"

"Brother Lü, you know my house. What if you take You, Ho, Wang and Xu and their men and go by the river route, while we five take the land route?"

"Very good."

"There's just one suggestion I'd like to make," put in Ho Wu. "Brothers, that swine Warden Qian can never be forgiven, either. Moreover, he's rich, worth tens of thousands. If we could get hold of what he has, we'd be well provided for."

"Fine," said Feng Gang. "I'm just afraid that Deputy Magistrate Niu will slip past us. We'll get two or three men to guard the crossroads, while the others go on to the Qian house."

That night, after wining and dining themselves, they surged out of the gate, each man gripping a weapon. What chance did the Qian household have to hold out against them? In less than an hour all the inhabitants had been killed and their possessions cleaned out. The neighbors who heard the cries and came to help were scared off by the number of assailants. One by one the men arrived back at the crossroads. Since it was already the fifth watch and Deputy Magistrate Niu had still not returned, they divided into two groups and went to meet him.

When Youkui and his men came to the river, they found three small boats tied up. Since there was no one in the boats, they leapt in and had their men push them along. The Phoenix Tail River runs through steep mountains for a distance of seven or eight miles, but the water is only a foot or two deep, making it impossible to use either sails or oars. There is also no way to pull the boats along with ropes; they have to be pushed.

The men went as far as the ferry dock, but saw no sign of the deputy magistrate's boat. Youkui and the others concluded that he must have taken the land route. They were about to go ashore when they heard someone on the bank shouting, "Isn't that a boat coming?" Ho Wu gazed into the distance and saw a dozen men surrounding a sedan chair occupied by none other than Niu Zao, and he told Youkui. The two men were going to go ashore and capture him. "You can't do that," said You Qi. "It's broad daylight, and there are too many people about. If we kill someone here, it will only call attention to us. Brother Feng won't be able to go on living at his place, and we'll never be able to rescue Brother Yao. Far better to leave the cur alone for the present! It'll be easy to pick him up later."

Youkui yielded, but with Ho Wu it was a case of "When sworn enemies meet, they know each other at a glance." Fuming with anger, he was reluctant to let Niu go, but You Qi and the others eventually managed to dissuade him.

As they went ashore and continued their journey, they saw a messenger approaching the sedan chair and saying something. Then Deputy Magistrate Niu started shouting, "Quick, arrest them!" Seven or eight men rushed over and seized Youkui and Ho Wu, who went with them to the sedan chair. "You, boy, you're Ho Wu, but who is he?" demanded the deputy magistrate. "Is he one of Yao Huowu's gang?"

The two men had not even opened their mouths to reply when the messenger reported, "Sir, there's no need to ask. The other day when I went to fetch Mistress Guan, Ho Wu pushed me down, and this fellow with the dark face was sitting right there with Yao Huowu at the inn."

"Since you two damned criminals belong to the bandit gang, you must be responsible for killing thirteen members of my household. Quick, put them in chains and bring them back to the yamen for questioning!"

The runners were about to put the chains on when Youkui shoved them with both hands and they fell down. Ho Wu then broke into the sedan chair, dragged Deputy Magistrate Niu out, and went off with him under one arm. You Qi and the others saw how dangerous the situation had become, and they drew their swords and came forward. The runners swarmed ahead, too, but You Qi gave a roar and cut two of them down, while Youkui threw another to the ground, killing him, and Wang Dahai dispatched an attendant. The shopkeepers were so scared that they locked their doors, and all the spectators fled. Awu, with Niu under his arm, said, "Let's go! Just ignore him." With their men carrying the Qian money, Youkui led the way and You Qi and the others followed as they traveled east. Niu, at Ho Wu's waist, kept crying out, calling for help, and several runners pursued them, together with a group of local people.

You Qi shouted to their pursuers, "We're under orders from Chief Qin of Army Gate Ridge. For every crime there's a criminal, for every debt a debtor, and we're not after anybody but Deputy Magistrate Niu. You want to die, do you?" Xu Zhen fitted an arrow to his bow and shot one of them dead. The rest withdrew.

After less than a mile they came to Feng Gang's house. Feng was a man of substance, and his house was large, with four or five fine horses in its stables at the rear. He had thirteen or fourteen servants, more than twenty tenant farmers, seven or eight grooms, as well as supplies of all kinds of bows, arrows, swords, and spears. The newcomers entered the central room, where Feng and the others had been waiting a long time, and they greeted one other. Ho Wu put the deputy magistrate down. He had already been squeezed half to death.

"Who's this?" asked Feng.

"Don't you know?" said Youkui. "This is His Honor Niu Zao of the Ebu district. We met him along the way and invited him to come with us."

Ho Wu stripped Niu naked and tied him to a pillar, and then they all sat down and told of the events that had just occurred. Before long food and wine were brought in. Ho Wu took a sharp sword and pointing it at Deputy Magistrate Niu roared, "Niu Zao, you dog of a slave! You cheated and killed people in Ebu, but that's not what concerns me. Why, after getting thirty taels from Warden Qian, did you slander my sister as an adulteress, force two people to kill themselves, frame Master Yao, and even try to arrest me? Now that I've arrested you, what do you have to say for yourself?"

"It was all my fault," groaned Niu, "but it's too late now for any regrets. I just beg you, Master Ho, to spare this old life of mine, and from now on I'll be a reformed character. It would be an act of great mercy on your part."

"You slandered my sister as an adulteress, and yet she killed herself to preserve her virtue. Your own elder daughter was committing adultery with some young fellow. Did you know that?"

"No, I truly didn't."

Youkui leapt to his feet. "The filthy swine! Why go on chatting with him? Finish him off, the sooner the better, or we'll all have a fit!"

"Now you listen to me, Niu Zao," said Ho Wu. "Warden Qian is waiting for you up ahead with a lot of silver dollars. Hurry up and find him." He slashed with his sword at the man's heart, and blood came spurting out at an angle; he had been cut in two, and his guts spilled forth. Feng Gang told someone to clean up the mess, while Ho Wu bowed in gratitude to everyone present and then joined them in their drinking.

"Now that Brother Ho has avenged himself against his archenemy, the only thing left is this matter of Brother Yao," said Wang Dahai. "What do you suggest, Brother Feng?"

"Let's not do anything in haste. I've already sent someone into town to find out what the situation is. When he comes back, we'll be able to get into town one by one. But after we've rescued Brother Yao, I doubt that we'll be able to settle down here. We'll have to think of some long-term solution."

"I've been giving that some thought, too," said You Qi. "Going to sea is not a good idea. Since Brothers Qin and Cao have set up camp on Army Gate Ridge, why don't we go and join forces with them?"

"That's not too suitable, either," said Feng. "Of course we could go there, but from what you all say Brother Yao is so great a figure that he may not want to be subordinate to them. I've seen how this Goat's Foot Ridge stretches on for over fifteen miles and contains a vital access road to both Haifeng and Lufeng. It would take only a few hundred men to hold it, and a force of ten thousand could not get past. We'd cut away the undergrowth, drive away the wolves, and settle down there."

"A great idea!" they cried. "We'll do as you say."

"I'm just a rough and ready fellow who's not skilled in the martial arts, but from living in this area I am familiar with local conditions, and that's how I came up with this idea. We'll have to wait until Brother Yao gets out and decides the issue. However, those of us here at the outset are very few. With you who have just joined us, we're only a dozen or so, and even if we include my household staff we'll still be no more than fifty. What can we do with a number like that? I've been thinking. On the road a mile or two west of the ridge there's a Hongyuan Temple, where the abbot, whose name is Konghua, has a complete mastery of the martial arts. He has over two hundred priests under him as his disciples, and all of them can give a good account of themselves. When it comes to lechery and robbery, this abbot will stop at nothing, but because he hobnobs with the local officials and is in and out of their yamens all the time, people have no way of bringing him to justice. What's more, the temple is very rich. We have only to kill Konghua, force his disciples to submit, and take over his money and provisions, and we have a solid foundation for our venture."

His speech sent his listeners into raptures. "Brother Feng," they said, "you really are a great strategist. We'll follow your orders."

Late in the afternoon Feng Gang's man raced in to report, "Yesterday the Haifeng magistrate received the news of the killing of Deputy Magistrate Niu's whole family, and he gave Master Yao a beating and sent him back to jail. Then today the magistrate heard that Niu had been abducted on the way back and that five of his personal staff had been killed as well as Warden Qian's entire family, and he gave orders that people arriving at any of the town's four gates be interrogated and searched. Because the battalion stationed there has not returned from marine patrol, there are few troops in town. Government forces will probably be sent down within the next few days to patrol the area."

"We mustn't delay," said Feng. "Only if we act now while they have few troops there and everyone is fearful will we be able to carry out our mission." He told Youkui, Ho Wu, and You Qi to break into the jail; Xu Zhen and Wang Dahai were to kill the soldiers guarding the wall and secure the town gates; Chu Hu and Gu Shen were to blockade the magistrate's yamen; he himself and Qi Guangzu would do the same with the military yamen; and Han Pu would lead the rest of the men and stand by outside the walls ready to back them up if necessary. At the second watch they would scale the wall and at the third watch spring into action. Everyone would reassemble at the Temple of Confucius and fight their way out together while shouting out the names of the Army Gate Ridge outlaws. There was to be no indiscriminate slaughter of the common folk. The men accepted his orders, put on their armor, and set off.

Turn to the next chapter to see what happened.

Chapter XII
Hearing of his brother's death,
a prisoner breaks out of jail
Taking advantage of a visit, an abbot gains a gem

Gongyang Sheng, the magistrate of Haifeng county, had served five years as an official after succeeding in the provincial examinations. Avaricious though he was, he was by no means a brutal man. Alcohol had long been his passion, either in the form of spirits or wine. He was well aware that Colonel Yao was a good officer who had merely lost his way at sea and bungled the operation but who had certainly not collaborated with any pirates, and when Deputy Magistrate Niu brought Huowu to his court, his first inclination was to pardon him—until he heard Niu say that the fifty-tael ingots were definitely Customs dues and that Huowu had been tortured a few times already without confessing. Then he learned that Niu had driven two members of the Ho family to their deaths, and he severely berated him and was determined to impeach him, but Niu kowtowed and begged for mercy, and Gongyang forgave him. When he heard that Niu's whole family had been killed, he told him to hurry back to his yamen. Suspecting that the massacre might be the work of Huowu's gang, he had Huowu brought out and put in the press and beaten. But Huowu remained as imperturbable as ever, and there was nothing Gongyang could do but return him to jail. Later still, he received the report that Niu had been abducted on his way home and that Warden Qian's entire household of twenty-three persons had been killed, and since these were major crimes, with consequences for his own career, he had Huowu brought out once more. This time he did not have him beaten, he merely roared at him: "You reckless fool! For your brother's sake I showed you kindness and didn't convict you. How could you connive at your gang's murder of officials, their robbery and violence, as if the law did not exist? I no longer care whether you confess; I'm going to refer your case to higher authority, and I doubt very much that you'll ever be able to get away to sea!" He told the department concerned to draw up a document to be submitted as soon as possible.

"I don't even come from these parts," protested Huowu. "How could I have any so-called 'gang'? My own death is not of any consequence. My one fear is that it might implicate my brother, and for that reason I hope you'll take pity on me."

"Just this morning I read in a report from the governor-general that your brother has been condemned to death and will soon be executed. As for you, you can find your own way to death." He gave orders that Huowu was to be guarded with the utmost care. At the same time he called up soldiers to arrest the robbers and initiated a rigorous search.

As he returned to his cell, Huowu was in a state of shock and despair. That murder must surely have been the work of Lü Youkui, he thought. But why didn't he come and see me instead of going berserk? And why did the magistrate come out with that remark about my brother being executed? If I simply accept the charge, it will certainly mean death for me when he reports to his superior today. But surely both of us brothers are not going to meet our deaths here in Guangdong? I'll break out of prison tonight and go and find out the truth. If he lives and I die, or if I live and he dies, at least one descendant of the Yaos will have survived. But if I escape, I'll have broken the law, and wouldn't that be flouting the advice that Brother Jiangshan gave me? After thinking about the matter from all angles, he decided to take the expedient course.

Sometime after the first watch, he twisted the manacles until their joints snapped, then removed the irons from his feet and the chain from around his neck and sprang over the wall in a single bound. The moon had gone down, and although the sky was full of stars, there was no moonlight. He walked through the neighborhood, but since he didn't know the way he took a random course that brought him back to the front of the yamen. There he heard shouting on all sides and assumed it was the men coming to arrest him. Nevertheless, he kept walking straight ahead in a westerly direction, undaunted.

It was now the third watch, and our heroes climbed over the wall and set to work. Youkui, Ho Wu, and You Qi hacked open the prison gate and stormed inside, searching everywhere but failing to find Huowu. Instead they seized a jailer and threatened him. He took them to the place in the basement where Huowu had been chained, but they found no trace of him there, merely some irons scattered over the ground. "Do you want to go on living?" they asked the jailer.

"I have a father and a mother like everyone else. Of course I want to go on living!"

"In that case," said Youkui, "you'd better tell us the truth. This Master Yao—did they murder him, or have they hidden him somewhere?"

"He was tried this evening and then held here, and the magistrate didn't ask about his illness.[1] I wouldn't dare tell you anything that wasn't true—I've always been a strict Buddhist."

Before he could finish speaking, an enraged Youkui had cut

him down with a single stroke. "I expect my brother has been murdered by that corrupt magistrate, which means I'm the one responsible for his death," he said with tears in his eyes. "Let's break into
the yamen and give vent to our hatred!"

You Qi hastily tried to dissuade him. "Don't start grieving just
yet. Look at how these irons on the floor have been wrenched
apart—Brother Yao isn't one to let somebody murder him without
a struggle! He may well have broken out of jail and escaped."

"You don't know what he's like," said Youkui. "He'd be absolutely opposed to breaking out of jail. Moreover, it was only this
evening that the hearing was held. How far could he have got?"
They lit a torch and shouted out to all the prisoners, "Those of you
who want to live, come and fight your way out of jail with us!"
The prison held upward of two hundred men, who burst into a
chorus of shouting, and most of them left the prison. Once Youkui
and the others were outside the gate, they ran into Gu Shan and
Chu Hu.

When this incident was reported to him, Magistrate Gongyang was having sex with a young concubine, and he was suddenly
rendered impotent by the shock. At once he ordered his men to
block the main entrance, while he himself wriggled under the bed.
Outside the yamen were runners, guards, jailers, and night staff—
over fifty in all, but they were no match for the five assailants, who
carved their way easily through them. Some of the defenders were
killed, some escaped—no one was left alive in front of the gate.
Unable to find Huowu, Youkui was determined to storm into the
private quarters, but the others managed to dissuade him: "Let's go
to the Temple of Confucius and wait for Brother Feng before we
decide what to do," they said, and Youkui had no choice but to go
with them.

As it happened, Feng Gang and Qi Guangzu had just arrived

there after routing the reinforcements sent from the military yamen. At sight of the five men accompanied by a large contingent of prisoners, they came forward and called out, "Ask Brother Yao to come and meet us."

At this Youkui burst out sobbing. "Our brother has been murdered by Gongyang Sheng! I hope with all my heart that Brother Feng will avenge this wrong for me. I'll willingly lead the charge and die without regret."

Feng Gang asked what he meant, and Ho Wu explained the situation and told of the advice You Qi had given him. "Brother You was perfectly right," said Feng Gang. "Brother Yao is surely not dead."

"None of you has any guts!" cried Youkui. "I'm going to kill that magistrate and avenge our brother, and I don't need any help from you." He started to go back the way he had come.

Feng Gang and You Qi tried to restrain him. "Don't be so hasty, Brother," they said. "Since you want to kill the magistrate, we'll need to go there first to capture and interrogate him in order to learn where our brother is. If you kill the magistrate first, he'll die before we've established the facts. And what good would that do, even if you killed a hundred magistrates?"

In the midst of the quarrel, three figures loomed up out of the shadows. The one in the lead roared, "Lü Youkui, who are you going to kill now? Come on, let's get out of here!"

Youkui saw it was Huowu and was so overjoyed that he threw himself on the ground. "So you're not dead, Brother? You had me worried half to death!"

Huowu helped him to his feet. "Brother, if you go around willfully slaughtering people, you draw me in, too. How could you go on these deadly rampages!"

Youkui didn't dare to defend himself. Feng Gang now stepped

forward. "Congratulations on breaking out of jail, Brother. Let's get out of town now and leave the discussion till later. I'm afraid there'll be soldiers coming after us, and then we'll be forced to take more lives."

"Who is this gentleman?" asked Huowu. "I've not met him."

"He's Brother Feng Gang," answered You Qi. "We depend on him for everything."

"Let's get out of town. I'll thank him later." They clustered around Huowu as they headed out of town, and not a single soldier tried to block their way. Han Pu soon brought his men to welcome them. The prisoners' chains were removed, and they were told to flee for their lives, but they all declared themselves willing to join the band. "Let's go to my place and discuss what to do next," said Feng Gang.

How long did it take, this journey of fifteen or twenty miles? The sun had just risen when they reached the Feng mansion. Feng Gang placed an armchair in the hall and asked Huowu to take a seat, while he bowed his head and kowtowed. "I have long revered your great name, Brother," he said. "It echoes like thunder in my ears. Meeting you today has satisfied my dearest wish. I hope that you will accept me as your student and employ me in whatever way you see fit."

"I haven't thanked you for your kindness in coming to my rescue," said Huowu. "When you suddenly salute me like this, I can't help feeling embarrassed." He hastily knelt down and kowtowed.

Ho Wu also came forward and kowtowed twice before declaring, "I hope that you will accept me, master. I'd be happy to render humble service for the rest of my life."

Huowu also raised him to his feet. On Ho Wu's behalf, Feng Gang explained why they had slaughtered Deputy Magistrate Niu's entire household.

"So he drove both your father and your sister-in-law to suicide? Of course he had to be killed. Brother Lü, I was wrong to blame you. Don't take it to heart."

Youkui roared with laughter. "Now that I've seen you again, I wouldn't mind if you beat me to death!"

"Now that you're out of jail, Brother, we'll make you our leader and discuss the matter of an armed uprising," said the men.

Feng Gang and You Qi pressed Yao Huowu down into the chair and everyone kowtowed before him, which made him so nervous that he leapt out of the chair and began kowtowing along with them. "What you brothers are talking about surely means that entire clans will be wiped out in reprisal. When I was arrested by the deputy magistrate the other day, do you know why I couldn't bring myself to escape? Firstly, because my conscience was clear, and secondly, because I remembered what Brother Li Jiangshan had told me, that I should never use my physical strength to resist the authorities or defy the court, which would only result in unpardonable crimes. That is why I submitted to arrest. But then yesterday I heard Magistrate Gongyang say that my brother had been sentenced to death, and because you, my brothers, had killed many people, I knew that it would be hard to avoid the death penalty myself. It occurred to me that in that case my brother and I would both die in Guangdong, which would mean the end of our family line. I knew that I was not guilty of any serious crime, so I had no alternative but to try to escape death. I intended to go to Guangzhou and find out my brother's situation. But now you want me to be both disloyal and immoral. In that case, how would I ever be able to face Brother Jiangshan again? I definitely cannot do what you ask of me."

"Honored brother," said Feng Gang, "please listen to what I have to say. I may be a crude sort of fellow, but my grandfather did serve as an official, and I once held a position myself. You surely don't imagine that I could bear to let myself be thought of as disloyal or unfilial, do you? The only problem is that our brothers have already committed heinous crimes, and if you were to flee to some distant place, they would never be allowed to live in peace. If troops should suddenly descend on Huizhou and Jieshi, wouldn't the brothers all be arrested and charged with capital crimes? You will have stayed true to the advice of one man, Li Jiangshan, but at the same time you will have condemned eleven of your brothers to death, which is something that I fear no humane and courageous person would do. As for your brother the colonel, since he has been awarded the honor of a class-two rank, it will naturally be for the emperor to decide whether he lives or dies, for the law to determine whether he is treated leniently or severely, and for public opinion to conclude whether what he did was wrong. At this point we might just as well send a man there to find out. If you insist on going yourself, well, in the first place Haifeng will certainly have issued wanted posters with your likeness on them, and you might not even get as far as Guangzhou. And secondly, even if you did get there by virtue of your martial skills, you'd still be of no help in your brother's case. In my humble opinion you should do the expedient thing for the present. One day, out of his great mercy the emperor will call on us to surrender, and by then you will be able to redeem yourself by virtue of your achievements."

At this point the others began to shout, "Once you leave, Brother, we're sure to die, and we'd rather die right here in front of you and show that we're dying for a friend." Drawing their swords, they made as if to cut their throats.

Huowu hastily stopped them: "Don't do that, Brothers, whatever you do! I'll go along with you for the present. But Brother Feng must continue to be in charge of everything, and I'll just have to obey his orders."

"Don't be so modest, Brother," said Feng Gang. "We decided the seniority question the other day." He told Han Pu to bring out the draft of the brotherhood oath, and everyone took his seat in the prescribed order. Feng Gang fetched some clothes for the prisoners to change into, and together with the servants and tenant farmers, they presented themselves in groups and were then regaled with wine and food in the outer rooms.

In the inner room the eleven men sat together at a single table. After several rounds Huowu stopped the drinking. "I've been honored with your friendship and support in a time of trial, and today you've also made me your leader," he said. "As we speak, Haifeng and Jieshi are surely sending troops here. I understand that Brother Feng has settled on a plan of action, and I would like to hear the details." Feng Gang told him of the discussions they had held the other day, and Huowu said, "I may be from another province, but I have learned something about the local geography and culture. Brother Feng's idea is quite correct; let's put it into practice. He will lead all of you up to Goat's Foot Ridge tonight and start laying the foundations of our camp. I will take Brothers Lü and Ho and recruit the monks of Hongyuan Temple. The only problem is that not everyone has a weapon. That's something we need to discuss."

"I have some weapons handed down from my ancestors," said Feng Gang. He told his servants to bring them out.

Youkui stepped forward and chose a broadaxe weighing fifty or sixty catties; he tried it out and found that it suited his grip. The others also made their choices. "I don't expect you'll be needing your iron staff, Brother," said Ho Wu to Huowu. "Could you let me have it as a weapon?" Huowu agreed, but then could not find a weapon to suit himself. He merely chose a sword weighing over twenty catties.

"Your marvelous strength is, of course, superior to everyone else's," said Feng Gang. "I have broadswords of three different sizes in the house. We used them for practice when we were studying for the military examination." He told his men to bring them out. Huowu tried them one by one and ended up choosing the middle-sized sword, one weighing about one hundred and thirty catties. (Note that a catty when weighing weapons in earlier times was equivalent to six current ounces. The sword that Huowu had was at least fifty present-day catties—he truly was an extraordinary warrior!) The servants were told to sharpen the weapons ready for use. The former prisoners, the tenant farmers, and others were also issued with weapons. Those not fully equipped would have to wait for more weapons to be made.

That evening Feng Gang told his whole family to pack up and head for the ridge, where he ordered everyone to cut down trees and build a stockade and also sew cloth for tents. He had his own house dismantled and told the carpenters to reassemble it up in the mountains. Meanwhile Huowu went with Youkui and Ho Wu to Hongyuan Temple.

> Besandaled, bareheaded, used to defying the law;
> They're disloyal to the court, these honest folk.
> As a refuge they build their camp upon mountains;
> "The mountain ox lives to a ripe old age," they jest.

Let us turn to the Niu household, in which everyone had been slaughtered except a fourteen-year-old girl named Yerong and a maid. The maid had previously attended Yerong's elder sister in

her room, but because the sister had feared that the maid's presence might impede the affair she was engaged in, she had sent her
off to sleep in Yerong's room, which was how she had been lucky
enough to escape the slaughter. In the outer quarters a nephew
of Niu Zao's named Shanmei had also survived. He had gone
out at night to relieve himself and taken the opportunity to hide
on top of the privy, where Youkui had failed to find him. In the
morning Shanmei got up and sent a runner to report the news to
the county magistrate. To his dismay the next day he received the
news of Niu's abduction, and realizing that Niu would surely be
killed, concluded that he couldn't stay in the yamen any longer.
He discussed the situation with Yerong and suggested that they
go together to the magistrate to lodge an accusation and told her
to pack up all her valuables. She had a couple of thousand taels as
well, and the cousin took charge of both valuables and money. Hiring two sedan chairs, he told Yerong and her maid to follow him
in the second chair. Now that he had all of her possessions tucked
away, he ceased to care whether she lived or died; he simply gave
his bearers a few extra taels, then had them double back and head
for Huizhou.

Yerong and her maid left the yamen carried by four bearers
and took the main Haifeng road. (The yamen runners, learning
that their superior had been killed, had all fled.) The bearers, realizing that there was no one else attending the girls, cozened them
out of money for drink the entire way and deliberately walked
slowly so as to prolong the journey. Passing by Goat's Foot Ridge,
they left the main road and headed for Hongyuan Temple, where
they stopped to rest and then went inside, bent on some kind of
trickery. All they said was that they were going in to get some tea.

Out from the temple came two priests who were sixteen or
seventeen years old, one named Zhixing, the other Zhihui. Each

carried a cup of tea on a lacquered tray that they brought to the sedan chair and offered the girls. The sight of Yerong quite took Zhihui's breath away, and he couldn't take his eyes off her. He proposed a secret pact with Zhixing: "What a gem that girl is! If we can get her inside, each of us will have a night of fun. But don't let the news get out to the abbot, or he'll come and seize her for himself."

He went up to Yerong and bowed, "You must be feeling bored in that sedan chair, miss. Why not come in and visit the shrines?"

"No, thank you, your reverence."

"Your bearers will be quite some time. In our Hongyuan Temple we have a famous living Buddha who always answers your prayers, whether to receive blessings or avert calamities. It's an opportunity not to be missed."

Yerong had never had a proper upbringing in the first place and now, hearing of a Buddha with marvelous powers, she thought she would go in and worship—and also take the opportunity to relieve herself. Telling the maid to take her arm, she entered the temple gate and prostrated herself before the Buddha statues. Zhihui then invited her to tour the various shrines. She flushed and said something to the maid, who relayed the request to Zhihui. "It's quite convenient," he said. "It's in an extremely private place. Let me show you the way." He led the two girls on a circuitous route that brought them to his own cell, where he pushed open the door and took Yerong in his arms, while Zhixing led the maid off to the adjoining cell and then came back to contend for possession of Yerong. By this time Zhihui had pulled down his trousers and his lower baldhead stood erect. "Look, it was my idea, and this happens to be my cell," he said to Zhixing as he came forward. "Let me have first turn, and then you can do as you wish. Two brothers shouldn't let something like this ruin their relationship!" As he said this, he suddenly entered her. Yerong tried to fight him off with her hands and feet; she screamed and twisted about from side to side, but Zhihui took not the slightest notice and continued until his essence spread everywhere and fresh blood spurted forth. Zhixing, who had been waiting hungrily for a long while, then reared up and mounted her. How could this young girl endure being raped by two priests? She was left gasping, at the point of death.

As it happened, the news did get out. Someone reported the girls' arrival to Abbot Konghua, who came striding along and scared Zhixing into abruptly stopping what he was doing. After cursing him out, Konghua glanced at Yerong, who looked both seductive and pathetic. "There's no need to be angry, my lovely," he said, helping her on with her trousers. "I'll certainly punish those two animals. Let's enjoy a cup of wine together and then have a wee rest."

Barely conscious, her eyes tight shut, Yerong murmured, "Thank you."

With his arms around her, the abbot asked Zhixing, "Did anyone come with her?" Zhihui went to the other cell and dragged out the maid.

"I'll let you two have that one," said the abbot. Embracing Yerong, he brought her to his secret quarters, where he was attended by five or six women in peasant dress and seven or eight handsome young priests. "My lovelies," he addressed them, "today I am taking a wife. Quick, bring us some wine so we can celebrate." He also gave orders to the young priests: "Go and tell them in the kitchen to prepare some wine so that the whole temple can celebrate my wedding." Before long great quantities of food and wine had arrived. The abbot raised a large cup and held it to Yerong's lips. "Please drink a cup of nuptial wine, my beauty," he said.

Sitting on his lap, she soon regained her senses. When she opened her eyes, she found an enormous, ugly priest with a brown beard and eyes that bulged out like brass bells holding her in his arms. She assumed that it meant the worst for her and began to weep. "Your reverence, please spare me!"

The abbot laughed. "Drink up, my beauty. There's nothing to worry about."

Afraid of him as she was, she had to take a sip. After quickly draining his own cup, the abbot picked up some food with his chopsticks and held it to her mouth, and she didn't dare refuse. Little by little, with the abbot drinking a cup of wine for every sip that she took, the wine began to affect them both. The abbot opened her blouse and stroked her breasts. With hands like iron rakes fondling such smooth and soft objects, how could he fail to be aroused? He undid her trousers and began to fondle her down below. "Your reverence," she cried, "please spare me that!"

"I'd gladly spare you," said the abbot, "but this little priest of mine won't let me. Luckily my two disciples have cleared the way, and it shouldn't hurt too much." He took off his clothes, and she didn't dare refuse him, thinking to herself, I expect I'll die tonight, anyway, so the sooner I kill myself the better. She tried to jump down, but he wouldn't let her. Standing up, he stripped her naked and laid her down on the bed. Although her private chamber was still tightly locked, the abbot's little priest thrust without mercy. Yerong pleaded desperately for mercy, but the abbot showed her no pity. Fortunately, "water soaked the gourd,"[2] and she did not die. Not until dusk did he stop. After wiping her temple of depravity, he embraced her again and still did not get dressed. He drank with her, and Yerong, prostrate in his arms, cried softly and prettily and begged him to let her go. "You'll enjoy yourself here every day," he said. "You'll be so happy, you'll never want to go back."

There is a lyric that describes this priest's evil qualities:

Bald, bald, bald—
There's nothing so vicious as a bald head,[3]
A ravenous eagle that hunts its prey
And then devours it, fur and all.
Torn is the flower's heart, but still he pounds away;
Tireless the bald one is, hard to subdue in bed.
Her cries are of grief over the flowers' fall.

The abbot threw on a monk's cassock and clutched her in his embrace, begining a wild drinking bout. Before long his desires soared again, and after drinking for a while longer, he subjected Yerong to a many-sided assault. Then just at the height of his enjoyment shouts erupted outside, and four or five monks rushed in and declared, "Master, stop playing about! A great big fellow has just fought his way into the temple."

Since only one man was involved, the abbot did not take the threat seriously. "A lot a fuss about nothing!" he growled. "Take him away, cut off his head, and be done with it."

"But there were forty or fifty of us, and we couldn't get near him! He's killed a good many already."

The abbot flew into a rage. Putting Yerong down, he took up two priest's swords and was just about to dress himself when Huowu burst into the room. There was no time to dress and so, naked as he was, the abbot advanced like a whirlwind, brandishing his swords. Huowu noted the ferocity of the attack, but because the room was too confined to allow free play for his skills, he feinted with his sword, then turned and ran, retreating to the main hall, where the abbot, a sword in his left hand, slashed directly at his face. Huowu dodged to one side, and as he did so, struck with his sword. The abbot parried the blow with both hands but felt its weight and did not dare take his opponent lightly. He fought furiously with every ounce of his ability, but he had overindulged in wine and sex, and in any case his skills were no match for Huowu's; after ten jousts, down he went. Terrified at the sight, the monks fled in all directions, but the front gate was securely guarded by Ho Wu's iron staff and the back gate by Youkui's broadaxe. Before long a few monks had been killed, and the rest had to go back, kneel down, and beg for their lives.

"I intended to kill all of you monks," roared Huowu. "If you want to be pardoned, you'll have to return to the laity as a group, gather up all the provisions in the temple, and come with me to Goat's Foot Ridge. If you lose just one item, or if just one man runs away, I'll kill the whole lot of you." The monks kowtowed. "We are willing to follow you and return to the laity."

Huowu ordered them to get up and go in search of other monks who were in hiding, then assemble in the great hall. Apart from those who had been killed, or who were too old or too feeble, they numbered over two hundred. Huowu then ordered them to gather up the money and provisions from all over the temple. The few village women as well as Yerong and her maid came and knelt before him, kowtowing and begging to be set free. "Go back to your families and don't ever do such a shameless thing again," said Huowu. They kowtowed and thanked him.

Only Yerong remained, her eyes streaming with tears, to tell her pathetic story. "I have no one to depend on. I would be willing to serve you as a maid or concubine. I hope that you will take me in."

"Since you're Niu Zao's daughter, by rights I ought to cut you down with my sword. But let the vicious abuse you've been subjected to serve as heavenly retribution. I'll leave you to find your own way to the grave. Who would want you?" He roared at her to withdraw.

When the monks had gathered up all the money and provisions, Huowu asked Youkui to go to the front gate, and the three
men guarded the group in front and behind as they climbed Goat's
Foot Ridge. Feng Gang had already erected several tents there,
and the men took shelter in them. The next day they went back to
Hongyuan Temple and dismantled the buildings and transported
the materials up the mountain. From the surrounding area they
also seized numbers of masons and carpenters, and the work of
building went on day and night.

After seven or eight days the building was about half done,
and they were just about to discuss the manufacture of armor and
weapons, when the scouts brought in a report: "Captain Liang
Shangren of Haifeng has joined with Major Wu Risheng of the
Jieshi left battalion to lead a thousand cavalry and infantry against
us. They're only three or four miles away from the mountain."

Huowu was jubilant. "They're bringing us our armor and our
horses!" He told Feng Gang and Xu Zhen to take a hundred men
and guard the batteries on top of the ridge; You Qi, Wang Dahai,
Gu Shen, and Han Pu were each to lead ten men and patrol all
around to prevent the enemy from taking an alternative route; Qi
Guangzu was to make haste to supervise the work of the craftsmen and artisans; while Huowu himself with Youkui, Chu Hu, and
Ho Wu would confront the enemy.

"But why use an ox cleaver to kill a chicken?" protested Feng
Gang. "You're the head of the camp, and you shouldn't be doing
anything rash. Let me go with them instead of you." Huowu consented.

Feng and the other men led two hundred troops, half of them
monks, as they rushed down the mountain. When they had gone
less than a mile, they saw numbers of government troops in the

distance, waving their banners and charging toward them in full cry. The lieutenant of the vanguard, Shi Buyuan, rode boldly forward armed with his spear, roaring, "Ignorant bandits, you dare to murder people and break prisoners out of jail and now you gather in the mountains and block the Court's thoroughfares. Get down on your knees and submit to capture!"

Youkui gave a great roar and rushed forward shouting, "Save your breath and bring your head up here so I can try out my axe on it!" Clang! went the axe, as Shi Buyuan parried it forcefully with his spear. He had already made two or three passes and was about to wheel around again when Youkui suddenly leapt onto the horse's back. Shi Buyuan thrust at him with his spear, but Youkui caught the spear and gave it a jerk, and Buyuan fell to the ground, where one stroke of the axe put an end to his life. Wu Risheng saw Buyuan fall from his horse and flew to his rescue, but Ho Wu sprang forward from the ranks and struck at the horse's head with his iron staff, and the head went down. Wu Risheng leapt from his horse and advanced together with the two lieutenants. Ho Wu had not received any training, but he used his iron staff to thrust to left and right of him. Feng Gang with his iron lance and Chu Hu with his two swords led the men as they advanced together in close formation. Youkui came with his broadaxe to help Ho Wu, and in a flash one of the lieutenants had fallen from his horse. The moment the weapon in Wu Risheng's hand grew slack, Youkui raised his broadaxe and brought it down, and Wu did not survive the blow. "Shoot your arrows! Fire your guns!" shouted Liang Shangren. He himself, however, spurred on his horse and was the first to flee. Feng Gang tried to cut him off, and Liang did not dare engage him but leapt from his horse and ran like the wind. The government troops, seeing that their officers either were dead or had run away, cast off their armor and fled for dear life. Feng Gang told his men not to pursue and kill them. The victors seized over a hundred horses and four or five hundred suits of armor, plus twenty or thirty cannon and other weapons, and they went back up the mountain with broad smiles on their faces.

Huowu came out of the camp to welcome them and arranged a feast to celebrate their achievements. He distributed the horses and weapons among his men, and placed the cannon in readiness to the north and south of the mountain. The four people patrolling the mountain were also rotated. Everybody drank heartily at the feast, at which Huowu said, "This revolt of ours is the product of careful deliberation. We are forced to take action. Brothers, first of all, we must not kill any of the common folk, and secondly, we must not rob any merchants. If we learn of any corrupt or cruel officials or crafty, unscrupulous rich men, get them to lend us money and provisions. All around the mountain we should put up banners with the words 'Wanted: Men of Talent and Learning,' and have someone keep watch over the banners. When the building is finished, we'll set up checkpoints to north and south in order to guard against a sudden attack by government forces. We should also set up a practice ground in some level place so that we can take turns training there." The men went off to carry out his orders.

Chapter XIII

Emerging from reclusion, he reviews commanders
A bandit for the present, he is awarded high rank

⤳

Bai Xishao was a commoner who lived in Boluo county and whose monastic name was Dun'an. He had built himself a small hut beneath Mount Luofu, and although he was poor, with nothing to his name apart from his lute and a few books, he had a mind well stocked with ingenious schemes, he could predict the future, and he was skilled in all aspects of military strategy. In his straw hat and his coarse cloth gown, he led a contented life. Three years previously he had divined that the coastal areas would suffer several years of armed conflict, after which certain individuals, he himself would share the same destiny, would serve the state by setting one group of bandits against another. The only thing he did not know was when the conflict would begin.

One day, as he was fishing beside the stream, he heard some passers-by talking about how some bandits had recently set up camp on Goat's Foot Ridge. Although the bandits didn't rob any of the common people or the traveling merchants, they had blocked the road through the mountains. Dun'an smiled. "You must have it wrong," he said to one of the passers-by. "How could bandits survive if they didn't rob anyone?"

"You don't understand, sir," said the man. "This bandit chief is the brother of Colonel Yao, and he wants to render service to the court. He is burdened by an enormous sense of injustice, and he kills only greedy and corrupt officials and robs only those who are ruthless in their pursuit of wealth. He doesn't bother honest citizens at all."

Struck by a sudden thought, Dun'an stopped fishing and went back to his hut. From what they say, he thought, this man Yao really does sound rather unusual. There has never been a bandit in the greenwood who has been able to repay his obligations to the court. Let me use the eight diagrams to try and divine his behavior. He heated up some incense, cast the milfoil stalks, and was delighted to obtain the Second Yang of the Army hexagram. The Second Yang at the lower level is where many yin images return; at the higher level it resonates with the Fifth Yang, he reflected. This man will receive the favor of the sovereign, who will confer on him a threefold commendation,[1] all of which fits my earlier divination. But he has no idea that I even exist, and I shall have to go and seek him out. He cast aside his medicine burner and his tea stove, said farewell to his thatched hut and his bamboo fence, and set off in the direction of Huizhou.

He soon reached Ebu, where people gathered in groups of two or three passed on the news: "Chief Yao has seized Goat's Foot Ridge, where last month he defeated a force from the Jieshi station. In the last few days the commander-in-chief has dispatched government troops to root out the bandits.[2] But it's not the bandits we're afraid of, it's the government troops; when they come, it'll be a disaster for us. Pack up and get out while there's still time." Dun'an took all of this in, ate his breakfast, and then went out onto the street and set off along the road. He had gone little more than half a mile up the mountain when he saw ahead of him a tall barrier with a banner bearing the words, "Wanted: Men of Talent and Learning."

By this time Goat's Foot Ridge held over one thousand troops, and a system had been set up: Yao Huowu and Feng Gang were quartered in the main camp in the center, Ho Wu in the forward camp, Han Pu in the left camp, and Gu Shen in the right camp. Jiang Xinyi had brought all the families up to the ridge and lived with them in the rear camp; at the southern checkpoint Wang Dahai and Qi Guangzu kept guard, and at the northern checkpoint Lü Youkui and Xu Zhen did likewise. You Qi and Chu Hu had set up a separate camp on the banks of the Phoenix Tail River to defend against a waterborne attack.

One day, as they were returning from military exercises on the training ground, they heard a report from the northern checkpoint that a scholar had come to see them, and Huowu promptly ordered him brought in. Xu Zhen then led in a man who entered with his head held high. Huowu rose to his feet and welcomed him, and Dun'an bowed and took a seat. Xu Zhen gave Dun'an's name, and Huowu said to him, "I'm just a military man with no other talents or wisdom, and I appreciate the fact that you've deigned to pay me a visit. I wonder what instructions you have for me."

"His Majesty is our ruler; he treats places near and far alike, and the common people everywhere rally to him. I don't understand why you've seized control of this mountain, General. Where do you intend to establish yourself?"

"Generations of my family have received imperial benevolence; how could I possibly rebel with an easy conscience? But my sworn brothers have been persecuted by corrupt officials, and my blood brother has been executed on the basis of a false accusation, and that is something I cannot abide. We need to rid ourselves of evildoers and kill off corrupt officials before submitting to the court and dying in battle. That is my sincere intention, as Heaven is my witness. That is why we take from the greedy and corrupt but don't dare to harm honest folk."

"You may be an upright man, General, but the petty amount of property belonging to corrupt officials cannot possibly provide for the hearty appetites of all your men, and eventually you are bound to impact honest folk as well. Moreover, Goat's Foot Ridge covers only a tiny area; how can you hope to control Guangdong province from here? If the governor-general should issue an order, asking the commander-in-chief's troops attack from the north, the Jieshi garrison attacks from the south, and the Chaozhou troops mount a surprise assault from the southeast, not only will you be outnumbered, you will be bombarded from a distance by cannon on three sides. This mountain is not very high, nor is it protected by any walls or moats. You gentlemen may have all the military skills in the world, but even if you grew wings I'm afraid you'll find it hard to get out of here. If you're not actively taking precautions against disaster, you're living in a fool's paradise!"

Huowu and the others rose from their seats in alarm. "We've lulled ourselves into a false sense of security—we really haven't thought about the disaster that will eventually follow. Give us the perfect plan, sir, and we'll certainly put it into practice."

"Goat's Foot Ridge controls a key thoroughfare linking Haifeng and Lufeng counties to Guangzhou. Unless you take those counties, you certainly won't enjoy any peace and quiet. According to my plan, you should first take Jieshi, then Haifeng and Lufeng, and finally Jiazi, after which you should send one officer with strong support to hold and defend the access to Huilai and another officer to guard this mountain and threaten Huizhou and Chaozhou and stabilize Jiaying. The money and provisions from the two counties, apart from the army payroll, should be stored in warehouses and eventually returned to the court. This is a plan designed to let you breathe a little more easily."

"Your analysis, of course, is perfectly sound. But I wonder why you would have us take Jieshi first instead of Haifeng or Lufeng."

"Haifeng has suffered a defeat and so naturally it's under martial law. Lufeng is an adjoining county—surely they've put a garrison in there by now. Moreover, it has high, thick walls, and it can count on help from Jieshi, so there's no guarantee you'd be able to take it. But Jieshi itself, which depends for its security on its distant location and difficult access, will definitely not be on the alert. In addition, the commanding officer has not yet returned from marine patrol. You would need only a few hundred men to attack under cover of darkness, and you are sure to take it. As it says in the *Art of War*, catch the enemy unawares, hit him before he's ready. Once Jieshi falls, the other two counties will be terror-stricken, and since they'll be cut off and without support, it will be simplicity itself to conquer them."

Huowu was delighted with the plan and wanted to make Dun'an his strategist, but he was afraid that the others might not accept him, so he ordered all of the brothers to gather at the main camp the next day for a conference.

In the Hall of Justice three seats were set up in the middle for Yao Huowu, Dun'an, and Feng Gang, while the rest of the men sat to the left or right of them. After they had drunk three cups of wine, Huowu opened the discussion: "I have your support, and we help one another as best we can, but we are all military men and know nothing of how to use the element of surprise in gaining a victory. We are fortunate that Master Bai has come to visit us. I would like to have him stay here for the time being and help us. Would you be in favor?"

"You've made a conscientious effort to recruit men of talent and learning," said the others, "but we don't know if Master Bai really has those qualities."

"His talent and learning are prodigious," said Huowu. He turned to Dun'an. "Let me ask you this, sir: Since ancient times two kinds of accolades have been bestowed on soldiers—famous general and great strategist. I wonder what sort of men they had to be and what sort of learning they had to possess in order to receive that sort of recognition."

"There's a fundamental difference between strategists and generals," said Dun'an. "It's the general's task to combine wisdom with courage, but it's for the strategist to devise a plan in the command tent that will determine victory hundreds of miles away. Not only is he the leader of the army, if he is to deserve the title of strategist, ever since the Three Dynasties he has also needed to be a mentor to his ruler. Jiang Ziya was the earliest of the great strategists, but Zhang Liang, Zhuge Liang, Wei Zheng, Li Jing, Zhao Pu, Liu Bingzhong, and in this dynasty Liu Ji, all belong in the same category. Sun Wu was the earliest of the famous generals, and the most outstanding of his successors were Han Xin, Zhou Yu, Guo Ziyi, Yue Fei, and Han Shizhong. In a second group the following would be selected: Yue Yi, Zhao She, Li Mu, and Bai Qi of the Warring States period, Zhou Yafu, Li Guang, and Feng Yi of the Han, Li Guangbi of the Tang, Cao Bin of the Song, and Xu Da and Chang Yuchun of the beginning of this dynasty.

"Those who appear to be great strategists but do not deserve the title include Guan Zhong, who served Duke Huan of Qi; Fan Li, who assisted Gou Jian; Chen Ping, who advised Gaodi of the Han; and Wang Meng, who reported to Fu Jian. Those who would appear to be famous generals but do not deserve the title include Xian Zhen, who was cunning and disrespectful; Sima Rangju, who never attained any great success; Sun Bin, who merely sought his own personal revenge; Tian Dan, who would stop at nothing to regain the state of Qi; and Deng Ai, who took undue risks in his invasion of Shu. Beyond these men, those who possess both good and bad qualities and deserve both praise and blame are simply too numerous to list."

The speech laid everyone's doubts to rest. "Your great talents, sir, should not be applied to petty tasks," said Huowu. "Since you have deigned to join us, I hope you will accept the position of strategist. We will gladly take orders from you." Dun'an readily accepted.

That day they went back to the training ground and gathered all of the soldiers together to receive their orders. Dun'an was asked to mount the tribunal, and Huowu drew the jeweled sword that he wore at his waist and presented it to him. After bowing twice, he said, "From my brothers and me down to the common soldier, if anyone should disobey your orders, behead him with this sword." Dun'an returned the bows and accepted the commission. All of the sworn brothers then paid their respects and sat down on one side. Mounting the tribunal, Dun'an proceeded to give explicit orders: "My rules are simple and easy to understand, strict but not hard to obey: those who rob the common people will be beheaded; those who commit rape will be beheaded; those who reveal military secrets will be beheaded; those who steal property will be beheaded; those who fail to advance on hearing the drum or to retreat on hearing the gong will be beheaded; those in the rearguard who don't scale the walls following the vanguard will be beheaded; those officers who fall back when one officer is defeated will be beheaded; and those who do not stay in the ranks but act without permission will be beheaded. Other, lesser offences will be punished, according to their severity, with floggings."

Each of the men bowed and voiced his acceptance of the rules.

Dun'an then gave the following order to Gu Shen: "Take two hundred infantrymen and go to the upper reaches of the Phoenix

Tail River and build a dam there so that the water drains away below it, then stand guard over the dam day and night. You'll receive further orders just in time to execute them." He gave the following order to Jiang Xinyi: "Take a hundred infantrymen and start moving trees and rocks so as to set up an ambush on both banks at the northern mouth of the river. Each man should have a musket and flaming arrows. If government troops enter the mouth of the river, you should not try to block them, just quietly await further orders." He also told Lü Youkui and Xu Zhen to prepare numbers of cannon, logs, and arrows at the northern checkpoint. "But if the government troops attack, you are not to engage them, just let the cannon drive them back—that would be the greatest service you could render." The men went off to carry out their orders.

Dun'an stepped down from the tribunal and with Huowu and others returned to camp, where he told the craftsmen to build such things as fiery dragons, fiery horses, fiery crows, thunderbolts, earth cannon, and flying chariots. Huowu had a question: "You've just sent soldiers out to Phoenix Tail River. I wonder what you have in mind?"

"You'll see within the next few days," said Dun'an. He drank steadily for three days on end and paid no heed to anything else.

Before long a scout on the northern route came in to report: "He Siguang, adjutant general of the commander-in-chief's brigade, has assembled three thousand troops with twenty officers. He has arrived at Ebu and set up camp there. Please decide on a course of action."

After rewarding the scout, Dun'an took out a command arrow and gave it to Han Pu. "Go to the southern checkpoint and order officers Wang and Qi to remove all swords, spears and banners from the checkpoint. Let them lead the troops under their command down the mountain and set up camp half a mile along the eastern route in order to prevent Haifeng from sending troops to attack us from the other side. Then assist the men in the camp." He took out another arrow and told the leaders under his own command to go to the northern checkpoint and convey the following order: "See that you strictly adhere to your previous orders. If you deliberately disobey, even if you emerge victorious, you will be beheaded. Only when you hear the cannon firing from the top of the mountain are you permitted to charge down and attack." He also took out two brocade bags and told someone to take them to Jiang Xinyi and Gu Shen, who were to carry out the orders contained in the bags.

He then told Feng Gang, Ho Wu, You Qi, and Chu Hu to lead four hundred soldiers equipped with firearms to lie in ambush on both sides of the Phoenix Tail River. When they heard cannon fire from the top of the mountain, they were to shoot into the river. He himself would join Yao Huowu in setting up the signal cannon on a steep point and then quietly awaiting news of victory.

> Great men of unparalleled fame—
> Watch their exploits on Goat's Foot Ridge.

Let us turn to Commander-in-Chief Ren Ke. He was a wise and courageous general who had been a close friend of Yao Wei-wu. When Yao made his crucial mistake and was impeached by the governor-general and governor, Ren was not only unwilling to add his name to the document, he even sent a letter to its authors begging them to forgive Yao and allow him to redeem himself by meritorious service, but the two men refused. On the assumption that Colonel Yao would surely not be sentenced to death, Ren had let the matter rest there. While out at sea he received a report that Goat's Foot Ridge had been occupied by bandits, but he was still not greatly concerned; only when he had urgent messages from Jieshi and Haifeng, as well as a communication from the governor-general and governor, did he realize that Yao Weiwu had already been executed and that the leader of the bandits was none other than Yao's brother, Huowu. Ren hated Huowu for flouting the law and showing no concern for his parents' honor, and so he issued an order directing General He Siguang to lead an army and root out the bandits. He told him to take Yao Huowu alive, because he wanted to conduct the interrogation himself.

He Siguang was the great grandson of Senior General Qiu Fu, who was active during the Yongle reign.[3] Because Qiu Fu's whole force had been wiped out after he crossed the frontier, Qiu He, his second son, had fled to Guangxi, where he changed his surname to He. As the commander-in-chief's outstanding officer, he could draw a two hundred catty bow and wield a one hundred catty staff, and Ren had always appointed him to head the vanguard, in which he had been consistently victorious. However, he relied too much on his personal bravery and took his opponents too lightly; furthermore he shared the Lord of Xinling's addiction to wine and women.[4]

After receiving his orders, He Siguang was just about to set off when he also received a call to arms from the governor-general and governor. And so he chose two thousand troops, cavalry as well as infantry, together with seven or eight officers of various ranks, whipped up his men's fighting spirit, and set off. But because their commanding officer was dissolute as well as courageous, his men imitated and even outdid him in acts of senseless savagery, looting every house they came to and raping every woman they set eyes on. Arriving in Ebu, they started fires to clear the ground for their camp. He Siguang ordered them to raze Goat's Foot to the ground before breakfast, and his troops duly advanced, shouting their war cries. However, cannon shot from the top of the checkpoint, together with rocks and logs, rained down upon them, and they could make no progress. "Since the bandits are prepared for us," said He Siguang, "let's have a good meal first and then find some strategy for destroying them." He ordered his men to heat their pots and cook their food in the open field, while he sent scouts all around to find out which tracks led up the mountain. Before long the scouts returned to report that there was no way up except by the road to the southwest; a new checkpoint had been set up there, but there was no one manning it, and the Phoenix Tail River was shallow, having recently dried up, so that there was no need for boats. "This gang of bandits assume that I'm going to attack from the north, and that's why they've stepped up their defenses here," said He Siguang. "Well, I'll change my plans and attack from the rear. I'll hit them like a clap of thunder—they won't have time to cover their ears—and none of them will survive! But we can't make a move during the daytime—I'm afraid they'd see through our stratagem. We'll pretend to attack the mountain and then advance at night along the Phoenix Tail River. They'll have no time to take precautions." His officers were greatly impressed with his plan.

He Siguang drank for much of the day, and then that evening, leaving a couple of hundred old and feeble soldiers behind to guard the camp, he began a diversionary maneuver with drums sounding and banners flying. Meanwhile, together with his officers he made an undercover advance along the Phoenix Tail River. There was no water in the river, and the troops, both infantry and cavalry, advanced freely and easily. But they had gone no more than three or four miles when they heard an earth-shattering rumble of cannon fire from the top of the mountain and in no time at all both banks were lit up with torches and they were assailed by countless weapons. He Siguang was shocked; he knew perfectly well that he had fallen into a trap. Hastily he shouted to his men to turn back, but the fiery weapons struck their armor and scorched them so badly that they panicked. The flaming arrows from the top of the mountain descended like a swarm of locusts, and when his troops reached the mouth of the river, they found that the road ahead had been cut. He Siguang looked back and saw that half the men under his command had already been burned to death. There was nothing else for it—he yelled to his soldiers to try to save themselves with a desperate lunge up the bank. He himself made a daring leap of some twenty feet. With one hand clutching a tree and the other brandishing his club, he swung close to the bank. Unfortunately the roots of the tree had been scorched by the fire and could not bear his prodigious strength. They snapped, and he tumbled headlong into the river. The water from upstream suddenly came surging down, and a thousand or more badly burned soldiers turned into overcooked fish, so that it was impossible to tell one person or creature from another—officers, soldiers, horses. Meanwhile the couple of hundred men left in the camp had been killed or forced to flee by Youkui and others, who also seized large quantities of supplies, weapons as well as food.

Huowu and Dun'an knew that they had won a complete victory. The next morning they sat in the camp while reports of success poured in from all sides. Dun'an ordered the troops from south of the mountain to return and invited everyone to the camp to celebrate with a feast. Huowu rewarded all the men with a share of the money and provisions that they had won and allowed them to take a day off and enjoy themselves drinking. During the feast, Dun'an said, "Now that Huizhou has suffered this major defeat, no one else will dare come up from there. Moreover, Commander-in-Chief Ren is still out at sea and will not be back any time soon. However, within a few weeks the governor-general's and governor's brigades are bound to spring a surprise attack. You officers mustn't beg off on the grounds of difficulty—you need to make the most of this quiet spell in the cool autumn weather by taking Jieshi and then Haifeng and Lufeng and making them into our base of operations."

They answered with one voice, "We will follow your orders."

Three days later Dun'an assigned You Qi and Lü Youkui to command the first of four detachments, Ho Wu and Han Pu the second, he himself and Feng Gang the third, and Xu Zhen and Gu Shen the fourth. Each detachment would consist of two hundred infantry and cavalry. Giving out that they were going to attack Haifeng and Lufeng, they marshaled their troops and set off. At the news both Haifeng and Lufeng manned their walls and stood guard day and night. However, the Goat's Foot troops did not bother Haifeng at all, and when they came to Lufeng, they pitched their camp well away from its walls for half a day and then headed that night for Jieshi. At midnight they arrived before Jieshi station, which had not mounted a guard, and Dun'an ordered his men to scale the walls. The two miles of wall were only a little over ten feet high and were soon overcome. Dun'an told the first detachment to attack the central battalion, the second to attack the left battalion, and the fourth to attack the right battalion. He himself with Feng Gang fought his way into the colonel's residence. The sub-prefect's yamen held no troops, so there was no need to bother with it. As the four detachments attacked, the battalion commanders, ridiculous as it may seem, were still asleep in their beds. The fighting continued until the fifth watch, when Dun'an took a seat in the colonel's residence, and You Qi and Youkui led in Captain Sha Xian and Major Zeng Yong, Han Pu and Ho Wu brought in Lieutenant-colonel Fei Shi's head as well as two lieutenants whom they had captured, and Xu Zhen and others led in Captain Chang Difu and

Sub-prefect Hu Zixing. Dun'an gave orders that two banners were to be erected calling on all troops to surrender and that notices be posted reassuring the populace. All the civil and military officials who had been brought in were to be held in custody and their family members investigated and separately detained, but none of them was to be put to death pending General Yao's decision.

Before long over two thousand troops were kneeling down at headquarters seeking to surrender, declaring that they wished to see Master Yao. Dun'an reassured them all, distributing one tael plus five pecks of grain from the sub-prefect's yamen to each man.

After fighting had ceased for a day, Dun'an told You Qi and Ho Wu to stay there with their four hundred men plus a thousand of the surrendered troops as a garrison. He himself led the other officers plus over a thousand surrendered troops back to Lufeng.

On hearing the news, the magistrate of Lufeng county, Gou Youxin, called Major Yang Dahe in to discuss the situation. "The other day when those bandits passed through here," said the major, "I wanted to lead my troops out to cut them off and kill every last one of them, but you insisted on a defensive posture, which is what has led to this disaster! Let's wait until they're heading back to the hills. I'll confront them, and then we'll talk."

"They seemed so bold and so fierce, and it was just after those defeats at Haifeng and Huizhou—that's why I decided on a strong defense. Now, with enemies in front and behind, I think it will be impossible to ask for a relief column, so we're completely dependent on your courage as we risk everything on a single battle. But you shouldn't underestimate the swine."

"Don't worry about that! You concentrate on defending the walls, sir, while I concentrate on the battle. Each of us must do his duty to the best of his ability." With one lieutenant and three or four sub-lieutenants he led twelve hundred troops outside the walls and set up camp there. About noon the next day the Goat's Foot troops could be seen in the distance advancing in imposing strength. Dahe hastily drew his men up in formation and, gripping his great sword, barred the way at the head of his troops.

As soon as Dun'an, who was aware that Dahe was a fine officer, learned that the Lufeng troops were blocking the road, he summoned Xu Zhen and Gu Shen and gave them certain orders. But he also gave them an additional, secret order, by which the rearguard would turn into the vanguard and beat a slow retreat. Leading over two hundred troops, Xu Zhen and Gu Shen rode forth and shouted: "What scurvy, death-defying officer dares to block our path? He must have donkey ears not to know how fearsome we heroic Goat's Foot warriors are!"

Slashing with his sword, Dahe roared back: "Vile, death-deserving criminals, I'm coming after you to get revenge for General He." Xu Zhen fought four or five jousts with him, then turned his horse around and fled. Next Gu Shen came forward and fought six or seven jousts before also fleeing on horseback. Bellowing with laughter, Dahe ordered his cavalry to go in hot pursuit of the two officers, who fought as they retreated. Youkui thought that the two had been defeated and was about to go forward himself, but Dun'an was quick to stop him, ordering him to retreat to a temporary position three or four miles away. On checking his troops, Dun'an found that he had not lost a single man, and that only twenty-odd had sustained injuries. The wounded were sent to the rear to recover.

When his men asked the reason for the retreat, Dun'an replied, "We're not interested in killing just one officer; our task is to take Lufeng. Major Yang has set up his camp near the town, and if he is beaten, he'll undoubtedly go inside the walls and stoutly defend them. Lufeng is known as Little Suzhou, and attacking it would take us some time. Now that we've tricked him into coming three or four miles outside the walls, we can use a stratagem to destroy him. We've lured the tiger out of his lair, and it will now be child's play to take Lufeng."

He ordered Youkui and Han Pu to lead six hundred troops flying Yang Dahe's banners to trick their way inside the gate that night and take possession of the wall and moat. Feng Gang was to lead three hundred troops and approach from the rear. Then at dawn, at the sound of cannon fire, both forces would attack in a pincer movement. He himself and Gu Shen, still wearing their armor, would cook a meal at the third watch and enter the town at the fifth.

Having won a victory, Dahe was mighty pleased with himself. He camped half a mile away from Dun'an and told his lieutenants: "Wu Risheng was incompetent and He Siguang fell for a ruse; that's why they were defeated. Tomorrow, gentlemen, you are going to see me capture them with a single, overpowering attack."

"We are counting on your awesome powers to kill them all," said his lieutenants.

Dahe drank to celebrate his achievement and ordered his men to sleep in their armor with their weapons close at hand, in case the bandits should mount a raid on their camp.

At dawn, before the men had finished their breakfast, they heard three cannon shots, and the Goat's Foot troops came surging forward. Dahe hastily grabbed his great sword and mounted his horse, then arranged his men in formation and galloped out in front of the ranks, shouting, "Bandit scoundrels, you dare to come and meet your doom!" Xu Zhen rode out alone and fought over twenty jousts, but was no match for him. Then Gu Shen urged his horse forward and joined the fray, while the lieutenants on the other side thrust at him with their lances. The battle was just at its height when Feng Gang attacked from the rear, and whenever he raised his halberd, men tumbled from their horses. Dun'an also ordered his own troops to advance.

Dahe now had enemies in front and behind, and his soldiers broke ranks and fled. Xu Zhen, unable to hold Dahe off, retreated, trailing his weapon behind him, and Feng Gang came forward to take his place. Gu Shen, who had already speared the lieutenants to death, urged his horse on to attack from the other side. Xu Zhen also wheeled around and rejoined the battle. Dahe gradually weakened. He had no more than three hundred men left and was forced to turn his horse and flee, with the enemy in pursuit. He raced to the city wall only to see Youkui and his men, who had taken the walls and moat, come charging out. Dahe had just reached the drawbridge, when he saw that it was futile to go any further and tried to turn back. Feng Gang, however, caught up with him at just that moment and cannoned straight into him, seizing him and calling out to the others to come and tie him up.

Dun'an entered the town and set up a tribunal in the hall of the magistrate's yamen, issuing a notice to reassure the populace and calling on the remaining soldiers to surrender. Youkui escorted Magistrate Gou in, while Feng Gang brought in Major Yang. Gou Youxin kowtowed three times and said, "I would not have dared to resist you, sire, but because Major Yang had such confidence in his own strength and courage, I gravely offended Your Majesty. I have a mother at home in her eighties, and I hope, sire, that you will show your infinite mercy and spare my humble life."

Dun'an laughed. "There's no need to talk like that, Your Honor! It's not up to me to say whether you ought to live or die. I'll keep you and your family in jail for the present while we await the people's verdict."

The magistrate kowtowed again and again. "I have always taken my duties seriously, and the people are not very pleased with me. I would beg you, sire, to extend your grace to me." Dun'an took no notice of his pleading and ordered him held in jail.

"Magistrate, how can you stoop so low!" thundered Dahe. "Come on, kill me first!"

"General Yang," said Dun'an, "you're a gallant man, and your fame echoes along the south coast. If you could join us in raising the banner of justice, if you could join us, it would be a great honor!" As he said this, he stepped down, undid the major's bonds, and helped him into the seat of honor.

"I was in charge of defending the walls of this town," said Dahe, "and they've been breached. I should have died in the attempt to defend them—there's no disputing that. How could I now bring myself to help you with your rebellion?"

"My brothers and I would never have dared to rebel—we did so only because we were driven to it. In the future, when an amnesty is declared, we intend to devote our efforts to the cause of the court. If you, General Yang, would deign to join us, it would be a matter of 'a man doing what he thinks is right.' We would never dare to detain you by force." He called to his attendants, "Bring General Yang's weapons and his horse around. I shall personally escort him out of town and let him do as he wishes." Dahe, seeing that Dun'an was showing him both grace and courtesy, and was also speaking frankly and openly with him, bowed low and expressed a desire to surrender. Dun'an was delighted and helped Dahe up and had him sit at his side. He then sent someone with a document to Haifeng, calling on the whole town to surrender, and also sent Youkui with three hundred troops up the ridge to report on the victory and invite Huowu to transfer his headquarters to

Lufeng. He had the magistrate's yamen in Lufeng converted into Huowu's quarters and withdrew to a private residence.

A few days later a reply came from Haifeng: "A public-spirited citizen named Dou Bipi has brought the local people together and seized Gongyang Sheng, and the whole town has pledged its allegiance to you. Liang Shangren has fled. Dou Bipi is outside waiting to see you." Dun'an called him in and praised him. He had Gongyang Sheng confined to prison, then meted out rewards and punishments and waited for the leader, who would decide on their course of action.

The following morning Huowu arrived. Receiving the two reports of victory, he had left Wang Dahai and Chu Hu to guard the mountaintop while he set off with Jiang Xinyi, Qi Guangzu, and Lü Youkui. On the way he received the news of Haifeng's pledge of allegiance, and so with his path cleared of obstacles he headed straight for Lufeng. Dun'an led his men out and formed them up to welcome Huowu into town. On entering the yamen, Huowu took a seat, and Yang Dahe and Dou Bipi came forward and paid their respects to him. Huowu offered praise and encouragement to both men.

"Fellow officers," began Dun'an, "by General Yao's power and authority and the combined efforts of all of our men, we have taken three county towns in the course of twenty days, and a fourth, Jiazi, is there for the taking. In my humble opinion we should honor General Yao with the title Duke of Fengle, as head of the government in this area. I wonder if you approve."

"Approve!" shouted the men. "The strategist's proposal meets with our unanimous approval! Today we endorse you, Brother, as Duke of Fengle."

"You shouldn't be so hasty!" said Huowu to Dun'an. "And you, my brothers, you ought not to approve his proposal. I'm just a military man who has taken refuge here for the time being. Through your and Master Bai's efforts I have managed to eke out a dishonorable existence and now, just when I'm most concerned about how to forestall the enemy, I cannot possibly start out by giving myself airs. Moreover, my strategic abilities are not equal to Master Bai's, nor are my courage and intelligence on a par with Brother Feng's. I urge you to reconsider."

"You're being far too modest," said Dun'an and Feng Gang with one voice. "We've already made our decision."

They surrounded Huowu and prostrated themselves before him. He declined again and again before finally accepting, and then only after changing the title of "duke" to "commander." Everyone approached and bowed again. After the ceremony they sat side by side and presented oral and written reports.

Next day they sacrificed to the gods and printed out the new appointments. Dun'an was to be the strategist in charge of important civil and military matters; Feng Gang was to be the general in command of the central detachment, supervising the troops on all the access routes; You Qi and Ho Wu were to be in charge of coastal defenses, controlling the routes to the Jieshi station; Wang Dahai and Chu Hu were to be in charge of the northern defenses; Jiang Xinyi was to be in charge of pacifying Haifeng; Xu Zhen was to be in command of the advance detachment; Han Pu was to be in command of the left detachment and also to administer Lufeng county; Qi Guangzu was to be in command of the right detachment; Gu Shen was to be in command of the rear detachment; Lü Youkui and Yang Dahe were to be distinguished generals of the left and right, respectively, and also commanders of the vanguard; Dou Bipi was appointed administrator of Haifeng, but he objected: "I brought men together to capture the magistrate, but I was only carrying out the will of the people. How can I become an official myself? There's a jail warden, Master Lin by name, who has held office for nine years and would satisfy the people's desires. I beg you to appoint him as magistrate. The people will be most grateful." Huowu granted the request and appointed Warden Lin Shitai magistrate of Haifeng while generously rewarding Dou. The post of sub-prefect in charge of the Huifeng defenses was eliminated for the time being because the duties scarcely existed. Lawsuits among the people were to be referred to the coastal defense officer for investigation and settlement. A notice was also posted calling for the recruitment of men of talent and learning. And a proclamation was sent out soliciting accusations against Gongyang Sheng, magistrate of Haifeng, Yu Xing, sub-magistrate, Gou Youxin, magistrate of Lufeng, Wu Shishi, jail warden, Qu Bo, sub-magistrate, Gong Nanjin, sub-director of schools, and Hu Zixing, sub-prefect of Jieshi, using such language as the following: "Is there a case of greed and extortion to be brought against any of these officials? When a tiger is in captivity, you needn't fear that it will attack you; when a fire has burned to ashes, you needn't worry that it will flare up again. Since justice resides in the hearts of men, why not bring charges in cases of injustice?"

When the troops had undergone a month's training, Feng Gang was appointed senior general, Yang Dahe general of the vanguard and Ho Wu general of the rearguard. Together they led fifteen thousand troops in an attack on Jiazi.

Chapter XIV

Faced with a cruel husband,
she bites her tongue and endures her shame
Meeting an artful woman, he hopes for sex but gets
feces instead

⤫

Yao Huowu's uprising on Goat's Foot Ridge took place during Su Jishi's mourning period, so let us now drop the subject of Lufeng and turn back to what was happening in Guangzhou.[1]

After the hundred days of mourning were over, Jishi left his house and began paying visits again. At first it was the officials in their yamens that he visited, then the traders, then the merchants, and finally his relatives and friends, such as the Wu, Shr, Qu, and Zhu families. Returning from one such visit, he changed back into mourning clothes and went as usual to the inner quarters where, after greeting his mother, his father's concubines, and his sisters, he arrived at Huiruo's room. She and Xia brought out some wine and they drank together. "My brother is getting married on the twenty-fourth," said Huiruo, "and he's asked both of us to go back for the wedding. Since we're still in mourning, do you think we should go?"

"If you're visiting close relatives, there's no taboo after the hundred days, so why don't you go? Anyway, I intend to spend a few days there." That night he slept in Huiruo's room, and their pleasures, coming like a sudden shower after a long drought, are not hard to imagine.

The following morning they had just gotten up when Wuyun came into the room. "We've just received a message," she said. "There's someone called Shr Bangchen who's come to see you." Jishi finished his morning wash and then went to the outer quarters and had his visitor brought to the study. Bangchen greeted him, bowing low. "Yesterday I received a visit from you, gracing my humble abode, and I've come to thank you most respectfully."

"I was simply doing the appropriate thing after your and the others' kindness at the funeral. There's no need to thank me."

"I've prepared a cup or two at my place to cheer you up," said Bangchen, after taking a seat. "I hope you'll honor me with a visit."

"I haven't had time to impose on any of you gentlemen. Why should I trouble you before any of the others?"

"I'm unworthy to be counted among your disciples, I know. This is just a small gesture of respect on my part. But if you don't honor me with a visit, I'm afraid I shall lose face with all of those friends." He bowed again.

Impressed by his candor, Jishi agreed, and Bangchen promptly took his leave. "This afternoon I'll send someone around with an invitation. I still have to go and ask Cousin Shy and Master Wu to keep us company." Jishi pressed him to stay for breakfast, but he adamantly declined.

Jishi then told Su Xing to get someone to write several letters thanking the relatives and friends who lived at a distance.

In the afternoon Shy Yannian came by and said, "Bangchen has invited me to be a fellow guest tonight. Twice he's sent someone over urging me to come. Let's go together."

"I've already accepted," said Jishi. "I'll have my men get a couple of chairs ready. We'll go together and save them from having to wait for one or other of us." They got into the chairs, and with Xiangqin, Heqing, and the Shy family's page Afu in attendance went directly to Double Gate Under.

Shr Bangchen was over forty, and his wife had died long

before, leaving him with a fifteen-year-old daughter, Shunjie. He lived near the registry, and had opened a curio shop there, next door to Zhu Zhonghuang and his brother. On this occasion he was inviting Jishi, in particular, as a way of establishing a closer relationship. He had tidied and cleaned his house, burned a little incense, and arranged for two girl singers to be present. The Zhu brothers were already there; they had been waiting for some time. When Jishi and Yannian arrived, Bangchen and the others came out to the sedan chair to greet them. Jishi alighted, took Bangchen's hand, and went inside, saying, "I'm embarrassed to be receiving your hospitality."

"A poor man's house won't be able to provide anything to your taste," said Bangchen, "but we've done our best. We Suzhou people are known as 'empty heads,'² but you mustn't laugh at us." He offered the newcomers betel nuts, and Zhu Zhonghuang handed them tea. Jishi and Yannian expressed their thanks.

"Why isn't Master Wu here?" Bangchen asked Axi, his page. "Go and invite him!"

"I've just been. I was told by his people to ask you to take your seats and say that he'd be along soon."

"Is it anything serious?" asked Bangchen.

"It seems he's had a quarrel with his wife," said Axi. "Let me go back and ask again."

"Where does he get the nerve to have a row with his wife?" asked Bangchen with a laugh. "When he gets here, we'll penalize him for overdoing the husband role."

"His wife is the sister of your good lady," Zhu Lihuang said to Jishi, "and I've heard that she's the essence of virtue and kindness. He must be the one who started it."

"Ever since his father got appointed treasurer," said Shy Yannian, "he's had a superior air about him—quite different from what he used to be like."

"You never said a truer word," said Zhu Zhonghuang.

"But how could anyone change like that?" asked Jishi. "I don't believe it."

"Bangchen invited Master Su here," said Zhu Lihuang, "so surely we're going to get something else beside all this chit-chat? Whatever you've prepared for him should be brought out, if only for the sake of appearances."

"Quite right," said Bangchen. "I've allowed our guest to get hungry. Come on, bring it out."

"There's no hurry," said Jishi. "Let's wait until Brother-in-Law Wu gets here, and then we'll enjoy your hospitality together."

As the plates and dishes were being set out, Daiyun came in from his sedan chair. He appeared to be half drunk. The others welcomed him in.

"Why are you so late?" said Bangchen. "I suppose you knew that I'd have nothing to offer you and deliberately filled up at the yamen first."

"I don't have time to drink," said Daiyun. "I haven't seen Brother-in-Law Su in ages, so I came over to keep him company."

"That's very kind of you," said Jishi. "But I'd still like to hear why you're so late."

"Let's all sit down first," said Bangchen.

Jishi offered the place of honor to Daiyun, who accepted without demur. Although Jishi didn't mind, Yannian felt that Daiyun was taking liberties. As for the second seat, Jishi wanted to yield it to Yannian, but Daiyun said, "Oh, do sit down, Brother-in-Law! I don't imagine for one moment that they'd dare take our seats." Everyone urged Jishi to sit down, after which Yannian, Zhonghuang, Lihuang, and Bangchen all sat down in order. Wine was served, and Bangchen handed the first cup to Jishi, while Zhonghuang and Lihuang handed cups to Daiyun and Yannian. They drank up.

Jishi then repeated his question, and Daiyun replied. "That Wen woman is getting to be more and more of a monster! Ever since last spring, when she came into my house, I've treated her well in every conceivable way. Then my father got the treasury post and took my mother off with him. Very few people were left in the yamen, and so I took a concubine named Yunjiao, just to liven things up. But every day since then that Wen woman has found something to pick a quarrel over. At New Year's, I told her off, and she calmed down a bit, but this morning I got up and went off to my father's place. Yunjiao arose a little late, and that woman actually barged into her room and started beating and cursing her. When I got back, I asked her why and she actually said, that my concubine had been having an affair with a page and that was why she had hit her. Now, my rules for the women's quarters are very strict. Others may not know that, but Brother-in-Law Su certainly does. When she tried to smear someone with that sort of slander, how could I help getting angry? I gave her a real hiding. The woman has a mouth on her like the River Huai. She said she wanted to kill herself, but I locked her up, and she finally calmed down a bit."

"The charge of adultery may have been false, but her jealousy was real enough," said Jishi. "You ought to have taken that into consideration and let her off."

"But you don't understand! If old Shy's sister were your concubine, and your wife got jealous like that, are you telling me you wouldn't get angry?"

Jishi said nothing, but Yannian flushed scarlet. Bangchen saw that the two men were furious with each other, and he broke in and urged them to drink up. "I've arranged for two singers to attend on Master Su and Master Wu. I wonder if you'd care to receive them now?"

"If you've got singers, why didn't you bring them out before?" demanded Daiyun.

Bangchen quickly did so. One was called Aqiao, the other Yu'er. They were only eleven or twelve, and both were still virgins. Standing side by side before the company, they bobbed up and down a few times as they curtseyed to everyone. Daiyun put one arm around Aqiao and drew her onto his lap. "Which group do you belong to, my dear?" he asked. "And how many songs do you know? Choose one of your favorites and sing it for me, and I'll drink a big cup of wine."

"I live on Datang Street in the city," said Aqiao. "So far I don't belong to any group. Please drink up and then I'll sing." With both hands she held out a large cup to him, and Daiyun drained it. With Yu'er playing the lute, Zhonghuang beating time, and Bangchen on the dulcimer, Aqiao tuned the instrument and sang in a soft voice:

> Two lovers have I,
> Equally dashing and debonair;
> I love you,
> But I love him too.
> At our secret tryst last night
> Below the western balcony,
> One was there for the tryst,
> The other to check up on me.
> As to what he found out,
> It was hard for me to respond,
> So I drank a cup of *pin* tea;[3]
> The *niao* put forth its blossoms,[4]
> While the *jie* was pulled aslant;[5]
> Let my two lovers do as I say and make their peace!

When she finished the song, Daiyun exclaimed, "Marvelous! Truly marvelous! But you're only allowed to love me, not Master Su as well." Jishi laughed. Bangchen told Yu'er to coax Jishi into drinking some more, and she handed him a large cup. She herself kept time—with Aqiao on the three-string and Bangchen playing the flute—and sang a southern song to the tune of "The Drunkard Returns." It truly "sprang from Beauty's lips and enthralled its audience." Jishi drained the cup, and everyone applauded the girl's singing.

"I don't understand singing," said Daiyun, "and I don't like Yu'er." He embraced Aqiao and declared with nauseating sentiment: "You're the only one I'm going to keep."

"Do be a little more serious, sir," said Aqiao. "It doesn't look nice."

"Who cares how it looks?" He went on to play several games of guess-fingers with her, and had to drink seven or eight more cups. The wine put him in an exuberant mood, and he began to paw her, leaving her no chance to escape.

"Since you love her so much, why don't you take her as your concubine and let us enjoy a matchmaker's cup?" asked Yannian.

"Just what I have in mind. But I can't do as I please until that shrew of mine has killed herself."

"But if your wife really did commit suicide, wouldn't your father-in-law have something to say about it?" asked Yannian.

"Oh, I'm not afraid of him! He's just a failed salt merchant, and he'd never dare to pick a quarrel with a newly appointed young gentleman like me. If the worst comes to the worst, I'll have him put in chains. I'll also accuse him of conspiring with a relative to embezzle tax money."

Stung by the accusation, Yannian snapped, "Conspiring with just what relative?"

"Oh, don't pretend to be so dumb, young Shy! Have you finished paying all the taxes that your family owes?"

"That's none of your business!"

Daiyun flew into a rage. "Daddy's the treasurer, so how can you say it's none of my business? Who do you have backing you up, that you can afford to be so wild? I tell you, if I don't sue you for it tomorrow, I'm no man!"

"And if I'm afraid of a young fellow like you with no rank to speak of, my name's not Shy!"

Jishi saw that things were getting out of hand, and he shouted at Yannian to stop and urged Daiyun to calm down: "There's no need to get so worked up, Brother-in-Law. Bangchen invited us here for drinks, to enjoy ourselves and have a good time, and if we have a row, we'll only embarrass our host. Do me a favor, keep it to yourself."

"You're an honest fellow," said Daiyun, "and I have no quarrel with you. Just don't spring to the aid of your maidservant's brother!"

"Who's a maidservant's brother?" retorted Yannian. "In that case you're the brother of Heh Guangda's maidservant!"

This made Daiyun even more furious. "Well then, which of us brothers has more clout?"

Jishi and the others tried again and again to calm Daiyun down, but he refused to stay until the end of the party and left fuming with anger.

Jishi also wanted to leave, but Bangchen blocked the door and urged him to stay, and he was forced to sit down again. "Don't be angry, Brother Shy," said Jishi. "And there's no need to be anxious, either. If he really does try to sue you, it won't amount to more than a few thousand taels, which I'll pay. He won't be able to extort it from you."

"You're right, sir," said Bangchen. "I never realized how much young Wu had changed. Even if his father had won his lowly office by the regular process, instead of being appointed to it just a few days ago, he could hardly survive the slightest challenge. However lovely the peony is, it still needs green leaves to back it up. How could he bear to alienate all his relatives and friends like this? Take no notice of him, Cousin Shy."

"He had no sooner come in the door than his arrogance was there on full display. I never picked a quarrel with him, he dragged me into it because of his wife. How could I possibly hold back?"

"Of course he's impossible to get along with," Zhu Lihuang said to Jishi. "But Cousin Shy has you to stand up for him, sir, so there's nothing to fear. And now let's enjoy ourselves over a few drinks."

With the two singers assiduously encouraging him, Jishi drank heartily. He gave each of them three taels, after which he and Yannian took their leave. At his gate, he had some more advice for his companion: "You don't need to worry about him, you know. You have me at your back, whatever happens." Yannian thanked him and went home.

At the main hall of his house Jishi stepped out of the sedan chair and walked through to the inner gate, where a number of serving women and maids bustled forward. They relieved him of his felt bag, and with two of them carrying lanterns and two others holding candles, he went to the west court, where he was welcomed by Xia: "You don't appear drunk," she said, "but you do look as if there's something on your mind."

He told her about Daiyun's abuse of Suxin. "Uncle made a great mistake in arranging that marriage," she said. "What a pity it is that someone as talented and beautiful as Suxin should be matched with such a scoundrel!"

Jishi continued. "Daiyun was also going to sue your brother for unpaid taxes, but I'll take care of that."

"I'd rather you didn't. Daddy never embezzled any tax money; he was driven to his death by the superintendent. My brother was too naive, and he was unfairly beaten for it. At the time we had nothing except the four bare walls around us; there was nowhere we could go to protest, and we had to let the matter drop. But resentment over the injustice of it all is constantly on my brother's mind. If Wu Daiyun doesn't prosecute, all well and good, but if he does, I would urge you not to squander the few thousand taels that it would cost you."

"How do you mean?"

"My brother may not be very capable, but he's strong-willed. On the other hand, I know quite a bit about the world. In a deadly feud like this, we can never forgive Wu Daiyun! With a few thousand taels to spend, if I can't take down the superintendent and destroy the Wu family, I'll write my name upside down for all to see!"

Jishi smiled. "So I've found myself a true heroine, have I? But your brother's a tough character whose behavior gives rise to a lot of complaints. Why bother to imitate him?"

"My brother's a hothead, and I need to have an idea or two of my own. Just now the governor-general and governor are at odds with the superintendent. Moreover, even if they were supporting him, there's still the emperor above them. Surely those few thousand taels will be enough to pay for travel to the capital? I wouldn't be willing to make a spectacle of myself, but all I would need to do is draw up a petition and get my brother to present it. He's been in trouble before, and this would only mean another taste of the rod; they'd hardly give him a death sentence! My dear husband, trust me on this."

As she finished, the tears were streaming down her cheeks. Jishi sent the maids out of the room and came forward and wiped away her tears. "Now, don't be sad. Let's wait and see whether Wu goes ahead before we decide what to do."

"I'm grateful for all your kindness. I don't dare go on any further, but if this affair does blow up, don't on any account try to intercede with Wu." Jishi promised, and got into bed with her. He slept until noon the next day, then sent someone to find out what Daiyun was doing.

On the same day that Daiyun returned to the yamen the Wen family heard of the quarrel between husband and wife. Mistress Shi sent a servant to fetch Suxin, but he was met with a volley of curses from Daiyun and returned home without her. Daiyun then marched into Suxin's room, accused her of getting her family to send for her, and gave her a savage beating in the hope that she would hang herself. But with a typical woman's temperament, Suxin, who had previously tried to kill herself in order to scare her husband, now adamantly refused when forced to do so. Unable to stand the beating, she had to plead for mercy. "I'll forgive you for the moment." Daiyun snarled. "I'm going to give you another hiding tomorrow!" He then went off to spend the night with Yunjiao.

Soon afterward he went to the treasury and discussed with his father how to punish Yannian.

"Don't meddle!" said Biyun. "They're relatives of ours. Why do you need to make such a fuss over it? What's more, it would be highly embarrassing to do anything that would offend Master Su."

"It's only because he's counting on Su Jishi's wealth to support him that he has the nerve to do this. I did think of including Su in the case, but he's such an honest soul that I let him off this time. One of these days, though, I'm going to put one over on him."

"What utter drivel! How has he ever offended us, that you should be so grossly unfair to him? When you got married, I borrowed three hundred taels from him. And when I got my promotion, his share of the presents I received was worth ten times that of anyone else's. You're showing a complete lack of conscience in wanting to harm him. Moreover, His Honor has just sent in a memorial about the true situation with the pirates, and both the governor-general and governor would dearly like to impeach him. Master Bao is a man who's constantly on the alert in these matters, and he won't support you if you prosecute." These words fell on Daiyun's ears like ice water on hot coals, and he withdrew in silence.

Returning to the river police yamen, he told a maid to heat some wine to cheer him up. Then he sat down with Yunjiao, and ordered a maid to undo Suxin's chains and bring her out from her room. He himself stripped her naked and then, holding a horse-whip in his hand, roared at her: "Well, slut, do you admit your guilt?"

Suxin, looking like the beaten cock in a cockfight, was so frightened that she knelt down in front of him. "I admit that what I did was wrong."

"Since you admit it, I won't whip you. Now, be so good as to take the jug and urge your mistress Yun to drink another cup of wine."

"I'll willingly serve her, but I beg of you, please let me put something on to preserve my modesty."

Swish, swish went the whip, leaving two red welts on her delicate flesh, as Daiyun snarled, "What modesty do you have left, you slut? Don't try to play the innocent with me!"

She didn't dare reply, but patiently bore the humiliation as she stood beside them pouring the wine. Daiyun took Yunjiao in his arms and crooned softly to her as he sipped his wine, fondling her breasts, kissing her on the lips—every kind of shameless behavior. After drinking for a while, he barked at Suxin: "Slut, cut some hair off your head and compare it with Mistress Yun's, to see if it's as good as her pubic hair." Suxin did not dare say anything, but she was so frightened that she started shaking like a leaf. Daiyun jumped up again and lashed out wildly with the whip. "Come on, off with it!" Still smarting from the pain, she was forced to cut off a lock of her hair and hand it to him.

He passed the hair to Yunjiao, and wanted to pull down her trousers and compare it with her pubic hair, but she refused. "This filthy, greasy thing—how could it compare with anything of mine?" She tossed the lock of hair into the fire, where it burned up.

Daiyun laughed outright. "You jealous shrew, do you realize now what a low creature you are?" he said to Suxin. "In a few days' time your brother will be getting married, so do me a favor and go back home. Clear out of this house once and for all, and save me from having a bitch like you in front of me all the time making your Mistress Yun angry. But you're not to take anything with you from your room." He went off to sleep with Yunjiao.

Suxin's thoughts ranged over the past and the future, but although she cried bitterly all night, she didn't dare make a sound.

> She rues the "Madcap" line in "Lift your gown";[6]
> No river now could wash away her shame.

When Jishi learned that Daiyun had taken no action, he put the matter out of his mind.

Soon Chuncai's wedding was at hand. His family sent servants out with invitations, and Huiruo and Xia, accompanied by menservants, women servants and maids went back to stay with them.

Merchant Wen settled the two women in Break-Cassia Studio and Play-with-Lotus Pavilion, respectively, and the dozen or so women servants and maids were quartered with their mistresses, while the five or six menservants and pages kept watch at the garden gates, taking orders and running errands. The side gate to Pity-the-Flowers Lodge, which led inside, was reopened.

Suxin had already returned, bringing with her the two maids who had accompanied her at the time of her wedding, and she was living in Hide Spring Dell. When she met Huiruo and Xia, she naturally told a tearful story of the misery she had had to endure. Huiruo was not greatly affected, but Xia felt deeply sorry for her. "Since that's the case, stay here with us while you decide what to do," she said. She also told Suxin how Daiyun had picked a quarrel with Yannian a few days before.

"I was held there like a condemned prisoner," said Suxin, "and I knew nothing about any of this. But you must beware of him. Now that he and I are completely estranged, whom does he see anymore?"

"Since he won't acknowledge his relations," said Xia, "we'll just have to get on with our lives and see what happens." And there we shall leave them.

The girl Merchant Wen was marrying his son to was Huajie, the younger daughter of Miao Qingju, the registrar of Nanhai county. On the wedding day guests filled the house, which rang with music and song. Preposterous though it might seem, Wu Daiyun actually attended for some reason, and did so in high spirits. Merchant Wen acted as if he knew nothing of the quarrel, and treated him in the usual manner, together with Yannian and Jishi in the reception room. Although Daiyun ignored Yannian, he apologized privately to Jishi for getting drunk and having too much to say. On Yannian's behalf Jishi made the excuse that he had had too much to drink and had behaved rudely.

After the banquet, all of the guests went off to escort the bride to the Wen house—all except Daiyun, who walked over to see what the bridal chamber was like. It was in Pity-the-Flowers Lodge, and Daiyun, after amusing himself there for awhile, walked on into the garden. The maids knew that Suxin was staying in the garden and didn't care to stop him. He was strolling along, recalling the secret trysts that he and Suxin had held in the lodge, when he saw a maid approaching whom he recognized as one of his own. "What are you doing here?" he asked.

"The mistress and Mistress Su are both staying in the garden. I'm here to attend on them."

"Where is Mistress Su staying? Take me there so that I can meet her."

The maid didn't dare refuse, but took him straight there. After crossing Fragrance-seeping Bridge, Daiyun saw a beautiful woman in an unlined gown of sheer white silk pongee, a black formal jacket of Huzhou silk, and a black gauze skirt. She had tiny, slender feet and a jet-black coiffure. The uniformly plain mode of dress served only to accentuate her charm and beauty. "Who's that?" he asked.

"That's Mistress Su."

No wonder Yannian got so much help from young Su, thought Daiyun. He had this stunning creature to offer him as a concubine. He quickened his pace and blocked her way with a bow: "Let me offer you my greetings, Cousin."

Xia was totally unprepared to have a man approach her in the garden, but despite her shock she returned the greeting.

"The other day your brother was at the Shr house, and he picked a quarrel with me, but for your sake I didn't try to punish him for it. Did you know that?"

Realizing it was Daiyun, Xia felt furious. She saw his shifty eyes darting about before fastening on her body. Furthermore, she felt his speech had a certain sinister quality to it. Nevertheless, she pretended to be delighted and replied, "I'm extremely grateful to you for your kindness, but unfortunately I have no way of repaying you."

"Since you'd like to repay a debt of gratitude, don't give me any money—whatever you do will be fine. You follow my meaning, I take it?"

"Apart from my own person, I have nothing to repay you with. I really wouldn't know how to go about it."

Daiyun chuckled as he stepped closer and pointed at her skirt. "The repayment would be on your person. It's quite simple." He appeared to be on the point of taking physical liberties with her.

She flushed and whispered to him, "That would never do, not in broad daylight and with a host of maids looking on! Don't be so impatient. If you're really interested, wait for me at the third watch beside the Play-with-Lotus Pavilion."

Daiyun was thrilled. "I shall faithfully do your bidding, but you will have to keep your promise." He squeezed her tiny hand and said, "Why are you wearing this silver bracelet?"

She turned to go, but then looked back and said with a smile, "I don't break my promises. It's up to you to keep yours." As she walked slowly away, she kept thinking to herself, this loathsome creature bullied my brother and humiliated my sister, and on top of all that he has the nerve to insult me! I can never forgive him. She went to Break-Cassia Studio and told Huiruo that Daiyun had made odious advances to her and she needed to avenge herself.

"We women on our own shouldn't take any great risks. He's not someone you'd ever want to cross."

"Why should I be afraid of him? He was just too brazen and shameless. This is the trick we'll play on him tonight.... We're going to vent our anger on him for Suxin's sake."

"I shall be scared out of my wits, whatever trick you play."

Xia left and began surreptitiously deploying her forces. That evening the new daughter-in-law entered the house and performed the usual rituals with Chuncai. Chuncai also had a private chat with Jishi, during which Jishi gave a faint smile and nodded his head.

As soon as Daiyun saw that the wedding rituals were over, he slipped into the garden completely unaware of what was in store for him and dodged about from place to place. Only when he heard the third watch did he walk over to Play-with-Lotus Pavilion. It was surrounded on all four sides by water, and to get to it you had to cross a white stone bridge on which there was no place to stop and wait.

There was still a lot of activity in the pavilion, and just as he was peering about to find somewhere to hide there came a sound at the window and a maid approached out of the shadows and whispered, "Is that Master Wu?"

"Yes. Quick, let me in. I'll reward you well."

"Our Second Lady says that your mistress and our elder mistress are both in there. It's a small room packed with people, and there's nowhere you can go to get away from them all. She's also afraid someone may come along and see you here. You should keep out of sight for a while under the bank of this stream on the left side. Before long I'll come and call you, but whatever you do, don't do anything rash. If you can't wait, please go back and come again tomorrow."

Daiyun was quick to reply. "I'll keep out of sight. You just see to everything." Slowly, step by step, he moved down the bank and hid himself. What a great schemer she is, he thought—not even an immortal could find me here. It seems she's an old hand at this game. The unfortunate thing is that my shrew of a wife is so full of gossip that she's holding up my fun. But never mind her; soon I'll be able to enjoy myself to the full. As these chaotic thoughts were running through his mind, he heard the window above him creak open and a basinful of water cascaded down upon him, drenching his head and face. What water is this, he asked himself; it's still warm. He felt it with his hand, then sniffed his fingers and began to rhapsodize. What a splendid bouquet it has! I expect it's the water she washed her face in. My clothes may be a little damp, but that won't deter me. He looked up toward the window, and was just about to step away when a slops bucket full of urine and feces emptied itself all over him. Not only did his body reek of the smell, even his mouth and ears received the full benefit. The stench was unbearable, and he quickly moved away, but the ground was now covered in water, and he slipped and fell into the stream, from which he was unable to clamber out, no matter how hard he tried. Meanwhile the contents of two more buckets spattered down on top of him. However, intolerable as his situation was, he did not dare utter a sound; he just lowered his head and put up with it. Then he heard a gale of laughter as a crowd of women left the pavilion.

He began frantically washing himself in the stream, still hoping someone would come and pull him out, but the door of the pavilion was already shut. However, a number of men with bells and rattles did come by on night patrol. "This pavilion's surrounded by water," said one of them. "I doubt there'd be any thieves here."

"We'd better shine our torches here and there, anyway, or else the master will bawl us out for not doing our job."

A boy with a white silk lantern came up to him and said, "There's either a big fish or a turtle under that bank over there." Two or three men ran over and shone their torches on the place and began shouting, "Oh, no! It's a thief!" Swarming around Daiyun, they pulled him out. "And a fine foul-smelling thief it is, too! He must have been dredging the privy." Gripping their truncheons and surrounding him on all sides, they rained blow after blow on him. He was forced to cry out, "I'm Master Wu, the son-in-law! Why are you hitting me?"

"We're the Su family's night patrol. If you're Master Wu, what are you doing in here in the middle of the night? Come on, let's pull him out. We'll tell the master and Master Wen and let them decide what to do with him."

"Look, I came into the garden to tell my wife something, but I slipped and fell into the privy, and I was just washing myself off beside the stream. How can I possibly go and see them in this state? Do me a favor, will you? Keep quiet about this."

"I think he's telling the truth," said an older man. "Let him go, brothers. Master Wu, I don't mean to tell you off, but this is where our young ladies are staying, and you oughtn't to be in here late at night. If it happens again, don't blame us if you get beaten to death." Without daring to retort, Daiyun walked off toward Hide Spring Dell, but Suxin was asleep and did not open up for him. He had to wait until dawn, when he seized the chance to run home unchecked by the Wen family.

Once home, he was eaten up with anger. He assumed the incident was a trick on Xia's part and calculated how he could pick a quarrel with her and get even, but after spending half the night soaked to the skin, he caught a chill. Then, because of the chill, and also because of the beating he had received, he fell ill and had to send for the doctor.

Chapter XV
Three scoundrels set a trap
Four beauties disappear

⁓

Jishi and his womenfolk stayed on in the Wen household until the third day, then took their leave and returned. After paying his respects to his mother and his father's concubines, Jishi went to Huiruo's room, where she told him the full story of the humiliation her sister had suffered at Daiyun's hands and of the trick Xia had played on him.

It made Jishi feel sick at heart to hear of Suxin's ordeal. "She brought this humiliation on herself," he said at last, "and it can't be helped. But Xia, you were a little too drastic in what you did, and our feud with Daiyun is only going to get worse. We're not afraid of him, but we don't want to make things more difficult for Yannian, do we?"

"Oh, I can't be worried about that," she said.

Jishi turned to Huiruo: "The other day, when his bride joined the household, your brother asked me a lot of foolish questions. Then a day or two ago I asked him how things were going, and all he would say was that Mistress Miao had ordered him not to tell anyone. That set me thinking that perhaps the simpleton had actually learned something from her."

"My brother may be simple-minded, but you'd scarcely expect him to tell you what he and his wife did in bed, now, would you? My father is going to follow established practice; he's heard that next year there's going to be a special examination, and he wants Chuncai to take it."

Jishi laughed. "Tell him not to work too hard. If he manages to pass, I'll expect you two to top the list at the next palace exam!"

At that point Wuyun entered with a letter in her hand. "This has just come in. They say it's from the capital, and that the messenger is waiting outside for a reply." Jishi knew that it would be from the Li family, and he opened and read it:

> From Guodong [Jiangshan] to his esteemed relative Zhancun [Su Wankui]:[1] More than a year has passed since I said goodbye to you on the Pearl River. With your noble aspirations, moral behavior, carefree spirit and sound virtues, your high principles and interest in learning, as well as your lofty desire to withdraw from society, what depression could you possibly be feeling?
>
> Since I arrived in the capital, I have found the lamplight of the streets in the heart of the city burning into me and the city's prosperity dazzling my eyes and deafening my ears—truly, the ethical spirit is not averse to material things! My son was fortunate enough to pass the metropolitan examination and be ranked in the third group in the palace examination. By the emperor's grace he was appointed to the Hanlin Academy and then directed to study in the Shuchang College. As for the marriage, it will have to be delayed again. I expect that Jishi has devoted himself to self-improvement. I only hope he reforms himself and does not turn away from his friends and take the wrong path. That is all I have in my mind that is worth offering to you. Shen Xiangxuan [Shen Jin] went to Zhejiang as acting grain intendant and wrote a special report to the emperor about the need to eliminate outworn practices. He has already been promoted to lieutenant-governor. Yao Huowu of Donglai is a man whose worth you appreciated and to whom you gave support. He is no ordinary person, but a tiger among men. If he is still in Guangzhou, you should support him and also instruct him on how to correct his failings.
>
> Respectfully, Guodong

As he finished the letter, Jishi remarked to Huiruo and Xia, "My brother-in-law has been admitted to the Hanlin Academy, which is a great honor for the family. Father made the right decision in his choice of a son-in-law. What a pity he couldn't have lived to see this day!" He wept, then got up and went outside. He asked the messenger for the details, and invited him to a meal, gave him travel money, and had someone write a letter for him to take back.

Just at that moment Shr Bangchen came in, bowed to Jishi and took a seat. "You were at your father-in-law's place for several days," he said, "and I didn't like to bother you by going there to see you in the evening. There's a small favor I'd like to ask of you, and I pray that you'll be kind enough to help me."

"If there's something you want to ask me about, please do so."

"I run a small shop, just as a means of supporting my family. Because the inventory has sunk rather low, I need to go to Zhaoqing to buy some stock, and for that I need a hundred taels of capital." As he spoke, he took out the deed to his house, which had a promissory note tucked inside it, and bowed as he handed them both to Jishi. "I would like to request the generous loan of a hundred taels from you. Both principal and interest will be repaid at the end of the winter."

"What are you saying? Take the money by all means, but I definitely don't want the deed. Return the principal in the winter— that will be enough. There's no need for any talk of interest."

Bangchen gave another deep bow. Jishi had a servant take out a hundred and ten taels, which he handed to Bangchen. "I don't have time to give you a farewell dinner, but here are ten taels toward your traveling expenses." Bangchen accepted the money, thanked him, and left.

Returning to his house, he gave orders to his daughter Shunjie: "Pack my bags for me. I'm leaving for Zhaoqing tomorrow to buy some stock."

"But Daddy, where did you get the money?"

"Master Su has a genuine affection for me, and he lent me a hundred taels and gave me another ten as a parting present. I'll leave the ten with you and the maid for your expenses while I'm away. I'll be gone between fifteen and twenty days. See you take care to keep the doors locked."

"I know. Isn't Master Su that agreeable young man who came here for the party the other day?"

"That's right. He's been extremely friendly." Next morning Bangchen got up and went next door to the Zhu house to say goodbye, asking the brothers to look after things while he was away. Then together with Axi he headed for Zhaoqing.

In the Zhu house Zhonghuang remarked to Lihuang, "I wonder how old Shr managed to con someone into giving him the money for another buying trip. He won't have any trouble celebrating the New Year this time around! You and I will be left carrying bags of salt in a snowstorm, bags that get heavier with every step. We don't have a pretext for getting money out of anyone."

"Yesterday on the corner of Haoxian Street I saw old Shr coming out of the Su place, and he was all smiles. I think he must have borrowed the money from there."

"Then all it cost him was a single party, and old Su fell for it! Let's lay out a little money on a party and invite him to it, and also Shy and Qu to keep him company and put in a good word for us. We shouldn't have any trouble getting a loan out of him."

"Su Jishi's father was known for arranging loans to officials, so if you borrow from him, you'll have to pay it back. We'd better have a talk with old Qu and see if he knows of any scheme for laying our hands on some money."

They had no sooner reached the corner than they found Qu Guanglang coming toward them in a state of intense agitation.

Zhanglang immediately called out to him, "Brother Qu, we haven't seen you for a few days, and you look a lot brighter than you did. Where did you hit the jackpot?"

"What fucking jackpot are you talking about? The day before yesterday I lost five hundred cash, and for two days straight I've not had a single penny to my name. I really and truly can't get by. I heard that Bangchen had managed to borrow some money from Su, and I'm on my way over to Bangchen's to ask for a loan."

"He's gone off to Zhaoqing," said Lihuang. "Let's go into town and have something to eat and drink." Guanglang needed only to hear the word "eat" to be on his way. They went through the Wenming Gate to Aroma House. Lihuang ordered a bowl of fried eel, half a bowl of casseroled pork, a large dish of fried noodles, and two catties of Taihe spirits, and the three men wolfed it all down. Lihuang brought up the matter of the loan Bangchen had received from Jishi. "He's just one of us, but we don't have his kind of luck."

"But if you take out a loan, you have to repay it," said Guanglang, "and that's not a good situation to be in. The trouble is, I don't have the few taels it would take to invite Su Jishi to a party. And even if I did, I wouldn't consider it a successful move unless I got at least a thousand out of him."

"Cut the big talk, Brother," said Zhonghuang. "I've heard that he's not keen on sex with men."

"All you've heard is that he's not keen on it, but are you quite sure that he actually *confines* himself to women? I went to see Master Wu yesterday, and he's lovesick over old Shy's sister."

"If it's Yannian's sister he's after, she shouldn't be too hard to get. Why the lovesickness?"

"You don't understand," said Lihuang. "His sister is old Su's concubine. Wu doesn't stand a chance."

"Is that so?" said Guanglang. "Well, we don't need to bother about young Wu. But look at old Shy. What a sorry state he was in after that court case! But ever since his sister entered the Su household, he's been going in and out by sedan chair all day long, swaggering about and having a high old time. Old Su clearly spends money on his women."

"That's all beside the point," said Lihuang. "You and I don't have any sisters, so obviously we can't do anything but talk. But old Shr has a daughter, and you might introduce old Su to her."

"If I did the same as old Shy did, I'd be like a student who's copied an old essay in an exam—bound to fail. Instead of that I've just thought of a brilliant ploy. We may not have any sisters, but we could always borrow one. It would only cost us five or six taels."

"If you've thought of something," said Lihuang, "tell us what it is so we can talk it over. We could always get the five or six taels from a pawnshop."

Guanglang whispered something in the ears of the other two; "So long as we do..., he'll take the bait, no doubt about it."

"Brilliant!" said Zhonglang.

After thinking it over for some time, Lihuang remarked, "There's no need to borrow the money from outside; we can always save ourselves the four dollars. Anyway, she wouldn't actually start doing it with him. My wife is still quite pretty, so let me go home and put it to her. However, when the money comes in, I'll need to have a double share."

"If you do that," said Guanglang, "things will go even more smoothly. Of course you'll deserve a double share."

Now that the plan had been agreed on, the men ate seven or eight bowls of noodles, paid the bill, and returned home.

The capital, they say, abounds in villains;
Plan an affair, and someone will cheat you.
But Guangdong's rogues are devilish cunning;
Even heroes say, "There's naught that you can do."

Meanwhile Jishi was living at home with nothing to occupy him. He spent day after day with Huiruo and Xia in the garden to escape the heat, whiling away the summer by chanting poetry, drinking wine, or picking lotus from a boat. When he heard that Daiyun had been taken ill, he was vastly relieved.

One day he was told that Master Zhu of Gaodi Street had called, and he went out to the reception room to see him. Zhu Lihuang came forward and bowed. "It's boiling hot today," said Jishi. "You didn't need to dress up so formally. Do make yourself comfortable."

"My brother and I have prepared some melons and fruit, and we would like to invite you to honor us with a visit. I felt that I had to come properly dressed for the occasion."

"But why go to all that trouble on such a hot day? Anyway, I don't have the time."

"I heard that you were free; otherwise I wouldn't have dared to come. But since it was so hot, I didn't come until evening. We won't be having any other guests, just in case there's another row."

"Since you put it like that, I suppose that if I don't go, I'll be spurning this very kind gesture of yours."

He gave orders to prepare a sedan chair, but Lihuang said, "I've already arranged for a cool chair. Because our place is so cramped, I'm afraid it might be demeaning to your entourage, so I would ask you to bring only a few servants with you."

"I won't bring any at all, then. I'll come with you."

"That's most considerate of you."

The two men stepped into the sedan chair and soon arrived at the Zhu house. Zhonghuang and Guanglang welcomed Jishi in, served him tea, and set out a meal that consisted entirely of ice-cold seafood and the finest of fresh fruit. "It's very hot," said Zhonglang, "and wine makes you perspire. Let's drink gaoliang spirits instead. They're more cooling, and you'll be able to relax and enjoy a few cups."

"Gaoliang is excellent, but it's too strong for me," said Jishi. "I'm afraid I couldn't drink very much."

"With your vast capacity, you have nothing to fear," said Zhonglang. "Moreover, it's vintage spirits, from several years back."

The three men took turns pouring the spirits for him. After they had been drinking for awhile, Zhonglang said, "Just drinking by itself is no fun. Let me ask you to suggest a drinking game for us, sir. The only trouble is that none of us is well read. You'll have to choose a game that's easy for us to play."

Jishi noticed a dice box with four dice on a little table to one side and picked it up. "Let's play dice," he said. "If you get a red, you don't need to drink. You just quote a line from any poem, lyric or song that has the word 'red' in it. If you don't get a red, you drink a cup and tell a joke. If you can't come up with a line that has 'red' in it, or if you can't tell a joke, you drink another cup as well."

"You've set the rules, sir, and we'll follow them faithfully," said Guanglang. "But you're the master of the game, and if anyone here manages to tell a joke and tells it well, you'll have to congratulate him by drinking a cup yourself."

Jishi agreed and drained the master's cup. He threw a one and three reds, and quoted the line "One sheet of apricot blossom red for three miles,"[2] then handed the cup to Guanglang, who stood up to receive it. "You threw three reds, sir," he said. "That means the three stars of wealth, rank and long life are shining down upon you as portents of great joy. If you have a few more reds, it will mean not just three stars, but three hundred or three thousand. Before I make so bold as to try and follow your rules, let me ask you to drink a cup to the God of Joy."

Zhonghuang poured out the liquor and passed it over, and Jishi had no choice but to drink it.

Guanglang threw four threes and said, "That's a little skewed, just like us Hangzhou people, so let me tell you a local joke. A well-educated friend of mine, perfectly correct in all that he said and did, would never stray a single step from the straight and narrow. His father's personal name was Jishi, so he never dared to use those two characters. Whenever he came to the poem 'A Fair Knight Seduced Her,'[3] he used to substitute 'Daddy' for 'Jishi.' When one day a relative of his received an appointment to the Hanlin Academy, he stuck the notice high up in his hall and everyone came to congratulate him. Among the visitors was a short-sighted fellow who couldn't read the characters in the notice and said to the Hangzhou man, 'Unfortunately, I have poor eyesight and can't see what it says about appointment to the Academy. Could I trouble you to read it out to me?' Without thinking, the man declared in a loud, ringing voice, 'Report of the success of Master Wang of your honorable household, who passed in the second group and by imperial order has been appointed to the Hanlin Academy as a shu-Daddy.'"[4]

Loud laughter followed the joke. "Old Qu called you Daddy several times, and now this Daddy will naturally have to do us a favor," said Lihuang. "After he has drunk up, old Qu will no longer be allowed to call him 'sir,' only 'Daddy.'"

"Stop making fun of me," said Jishi. "The joke was well told, though." With a smile he drank up, after which it was Zhonghuang's turn. He threw a straight and quoted the line "A myriad purples, a thousand reds—all is spring."[5]

He passed the cup to Lihuang, who failed to throw a red, but drank up and told a joke: "When the country folk of Jiangxi have a baby, whether it's a boy or a girl, they name it after the first thing they see following the birth. In one family two sisters-in-law became pregnant one after the other. The elder one gave birth to a daughter and sent her husband out to see something and then come back and name the baby after it. He went into the garden, where he happened to see a woman raising her buttocks to relieve herself and in the process exposing her vagina to his gaze. Returning inside, he named the newborn infant Vagina. Later the other sister-in-law gave birth to a son and saw a man walking past selling bamboo baskets, so she chose the name Basket. Unfortunately, when the children were a year old, Vagina died of smallpox, while Basket grew up and began attending school. As he was coming home from school one day, he bowed to his mother and aunt, and the aunt was reminded of her own sad loss. 'What a pity my Vagina died!' she said to her sister-in-law. 'If she was still with us, my Vagina would be even bigger than your Basket.'" The joke was greeted with loud laughter.

Guanglang quickly poured another cup of spirits and handed it to Jishi, saying, "Didn't you hear that, sir?" he asked. "Zhu Lihuang's wife has a vagina as big as that. Drink another cup and you can try and see it for yourself." Lihuang lashed out at him. After drinking a cup, Jishi asked Zhonglang to come up with a quotation, which he did, followed by another "Fan Li Visits Xishi" act.[6] With the three men conspiring together, Jishi drank another seven or eight cups.

By the first watch he was feeling mellow and got up to leave, but his companions insisted that he stay. "I've brought someone along to encourage you to drink," said Guanglang, "and you must do her the favor." From beside him he produced the figurine of a Western beauty about seven inches tall that held a large cup filled with spirits in her hands. Guanglang touched the figurine in some fashion, and there it was standing in front of Jishi. Jishi happily drank the spirits, and more was poured. Strangely enough, when anyone else touched the figurine, it invariably turned to face Jishi, but when he touched it himself, it didn't budge. The large cups of spirits were by no means easy for Jishi to drink. He didn't want to have any more, but his hosts put on a great show of solicitude and plied him with four or five more cups, until he completely lost consciousness.

"The trap is set," said Guanglang. "Now we just sit back and wait for news of victory." The Zhu brothers carried Jishi over their shoulders into the bedroom and laid him down on the bed. Lihuang then called in his wife, Mistress Ru, and the men slipped out of the room.

Mistress Ru was twenty-two or twenty-three and quite attractive. Her husband had told her to wait until Jishi sobered up and then start sleeping with him, at the same time screaming for help. Outside the room three or four rogues would be stationed to catch the adulterer in the hope of extorting money from him. Mistress Ru had been peeping at Jishi for a long time from behind the screen and had seen him drinking with his bare back toward her, a soft, smooth back that she found irresistible. What's more, her husband was encouraging her to commit adultery with Master Su, so that she felt that she shared a predestined bond with him. Her room was on the west side of the reception room with its own courtyard. Shutting the courtyard gate, she went back into her room and placed the lamp beside the bed. She felt Jishi all over, then pulled off his trousers of pure white unlined silk, revealing an object shaped like a fresh mushroom. Holding it in her delicate fingers, she began stroking it rhythmically up and down. Jishi, who had been drinking gaoliang, was more virile than ever and offered a dazzling sight—bold and inviting. Mistress Ru felt as if she had come upon some priceless jewel, and she hastily stripped off her clothes and mounted him as if she were riding a horse. Those two hopeless fools, she thought, they're not just using me as a lure, to make friends with him and then get a little money out of him. Oh no, they're embarking on a ruthless strategy that will only offend this marvelous creature. I'll let him get away and then hope for a long-term relationship. As these thoughts whirled through her head, she continued moving up and down. Although thoroughly drunk, Jishi half awoke and, thinking he was in his own home, turned over and, clasping her to him, began thrusting with some urgency. By the time he had finished, Mistress Ru felt limp and numb.

She wiped herself clean and then embraced him. "Sir, do you know who I am?" she asked. Jishi leapt up and looked at her, then asked who she was. She told him about the plot against him.

The shock of this revelation drove the alcohol right out of his system. "But I'm an honest citizen. Why would they play such a deadly trick on me? I only hope you'll save me!"

"Don't you worry, sir. If I didn't plan to save you, I wouldn't have told you any of this." She helped him on with his trousers, then accompanied him into the courtyard. "The Shr family live next door," she said. "The father's away, and the only one at home is the daughter, who's a friend of mine. Climb over the wall and hide there until dawn before you go back. No one will dare to offend you again. However, you must not forget me. If you miss the love we shared tonight, well, there's nothing but empty land outside my back door, and you're free to come in at any time. The men are always out gambling, never at home."

"I wouldn't dream of ignoring the love you've shown me. But won't they make life difficult for you after I've gone?"

"Don't worry about that; I know what to do." Fetching a short ladder, she helped him over the wall, then put the ladder away but left the back door open. After taking a moment to collect herself, she burst into simulated sobs. The men outside broke in to find her wearing nothing but a pair of unlined trousers.

"I called for my husband!" she screamed at them. "What are you doing in here?"

"A fine thing you've been up to! We're here to catch the adulterer," said the first one to enter.

Mistress Ru slapped him across the face. "What adulterer are you talking about?" she screamed. "The wretch has run away!" While the men looked at each other in bewilderment, she rammed her head into Lihuang, screaming, "You can't even support your own wife! You order me to make a disgraceful exhibition of myself, and on top of that you tell all these people to come in here and humiliate me. Oh, why do I want to go on living?"

Lihuang was struck dumb with astonishment. Guanglang took one look out the back and said, "He's escaped through the back door, but he can't have got very far. Come on, let's catch him first and then decide what to do." Lihuang and the others went racing off in pursuit of Jishi.

Meanwhile Jishi had climbed over the wall in hopes of finding a place to hide and was walking toward the house. However, the poorer classes do not close their doors in hot weather, and Shunjie, having slept for a while, was keeping cool by sitting naked in her room. When she saw the shadow of a man slipping into the house, she set up a cry of "Thief! Thief!"

Jishi was afraid that her cries would be heard next door, and he rushed into her room and knelt down in front of her. "I'm no thief. I'm the victim of a plot, and I've come here to hide out for a little while."

Shunjie gathered from his manner of speech that he was not a burglar, but she was afraid that he might be intent on raping her, and she was so terrified that she shook like a leaf. "You come into someone's house in the middle of the night," she said, hastily pulling on her clothes. "Have you no fear of the law? Get out this minute, or I'll raise the alarm and have you arrested and taken to court."

"I wouldn't dare go into any other house, but your father's a friend of mine. That's why I've taken refuge here. My name is Su Jishi. You must have heard of me."

"If you really were Master Su, you wouldn't be coming into our house at this hour of the night!" Hastily she lit the lamp and peered at him. "You really are Master Su!" she said, helping him to his feet. "But why are you in such a state?"

Jishi told her what had happened that evening.

"You've suffered a shock," she said. "I said some offensive things just now. I hope you'll forgive me." She began kowtowing before him.

He quickly helped her to her feet. "I just hope you'll take pity on me and let me stay here until dawn. I'd be ever so grateful."

"I'm the only one at home, but the compromising situation we find ourselves in can't be helped. I'm only afraid that when you leave here you'll fall victim to some murderous scheme. I have an idea that would allow you to disguise yourself and also get home safely. Would you be willing to try it?"

"What is it?"

"My father loves to put on plays, and we have all the actress costumes here. Let's dress you up as a woman, and at dawn you'll be able to deceive the maids. Just get into a sedan chair in here, draw the curtains, and go straight back to your compound. Wouldn't that be a good solution?"

Jishi was delighted with the idea. "I've always wanted to be a girl, and today I shall get my wish. Please go ahead and dress me up."

Shunjie overcame her modesty sufficiently to bring out the head ornaments and fit them on him one by one. Jishi noticed how pretty she was, and felt his passions stirring. She gave him her own satin gown and silk skirt to put on, and he looked the picture of a beautiful girl. She then brushed his hair up all around. As she did so, he put an arm around her shoulders. "Let's look in the mirror together," he said. "Don't you think there's a certain resemblance between us?"

She gave him a stern look. "I took you for a sincere gentleman, sir, and that's why I put all modesty aside. Male and female shouldn't touch—how could you treat me with such a lack of respect?"

Jishi flushed scarlet. "You're right," he mumbled over and over, taking a seat with due respect.

"How old are you, sir?" she asked, clearly embarrassed. "And how many are there in your family?"

"I'm fifteen," said Jishi, "and I have my mother at home as well as a wife and concubine. I offended you just now, and I fully deserved your rebuke. But you were kind enough to save me, and I do need to find some way of showing my gratitude. I'd be willing to act as your matchmaker, if you would like that."

Shunjie assumed that he wanted to marry her and that this was merely an artful way of proposing. "One's father takes the lead when it comes to arranging a marriage. If you want to marry me, my father would never dream of refusing you, but I can't take the lead."

Jishi was filled with respect for her. He sat there until dawn, when Shunjie sent a maid out to hire a sedan chair to "take this lady to the Su compound on Haoxian Street." The maid, who had no idea what was going on, called in a sedan chair and Jishi stepped into it after expressing his thanks. Shunjie's passions were aroused. "My father will be back before long," she whispered, "and he will certainly come to see you. If you have something to say to him, you might as well say it to his face." Jishi nodded in agreement.

The bearers took him straight to the Su compound, where they said that their passenger had come from the Wen family to see the mistress, and Jishi was carried through the inner gate before stepping out of the chair. Huiruo and the others were astounded—until they heard his explanation and realized that

Scorpion-like is human friendship;
Beware the shaft behind the smile.

Let us turn to the thoroughly satisfying sexual relations that Mola was enjoying in the superintendent's yamen. After three months had gone by, Aqian, whose womb had been the recipient of frequent watering, gradually developed back pain and a weakness in her legs and also lost her taste for food and drink—she was pregnant, and the superintendent's joy knew no bounds. However, because he had received urgent reports from the various Customs posts and had heard the news of the commander-in-chief's loss of troops and the fall of Haifeng and Lufeng, he concluded that the area's duties were uncollectable and became extremely nervous. Fortunately he had previously submitted a memorial on this very subject. He heard that the governor-general and governor had already dispatched a general in charge of coastal pacification to attack and capture the rebels, and he was on the point of sending another memorial setting out the facts when he received his earlier memorial back again with stern comments. It stated that no excuses would be tolerated, and that Governor Qu Qiang should take counsel and deal with the situation as a matter of urgency. On receiving the rescript, Heh ordered Master Hao to draft a memorial based on the facts and then strolled over to the inner quarters to confer with Mola: "The White-robed Goddess has been most effective in answering our prayers for a son. Do you know of any charm that might cause these rebels to withdraw?"

"Amidha Buddha! Are there such things as rebellions in this peaceful world of ours?" exclaimed the priest. Heh told him about the recent events in Haifeng and Lufeng, which touched on a secret concern of Mola's, and he gave a confused answer: "The stupid fools! They'll soon perish. Why do we need to use the power of Buddha on them? You needn't worry, Your Honor." Heh bowed and left.

On hearing of the turmoil along the coast, Mola thought: I've long had a secret desire to seize the coastal areas. The only question is: who has struck so fast? Huizhou is not important, but if someone else should get possession of Chaozhou, all my hopes would be dashed. I'll seize this chance, while the Chaozhou garrison has been transferred elsewhere, to attack the city. It'll be a case of the old fisherman picking up the prize.[7] That evening he talked it over with Pinwa and the others and told them that he wanted to travel back to the island. The women were all under his sway, and they swore categorically that they wanted to go with him. "Wherever you go, Master, you must take us with you. If you go without us, we'll curse you all day and every day."

"There's no problem about our going together. Tonight I'll leave here and arrange a date for us to start."

He flew up onto the roof, leapt over to the city center, climbed over the Jinghai Gate, and walked along the coast. After he had given the secret password, a ship let down a dinghy that rowed over to him. He gave orders that the following night one hundred soldiers should be dispatched to infiltrate the city. At the beginning of the second watch they should set up an ambush at the right entrance of the Customs building, while forces from outside the city would stand ready to see them back to the ship. He then returned to the yamen and went to Pinwa's room, calling out to her to wake her up. He told her to get the other women to gather up all their fine clothes and jewelry the next day and be ready for a midnight departure.

Next morning Pinwa told the other three, and each of them gathered her things together without letting her maids know. At the end of the second watch, Mola intoned a charm of some sort that sent all of the maids into a deep sleep. He suggested that the women bring Aqian with them, but they weren't willing to do so. He took the money stored in Pinwa's room as well as everyone's personal jewelry, which was worth over a hundred thousand altogether, and moved it to the hall, then faced southeast and gave a deep breath. Suddenly a great wind sprang up that swept all the money and jewelry outside, where it was recovered and taken away. He also told the women to dress up as men and held one under each arm as he leapt out of the window and then repeated the procedure with the other two. After bringing them to the ship, he hoisted five large sails and headed for Mt. Fuyuan.

When dawn came in the city and the maids and servants got up, they found the rooms empty and the four women gone and at once reported the fact to Heh. Astonished, he went straight to the courtyard to see for himself, and then called Bao Jincai in to discuss the situation. "I would suggest you ask the Living Buddha, sir," replied Bao. "I suspect that he may be up to no good."

"How can you possibly call a living Buddha a thief!" roared Heh. "Moreover, what use would he have for women?" Bao did not dare reply, but accompanied Heh to the Buddha Hall, which was utterly deserted. "You were quite right about that priest; his actions are suspicious," said Heh. "Go out and announce that the priest has stolen the customs dues and run off with them. Tell the runners to search everywhere for him. Don't let word get out about the women, though."

As Bao went off to carry out his instructions, Du Chong went with him. Under the eaves to the north of the yamen he found a gourd and a small package and quietly tucked them away.

As Heh's embarrassment turned to rage, he began to shift the blame to Wu Biyuan, and promptly summoned him. "You were the one who recommended Mola, and I'm ordering you to catch him. If you can't find him, you'll be held personally responsible for paying the two hundred thousand taels of Customs dues." Wu Biyuan did not dare to defend himself, but kowtowed and went out and joined the runners in their search for Mola. No trace of him was found.

After three days, Heh called Biyuan in. "Have you caught that priest yet?" he asked.

"I've done everything in my power to find him, but no one knows where he came from or where he has gone. Outside Jinghai Gate a bag was picked up that was full of women's clothing, but I don't know if it came from the yamen or not. If it's part of the stolen goods, the priest must have gone to sea!" He presented the bag to the superintendent.

Heh knew well enough that it contained his concubines' clothing, but he was not prepared to admit it. "Two hundred thousand in dues has been stolen from here, nothing else," he said. "Are you using this to stall for time, in the hope that in the meantime I'll be reassigned to some other post? Since you vouched for the man, you must know where he is. I expect you colluded with him in the robbery!"

Biyuan hastily kowtowed. "I would never dare do any such thing!"

"All I'm concerned about is the fact that you recommended a bandit priest. I mean to recover the stolen goods from you."

"My whole family relies on Your Honor for support. How can I ever afford to repay the money? I beg Your Honor for a special act of mercy."

"I can't *stand* that sweet talk and smooth manner of yours!" He ordered Biyuan to hand over his treasurer's seal and sent the magistrate of Nanhai to confiscate his property at both yamens and consign it to the treasury. Although Biyuan banged his head resoundingly on the floor, Heh took no notice of him.

Let us stop here. Read on in the next chapter.

Chapter XVI
Reunion, as Qiao rejoins her lord
Justice, as Shangguan punishes scoundrels

Wu Biyuan had been struck by a sudden calamity. Heh wanted to strip him of his office and confiscate his property, but fortunately for Biyuan, Bao Jincai went down on his knees and pleaded for mercy on his behalf. Heh acceded, and for the time being did not remove Biyuan's seal of office, but set a deadline for the recovery of the stolen property. He also expelled Biyuan's daughter from his household and gave her father permission to sell her in order to help make up the stolen money. Biyuan kowtowed before him in tears, and then brought Qiao and Yeyun back to his river police yamen and explained the situation to his son. Daiyun was scared out of his wits; he had no idea what to do, beyond suggesting that his father try to implicate a few of their enemies and force them to repay the money. Biyuan, however, had a modicum of sense and paid no attention to his son; he simply searched out all the money that Daiyun had in the house, which came to about ten thousand taels, and took it to the treasury. He also fetched his own life's savings, which brought the total up to thirty thousand. First of all, he sent Bao Jincai two large pearls and four gold bracelets in the hope that he would persuade the superintendent to extend the deadline. Bao knew there was every reason to deplore the punishment meted out to Biyuan, and he was also on good terms with him, so he argued the case strongly in front of the superintendent. "Wu Biyuan didn't really conspire with the priest, and it's quite true that the priest has gone to sea. These thirty thousand taels represent Biyuan's salary over the past seven or eight years. Now all of a sudden he's lost the lot, and he's worried to death! Because he's so attached to his little post, he's trying his hardest to complete the payment. If Your Honor removes him from his position, he'll be desperate enough to appeal to the governor, and Governor Qu, because of the penalty he received, is just looking for something to accuse us of. You may not fear him, Your Honor, but you'll end up as a public laughing-stock. In my humble opinion, you should graciously commute some of the payment, get Biyuan to contribute a bit more, and then reassess the situation."

Heh pondered the suggestion for some time. "I see that he can't come up with very much," he said at last. "I'll reduce the sum by half and have him remit twenty thousand within the next three days. The remaining fifty thousand is to be paid in full by the end of the year. This is a special act of mercy on my part." Bao told Biyuan, then took him in to kowtow in gratitude before the superintendent.

Biyuan returned to his yamen and talked the matter over with his wife, Mistress Gui. She brought out her own private savings as well as her clothes and jewelry which, when put together with the contents of their daughter-in-law's room, came to only a little over four thousand. He also called on the traders as well as the clerks of the various Customs posts and asked them for loans. Because he had always been friendly with them, and also because he still had his seal of office, he received contributions from all quarters totaling another three thousand. But there was nowhere he could go to find the remainder. When he returned home that evening, Mistress Gui happened to be drinking wine with Qiao, and they both got up to greet him. Biyuan's face was the picture of fury as he said to his daughter, "It's all because of you, you ungrateful little hussy, that I've been so badly hurt! Now he says I should sell you, but as an official, how can I possibly sell my own daughter? What's more, you may be good to look at, but you're no good for anything else! Why would anyone want you?"

Qiao gave a faint smile. "When did I ever get you into trouble, Father? At first, you told me to worship the Living Buddha. Thank goodness I didn't do as you said! If I had, I'd have gone off with the other women and that priest. Then I'd really be collaborating with bandits, and you'd really be in trouble!"

Biyuan was startled. "Who did you say fled with the priest?"

"You mean you don't know? The superintendent's angry because the priest abducted his four concubines, and that's why he's been hunting for them so furiously. The truth is, they didn't steal very much of his money."

"So that's what happened! Then that package that was found the other day must have been part of the stolen property! The trouble is that we come under his control, and there's nowhere we can go to protest this injustice. I'm faced with a three-day deadline, and I'm still thirteen thousand short. How can I help being worried?"

"You don't need to repay the money, you know, but if you insist on doing so, there is somewhere you can borrow it."

"What would a girl like you know about such things? If it wasn't to borrow money, why do you think I've been running around all day? But thirteen thousand—where am I going to find someone who'll lend me as much as that?"

"Have you tried Daiyun's brother-in-law in the Su family?"

"I did think of it, but Daiyun has offended him on several

occasions, and he's driven your sister-in-law back to the Wen household, so our relationship with Su is broken beyond repair. The other day your brother was even thinking of taking him to court! Actually I don't think he's treated us at all badly. I've still not returned the three hundred taels that he lent me last year, and he's never once mentioned it. But I'd be too embarrassed to go and ask for another loan."

"I'm not being shameless when I suggest this, but just consider you're selling me. Send me to the Su household, and I'll guarantee you a loan of ten thousand or more with myself as surety. I've gotten you into trouble in the past, but this would be a case of selling myself to save my father."[1]

"My dear child, if you really can save me, I'll consider that what happened in the past was all due to my senility, and that your talents were wasted. In the future I'll depend on you to correct me when I do anything wrong! I'll send you over there tomorrow, but whatever you do, see that you please him, so that he's willing to lend me the money. It doesn't matter if it takes a day or two."

She flushed. "I'm only trying this because there's no alternative. But it would never do to let the superintendent know."

"I understand. Tomorrow I'll write a secret note giving the date and hour of your birth and add a card with 'Visit to a Relative' on the outside. No one will ever know." That night Biyuan tried to make amends with his daughter, and after he had drunk his fill, they parted.

> He gave up his daughter for a promotion;
> He lauded a priest in order to fawn.
> The priest went off, and the daughter came home;
> Now he's happy to bear the public's scorn.

Meanwhile, Jishi, having escaped the trap set for him by the Zhu brothers, had been living quietly at home. The twenty-fourth of the seventh month was his birthday, but because he was in mourning he did not bother any of his friends and relatives. Instead, with Huiruo, Xia, Pearl, and Belle he took turns playing host at a series of parties. On one day of cool autumn weather it happened to be Xia's turn. She prepared some yellow mandarin and white oranges, fresh late-crop lichees, fresh longans, and the like, and everyone gathered in the west courtyard. "Today you've struck a poor hostess," she said, "one who's not providing anything to go with the wine. I shall need to get our two young ladies as well as my sister to compose a few more good poems, so that our session won't be dull."

"Good wine goes with bad poetry, but when it comes to fine food only fresh fruit will do, that's clear," said Jishi. "Let's take fresh lichees as our topic, with no restrictions as to form or rhyme. The poems we wrote on withered lotus flowers the other day were too plain, while those on the new chrysanthemums were too ornate—none of them quite suited the form. Today we'll have to be a little more careful."

"We're all beginners, anyway," said Pearl. "We'll just have to do the best we can. You're the one who will have to decide."

"Let's drink a few cups first to liven things up," said Xia. "If your poem turns out to be no good, sir, so long as we still have that actress's costume from the other day, you can put it on and we'll consider you a woman." Everybody laughed. The maids poured out the wine, and then each of them drank three cups, after which the writing materials were distributed.

"Mine's a seven-word quatrain," said Jishi. "I couldn't help being rather slapdash."

On Fragrant Hill I found a picture—
Membranes of silk and skin of jade;
Pink and white are Beauty's fingers;
From Changle it comes, a surpassing taste.

"That sort of poem just isn't effective," said Xia. "It's not specific enough in its description, nor does it imply anything beyond the words.[2] It's not worthy of the food I'm offering you."

"I was only trying to get a better poem out of you," said Jishi. "Why do you have to be so critical?" He then looked at Huiruo's contribution, which consisted of two quatrains:

In slender fingers, pure of taste and hue;
On a dish of ice like crystals sparkling;
Don't say this province is short of marvels—
This heavenly fruit has claimed first place.

Red silk, crimson snow, gorgeous tapestry—
It makes those western grapes seem commonplace;
Once you discover its genuine flavor,
The Cai's guide and Bai's painting could be both deleted.[3]

Xia's contribution also consisted of two quatrains:

Swift horsemen have come often to the south;
A new play blames Guifei for the lichees.[4]
I wrote a "Lament on a Dangling Hairpin,"
And sought not a smile from the mundane world.

Despite the Chens' Purple, the Songs' Fragrance—
Devotees say Eighteenth Daughter is best.[5]
If gentle rain and dew can bring forth fruit,
People will say it's the champion of all.

"It's elegant like the topic, and full of the right kind of tribute," said Huiruo. "Mine can't help seeming wretchedly poor by comparison."

"Hers are fresh, while yours are exquisite," said Jishi. "I doubt that there's a place for me amongst you women. Let's see what my sisters have written."

"We've recently been reading Wei-Jin poetry," said Pearl, "and we've cobbled together a few lines. I don't know if there's any resemblance, but please tell us, all of you, what you really think."

Pearl's was in two verses:

Then there is the lichee,
Like syrup, like honey,
Treasured in Lingnan,
On a par with longan.

Then there is the lichee,
With its flowers and fruit,[6]
Be gracious to a princely man,
Constant and serene.[7]

Belle's was an old-style poem:

Richly grows the garden fruit,
Erect and tall the trees,

Both sturdy and exquisite,
Dense leaves damp with morning dew.
As the tides turn morn and eve,
The years go around and pass.
Flowers in the spring, fruit in summer,
Uneven they hang without number.
Like bright fabric and pearly ornaments,
Their skin truly appealing.
Newly red, you part them with your hands,
And hold them delicately in your mouth.
Their color and scent truly unchanged.
Their liquor, sweet, spurts forth.
I'll support them with a new poem,
And laud them with a rhapsody.

Both Huiruo and Xia were full of praise: "Your poems truly echo the *Poetry Classic* itself! They don't just follow in the footsteps of the Wei-Jin poets!"

"Now, stop all this wild talk, and let me give you a fair appraisal," said Jishi. "Belle's description is close and detailed and could pass for a moment as like Six Dynasties poetry, but Pearl is trying for a superficial likeness to the *Classic* when what she writes merely suggests the 'Airs of the States.'"

"The airs, the odes, and the hymns—are they different forms, then?" asked Pearl.

"Of course they are! Superficial scholars held that the airs and odes were distinguished in terms of their social level.[8] 'The Wine-millet' is among the airs, and those scholars maintained that the ruler had declined to the level of a feudal lord and that was why the Sage relegated that particular poem to an air. What they didn't realize is that the social level of the royal house was absolutely no reason for the Sage to relegate the poem—that was a mistake made by the writer of the preface.[9] In editing the *Classic*, the Sage referred to the terms airs, odes and hymns, which are merely the forms that the ancients used in writing their poetry; the distinction between emperor and feudal lord had nothing to do with it. What the Sage called the airs came from ordinary language, the language of the common people, of those in menial occupations, of women and girls, and it was simple and easy to understand.[10] He called others odes, because their diction was elegant and graceful, and he called still others hymns, because they lauded the emperor's achievements and virtues. As we look at the airs, we see that they are in three or four verses, each of which has only a few lines, and among the verses there is a great deal of verbal repetition. 'Tree with Drooping Branches'[11] is in three verses, forty-eight words in all, but only eight of them are not repeated. 'The Plantain'[12] is the same. 'Deep Rolls the Thunder'[13] is in three verses, with seventy-two words in all, only six of which are not repeated. The expression 'Well, all is over now' is repeated three times in 'The Northern Gate'[14] and 'She was to wait for me at Sangzhong' three times in 'Sangzhong.'[15] This kind of example could easily be extended.

"The odes, however, are different, no doubt because they were written by gentlemen, but there is still a distinction to be observed between the lesser and the greater odes. The lesser odes, although elegant and refined and not duplicating the form of the airs, still contain repetition and, odes though they are, exist on a lower level than the others. The poems, though elegant and refined, do not rise to the level of simple dignity. As for the greater odes, only someone deeply versed in the Way can speak of them. The airs and the odes, greater and lesser, all speak of the ruler's good and bad qualities and contain either praise or condemnation. The hymns have praise but no condemnation; like the poems of later times written at the emperor's behest they set forth his merits and virtues. This is how the airs, odes, and hymns differ from one other."

"Your discourse on the airs, odes, and hymns is something we've not heard before," said Xia. "I expect it comes from the work of Master Li."

In the midst of this high-flown discussion, a maid brought in word that the daughter of Treasurer Wu wanted to see the master and mistress, and that her sedan chair had already passed through the inner gate. Jishi was startled. Qiao was in the superintendent's household, he thought; how did she ever get out? And why has she come here? Hurriedly telling Xia to go and welcome her, he had his two sisters keep out of sight for the time being. Before long Qiao came in holding hands with Xia, while Yeyun followed with the maids. As soon as Qiao saw Jishi, she kowtowed, bobbing up and down, the tears starting from her eyes. Almost overcome with sadness himself, Jishi hurried to help her to her feet. "My dear, how did you manage to get here?" he asked.

Qiao told Yeyun to hand Jishi her father's letter as well as the card and horoscope, and as he read the letter, his joy was mixed with sadness. "I am grateful for your father's kindness," he said, "but there's one thing that troubles me: how could I bear to demean you like this?"

"If I'm able to depend on you as a husband, I shall not be ashamed to offer myself to you. I beg you not to reject me as unworthy. I will be deeply grateful."

She then asked Huiruo to accept her kowtows, but Huiruo refused again and again, demurring for a long time before finally accepting half the number. Qiao also asked Xia to accept her kowtows, and Jishi told them to kowtow to each other. He then asked Xia to take her to pay her respects to his mother, his father's concubines, and his sisters, before bringing her back. He assigned her the rooms opposite Xia's, transferring two maids to wait on her, and then held another banquet at which they drank heartily and enjoyed themselves. In the evening he went to Qiao's room, and each of them told the other many of the things that had happened since they parted, shedding a few emotional tears in the process. Only then did Qiao bring up the question of the loan to her father. Jishi responded generously. "I'll go over there myself tomorrow," he said. "You stay here with us, and in the new year, when the mourning is over, I'll choose a date for our wedding. I'll tell your father and let him decide." Qiao was overjoyed, but Jishi went back to Xia's room to spend the night.

The next morning he told his men to draw the money and went himself to the treasury, where he first thanked Biyuan, then handed him the money and told him of his plans to marry in the spring. It goes without saying that Biyuan was most solicitous of his visitor. Before returning home, Jishi also paid his respects to Mistress Gui.

Biyuan sent the money in the same day. Heh ordered him to pay the rest promptly; if he deliberately delayed, he would definitely lose his position. Biyuan promised to do so.

> He's safe for now from immediate danger,
> Small comfort to a heart that's full of grief.

Let us turn back to the Zhu brothers. After their futile pursuit the other night, they came back and submitted Mistress Ru to a close questioning. She simply told them that she had been asleep when for some reason Jishi had left her. She then rounded on her husband for shaming her and began hunting for a knife or rope with which to end her life. Lihuang was forced to change course and console her over and over again. He also had to pay several taels to get rid of the men who had been hired to catch Jishi in adultery. For these actions he put all the blame on Guanglang, who replied, "Your wife disgraced herself to no purpose and you lost some money, but you're not going to let matters rest there, are you? If we can't succeed by the soft approach, we'll just have to try the hard one. Let's all do our best to pry out his personal secrets and then bring suit against him. There's nothing a rich man fears so much as being taken to court, and you can be sure that he'll coming begging to be let off."

Having settled on a plan, they spent every day looking for something to accuse him of. This happened to be the time when the robbery at the Customs yamen came to light, and when they heard that Wu Biyuan had given his daughter to Jishi as a concubine, they realized that Daiyun would have opposed that arrangement and went to the river police yamen to see him.

Daiyun had only recently recovered, and he sent out word that he was not receiving any visitors. They replied that they had an important matter to discuss with him, and a servant ushered them in. "Congratulations on your recovery," said Guanglang. "We've come specially to wish you well. I wonder how that matter with the Customs turned out."

"That was all my father's stupidity. We never embezzled any money, so why should we have to repay it? And even if we did have to repay it, there are other ways of doing so. Why go to the length of giving my sister to young Su? It's a disgrace!"

"With anyone else it wouldn't matter," said Lihuang, "but young Su helped young Shy pick a fight with you. And now that your sister has been given to him—think what that makes you! I don't know how you put up with it!"

"Well, that's the way it is. In any case I can never approach the Su household, and my relationship with the Wens is over. My family has to pay fifty thousand taels, which is more than my father can come up with. When I get my strength back, I'm going to work off my anger by bringing charges against the Su, Shy, and Wen families and forcing them to pay back the money."

"That's definitely something you ought to do," said Guanglang. "If you hadn't brought the subject up, we would never have dared to mention it. Your charges would naturally be brought before the superintendent; just ask him to contact the prefect of Guangzhou. The Nanhai magistrate is a notorious money-grubber, while the Panyu magistrate is a friend of the Sus—don't fall for any of *their* tricks! We, too, were planning to bring charges before the prefect, but out of respect for you we felt we should inform you first."

"What would the charges be?" asked Daiyun.

"Your father gave his daughter to him, so isn't he guilty of taking a concubine during the mourning period? If he's charged, he'll not only be ruined, he'll be stripped of his rank. And we'll be credited with giving you a helping hand."

"Excellent!" said Daiyun. "You don't need to worry about offending me. Go ahead and press charges."

Now that all four of them saw eye to eye, Daiyun invited his visitors to stay for drinks.

At this point Bangchen returned to town with a large quantity of goods for his shop. He also brought Jishi such things as Duanxi inkstones and dragon beard mats. Jishi accepted them and invited him to stay for drinks. As they sat together, he said, "I've heard that your daughter isn't engaged yet. I'd like to find a wife for Cousin Shy, and I was wondering if you'd agree to the match."

"I wouldn't dream of opposing any instruction from you. The only problem is that my wife is dead, and I shall need go home and discuss the idea with my daughter."

"I'm acting for Cousin Shy in this matter. You must make that clear to her first."

Bangchen took his leave and returned home. "You're no longer a child," he said to Shunjie. "Today I visited the Su house and Master Su proposed a marriage for you, but you're the one who will have to make the decision."

"What did Master Su say?"

"He said he wanted to act as matchmaker for Cousin Shy, and I agreed."

Shunjie said nothing, but the tears streamed down her rosy cheeks.

"If for any reason you're unwilling," said Bangchen hastily, "don't hesitate to say so. Just now you were all smiles. Why these tears all of a sudden?"

"I don't have anything to hide, but I might as well tell you what happened." She proceeded to give her father a detailed account of how Jishi had hidden in her room.

"I see. We don't need to go into the Zhu brothers' treacherous behavior, but since you didn't accept Master Su's overture, he naturally cares for you and respects you. He wouldn't want to demean you by making you his concubine. Moreover, he already has a number of women. In the Shy family, Master Su is in charge now—it's not the way it used to be. Personally, Yannian is not unrefined, and as his wife, you'd live well. Don't get the wrong impression." Shunjie thought it over for some time before accepting.

Bangchen sent someone to tell Jishi, who informed Yannian and chose a date for the delivery of the betrothal gifts. All of the jewelry and other valuables, costing a thousand taels, were provided by Jishi, and when the betrothal gifts were delivered, it was the Su family's servants who delivered them. The opinion on the street was that Yannian had married up in society. Because the Zhu brothers were at odds with Jishi, Bangchen did not tell them about it, nor did he invite them to the wedding feast.

A few days afterward Qu and the Zhu brothers lodged an accusation at the prefect's yamen. Prefect Mu Yong had been promoted to the Nanshao circuit, and the new prefect, who had been transferred from Zhaoqing, was Shangguan Yiyuan, a graduate of both civil service examinations. He was a scrupulously honest official, one whose judgments were rendered with a keen intelligence. Common folk who were content with their lot he cherished like his own children or grandchildren; the law-abiding gentry he respected like teachers or friends; but as for cunning rascals, toadying, self-seeking local officials, and shameless licentiates and Academy students, they were thorns in his flesh, and he did his best to eliminate them in accordance with the law. He read the accusation:

> The filers of this lawsuit, Zhu Zhonghuang and Zhu Li-huang, request an investigation into a case of remarriage during the mourning period and of neglect of Confucian doctrine. We two brothers were friends with the senior licentiate Su Fang. In the first month of this year, his father, the salt inspector expectant Su Wankui, died, but Su Fang failed to follow the rules of mourning and instead indulged in drinking and whoring. We offered him our sincere advice and exhortation, but he took not the slightest notice. Then suddenly, on the eighteenth of last month, he took the daughter of Wu Biyuan of the river police as a concubine, and again, on the fifth of this month, he arranged to marry the daughter of Shr Bangchen, also as a concubine. Our friendship with him was one of moral principle, and time and again we tried to persuade him to cease this behavior. But he relied on his wealth to disregard all decorum and was moved to anger by his feeling of shame, uttering intemperate threats and directing his brutish servants to give us

a savage beating. We had to crawl home, as our fellow student Qu Guanglang will attest. We were most distressed that Su Fang took two concubines one after the other when his mourning had not yet lasted a full year and then met our sincere advice with insults, choosing to ignore the facts of the case. We entreat Your Honor to personally investigate and deal with this matter in order to uphold Confucian doctrine and have the case serve as a warning against extravagance and license. Gratefully submitted.

By the time he had finished reading it, the prefect knew that it was a case of defamation of character following a failed attempt at extortion. He was about to reject it when he recalled that recently Customs had issued a general directive about the recovery of the stolen goods, and so he appended an order directing the department to put together a case and assemble the plaintiffs, defendant, and witness to attend a hearing within the next three days.

After the accusation was accepted, Zhu Zhonghuang sent a message to the Su house that contained a good deal of threatening language. It concluded by saying that the person who had caused the problem should be the one to correct it, and if the master would put together several thousand taels, the affair would be over and done with. Jishi replied, "Since the case is before the prefect, we'll naturally have to look to him for a decision. My honorable brother need not concern himself." Later a runner brought the summons, and Jishi wined and dined him and gave him forty taels. The runner thanked him, and then went in order to the Wens, the Shrs, and the Shys, each of whom offered him presents. Only the Zhus and Qu had nothing to offer and found themselves locked up in the duty room to await questioning.

Jishi knew that the two cases would be tried together, and he went first to the Wus to call on Biyuan, who was highly embarrassed.

"The little swine deceived me over this. I've already notified the superintendent, and today I sent a man to the prefect's yamen with a submission. Don't worry; I still have some self-respect, and I'm certainly not going to implicate any of you."

He showed Jishi a draft of his submission to the prefect. It simply stated, "I'm a lowly official, and I have no money deposited with relatives. My son Daiyun favored a concubine over his wife and drove the wife out of the house. Animated by resentment, he then brought false charges. I beg that he be punished as a warning to others. As for my daughter, I followed the personal direction of the superintendent in selling her, and I sold her to Su Fang as a maid. He has not taken her as a concubine."

Jishi took his leave of Wu Biyuan and went home. Later he went to the Panyu magistrate's yamen and gave a truthful account of the incident from beginning to end, asking the magistrate to pass the information on to the prefect. Magistrate Ma remembered Jishi from the farewell for Director Shen and knew him to be an honest student, and so did not decline the request, but promised to look after his interests. The situation may be described as follows:

> When the flames reach the pig's head, the pork is done;
> When friendship is brought to bear, the case is won.

Governor Qu of Guangdong was a man with an excessive quantity of moral rectitude but a conspicuous lack of ability. He also had a stubborn crankiness that came from his obsession with examination essays and the like. The places to which he was posted bristled with problems, but he had no idea of what to do about them. He had received an imperial reprimand because of the superintendent's memorial claiming that pirates were running rampant throughout the province, and he was itching to settle the score. Later, when trouble broke out along the coast, he could have joined the governor-general in a memorial, but he heard that the superintendent was writing a second memorial based on the facts and realized that his own position could be in jeopardy. So instead he sent men out to uncover any misdeeds that the superintendent had committed.

On this particular day members of the provincial government, prefects, and magistrates all came to his yamen, and Governor Qu questioned the prefect and the two magistrates responsible for the administration of Guangzhou. Magistrate Qian of Nanhai county, catering to the governor's wishes, gave a detailed account of how Heh had brought pressure to bear on the traders and raised duties by twenty percent, demanded more money from standard practices, driven a customs clerk to his death, chosen prostitutes for himself, and invited a monk to pray for a son; later, when the monk stole money from him and fled, the superintendent had insisted that Treasurer Wu Biyuan make up the loss. Governor Qu had the list of charges recorded, and then asked Prefect Shangguan and Magistrate Ma, "Is what you have heard about him more or less the same as that?"

"I don't know about the rest of the charges," said Prefect Shangguan, "but the twenty percent increase in duties is accurate enough. There's also a case of 'Hiding stolen goods and forcing repayment' that is currently before my court, but I've yet to hold a hearing on it."

"If there aren't any stolen goods, how can they be hidden?" asked the governor. "Examine him closely. If Wu Biyuan has been treated unjustly, allow him to appeal." The prefect said he would do so and took his leave.

Magistrate Ma visited the prefect and on Jishi's behalf gave him a faithful account of the two matters. "I already knew all that from a river police report yesterday," said Shangguan. "But what has Su Fang's conduct been like in the past?"

"I'm none too clear about that. He's related by marriage to former Grain Director Shen, which is how we came to know each other. But we've never had even a brief note or letter from him."[16]

"That's admirable."

Prefect Shangguan showed the magistrate out and then called in the runners in the case. "Have all the plaintiffs and defendants in the 'Hiding the stolen goods and forcing repayment' and 'Taking a concubine during mourning' cases been brought in yet?"

"Yes, Your Honor. At your request, Master Wu of the river police and Senior Licentiate Su Fang are both here in person and await your pleasure." Prefect Shangguan immediately gave orders that Wu Biyuan should see him in his private quarters.

Wu Biyuan came in, kowtowed three times, paid his respects, and then stood to one side. The prefect offered him tea and said, "Your son testified to the superintendent that you had money deposited in someone's house. Why are you now testifying that you don't have any?"

"How would anyone with a minor office like mine have that much money? Because Master Heh was forcing me to pay, I borrowed money from relatives and handed it over. Half the amount remains to be paid, and the deadline has been extended half a year. Because my son Daiyun did not get along with his wife, he concocted some false charges, for which I hope Your Honor will punish him. My family discipline has been lax, and I beg a favor from Your Honor." He prostrated himself.

"You gave your daughter to Su Fang as a concubine. How did that come about?"

"Superintendent Heh originally wanted my daughter to join

his household and attend on him. Recently, because the priest robbed him and fled, he has been forcing me to repay the stolen money and has even driven my daughter out of the household and ordered me to sell her. Although I have only a minor office, how could I possibly sell my own daughter? Because I borrowed money from Su Fang, I sent my daughter to him. But he was unwilling to accept her and has still not been intimate with her. All of this is a source of great anguish for me personally. I pray that Your Honor will understand."

"How is it that when the priest robbed him and the superintendent told you to make good the loss, you actually did so? Isn't that an admission that you're really in league with the robbers?"

Biyuan kowtowed again. "In the third month Superintendent Heh suddenly put this question to me: 'There's a priest in town who has extraordinary powers and who is capable of miraculous transformations. Did you know that?' Very unwisely I replied by passing on the false information I'd been given that the priest excelled at praying for sons, and Superintendent Heh promptly invited him into his household. The priest then abducted four concubines and took them away to sea. And so the superintendent took a deep dislike to me for my recommendation and ordered me to repay the missing money. Not only did I not conspire to flee with the robbers, the truth is that not very much money was actually stolen from the yamen. But there is really nowhere I can go to lodge a complaint."

"You're far too submissive," said the prefect with a laugh. "You need to bestir yourself, give up your treasurer's position, and return to your old job at the river police. At the same time you should provide a detailed report for your superiors. I stand ready to support you." Biyuan thanked him, kowtowed once more, and took his leave.

Having dismissed Wu Biyuan, the prefect mounted his tribunal and ordered the litigants brought in. By now it was clear to him what had happened. First he called Jishi, who took one step forward and then dropped to his knees. The prefect noted his polite, refined manner and asked, "You're a senior licentiate by purchase, is that correct?"

"Yes. At twelve I started as a student in Panyu county, and at fourteen I became a senior licentiate by purchase."

"Since you're a licentiate, how could you bear to take a concubine during the mourning period?"

"Wu Biyuan and I were related by marriage, and Wu Daiyun was a fellow student. Because Biyuan borrowed some money from me, he sent me his daughter. I didn't dare accept her and politely declined several times, but he insisted, saying that, since we were related, there was no harm in her living with us for the time being. I had no choice but to invite her to stay in the house and live with my mother until the mourning period was over, when we would become engaged. As for Shr Bangchen's daughter, I was the matchmaker in her betrothal to Shy Yannian. Here is a list of betrothal gifts that is available for your inspection. Why would anyone bother you, sir, by gratuitously fabricating such a charge?"

"Well, a young man like you must have done something to offend his friends so badly that they would fabricate charges against him."

"I may be young, but I would never dream of doing anything to offend my friends. But I hesitate to reveal just how cunning those friends were."

"I appreciate the truth above all else. Go ahead and tell me."

Jishi gave a detailed account of the incident in the sixth month when they got him drunk and he managed to escape.

"Since they did this to you, why didn't you bring charges?"

"Mistress Ru allowed me to escape. I was reluctant to involve her in a lawsuit."

The prefect nodded. "Quite right! You may go home now, while I punish them severely for you." Jishi thanked him and left.

The prefect also called in Shr Bangchen and asked him a few questions. Bangchen showed him the list of the presents, and the prefect told him, "You have no involvement in this case. Now go home and abide by the law." Bangchen stepped down.

Next the prefect called in the Zhu brothers and Qu Guanglang and roared at them, "You pack of scoundrels, you brought false charges! Tell me the truth at once about your attempt at extortion."

"We would never dare to bring false charges," said Zhonghuang. "Wu Biyuan's daughter has been sleeping with Su Fang now for over twenty days."

"Wu Biyuan and Su Fang are related," said the prefect. "Surely you'd allow them to associate with each other? Shr Bangchen's daughter is betrothed to Shy Yannian—how can you drag Su Fang into that? You wouldn't forbid Su Fang to act as matchmaker for a relative, would you?"

"Wu Biyuan's daughter is Su Fang's concubine," said Zhonghuang. "You need only ask Wu Biyuan's son, Wu Daiyun, to learn the truth. Su Fang did intend to take Shr Bangchen's daughter as his concubine, and it was only when he saw that we had filed an accusation that he colluded with Bangchen to concoct a list of presents in the hope of getting off. I beg Your Honor to find out the truth by closely interrogating Su Fang."

This answer infuriated the prefect. "Wu Biyuan's the father, Wu Daiyun's the son. You're not suggesting that the word of the girl's father's can't be trusted, are you? Shr Bangchen's daughter is still not married, so how can you charge Su Fang with taking her as a concubine?" He gave the order to his attendants: "Haul these three scoundrels off and give them thirty strokes each!"

Qu Guanglang kowtowed. "I'm just a witness in the case, Your Honor, and I haven't even testified as to the truth of the charges. What reason do you have for beating me?"

"I'm beating you for this reason and this reason only—the fine thing you pack of scoundrels got up to one night in the sixth month." This remark reduced all three men to silence. After they had been beaten, the prefect ordered them transferred to the Panyu county jail, from which they were to be escorted back to their native places. They appealed again and again, but only Lihuang was pardoned.

The prefect also ordered Daiyun to come before him. Daiyun knew that the hearing had not gone well. He walked up, kowtowed, and begged for forgiveness. "Why did you disobey your father's order, secretly slander relatives, and join these jackals in a conspiracy? Haul him off and beat him!" Like the others, Daiyun also received thirty strokes, which raised welts on his back and broke the skin. The prefect ordered the runners to take him to the river police yamen, and told Wu Biyuan to turn him out of the house and send him back to his native place at once. Masters Wen and Shy were not called, and were sent home.

The next chapter continues the story.

Chapter XVII

Wu Biyuan lays his complaint before the censor
Su Jishi flees to Qingyuan to escape danger

⤙⤚

After Jishi won the court case, he told his men to give the runners twenty taels and invited Wen Zhongweng, Shy Yannian, and Shr Bangchen back to his house, where they enjoyed a long drinking session. The next day he went to the Panyu county yamen to thank Magistrate Ma, who told him, "Although Prefect Shangguan is a man of great rectitude, the outcome of this case has to be credited to the governor. Lately he's been eager to find something to use against the superintendent, and that's why the case went so smoothly." Jishi took his leave and visited the prefect's yamen, where he handed in a card expressing his gratitude. He then went on to the Wu household.

Biyuan did not dare defy the prefect's ruling that his son should return to his native place, but he treated the runners handsomely and begged them to ask their superior whether they could wait until Daiyun's welts had healed. He also took note of what the prefect had told him to do. On the one hand, if he didn't bring the charge, he was afraid of the endless complications he would be involved in, but on the other hand, if he did bring it, he would regret the loss of his treasury position. It was a case of "damned if you do, and damned if you don't." Just then Jishi arrived, and Biyuan welcomed him in. "Daiyun was treated unfairly yesterday," said Jishi. "I had already left, and I didn't like to go back and plead for leniency, but I do feel badly about it."

"The swine was out of control," said Biyuan. "The fact is I asked the prefect to punish him, and now he wants to send him to our native place under guard. There's just one thing: I'd like you to persuade the Wen family to let his wife come back and go with him."

"That's only natural, but I wonder how Daiyun would feel about it."

"He's always been so stupid, but of course I'll tell him he has to change his attitude. There's one other thing: yesterday the prefect told me to quit my treasurer's post and return to my original position. He also told me to inform the authorities that the superintendent was unjustly forcing me to pay the dues money; if I did, he said he'd back me up. But when I think how powerful the superintendent is, if by some chance he does make trouble, it's not the high officials who would be affected, just the lowly ones like me. Moreover, if I can't get out of the fifty thousand debt, and if I leave this position, how am I ever going to repay the people I've borrowed money from? What do you think I should do?"

"In my opinion, you would be doing the right thing by bringing the charge. Since you were given a direct order, you can certainly go ahead with it."

While Biyuan hesitated, unable to make up his mind, the lieutenant-governor issued a directive ordering him to return to his river police position; Salt Inspector Xie Jiabao of Shiqiao would take his place temporarily at the treasury. He also ordered Bi Qingru, the records secretary of Guangzhou prefecture, to supervise the transfer. This was the subject of the prefect's report that morning to the governor; in fact he had directed Biyuan to leave his post precisely so that he could inform the superintendent of it. His order providing for supervision of the transfer showed an even greater attention to detail. Biyuan read the directive, then saw Jishi out.

Afterward Xie Jiabao and Bi Qingru arrived and together reported on this new development to the superintendent. Heh was not greatly concerned; he simply issued an order that the fifty thousand taels should be paid immediately. Biyuan consented to the transfer, then handed over the duties of his post. Fortunately, he had not embezzled any money, and Xie Jiabao duly received the documents and accounts belonging to the post, wrote out a receipt, and reported to the superintendent. Meanwhile Biyuan packed up and returned to his original position, where he consulted an experienced clerk. Within five or six days eight documents went out together from the offices of the magistrate, the prefect, the censor, the three high provincial officials, the governor, and the governor-general. Governor Qu arranged the superintendent's misdeeds under ten headings and sent a draft memorial to Hu Cheng, governor-general of Guangdong and Guangxi, for his joint signature.

> If you don't want people to know,
> It's better by far to refrain.
> The general opinion is fair—
> A fool sets his folly in train.

Jishi returned home and spoke to Huiruo about the desire Wu Biyuan had expressed to have Suxin rejoin his son. "It wouldn't suit Qiao's brother, and I fear that Suxin herself would definitely refuse," she said. "Ever since she arrived here in the fifth month, she's been on a prolonged Buddhist fast. She asked Daddy if she could have the Play-with-Flowers Pavilion, and she spends all her time in there practicing the faith. She'd never agree to leave!"

Jishi felt a pang of anguish. "I'll have to tell your father first before we decide what to do," he said. That night he went to Xia's room to sleep, but since she was in the final month of her pregnancy and felt it would be unsafe to sleep with him, she urged him again and again to go to Qiao's room instead. Jishi had long wanted to do just that, but he had been afraid to incur public criticism.

"What are you afraid of?" Xia asked. "You surely don't imagine there'll be another lawsuit brought against you? I'll tell the maids they're not to breathe a word about it."

Hardly knowing what he was doing, Jishi made his way to Qiao's room, where they spent half the night in lovers' talk. We need hardly say what other intimacies they engaged in.

The next day Jishi paid a visit to the Wen household. Zhongweng was not at home, but Chuncai received him and took him into the inner quarters to pay his respects to Mistress Shi. "You suffered the strain of a trial day after day," she said, "and still you put yourself out for us. I heard that the other day that beast from the Wu household got a beating. Perhaps it'll serve as retribution for what he did to my daughter. I also heard he was to be sent back to his native place. Has he left yet?"

"That's precisely why I've come. Yesterday Uncle Wu told me that he wanted Suxin to return and go with his son to his native place, and he asked me to come over here and ask permission. Since your husband isn't at home, perhaps you ought to talk to her about it."

"My husband and I have already discussed it with her, and she's rejected it again and again. She's determined to practice the faith. I think that that Wu beast is so heartless that even if she did go, she'd have a miserable life with him. But she's too young to do what she's doing, and sooner or later she's bound to complain. You've known her a long time. Why not tell her so to her face and see how she reacts?"

Jishi accompanied Mistress Shi into the garden. As they came to the pavilion, they heard the clapping of wooden fish.[1] Suxin was inside murmuring the words of the sutra she was reading, and at sight of Mistress Shi and Jishi she slowly closed the scroll and stood up to receive them. Jishi bowed, and she curtsied in return. They had just taken their seats again when Jishi asked, "What was that sutra you were chanting so devoutly?"

"There's no way I can repent my sins. All I can do is rely on the bodhisattva Guanyin to relieve my pain and suffering. Well, distinguished brother-in-law, why have you paid me this sudden visit?" Mistress Shu explained the reason.

"It's not that I want to meddle in things that are none of my business," said Jishi, "but Uncle Wu insists that if there were ever to be a reasonable solution, I would have to beg you to go back to your husband. I hope you'll give a thought to the feelings of your parents-in-law. Even Brother-in-Law has had a change of heart. When he saw me yesterday, he was ever so embarrassed and asked me to convey his best wishes, so let me apologize here and now on his behalf. Bend a little, for my sake." As he said this, he left his seat and bowed. Suxin saw that he was still the same gentle and considerate person he had always been, and it brought back to her mind all that had passed between them, and she felt sad and wistful, and the tears streamed down her cheeks. After moaning for some time, she finally came out with this remark: "As you wish, Brother-in-Law. My task is done."

Jishi also shed some private tears, then hurried out with Mistress Shi.

A maid set out wine and food. Chuncai joined them, but he thought it too boring simply to drink and wanted to play a literary game. Mistress Shi objected: "I don't know how to play those games. You mustn't make fun of me. Ask the concubines to come out. Wouldn't it be better if all five of us played dice as we drank?"

"That's fine," said Chuncai. "But it's no fun if there aren't enough people. Let's get my wife out, too. She's a very good drinker."

"What utter nonsense!" said Mistress Shi. "With her brother-in-law here, she'd never be willing to come out."

"What's to stop her?" asked Chuncai. "I'll go in and drag her out. If she refuses to come, I just won't sleep with her tonight."

"Stop that crazy talk this minute!" cried Mistress Shi.

Jishi was still chuckling to himself when a maid brought in a package and handed it to him. "This is for you from the mistress," said the maid. "She wants you to take it home and read it, then you'll understand." Jishi slipped it into his sleeve.

"What did she have to say?" Mistress Shi asked the maid.

"After crying for awhile, she wrote something and then cut off all her hair," said the maid.

Mistress Shi and the others were aghast. She at once went in to see her daughter, then emerged and said, "She's set her heart on becoming a nun. Please explain the situation to the Wus." Jishi promised to do so, and then, in low spirits, took his leave and returned home. In Huiruo's room he explained what had happened, and Huiruo, too, shed tears. Jishi then took the package from his sleeve and opened it. It contained a lock of raven hair and several lines in a tiny, standard script that were both tragic and moving:

> We were two innocents, you and I, when I wrongfully received your loving affection. In darkened pavilions and behind closed doors we pursued our frivolous love. Then suddenly I met an utterly irresponsible person and lost my virtue to an unsuitable husband. It is not because I am an aging, discarded wife that I suffer, nor because, Oh, Mother, he played me false.[2] The retribution is of my doing, and whom shall I blame but myself? In recent years I'm so haggard and drawn that I

scarcely look human whose remorse has culminated in illness. I am grateful to you for your kindly advice—it was both generous and sincere. I used to consider myself "a pretty face condemned to a sad fate"[3] and beat my breast over it, but I am not to be compared with the abandoned wife of the Dou family,[4] and I feel even more ashamed of my own complacency. Luckily, my misdeeds have not gone too far, and "if I turn back, the shore is at hand."[5] The willow twigs and water of the Buddha-truth may not be sufficient to wipe away my shame, but they can surely cleanse my mind and banish my cares! With this lock of hair, I thank you. This life is now over!

After reading the message, Jishi and Huiruo sobbed for a long time, and he told her to put it securely away. He also wrote a letter setting out all the facts and sent it to Wu Biyuan, who naturally had to accept the situation. There is no need to go into further detail.

A few days later, Xia gave birth to a baby boy. Because the conception had occurred before her father-in-law's death, the birth did not violate the code of mourning. The news was circulated, and guests filled the house. Since Xia was in confinement, the management of the household was temporarily turned over to Qiao, who was kept busy for several days, through the Bathing of the Baby ceremony on the third day, when the name Desheng was chosen for the infant.

It was also time for Wu Daiyun to set out, and Jishi himself went to see him off and gave him two hundred taels as a parting present. Shameless as ever, Daiyun simply said "Thanks" and pocketed the money.

Returning home, Jishi consulted Xia about Yannian's wedding. "It's only a dozen days away," she said, "and I don't expect that I'll be up by then. Get Qiao to handle it—it makes no difference." He duly asked Qiao to see to the preparations.

At dusk word was brought in that there was a northerner

at the gate with an urgent message to deliver. Telling someone
to bring a lantern, Jishi went out to meet him. The visitor came
forward, kowtowed, and paid his respects. Jishi noted that he was
about seventeen or eighteen years old, splendidly dressed and very
handsome, and suspected that he must have been sent by Jiangshan. "Where have you come from?" he asked.

"Sir, might I ask if we could go somewhere else to talk?"

Jishi took him to the study and dismissed the servants.

"I'm on the superintendent's staff," said the visitor, "Du Chong
by name. I received great kindness from your father. But now you
are in trouble yourself, sir, and I've come specially to explain."

"So you are Du Chong! My father was indebted to you for
looking after his interests. But what is this trouble that you're talking about?"

"Just now I went with Master Bao to see the superintendent,
and His Honor, who had read the prefect's report releasing you
and the other gentlemen, wanted to demand the repayment of
the money. Then he listened to Bao, who told him that the priest
had some connection with you and that he ought also to hold you
responsible for getting him to come back. You'll probably have
runners here tomorrow, and you need to be prepared."

Jishi was taken aback. "Thank you very much," he said. "Please
sit down for a minute." Telling his servants to look after Du Chong,
he dashed inside to talk things over with his family. Alarmed
though they were, none of them knew how to advise him.

He then called Su Xing in and told him about this development.
"Since the governor-general and governor are both in residence,"
said Su Xing, "you don't need to fear a lawsuit from the superintendent. But just as there's never time to cover your ears before
a thunderclap, I'm afraid you'd lose out in the first instance. Your
best course, sir, would be to absent yourself for the time being.

The superintendent won't be able to find you, and he'll surely make a great fuss, but I'll file petitions with the prefecture and the two counties, and then wait until everything calms down before I ask you to come back. Would that be at all possible, do you think?"

"Good idea!" said Jishi. "If I want to keep out of trouble, why shouldn't I leave for the time being? You'll have to take good care of the household while I'm away, though. His Honor Shen has been appointed lieutenant-governor of Jiangxi, and he once invited me to visit him. It would take less than three months to get there and back. I'll go and stay with him."

"In my opinion, sir, it would be better if you hid out somewhere closer than that, so that we servants could bring you frequent messages. If you go too far away, it will be harder for us to reach you."

"But what messages would you need to send over the next few months?" asked Jishi. He told his womenfolk about the suggestion, and although they were reluctant to see him leave, they felt he had no choice.

He told Wuyun to do his packing. Huiruo and the other women were miserable, and Qiao kept on weeping. "I'm the one who dragged you into this," she sobbed. "I'm ready to die to repay you for your kindness, but I doubt that my death would do any good."

"Stop worrying, all of you!" exclaimed Jishi. "The only problem is that the superintendent's runners will be coming here, and they're bound to make a scene—you'll have to resign yourselves to that. But first and foremost, Xia must not have to face any more complications." "It's important that you take good care of yourself," he said to her. His womenfolk all said that they quite understood.

Xia also held a private discussion with Huiruo and Qiao, "The master needs a woman to attend on him," she said. "Unfortunately, we three can't go because our feet are too small, but I've noticed that Qiao's Yeyun is nice-looking and smart and also has natural feet, so she could go with him dressed as a page. In that case, you wouldn't have anyone to attend on you, Sister Qiao, so let me send Chuyao over to you."

"Quite right!" said Qiao. "Let's get Yeyun out here and dress her up as a boy."

In the outer quarters Jishi issued a number of orders. He told Su Bang, Aqing and Awang to accompany him and directed Su Bang's son, Arong, to take over his father's management responsibilities for the time being. Then Du Chong came up and kowtowed. "Now that I've revealed that secret, I think it would be very hard for me to go back to Customs. I beg Your Honor to take me on and let me attend you on your journey." Jishi naturally agreed, then turned and went in. His bags had already been brought out, and Yeyun had been suitably dressed up. Qiao had drawn up the hair on her temples, and she wore her master's turquoise blue cotton gown with a black wool and lambskin tunic, as well as a cap and boots. She came forward and kowtowed.

Jishi was outraged. "I'm not even out the door, and some young lout has the gall to come barging into the inner quarters! Quick, throw him out! And tell Su Xing to give him a good hiding!"

Xia burst out laughing. Only when Huiruo had explained the situation did Jishi brighten up and thank them. He said goodbye to his mother, and all of the women, with tears in their eyes, came out to the inner gate to see him off. The bearers erected the canopy, and Jishi stepped into the chair. They shouted for the city gate to open, and then embarked on a boat. The women who were left behind did not sleep a wink that night. When dawn came, they rose, and Su Xing ordered Wu Fu to lock the main gate. People came and went through the side gates.

That afternoon two runners from the Customs, Zheng Zhong and Li Xin, arrived, and Su Xing invited them to sit down. "Quick, ask Master Su to come out," they said. "We need to see him about something."

"The master left home the other day," said Su Xing. "He's gone to visit Master Shen in Jiangxi. What do you want to tell him?"

Zheng Zhong pulled a warrant from his pocket and handed it to Su Xing. "Since your master isn't at home, what are we going to report?"

Su Xing noticed that the warrant contained the names of Su Fang, Shy Yannian and Wen Zhongweng, and feigned surprise: "What an extraordinary thing! This case has already been tried by the prefect, so why is it being tried all over again? But when officials make a mistake, it's not the messenger's fault. Although the master isn't at home, I'll go and inform the mistress. We must also provide you with some small gifts."

He gave orders that food be prepared for them, then took a turn around the house before coming back to say, "The mistress says we should wait until the master comes home to decide what to do. These twenty taels are intended as tea money for the two of you. Please don't be offended that it's so little."

"Coming from any other family, such a gift would certainly be inappropriate, but we enjoyed a long association with your late master, so we won't argue the point. However, you do need to send someone after your master to get him to come back and deal with this matter. This is serious business. Within two or three days we'll have assembled everyone else. If your master isn't back by then, we'll come and invite you instead."

Su Xing was quick to agree. The two men left and went to the

Shys and the Wens, where they got nothing more than a little more money to take back with them to the yamen.

In court the next day they reported that Su Fang had gone to Jiangxi, that Wen Zhongweng was ill, and that only Shy Yannian had been brought to the hearing. Heh flew into a rage and gave each of them twenty strokes of the rod. He then ordered Wang Xing and Ru Hu to join the two runners in bringing in all of the missing men.

By this time Su Xing had arranged with the Shy and Wen families to submit a petition to the prefect. On hearing the latest news from the Customs, he knew there would be a fearful ruckus, and so he put away for safekeeping all the fine and breakable objects in the central hall. From among the servants he chose a certain Sheng Yong and promised him a hundred taels to take his place before the Customs. He then told everyone to look after the property carefully, while he himself went back before the prefect to lodge an appeal.

Before long the runners arrived. Zheng and Li took little part in the proceedings, just sat and moaned with pain from the beating they had received. Wang and Ru, however, snapped and snarled like mad dogs. When they saw no one was paying any attention to them, they took seven or eight assistants and searched through the entire house, knocking over numerous screens, tables, and chairs. They stormed into the main rooms, searching everywhere but failing to find any trace of Jishi, merely stealing a few odds and ends in passing. On returning to the reception room, they wanted to question the person in charge.

"Our master has gone to visit a relative," said Sheng Yong. "How could he possibly have known about this affair in advance? Every house has its outer and inner quarters, and you're relying on the superintendent's power to run amuck here and steal our belongings. Don't you realize the governor-general and the governor were in residence, there's still the law of the land to reckon with! I'm the one in charge here—and you've bitten off my prick!"[6]

Wang Xing flew into a rage, struck him across the face, and ordered his assistants to put him in chains. He also told the assistants to go to the house opposite and also put Shy Yannian in chains. He then took a seat in the reception room and went into a wild rant in hopes of extorting some money.

At the prefecture Su Xing was waiting for the prefect to ascend his tribunal when he received a detailed report of the ruckus back at the house and set up a cry of protest outside the gate. Prefect Shangguan called him in: "I read your petition yesterday, and I know how to deal with it. Why are you making all this racket?"

Su Xing hastily kowtowed and answered through his tears: "My master is away from home, and at this very moment a dozen men sent by the superintendent are running wild in the house and even, to their shame, intruding into the women's quarters! I was so overcome by the very thought of it that I cried out in protest. I beseech Your Honor to take pity on us and come to our aid, succoring the weak against the strong."

In a towering rage, Prefect Shangguan gave orders to clear the road and, with Su Xing in attendance, went straight to the gateway of the Su compound on Haoxian Street. The few runners who were there saw an official coming in and, assuming it was their own superior, scrambled to their feet. The prefect ordered them held. Telling Su Xing to lead the way, he surveyed conditions throughout the compound, then came out and sat down at the side of the street and gave the order: "Bring those brutes here!"

Wang Xing and Ru Hu kowtowed before him. "We are under orders to detain people for questioning in connection with the payment of Customs dues," they said. "We have an official arrest warrant here."

The prefect glanced at it and gave a sour smile. "You barefaced scoundrels! I've already adjudicated this case. Without the slightest justification you've looted someone's house and gone through all the rooms—what kind of behavior is that? This has nothing to do with the traders' dues, so how can the superintendent issue an arrest warrant? If he can do that, what's the point of having local officials? Haul these men off and beat them!"

"Don't get carried away, Your Honor!" protested Ru Hu. "We're runners for the Customs superintendent, and as such we don't fall under your jurisdiction. I don't think you'd want it to come out that you'd beaten us!"

"Do you mean to tell me that I can't govern the people of this city?" roared the prefect. He flung down all of his tallies, and each man received forty strokes. He then gave orders that they be locked up in large cangues and put on public display.

He also called in Zheng Zhong and Li Xin and was about to beat them, too, when Wu Fu knelt down and pleaded for them: "I'm a senior servant in the Su household. These men, Zheng Zhong and Li Xin, not only took no part in the disturbance, they didn't even say anything. It was those two over there who led the others on to loot the place. Your Honor is an upright official, and I wouldn't dare tell a lie!"

"I shall forgive you for the present," the prefect told the two runners. "But I want you two toadies to go and tell your superior from me that I shall personally deliver this warrant to the governor-general and governor with my final report." He ordered the two men to release Yannian and Sheng Yong and told them: "I have already adjudicated this matter with complete impartiality. If Customs should send any more runners, just bring them to me under guard and I'll deal with them for you." The two men thanked him and stepped down. He then ordered all the other runners to be given thirty strokes each. He also summoned the local constable: "Why didn't you report this incident to me? I'll overlook it this time, but see that you keep a close eye on those two criminals in the cangue. If they should get away, I'll hold you directly responsible for it and also for your failure to report." The constable stepped down. Next Su Xing came forward and kowtowed, and the prefect told him to clear away the smashed furniture and draw up a petition. He then took a sedan chair back to his yamen.

When Zheng Zhong and Li Xin reported back, Heh exploded in anger. He called in Bao Jincai and said he wanted to bring charges against the prefect. Bao, who was, after all, a shrewd and capable operator, advised against it. "As I see it, no prefect would dare do anything as bold and drastic as this," he said. "There must be something behind it. The prefect said that the warrant would be presented to the governor-general and governor along with his final report. The charge of unauthorized use of authority to harass the populace is of small account; what I fear is that the governor and governor-general have already sent in a memorial attacking us on some pretext or other. Only with their backing would the prefect have the nerve to do anything like this."

Heh shuddered. "Let's put that aside for the moment," he said. "Send someone in secret to find out what's going on. When we have his report, we'll decide what to do."

Bao Jincai was nothing if not efficient. Within a few days he had found out what had happened and passed the word on to the superintendent, adding: "The man I sent out said that today an urgent message had come in—Chaozhou has been seized by a priest, Prince Daguang. That priest is none other than Mola, who has appointed four royal concubines. If this affair heats up again, it'll be even worse for us."

Heh was shocked, and lost no time in ordering that the files in the dues case be burned, that the twenty percent increase in customs fees be rescinded, and that the practice of extortion be forbidden; meanwhile he would patiently await the emperor's direction. What a ridiculous figure he cut! Wine and sex no longer served to relieve his anxieties, and he passed the time in a state of dazed depression. Bao Jincai had nothing to suggest—he merely sent someone posthaste to the capital to distribute bribes—and in the panic of the moment he failed to notice that Du Chong had fled.

Meanwhile Du Chong was accompanying Jishi as their party of six passed through Foshan and headed for Shaoguan. The head boatman reported that bandits were running wild throughout the region and that one couldn't travel by night, but Jishi, who wanted to get back as soon as possible, told him to press on day and night, and the boatman didn't dare object. On the second night, at a place near Qingyuan Gorge, Jishi was sound asleep with Yeyun, Su Bang and Awang were asleep in the bow, and Aqing and Du Chong were sitting in the stern. Among the boatmen was an old man, Long Three, who could sing a "Night Travel" shanty. They encouraged him to sing, and as he rowed he sang this song:

> So many stars in the sky, the moon is not so bright;
> So many fish in the pond, the water's a dirty brew;
> So many officials at court, there's scarcely room to stand;
> So many clients she has, she can't recall who's who.

His listeners praised the song, and then he sang a second one:

> A priest and a nun are in bed together,
> ★★★★★★.[7]

A Buddhist novice comes in sight,
And lifting aside the curtain, asks:
"Reverend master, reverend mistress,
Together with that young acolyte
What sort of ritual are you performing?"
The priest replies: "A land-and-water rite."[8]

In the midst of the applause came a sudden burst of shouting, and a number of small craft attacked them. The robbers wounded one sailor and forced their way into the main cabin, while the boatmen escaped by leaping into the water. Terrified, Jishi and Yeyun clung together, not daring to utter a sound. But the robbers had other things on their minds than slaughter—they cleaned out the boat's contents and left without killing a soul.

At dawn Jishi got up, and Su Bang came and said, "You've only just left home, sir, and already you've run into trouble! Jiangxi is out of the question now. But before we decide where to go, it might be best to find somewhere near here to stay while sending home for more travel money."

"You're perfectly right. Go ahead and find us a place to stay." Less than two hours later Su Bang returned to the boat and reported, "There's a family named Bian living less than a mile from here. They're scholar-farmers who have a house with a fair number of rooms.[9] I told them about our situation, and without hesitation they agreed to take us in. They're waiting for us now. You can't find a good sedan chair in the countryside, so I've hired two carts instead.[10] Perhaps you and Miss Yun could make do with them."

With their possessions reduced to a few sets of bedding, what a pitiful sight the six travelers presented as they entered the village and arrived at the Bian household! Yeyun took off her gold bracelets and covertly passed them to Jishi, who told Su Bang to exchange them for cash. At that point Farmer Bian came forward and kowtowed, and Jishi hastily helped him to his feet.

"You don't understand, sir," said Bian. "We don't have money shops in the country. And where would you spend your money, anyway? If there's anything you need, we'll provide it, and you can repay us later." Jishi expressed his gratitude. Borrowing twenty taels, he paid the bearers and sent Su Bang back to Guangzhou by boat. The remaining money he gave to Aqing for incidental expenses.

Bian treated them with great respect. He showed Jishi to a study with three rooms, one of which faced the outside, so that he could rest. He killed a chicken and cooked millet for their breakfast and was personally most solicitous. An embarrassed Jishi asked him to come forward. "Please tell me your name," he said. "I'll certainly make this up to you later."

"My name is Bian Ming, and I have long benefited from your kindness. Now that I've been favored by a visit from you, my only fear is that I won't be a good enough host. How can you talk of making anything up?"

Jishi was startled. "But we've never even met! How can you talk of any kindness on my part? You must be mistaking me for someone else."

"My family have been scholar-farmers for generations. We own fifty mu of uncultivated land in Hua county. My father took out a loan of two hundred taels, but because of a succession of bad seasons, he didn't pay off either principal or interest. This spring you were kind enough to cancel our debt, but I fully intend to repay the principal this winter. I never expected that I'd be able to meet you, sir, and I'm absolutely delighted."

"But that's all in the past," said Jishi. "Meanwhile I'm imposing on you and I need to open a detailed account to be paid off later. No ordinary family can provide for appetites like ours for very long!"

"I wouldn't dream of allowing any such thing," protested Bian Ming. That evening he invited Jishi into the inner quarters, where he had prepared some wine that he asked his womenfolk to serve. Jishi demurred several times, pulling Bian Ming over to sit beside him and telling Yeyun to pour the wine instead. After they had been drinking for some time, a boy of thirteen or fourteen walked in, and Bian Ming told him to come up and bow to their guest. Jishi helped the boy to his feet and asked, "And who is this young gentleman?"

"He's my boy Bian Bi, style Ruyu. Last year he had the good fortune to start school and this year he's continuing his studies with a tutor."

"So he's your son! What a fine, upstanding lad! I'm sure he's very bright." He pulled the boy down beside him and asked him questions about the classics, histories, poetry, and so forth, to each of which the boy gave answers so fluent that they made Jishi feel quite inadequate himself. When the drinking was over, he took the boy by the hand and led him to the study. "With a talent like yours, you shouldn't be burying yourself in the country, you know. I'd like to invite you to come to my house and study together with me. What do you say?"

"Famous men have appeared in every generation since ancient times," said the boy with a smile, "and in general it's been the spoiled offspring of the rich who have lived in the cities while the men of outstanding talent and virtue have lived in the country. Although I'm still very young, I do rather think of myself as one of the ancients. You may do as you please, sir, but I would definitely not presume to go with you."

"But that's just too pedantic!" replied Jishi, also with a smile. "Famous men from ancient times have never come exclusively from either the city or the country. Moreover, those famous wise men and heroes of yours have always started out in the country but ended up at court."

"To distinguish oneself at court—of course that's the proper role of an educated man. But I've never heard of a famous man who ended up in the city."

"You surely don't suppose I want to hold you *captive* in Guangzhou, do you? It's merely to allow you to appreciate things that may seem strange to you, to resolve any doubts you may have, and to profit from other people's good points, that's all. There's also something I'd like to ask your help with. Not long ago a few friends and I established a Fresh Lichee Poetry Club, but the poems we wrote were rather poor. I was wondering if you could advise us?"

"I'm tired of the classics and histories. I'm no good as a poet, but since you've given me a topic, I shall have to do what I can with it." He dashed off the following:

> The hidden plum strives alone for glory;[11]
> Its painstaking spirit is self-assessed.
> Don't mock the country as unproductive;
> Ask it to stand out and surpass the rest.

"'Poetry conveys the poet's aspirations,'" said Jishi. "In the future, Brother, you'll not be second to anyone. Your diction is strong and elegant. You certainly have a talent that will make the nation proud." Ruyu modestly demurred, then said goodbye and went in.

The next day Jishi went back to the schoolroom to meet the

teacher and read Ruyu's examination essays. The teacher proved
to be an ignoramus, a semieducated licentiate, but Ruyu's most recent essays showed classical elegance combined with great vigor. Jishi praised them again and again, and then went back and asked to
speak to Bian Ming: "Your son has a matchless talent and is certain
to enjoy a rapid rise to fame and fortune. I have a sister who is the
same age as he is, and I would like to propose a marriage between
them. I wonder if you would deign to accept my proposal."

Bian Ming was quick to bow. "Sir, I'm completely overwhelmed by this! I'm a mere villager—how can I make a sudden
leap into the ranks of the high and mighty? Whatever you do,
please don't pursue that idea—I fear it would make you look ridiculous and destroy your reputation."

"My mind is made up. You mustn't be overly modest."

Bian Ming kept on making excuses, but he finally had to
accept the proposal. They decided to celebrate the engagement the
following year. Ruyu was called back again, this time to greet his
future brother-in-law.

Jishi had spent three days waiting in vain for Su Bang's return,
and he began to feel depressed. Telling Awang to stand guard at
the house, he and the three others went for a stroll through the
fields. The trees were gradually losing their leaves, the grasses were
withering, and a cool west wind refreshed them. Thanks to those
bandits I've found myself a brother-in-law, mused Jishi, one who
will turn out to be the equal of Academician Li. That puts one of
my concerns to rest—I can inform my ancestors of it without fear
of reproach. But can I ever succeed myself? If I had a talent like
Ruyu's, I'd spend my life as a scholar. Then another thought struck
him: What would I want with fame, anyway? If I can live a contented family life and enjoy myself daily in wine and poetry with
my womenfolk, I will enjoy a happiness that I wouldn't exchange

with the highest in the land. The only trouble is that I don't know how that matter turned out at home. With these thoughts running through his mind, he walked a mile or two without realizing it, and then, when his feet became a little sore, he took Yeyun off to rest by the side of the road. Down the road at that moment there happened to come a dozen mounted men, reining in their horses and proceeding slowly. When they caught sight of Jishi and his companions, one of the men jumped down from his horse. "Where have you come from?" he asked. "And where are you going? Are you a civil or a military licentiate?"

"Our master is a famous senior licentiate from Guangzhou; he doesn't know anything about military affairs," said Aqing. Hearing this, the men dismounted and came forward, then proceeded to drag Jishi, Yeyun, and Du Chong onto their horses. As he held Jishi on his horse, one of them said that their leader had issued an invitation. Aqing ran forward and tried to pull his master back, but the men cracked their whips and raced off.

Chapter XVIII

Vice-president Yuan impounds Heh's possessions
Governor-general Hu withdraws to Huizhou

With Jishi firmly in his grasp, the mounted man galloped off. When Jishi cried out for help, he answered, "Don't worry, sir. We're under orders from our leader to recruit men of talent and learning, and we've come specially to invite you to join us. Provided you're not just posing as a licentiate, and have some genuine talent and learning to offer, you'll enjoy a great many advantages with us."

In no time at all they had traveled over thirty miles. Along the way they ate some dry rations and after a day and a night came to a mountain peak. With its sheer walls the camp was impregnable, and it bristled with armed men. One of the mounted men entered and reported their arrival, after which two men in official garb came out and welcomed them in and invited them to sit down. "May we ask your names?" they began.

"I'm Su Fang, from Guangzhou," said Jishi, his alarm receding, "and these two are my pages. Could you tell me why you've invited me here? I would also like to ask you your names and what positions you hold."

"We are Wang Dahai and Chu Hu, officers on the staff of the Com-mander of Fengle, and it is our duty to guard the northern approach. Our leader is eager to find talented men from through-out the region. In their ignorance, our soldiers caused you needless alarm." He called to his staff to serve wine to the newcomers to ease their apprehension.

At this point Jishi realized that he had fallen into the hands of the Lufeng bandits, and he began to feel apprehensive and tried to excuse himself. "I'm just an ignoramus, I'm afraid—I certainly don't qualify as a man of talent. I beg you, General, to let me go home. Choose someone else instead of me. Otherwise, I fear that you'll be blamed for recommending the wrong person."

"The students who boast about their achievements are the stupid ones," said Wang Dahai. "You're so modest that you must have true talent." He issued an order: "Get a sedan chair ready. I'm taking this gentleman up there myself."

By this point Yao Huowu had already seized Jiazi. Brigade General Zhong Yu, commander of the Chaozhou garrison, led five thousand troops in an attempt to retake the town. Feng Gang was no match for him, so he locked the gates and mounted a resolute defense. Later Qin Shuming and Cao Zhiren of Army Gate Ridge, hearing of the initial achievements of Huowu and Feng Gang, brought their entire force over to their side. Dun'an selected Qin Shuming's sister Shaoying as Huowu's consort, while he himself led Lü Youkui, Qin Shuming and others to the aid of Jiazi, routing Zhong Yu's forces.

At the same time Mola, using light craft attacked and took Chaozhou and proclaimed himself Prince Daguang. Zhong Yu could neither advance nor retreat, and for the time being he had to go into Jiaying and mount a last-ditch defense there. Fortunately for him, Mola, having taken Chaozhou, was perfectly satisfied. He set up a number of palaces and gave himself up to drink and debauchery by day and night. He appointed his four disciples Guardians of the Faith and made his eight fierce chieftains generals, and ceased to concern himself with military matters.

After forcing Zhong Yu to retreat, Dun'an told Qin Shuming and the others to guard the town while he himself returned and prepared for battle. In consulting with Huowu, he gave him this advice: "Zhong Yu has all he can do to defend himself, so there's no need to worry about an attack from the east. But I'm afraid that the governor-general's and commander-in-chief's brigades will both come here. We shall have to step up our defensive measures." It was at this point that a cavalryman came in and reported that General Wang was bringing a man of talent to see them. Huowu was delighted, and told Dun'an to go out and receive him.

Before long Jishi entered the yamen, with Yeyun and Du Chong close behind. He realized he was meeting the leader and went forward and kowtowed. Huowu responded in like manner and made room for him to sit on his left, while Dun'an and the others sat on his right. After Wang Dahai had given Jishi's name, Huowu said, "I'm just a fighting man from Donglai without any refinement to speak of. Now that you've been gracious enough to come such a long way to visit us, Master Su, may I ask what instructions you have?"

"I'm merely a young and ignorant nobody without the slightest talent or ability. I just happened to be going for a walk in the country when I was seized by your men. If you are kind enough not to impose the death penalty, I would be extremely grateful if you'd allow me to return to Guangzhou."

"So your family live in Guangzhou, do they? There's a trader there by the name of Master Su, style Wankui. Do you know him, by any chance?"

Jishi stood up. "He was my father. He died in the first month of this year."

Huowu quickly bowed again. "So you're my benefactor's son? I didn't realize your father had passed away. When will I ever be able to repay his generosity?" His face streamed with tears.

Jishi bowed in turn and helped him to his feet. "I wonder how you came to know my father?"

Huowu told him of the incident in the capital and of his father's generous assistance. "I expect you also know Li Jiangshan of Jiangsu," he said.

"He used to be my teacher, and we're also related by marriage. He went back home the year before last. He's the father of my sister's fiancé. His son has been inducted into the Hanlin Academy, and it doesn't look as if he'll be able to get back to Guangdong." That brought Jiangshan's letter to his mind, and he asked, "Might your personal name be Huowu?"

"That's right. I expect your father mentioned me?"

"No, it was Master Li, in a letter." Jishi produced the latter and read it out.

Huowu heaved a sigh. "He did indeed give me that advice, and I have let him down. How will I ever be able to face him now?"

The others tried to console him. "You're just hiding out here for the moment; if you receive an imperial pardon, you'll be able to repay your debt of gratitude to the court. There's no need to be too concerned." Huowu ordered his men to prepare wine and food and offer it to his guests. He then turned to Jishi, "You have wealth and a good position; whatever gave you the sudden idea of going for a walk in the country?"

Jishi told him about the situation at home, and Huowu was enraged. "What sort of creature is this Superintendent Heh that he dares take the law into his own hands?" he demanded. "To avenge what he's done to my benefactor, I shall raise an army and go and bring back his head!"

"There's no need to be so angry, General," said Dun'an. "The court has laws to deal with the superintendent's corruption. But I doubt that Master Su will be able to stay here very long. Let's send spies to Guangzhou to find out how matters stand there before we escort him home." Huowu agreed, and sent out capable spies on horse and foot, giving them four days in which to report back. After dinner he took Jishi and the others to the residence to rest. He treated them lavishly and settled them in the finest accommodations, and also detailed four of the women in the camp to attend on them as well as two soldiers to stand guard. Everyone took turns hosting them, beginning with Dun'an and Feng Gang.

Four days later the spies reported that all was quiet in the Su compound. The superintendent had been impeached, but the imperial response had not yet been received. They also reported that Commander-in-Chief Ren had attacked Chaozhou from the sea, but that the issue was still in doubt and the governor-general was assembling forces from various quarters. In all likelihood the first month of the new year would see a pitched battle.

Jishi heard this news as he bade them farewell. Huowu realized he couldn't persuade him to stay, and he personally led the other officers in escorting him a long distance before holding the farewell ceremony. Raising his cup at the ceremony, he said, "After you leave us, you must take the greatest care. And if among your friends and relatives there is anyone who can ask the court for clemency and a pardon for my capital offence, I hope you will give a good account of me. I shall be eternally grateful."

Jishi readily agreed. Huowu also gave him four large chests. "I hope you will accept these trifling farewell presents," he said.

Jishi did not presume to refuse. Huowu ordered Qi Guangzu and Han Pu to escort him and his companions by road and then return and guard the ridge pending a transfer in the spring. Jishi bowed and left. He went straight to Pingshan, then parted from the two men and continued by boat to Guangzhou.

Some forty days had passed since he fled. The members of his household, who had been filled with apprehension after receiving reports from Awang and Aqing, were now overjoyed at his sudden return. Yannian had married, and he and his wife came by to pay their respects. All Jishi's other friends and relatives also called on him. And that evening, when he opened the chests that Huowu had given him, they proved to be full of gold and silver, at least a hundred times the value of the gifts that Huowu had received from Jishi's father.

> Return a hundredfold?[1] It matters not;
> It's depth of gratitude that moves the heart.

After Heh Guangda's impeachment, he spent his days plunged in despair. Early in the twelfth month, Aqian gave birth to a son, which afforded him some relief, but suddenly there came a report that two imperial emissaries had arrived. Officials from both provinces would greet them at the number 1 dock, and the superintendent was requested to go there immediately and receive the imperial edict. He set off at once, clearing the road before him, but by the time he arrived the two emissaries had already come ashore and stood facing south while the assembled officials made the nine kowtows and prostrated themselves to hear the proclamation.[2] The emissaries held the edict up high and read it out:

> Imperial edict: The purpose behind the nation's establish-
> ment of the positions of governor-general and governor was to
> unite the civil and military administrations and coordinate the
> general policy. The establishment of the superintendent's posi-
> tion was to increase the nation's taxes and levies and to benefit
> the merchants and the general public. According to a memo-
> rial from Heh Guangda, the superintendent of Customs in

Guangdong, pirates were running rampant, bringing trade to a standstill and leading to delinquencies in the tax revenues. We have already ordered the department concerned to transmit an order reprimanding the governor-general and governor and instructing Heh Guangda that he cannot use this as an excuse for evading his responsibilities. Shortly thereafter Governor-general Hu Cheng, Governor Qu Qiang, and Superintendent Heh Guangda separately memorialized that the coastal access to Huizhou was being harassed by Yao Huowu and others. This was due to the governor-general's and governor's lack of administrative control. Hu Cheng has not been in office long, and we are treating him leniently by removing him from this position but allowing him to continue to serve. Qu Qiang is hereby demoted three ranks and transferred to be the military intendant for Huizhou and Chaozhou, where by good service he may atone for his misdeeds. The governor's duties are to be given to Lieutenant-governor Pan Jin in an acting capacity until such time as a replacement is chosen. In addition, with regard to the ten charges of robbing the state and mistreating the public that Qu Qiang has brought against Heh Guangda, since Qu Qiang has always been scrupulously honest, no doubt the charges are not without foundation. One of whose forebears had achieved great credit, Heh Guangda has never consolidated his reputation. We offered him an excellent appointment, but he has behaved with such a lack of restraint as to betray the kindness that we showed him. We order that he be summarily dismissed from his position, and that the two special emissaries, Yuan Xiu, vice-president of the Board of Works, and Li Yuan, supervising censor of the Henan circuit, deal with this matter justly, and also conduct a search of his yamen for evidence of items that he has embezzled. As for the superintendent's duties, we order Provincial Judge Lian Ming to take them over in addition to his current responsibilities.

As soon as the edict arrives, each of you is to respectfully follow orders and put it into practice.

After the officials had expressed their gratitude with three cheers, the emissaries gave orders for the arrest of Heh Guangda, telling Mu Yong of the Nanshao circuit to stand guard over him. Then Governor-general Hu, accompanied by Lieutenant-governor Pan and Provincial Judge Lian, as well as the prefect and magistrates and various other officials from the city, proceeded to the Customs superintendent's yamen. There the imperial emissaries and governor-general sat at the head of the hall while the other officials lined the sides. First they clapped in irons the people named in the memorial—Bao Jincai, Ma Bole, Wang Xin, and Bu Liang—and drove Heh's wife, daughters, concubines, and maids into a large empty room and locked them in. With Nanhai county runners keeping watch on the rear gate, and Panyu county runners guarding the door to the inner quarters, and the gates of the courtyards all secured, they told the Guangzhou prefect to accompany the Hua county and Xinhui county magistrates in leading their runners in a thorough search of the buildings, a search that took them about four hours. They reported the total figures for each of the various items, and then Imperial Emissary Li took up his brush and recorded them as follows:

Four good luck ruyi of Han jade;[3] six good luck ruyi of Hetian jade; one Guanyin of Han jade two feet tall; one dish of red jade one foot six inches in diameter; three green jade dishes two feet in diameter; 124 disks, trinkets, and miscellaneous ornaments of Han jade; 252 baubles and miscellaneous belt ornaments of green jade; 84 belts ornamented with jade; two pearl bracelets; 22 bracelets of precious stones; four vases of green jade; 28 chiming clocks; 182 foreign-made watches of various sizes; 24 screens of foreign glass; 16 beds of foreign glass; 120 pairs of lanterns of foreign glass; 180 pairs of glass lanterns in a variety of colors; one table of four-inch thick crystal; eight chairs of four-inch thick crystal; 104 hanging screens of foreign glass; 800 lengths each of crimson, blue and black woolen material; 400 lengths each of crimson, blue and black woven fabric; 800 lengths each of crimson, blue and black camlets; 1,000 pieces of Dutch camlets of various colors; two coats of gilded peacock feather; 14 coats of sable fur; 24 coats of fine horse leather; 12 coats of lynx fur; 18 coats of sea otter; 28 coats of black fox; 48 ermine coats; 28 squirrel coats; 84 black and white leather coats studded with pearls; 864 items of miscellaneous male and female leather clothing; 5,113 items of male and female clothing; 1,212 coverlets and mattresses of woven colored-pattern silk and wool; 1,820 rolls of Nanjing satin, Hangzhou silk and silk gauze; 58 pieces of marten fur; 30 pieces of sea otter fur; 800 pieces each of ermine and squirrel fur; 418 foreign rugs and Tibetan carpets; two pearl rosaries; five catties 12 ounces of pearl beads; six red-gold dishes; 12 red-gold wine jugs; 80 red-gold goblets of various sizes; 40 jade goblets of various sizes; 80 cups of foreign glass; 1,200 items of red gold First Graduate ingot-shaped ruyi and fruit-shaped baubles of various kinds; 42,012 ounces of red gold; 12 silver dishes; 24 silver jugs; 800 silver goblets of various sizes; 522,103 ounces of white silver; 450 items of pearl jewelry; 612 items of gold jewelry; 2,500 items of silver jewelry; 582 tables and chairs of sandalwood, rosewood, or nanmu; 2,004 strings of coins; 1,803 gold dollars; 42,008 silver dollars; one white jade chamber pot with beautiful-lady portrait; 18 silver chamber pots.

The emissaries stamped each page of the inventory with their seals of office. Then they examined the dues, and found that the amount in default came to 1,640,400 taels, one qian, six fen, five li. The Panyu magistrate prepared his official residence for the emissaries and invited them to rest there, and the prefect of Guangzhou issued a warrant for the arrest of those named in the imperial edict and interrogated them closely. Since the memorials had stated the facts, how could the charges be anything but true? However, all of the blame was placed on Bao Jincai and the three other men, while Heh himself was judged to have been so addled by drink and sex as to be unable to control his subordinates, with dire results for the merchants and the public. The emissaries asked that the tax delinquency be made up from Heh's private fortune and that any remaining sum be found by confiscating his property at his native place. Their recommendation went up to the Emperor, whose benevolence was as vast as the sky itself and who cherished fond memories of his old servitors. While he had Bao and the others dealt with according to the law, Heh was merely told to stand guard over his ancestral graves and reform his conduct. But all of this belongs in the future.

That day, after the emissaries had completed their investigation, Censor Li remarked to Vice-president Yuan, "I have a relative by marriage who lives here. The other day when we left the capital, my father told me to visit him. Now that we've completed our official business, I should like to do so. Would you be in favor?"

"May I ask what his name is and how he is related to you?" asked Yuan.

"He's Senior Licentiate Su Fang, who was waiting to be called as a witness yesterday. He is to be my brother-in-law. Before I succeeded in the examinations, my father was his tutor. He arranged my engagement, but the betrothal presents have not yet been delivered. My father ordered me to bring some with me, and after this mission is over, probably next year, I'll ask for leave to come back and marry her."

"But of course you must go and see him! I wonder if you'd allow me to serve as matchmaker and drink a betrothal toast?"

"Since you are so gracious, let me bow before you and thank you on behalf of my relatives. Today I'll go and visit them, and tomorrow I'll trouble you to bring the betrothal presents. The day after that we'll set off." He left his seat and began to bow respectfully, but Yuan at once helped him to his feet. "That ritual is for your parents," he said. "I wouldn't presume to respond to it. Off you go, and when you return, we'll enjoy the acting governor's hospitality together." With a flushed face Li Yuan ordered his men to head for the Su compound.

Li Yuan, the son of Li Jiangshan, had received an appointment as compiler before the end of his three-year course in the Study Department of the Hanlin Academy. This year he had been recommended first to the censorate on the Henan circuit, and then to the position of provincial censor. The Emperor had been impressed by his brilliant mind and forthright manner, as well as by his remarkable physique, and had specially appointed him to handle the Guangdong Customs case along with Vice-president Yuan. A messenger had already informed Jishi that Li Yuan was coming to the compound, and a banquet had been prepared at which the decoration reflected both the nuptial and the mourning themes. A servant brought in his visiting card, and Jishi welcomed his visitor into the reception room. Censor Li had all of the colored silks, red cushions, table covers, and so forth that represented the nuptial theme removed, after which the two men kowtowed to each other. "I didn't realize that the imperial emissary was my brother-in-law," said Jishi. "It was very remiss of me not to go and welcome you."

"I was attending to the emperor's orders, and I'm late; please forgive me. I'm afraid I offended you yesterday."[4]

"Not at all. That was by order of the court. I'm infinitely grateful to you for your consideration." Getting to his feet again, he asked after the censor's father and mother. Censor Li also stood up and replied that they were both in good health, and then asked to pay his respects to his prospective mother-in-law. Mistress Mao soon emerged with an entourage of maids and serving women. Censor Li wanted to give four kowtows, but she would only accept half that number before walking slowly back to the inner quarters. After changing into mourning clothes, he kowtowed before Wankui's spirit tablet and then went in to the banquet. In the course of the meal, he said, "My father told me to bring the betrothal presents, and because of the tight time limit imposed by the emperor, I will have them delivered tomorrow. I have invited Master Yuan to act as matchmaker along with Master Wen. Next winter I will certainly have to ask for leave to come back and marry." Jishi agreed to all of these arrangements.

A servant reported that the Nanhai and Panyu magistrates had come specially to wait upon him. Censor Li promptly said goodbye and went out and with genuine modesty begged them again and again to return to their yamens. Jishi also bowed and thanked them for him, and the two magistrates finally left. Censor Li then went to the Wen household and met Wen Zhongweng, the other matchmaker. He thanked him, and on leaving said he would wait for him at the Su compound. He then returned to the residence and accompanied Yuan to a banquet at Acting Governor Pan's yamen.

The next morning Jishi ordered Su Xing to see to all everything, while he himself took a sedan chair to the residence and sent in a letter of invitation and a visiting card. The emissaries invited him in, offered him tea, and engaged him in conversation, after which he took his leave. By the time he returned, Wen Zhongweng had arrived. In the afternoon Vice-president Yuan asked his entourage prepare his visit in the highest permissible standard, and leaving behind his civil and military escort came to the Su compound in a large eight-man sedan chair. All the decorations now reflected the nuptial theme, and he was ushered in with music and song. The betrothal gifts consisted merely of a pearl-studded cap, a jade waistband, a suit of court attire, twelve gold hairpins, twelve pieces of lined palace satin, one hundred pieces of colored satin, eight pairs of palace flowers,[5] plus one object of great rarity that no one else possessed—an order, wrapped in yellow silk conferring the title of "Dame" at the fifth rank. Jishi hastily set up an incense table and invited his mother and sisters to dress in their finest clothes, while the maids and servants were dismissed. He went with the women to the hall, where they gave nine kowtows before accepting the gifts. At the same time Jishi entertained the two matchmakers. The players came on stage and congratulated them, handing over their repertoire, and Vice-president Yuan chose half of the play "A Bed Full of Tablets." After three rounds of drinks, he got up and took his leave, explaining to Jishi, "Your brother-in-law and I have been invited by Prefect Shangguan to visit Mount Yuexiu to see the plum blossom, and I've kept him waiting a long time already." Jishi did not dare to detain him any longer, but escorted him out, and he left with great fanfare. The presents given by Jishi in response were naturally very generous.

The next day Jishi had farewell gifts prepared and waited at the dock with them. In the afternoon the two emissaries embarked, and Jishi sent in his card. Vice-president Yuan accepted only four offerings, but Censor Li accepted them all. He also invited Jishi on board and engaged him in conversation. Jishi ordered his servants to leave them alone together, and Censor Li's men also left. Jishi then told of the letter he had received from Jiangshan in the spring and also of his own abduction to Lufeng and the message Yao Huowu had entrusted him with. Li was astonished. "What an extraordinary thing! I'll keep this in mind, and when I get back to the capital I'll talk to Father about it." By this time the civil and military officials were swarming around them. Jishi quickly said his farewells and then left as the emissaries had the drum sounded for their departure.

He spent the night at home, then next day went and thanked the Nanhai and Panyu magistrates for their visits. He also called on the prefect and sent in a note thanking him for the way he had dealt with the Customs runners. Prefect Shangguan suddenly sent out word for him to come in, and then invited him to sit down and drink some tea. "The other day, when you were away from home, I had those brutes put in cangues for your sake," he said, "but now that Master Heh has gone, why don't you get one of your men to come and submit a petition that they be given lenient treatment and released?" Jishi quickly bowed and undertook to do so. This was a case of Prefect Shangguan teaching Jishi to treat people favorably so that they would not bear him any ill will. Where in the world would you find such a circumspect and thoughtful person as this prefect? Jishi did have such a petition submitted, and the two runners came and thanked him for it.

It was the end of the year, and the farm managers arrived with their rental money to settle accounts. Su Bang was fully occupied, and so Jishi told Awang to take a letter together with some handsome presents to the Bian family of Qingyuan expressing his thanks. The letter told of his return, reaffirmed the betrothal, and urged Ruyu to come into town during the spring to continue his studies. Jishi ordered Su Xing to see that New Year gifts were sent to officials and others. "This year it will be necessary to add gifts for the prefect, for Miao, the registrar of Nanhai county, and for the Shr family," he said. Jishi also went into the inner quarters, where Xia handed him the list of young servants and maids who were of age to marry. Jishi crossed out only one name, that of Wuyun. "Let's not be too hasty," he said.

"She didn't want to go," Xia said, "and now I can see why." Jishi smiled, and sat down and played with the baby.

A maid came in to say that Su Yuan's son, Su Fu, who had been adopted by another family, had gone to the capital in the spring and managed to obtain some kind of position for himself. He had received his appointment papers and was paying a visit home before taking up office next spring. His mother had brought him in to kowtow to the old mistress, the master and the ladies. "Have him come in so that I can take a look at him," said Jishi. Su Yuan's wife brought in a man in his thirties. Jishi stood up, but Su Fu didn't dare go forward; he just knelt down outside the door and kowtowed three times.

"What office did you purchase?" asked Jishi. "Where will you be serving? And when do you set off?"

"I am grateful to you for all your kindness, sir," replied Su Fu. "At the time of the earthquake in Gansu I followed the established practice and bought a rank at the ninth grade, principal class. I've been appointed grain registrar of Jingxi county in Changzhou prefecture of Jiangsu, and I set off in the third month of next year."

"Since Mistresses Shy and Wu are both here, come and take this chance to kowtow to them," said his mother. "Then I'll take you to pay your respects to the old mistress and the mistress."

Sun Fu kowtowed, not daring to look directly at the women. Flustered, Xia and Qiao curtsied and congratulated his mother.

"It's all thanks to the master and to you ladies," she said, before leading her son off.

Let us bring this digression to an end. Before long the last month of winter had given way to the chill of early spring. Governor-general Hu, hearing that Commander-in-Chief Ren had not yet won a decisive victory in Chaozhou, had himself assembled troops from all quarters, fifteen thousand in all, with Adjutant Ba Bu of his own brigade, Brigade Generals Chang Yong and Fan Ruilin, and Lieutenant-colonels Gao Baoguang and Ho Lang, plus over twenty other officers. The newly appointed colonel at Jieshi, Qian Lie, had returned to Guangzhou by sea, and because he had lost his post, he asked to be put in the lead of the advance detachment. The troops held a sacrificial ceremony before setting forth from Guangzhou, and all of the civil and military bureaucracy turned out to see them off. Before long they arrived at Ebu and set up camp there.

The officers guarding the ridge, Wang Dahai and his colleagues, had already received the news and sent a messenger racing off on horseback to ask for reinforcements. Leaving Qi Guangzu behind to defend the pass, the three leaders selected one thousand five hundred men to go down and attack the enemy. Chu Hu urged his horse to the front, and Qian Lie engaged him with his lance; the two men fought over thirty jousts, with neither emerging victorious. Wang Dahai then came up in support of Chu Hu. Ba Bu wanted to show off his ability before his superior, and he rushed out to join the fight, wielding his broadaxe and roaring, "What bandits are these who have such gall? Dismount and submit at once! The governor-general is here!"

Dahai said nothing in reply, but thrust with his lance. Ba Bu moved deftly aside and, raising his broadaxe, hacked at him. He was of unparalleled strength and bravery, and Wang Dahai was no match for him; after eight or nine jousts, he could hold out no longer. Han Pu rushed forward, his sword raised, but Gao Baoguang was there to engage him. Governor-general Hu ordered a general advance, and Fan Ruilin and his troops surged ahead. Chu Hu and his men could not withstand the charge, and their beaten troops fled back. Governor-general Hu then ordered an attack on the pass, but cannon balls and rocks rained down upon them, and they were forced to retreat to their camp, where they drank to celebrate their success.

Having lost a battle, Wang Dahai returned to the pass and discussed the situation with the other officers. "We're outnumbered, and the reinforcements haven't arrived. We shall need to take great care night and day in guarding this place."

"You're right," said the other three. "We asked for reinforcements the day before yesterday, and they should be here by now. Let's send another man there on horseback to urge them to hurry. If this pass is lost, everything is lost!" They took turns inspecting the defenses and the following day did not venture down the mountain, but simply endured the enemy's taunts.

On the afternoon of the second day, their scouts reported, "Our leader himself is bringing a force here, together with the strategist. The vanguard, commanded by Generals Lü and Qin, has already reached the ridge." Dun'an had realized that the governor-general would be there in person and that they would need an able and experienced officer to lead them, so he had sent Ho Wu to Jiazi and summoned Qin Shuming to join the force; that was why they were two days late. When Wang Dahai and his colleagues heard that their leader himself was coming to direct the fight, they fairly leapt for joy. Morale soared, as the men lined the road to welcome Huowu and his men to the pass. After greetings had been exchanged, they told how they had lost over four hundred men in the fighting two or three days before.

"Both victory and defeat are to be expected in war," said Huowu. "Don't worry about it. Tomorrow we'll go down and engage them again and find out their deployment. Then we'll ask the strategist to produce a plan."

The next day Huowu gave orders to open the pass, and eight thousand foot soldiers and cavalry poured down the mountain and formed up at the bottom. The two armies now faced off, each arrayed in a half circle. Governor-general Hu noticed the Fengle

Commander's banner and gave orders to his men: "The chief bandit is here in person, and that will save us a lot of trouble. All you officers must do your utmost to capture him." The words were hardly out of his mouth when two officers, Chang Yong and Ho Lang, galloped out to do just that. On the other side, Lü Youkui and Yang Dahe engaged them in close fighting; Fang Gang hoisted his halberd and came to his comrades' aid, and Fan Ruilin attacked with leveled spear. The six men were fighting in pairs—a splendid sight.

"Why don't you want to join in?" Governor-general Hu asked Ba Bu.

"There's no point in capturing bandits unless you capture the chief," said Ba Bu. "Don't you worry, sir."

Dun'an noted the ferocity and courage of the new officers as well as their mastery of battle tactics, and he at once sent secret orders to Chu Hu, Wang Dahai, and Qi Guangzu to take their troops and attack the governor-general's army from the rear. As Huowu was enjoying the sight of the six officers fighting, Qian Lie, who had heard what the governor-general said and wanted to claim top honors, grasped his spear and came racing in from one side like a white whirlwind. Huowu, calmly professional, slashed with his sword, shouting "Vile bandit, you've come to your doom!" and bringing the sword down with the force of an avalanche. Qian was no match for him, and after four or five jousts Huowu feinted and let Qian thrust forward with his spear, then slashed him across the middle, cutting him in two, a sight that shocked the governor-general.

Ba Bu raised his broadaxe and sprang forward. Huowu was about to cut him down, too, but Qin Shuming had already lifted his mace and engaged him. However, Huowu's blood was up, and he raised his great sword and advanced to cut down the governor-general. Gao Baoguang hastily seized his spear and parried the blow, but Huowu's sword snapped the spear in two and also severed Gao Baoguang's leg and struck down his horse. Terrified, Governor-general Hu turned his horse and fled. Luckily for him, a dozen of his officers came surging forward. Huowu summoned all of his martial powers and cut and thrust, and many a man tumbled from his horse. With Wang Dahai and his forces attacking from the rear, Ba Bu and the other officers, fearing the loss of their commander, fled with their weapons trailing behind them. Combining their forces, Huowu's men pressed their pursuit for several miles.

When Governor-general Hu assembled his defeated army, he found that he had lost two generals, a dozen officers, and over four thousand men. He was utterly baffled. "Those bandits are so brave and so skilful," he said. "How can we destroy them?"

"Don't you worry, sir," said Ba Bu. "Tomorrow I'll use the feigned defeat tactic to capture them. That bandit general would have been beaten today, but I was taken in by their pincer attack from front and rear and feared that we would lose you, so I had no choice but to retreat."

"We're completely dependent on your prowess. After your triumph, I shall naturally report the news to the Emperor." Ba Bu thanked him. The officers went off to sleep in the camp, all except Ba Bu, who spent the night attending on his commander. At midnight, they were caught by surprise when Dun'an, who had divided his troops into eight columns, attacked them from all sides, showering them with fireballs, flaming arrows, and the like. The whole camp was startled awake, but by that time the flames had begun to spread. The men had no time to put on their armor or saddle their horses; instead they fled for their lives in all directions. Ba Bu, guarding Hu Cheng, gallantly charged out through the flames, only to come up against Lü Youkui. A dozen jousts were sufficient to show that Youkui was no match for Ba Bu, and Feng Gang spurred on his horse to come to his aid. But Ba Bu didn't dare go on fighting—guarding Hu Cheng and blocking and parrying to left and right, he fought the attackers off as he fled. Then he ran into Qin Shuming and fought with him before finally reaching the highway. The foot soldiers and cavalrymen injured in the fire gradually reassembled, and when a check was made, it was found that Ho Lang, one of their officers, was missing, and that their remaining troops numbered no more than three thousand. They were forced to retreat to Huizhou and mount a defense there until they could assemble more troops and avenge the defeat.

For their part Huowu and his men had won a great victory. They had also captured Ho Lang and brought him back to the pass. When Huowu heard that Hu Cheng had withdrawn to Huizhou, he told Qin Shuming to join Wang Dahai in guarding the pass. He himself led his men back to Lufeng, where they placed Ho Lang under house arrest.

Read on in the next chapter.

Chapter XIX

A girl suffers a tragic fate at New Year's
An in-law embarks on a literary career

~⚬~

At New Year's Jishi sent a man into the countryside to invite Ruyu to Guangzhou, and Ruyu's father sent back a letter setting the twenty-fourth of the month as the date of the engagement and the twenty-sixth as the date for Ruyu's travel to the city. Meanwhile Jishi went out daily offering compliments of the season to the various families they were close to. One day at Bangchen's his host pressed him to stay awhile, and they drank until late at night, when Bangchen remarked, "Because my neighbors, the Zhus, lost that lawsuit last year, Zhonghuang was sent back to his native place and they were left with nothing to their name. Then at the end of last year Lihuang slipped away to avoid paying his debts, and we still don't know where he went. His wife, Mistress Ru, is suffering terribly, and she told me with tears in her eyes how much she was longing to see you again. I wonder if you'd care to honor her with a visit?"

"She showed me great kindness, and it's been on my mind ever since. But it wouldn't look good if I were to call on her."

"If you want to see her, there's no reason why you shouldn't. Our back doors are close together, and provided you go through my place, nobody will ever know." Jishi agreed to visit her. He sent Qinghe home to say that he could not be back that evening because he was spending the night with Bangchen, and the servant went off, leaving Xiangqin and Sishu to attend on him. Jishi continued to drink until he was pleasantly inebriated. Meanwhile Bangchen had informed Mistress Ru of his visit.

After her husband's departure, she had had nothing left in the house, and because she was behind with her rent, the landlord had let the rooms at the front to someone else, leaving her with just one inner room and a tiny side room accessible through the back door. Fortunately, during Shr Shunjie's visit home a month after her wedding, she had given Mistress Ru two silver dollars, and with these she struggled to make herself two meals a day. For this New Year's festival she had on only a shabby silk lined jacket, a black cotton vest, and a worn black skirt of raw silk—everything else was in the pawnshop. When she heard that Jishi was about to visit her, she quickly tidied up the room, heated a basin of water, washed herself all over, and then did her hair and reapplied her makeup. Unfortunately, she had not so much as a cup of wine or a scrap of food to offer him. Moreover, threadbare clothes are hardly suited to the pursuit of pleasure, any more than cold and tattered bedding is conducive to making love. As she trimmed the lamp, shed a few tears, and silently resigned herself to her situation, she heard the knocker sound and quickly wiped away her tears and went to open the door.

In walked Jishi, unescorted and without a lantern. Mistress Ru put the latch on the door and showed him into her room, then asked him to sit down while she kowtowed. He quickly raised her to her feet, and she fell into his arms, crying, "My husband got what he deserved—we don't need to worry about him. But the fact that you took me as you did showed that we share an unexpected bond, so why did you cast me aside? I may be ugly, but you still ought to have been mindful of the warmhearted help that I gave you, not to mention all the misery I've had to put up with since."

He quickly wiped away her tears. "Of course I thought of the kindness you showed me, but your husband was such a scoundrel that I was frankly a little afraid of him. Then he brought that law-suit against me, so I kept putting off trying to see you. I'm here to-day to ask your forgiveness." At that point he noticed that she was wearing thin clothes and that her hands were ice-cold, and he took off his squirrel-fur tunic and gave it to her to put on. "Don't be sad. I'll make it up to you."

"I wouldn't dream of complaining about you. All I regret is the bad luck I had in marrying such a scoundrel! Now that you've deigned to call, I'll be able to die without regret."

Jishi was busy consoling her when he heard an urgent knocking at the door behind him and felt alarmed.

"Don't worry, sir," said Mistress Ru. "I'll see to it." She told him to sit down while she went and opened the door. It turned out that Bangchen, in order to please them, had sent two men over with wine and delicacies, plus two sets of bedding. Without a word they offered the articles to Mistress Ru, who accepted them and then shut the door again. Coming back in, she spread the bedclothes on the bed and set the wine and delicacies on the table. Then she poured a cup of wine and handed it to Jishi. "This is of-fering borrowed flowers to Buddha,"[1] she said, "but do drink a few cups." She was about to kowtow again when Jishi took the cup from her hand, helped her up, and sat her on his lap.

"We're done with the bowing," he said. "There's no need for any of that." Because his mouth felt dry, he poured another cup and held it to her lips, and she drank, too. According to the old say-ing, wine is the handmaiden of sex. They kept on pouring wine for each other until Jishi entered the realm of drunken bliss. Mistress Ru had no great capacity for wine, and after four or five cups her eyesight became blurry and her sensual desires were aroused. As she undid his belt, Jishi's own passions stirred, and he started to undress. Intent on winning his favor, she said, "Don't tire yourself out, sir. Just sit there on the bed. I know what to do." She threw herself on top of him and sported with him for a considerable time.

Next morning he put on some clothes and went out. Once home, he told Du Chong to covertly take four sets of clothing and two hundred taels and, accompanied by Axi of the Shr household, to go and offer them to Mistress Ru. She rewarded the messengers with ten taels. From this time forth, Jishi took advantage of Lihuang's absence to visit her frequently. Mistress Ru bought herself a maid, and also rented an outward-facing room. Gradually she began to dress in a more eye-catching manner.

On the twenty-fourth of the first month the Bian family prepared betrothal presents and sent them along with Ruyu's teacher, Bai Ruhuang, as matchmaker. Jishi treated the occasion with full ceremony, and his return gifts were distinctly lavish. The next day he sent men to tidy the three-room Peach Song Bower and prepare it for Ruyu. On the twenty-sixth Bian Ming brought his son to Guangzhou, and the Su family invited a large number of relatives and friends to join them. From this time on, Ruyu lived in the back garden of the Su compound. Jishi assigned four pages to attend on him and often dropped by himself to discuss the classics and histories; on any given day he might go there two or three times. At first Ruyu had taken Jishi for a callow youth, but he came to appreciate him as a gentle and cultivated person quite different from the general run of young men and developed a deep respect for him.

> He sees this is no affluent young fop,
> And learns the world is larger than he thought.

Let us now tell how Mola, having taken Chaozhou, considered himself a matchless hero whom no one in the world would dare to challenge. General Ren led his troops up to the city, but Mola won two battles in quick succession. Fortunately Ren maintained strict discipline among his troops and so did not suffer a major defeat. However, he lacked good officers and had to withdraw for the time being and camp at Huizhou. Having learned from his scouts of Ren's withdrawal, Mola returned to the city to celebrate his triumph. At the New Year's festival he issued an edict ordering the entire city to display New Year's lanterns; if anyone were to disobey, his whole family would be put to death. Now, Chaozhou was a wealthy place; northerners used to say, "If you visit Guangdong, you're wasting your time if you don't go to Chaozhou." It was a thriving city, and when the order came down by martial law, all the households, great and small, vied with one other in the novelty of their lanterns. Young men and women throughout the city actually forgot that they lived in a world ruled by bandits and, as if sharing their pleasures with the common people, woman neighbor called out to woman neighbor and family to family in a hectic celebration. Mola ordered Hai Yuan, First Defender of the Faith, and Hai Zhen, Fourth Defender, to take three thousand mounted men and set up camp outside the city in readiness for any contingency. He also gave secret orders to the two other Defenders, Hai Heng and Hai Li, to take mobile units and patrol the streets every day. If they came upon any exceptionally beautiful women, they were to record their names so that His Majesty could make his choice from among them.

Next door to the assistant salt comptroller's yamen lived an Imperial Academy student named Tao Zhuo, who was quite wealthy. He had a son, Xianrui, and a daughter, Zifang, who had just turned fourteen and was a dazzling beauty. One day her father went to a relative's to enjoy the lanterns, and Zifang arranged with Yinjie, the daughter of the locksmith Jia Zhen, to go out on the street and look at the lantern display. Yinjie was seventeen and above average in looks, she had deceived her parents and done some unseemly things—they sauntered about accompanied by a bevy of maids until after the second watch, taking in the fantastic spectacle of streets flooded with illuminations:

> Ram's horn lanterns, shining high in the sky;
> Glass lanterns, exceptionally brilliant;
> Multicolored lanterns, embroidered around with pearls;
> Eight Treasures lanterns, inlaid with gold and jade;
> Flying Tiger lanterns, baring teeth and claws;
> Galloping Horse lanterns, lightning flashing over painted
>   clouds;
> Carp lanterns, leaping from wave to wave;
> Lion lanterns, belching clouds and smoke;
> Unicorn lanterns, with the animals dancing together;
> Phoenix lanterns, with the birds hailing their king;
> Embroidered Ball lanterns, dripping with glistening pearls;
> Immortals' lanterns, with mists rising off the sea;
> "May Everything Go Your Way!" lanterns;
> Two Dragons Playing with a Pearl lanterns;
> Three Heavenly Bodies lanterns;
> "May All Four Seasons be Peaceful!" lanterns;
> Five Blessings Come to Court lanterns;
> Six Tortoises Traverse the Sea lanterns;
> Seventh Eve Prayers for Cleverness lanterns;
> Eight Tribes Offering Treasures lanterns;
> Nine Grades of Lotus Thrones lanterns;
> Ten-Sided Ambush lanterns;

Flashing and sparkling,
High up and low down,
Vivid and brilliant,
Charming and beautiful.
Indeed,
When eyes are dazzled, the true is not false;
When forms are illusory, all sense is void.

Zifang and Yinjie were walking along holding hands and giggling as they crossed Front Street and came to the Haiyang county yamen. It was midnight, and there were not many people about. The yamen was currently occupied by Hai Heng, the Second Defender, and he had erected a festival tower in front of it. Actors were performing there outside the main gate, and Hai Heng was drinking and enjoying the lantern display when his men reported: "There are two girls out there, both young, who are first-class beauties. Please come and look them over, sir, and decide for yourself."

Hai Heng descended the tower, took one glance at the girls, and exclaimed, "Excellent! There's no need to enter any more names in the book. Bring them in at once, lads, and get the sedan chair ready. We'll take them to the palace immediately. This means that our patrolling the streets has been successful." At his command the soldiers, several score at least, surrounded the two beautiful girls and forced them into the chair, after which Hai Heng took them away.

Mola was enjoying a boisterous celebration with a group of women when a close aide reported that Hai Heng was waiting outside with two girls whom he had selected. Mola ordered them led in and told Hai Heng to go off and mount a careful watch on the city walls. Women servants ushered the girls in.

Zifang and Yinjie prostrated themselves on the ground, not

daring to look up. Mola's retainers pulled them to their feet, and Mola examined them closely before expressing his admiration: "They truly are exceptional!" Jumping down from his seat, he pulled them up and threw his arms around them and hugged them, then told his serving women to serve some wine to celebrate the occasion. Zifang didn't dare drink anything, but Mola told Yin-jie to sit beside her while he forced her to do so. Little by little he bared her bosom, revealing soft breasts and nipples, then played with them for some time before his passions were aroused and he ordered the cloud bed prepared.[2]

Mola had recently had two beds set up, a cloud bed and a rain bed, both of foreign manufacture. The cloud bed was for intercourse with very young girls. If he seized a young girl who knew nothing of sexual enjoyment, all he had to do—lest she thrash about with her arms and legs—was to push her onto this bed, and a mechanism would automatically pin down her arms and legs and allow him to vent his lust without restraint. The rain bed was even more ingenious. During the sexual intercourse, he merely had to lie on the woman's body and activate a mechanism, and he could thrust at will; at the critical moment they could meet perfectly together. On this occasion the serving women stripped off Zifang's clothes and pushed her down on the cloud bed. What did a young girl like Zifang know about such things? No sooner was she lying on the bed than she found it impossible to move her arms, while her feet were held up in the air, far apart. In her panic she cried out pathetically. On each side of her the four women servants suppressed their smiles behind the lanterns that they were holding. When Mola took off his clothes and approached, how could he fail to be aroused by such a sight? Without asking whether she had had any experience, he simply drove into the bower of bliss. Zifang was in such pain that she began squealing like a slaughtered pig.

She was unable to move either her hands or her feet. All she could do was plead with him again and again to have mercy, but Mola cared only for her beauty—what sympathy did he have for her tiny, delicate frame?—and deployed his full array of techniques. At first she screamed, then she pleaded pathetically, and finally she could make no sound at all, while he continued to violate her with every ounce of his strength. Her spirits faded, and soon she was on her way to the world of the dead, where countless eons would have to pass before she would reappear in the material world. How tragic that this surpassingly beautiful girl should be raped and die while still so young! "The lady has fainted," Mola's servants reported. He ordered the mechanism opened up and the girl helped into a back room to recover, while he himself, his desires still not sated, turned to Yinjie in her place. Having witnessed his fierce onslaught, Yinjie was petrified, and no sooner was she on the cloud bed than Mola raised his lance and attacked. Fortunately for her, however, she was already an initiate; she had had someone in her own household to prepare the way. Moreover, she was a few years older than Zifang, and so, although she suffered terribly, she was able to more or less endure the pain. Fortunately for her, she managed to fight the bald head to a standstill, after which more cups and dishes were set out and an excellent wine was served.

On their knees, the serving women reported: "The lady cannot be revived."

Mola roared with laughter. "Why couldn't she stand a little fun? Take her away and bury her."

"You people die every day and then come back to life," he said to his concubines.[3] "Where does she get this violent spirit of hers?"

"She was simply too young," said Pinwa. "She couldn't take that magic weapon of yours. In the future, Father, you really shouldn't condemn these little lassies to death."

"Oh, what good are virgins, anyway? They can't compare with you people." Throwing an arm around Yinjie, he added, "This one was all right, though." He gave her the name Pin'e and told someone to award her father one thousand taels and a post at the third rank.

When Commander-in-Chief Ren, who lacked capable officers, heard that Governor-general Hu had also not managed to win a complete victory, he discussed the situation with Intendant Qu and then asked the governor-general to join forces; together they would smash Mola and then execute a pincer movement against Lufeng. He also directed Zhong Yu to leave half of his men behind to guard the city, while Zhong himself led the rest to assist the army. Early in the fourth month they would join forces and advance together to root out the rebels. That was why, although Mola had held a lavish lantern display, he had had no fighting to deal with.

Let us turn to Ruyu who, from the time he arrived in the Su compound had been working hard every day at the classics and histories. Because he knew that his prospective brother-in-law was a member of the Academy while he himself was a mere penniless student, he was afraid that the staff would look down on him. However, the servants and pages all heeded Jishi's orders, and none of them dared slight Ruyu in any way, for which he was more than a little grateful. Chuncai, although his writing was both incoherent and illogical, had a simple and honest nature. His father, who wanted him to study seriously for the examinations, had entrusted him to Jishi, who had then passed him on to Ruyu. And so Chuncai spent each day in the garden with Ruyu before going home to sleep and in this way gradually acquired a rough knowledge of composition. When the topic was "The pond-keeper cooked the fish,"[4] he wrote as his exordium, "Who can cook fish? Fish is something I like." His father thought he had a rare talent, but others couldn't help laughing at him.

One day in the third month Jishi had just come back from a banquet at the traders' association. The twentieth was Pockmarked Pan's sixtieth birthday, and Jishi wanted Ruyu to compose a congratulatory piece in his stead. Hurrying over to the garden, he met Ruyu and Chuncai and urged the former to write the piece. When he saw the peach trees in full bloom, he told his servants to prepare a party to celebrate the event and even felt inspired to write a poem on the subject himself. Chuncai was eager to play a drinking game, but Ruyu said, "Composing a poem *is* playing a drinking game—you can use poetry in the game. You shouldn't be so set in your ideas, Chuncai. With that 'Flowering Peach' poem I wrote yesterday I was a bit too careless, while your effort was just bizarre."

"Please show me," Jishi said. Ruyu fetched two sheets of paper. Jishi read Ruyu's first:

> No need beneath the blossoms to think of Pingyang;
> Brocade curtains, fold on fold, vie in brilliant hue;
> Who planted the myriad trees in Xuandu Temple?
> Spring breeze brushing my face, I'm moved by Master Liu.[5]

"These peaches were planted before you ever came here," said Jishi. "Why do they move you so deeply?"

"Since the trees planted after the poet's departure could still move the poet, surely the trees being here before my arrival and enjoyably standing in the wind can touch me. How many flowers do we see bloom in the course of our lives? Anyway, this was just a humble offering designed to bring out better things from others."

Jishi praised it, then turned to Chuncai's poem:

The peach trees are in bloom,
With abundant leaves and red fruit.
Pick a lot and cook till tender;
Planted well, they're like Peach Blossom Spring;
Fully grown, they tower over the rooftops.
The spring wind enters the smiling garden;
Last year the qian looked at them alone;
He hadn't yet married the kun.

Jishi laughed. "I understand the first two lines, but what does the third line mean?"

"Everybody eats peach blossom porridge," said Chuncai. "When we pick a lot of blossom, wouldn't we want to cook it and eat it?"

"The fourth line's a reference to the Peach Blossom Spring, but what about the fifth and sixth lines?"

"You haven't read the *Classified Allusions*,[6] and that's why you don't understand the reference to peach blossom waters rising up.[7] Look, aren't these peach trees taller than a house? The sixth line is merely taken from the *Thousand Poems*; there's no explanation for it."[8]

"What about the characters 'qian' and 'kun'?"

"The other day Brother Bian taught me that 'qian' meant heaven as well as male, and that 'kun' meant earth as well as female. This time last year I was still unmarried, wasn't I?"

"Bizarre is certainly the word for it! Now let's play a drinking game." They began playing dice and drank for some time. Jishi had just come back from a drinking session, and since this was wine on top of wine, he inevitably became very drunk. He escaped and fled into the inner study, where he took off his outer clothes and sprawled across the bed.

A maid brought him some tea, but he took just one sip of it and then told her to call Wuyun in to massage his legs. It so happened that Wuyun was looking for Jishi in order to report to him and was waiting quietly outside as the maid shut the door. Jishi told her to climb onto the bed and gently pummel his legs and also give him a full body massage complete with exercises for the sinews and muscles.

As she did so, he caught her around the neck. "Where are your mistresses?" he asked.

"They're all with the old lady playing cards in First Lady's room. Mistress Shy told me to come and ask you something. Tomorrow morning Su Fu is setting off to take up his position, and his mother has brought him in to kowtow and say goodbye. Should they pay for his travel?"

"Oh, let's give him a couple of hundred taels and be done with it. Why do they ask?" He stretched out a hand to feel her breasts.

"Stop fooling around, sir! At New Year's in Mistress Shy's room you took all kinds of liberties, and she saw what you were doing and smiled, then pulled a face just to embarrass me. If you're really so fond of me, why don't you take me openly as your concubine? Last year I didn't want to leave here because I appreciated how kind you'd been to me."

"I know about that, but it would be very inconvenient to do anything just now. I told Mistress Shy about you today. Let's have a little preliminary tête-à-tête tonight."

She shot him a sidelong glance. "You love this sort of rigmarole, don't you? I've noticed that Mistress Wu is also neither one thing nor the other. What's the point of it all?"

"You don't understand." He tugged at her hand and told her to fondle his penis. She had no choice but to put her hand inside his trousers and take a firm grip. Then, placing her cheek against his, she said, "Dear master, I don't think I could take this. Put it only halfway in tonight."

Jishi pulled her head around and kissed her. "Don't be afraid. I know how to enter little by little. Look how nice and soft the head is!" They dallied for a while before she opened the door and went out.

A maid, Cuiluo, ran up to her and whispered, "Dear sister, do lend me a tael. My mother's waiting to buy some linen, and tomorrow you can deduct it from my savings!" Wuyun promised to help, then went directly to the main room.

Jishi slept until dusk, then went to Xia's room. He had his supper and was about to go to bed when he remarked to Xia with a grin, "There's a favor I'd like to ask of you. I wonder if you'd agree?"

"What are you being so secretive about?"

"I've wanted to have Wuyun for a long time, but it's not convenient just now to take her as a concubine. I'd like to sleep with her tonight, and I need you to cover for me."

She smiled. "All this to-do over a little thing like that! The First Lady puts up with us, so we can hardly afford to be jealous of others. If I were a jealous woman, I wouldn't have waited this long! The other day you spent three or four nights out of town at the Shr house. Just how did *that* come about?"

"It was late, and the city gates were shut. I couldn't get back in time, that's all."

She pressed a finger against his cheek. "Aren't you ashamed of yourself? You just happened to be at the Shr house late at night, and they just happened to shut the city gates—what a *coincidence*! I'm very much afraid that you wanted to go charging into a certain neighbor's house by one means or another."

Jishi laughed. "My dear girl, how did you know that?"

"If you don't want it known, you'd better not do it. Even a body that's buried in the snow comes to light when the snow melts. I know you're not very obsessed with that woman—you're just too kind to turn her down."

"I didn't greatly care for her at first, but these last few times I've been unable to leave her alone."

Xia flushed. "Don't talk such rubbish! Off with you now. Come back all the sooner, so the maids don't find out."

Jishi left with a broad grin on his face.

That night he made tender love to Wuyun, satisfying a long-cherished desire, and returned to Xia's room before dawn. She pulled him inside her bedclothes, they embraced, and then he made postcoital love to her. From this time on Xia gave Wuyun special treatment.

> She may not have been free of jealousy,
> But to win a good name she meets his wish.

Let us turn now to Zhu Lihuang, who had fled Guangzhou to escape his debtors. He was intent on going to Chaozhou and seeking refuge with Prince Daguang in the hope of gaining riches and rank, but because Commander-in-Chief Ren's forces, encamped some thirty miles away, were stopping and questioning all travelers, he could get no further. He hadn't a penny to his name, and he needed to find work where he was, in Wuguizhen. However, as a social parasite, he was unsuited to any sort of work, and within ten days he had changed employers three times. The fourth family he worked for was surnamed Fan, and it consisted of a mother in her fifties and a daughter of fifteen or sixteen. The pair depended for their living on traveling merchants who stayed the night and paid for their pleasure. Lihuang lived in their house and did nothing but carry hot water, draw fresh water, buy wine, and make tea—suitable tasks for an inveterate idler. He drifted along in this fashion for a considerable time before realizing that the girl was only a foster daughter that the mother had bought. The Fan woman had originally intended to take a boat to Chaozhou, but since the way was blocked by troops, she had rented a place here for the time being. Although her surname was Fan, the girl's was Niu—in fact, she was none other than Niu Yerong, the daughter of Niu Zao. After Huowu killed Konghua and took all the monks up to the ridge with him, Yerong had had no one to turn to. Her only course was to go home with one of the village women in the temple. The woman's husband had enjoyed her for a time, but he eventually found that he could not afford to keep her. At that point the Fan woman and her husband, who trafficked in girls and were greatly impressed with Yerong, bought her for a mere thirty taels. When the pair got to Huizhou, the husband fell ill and died, and his wife and the girl came on here, where day and night Fan instructed Yerong in a range of bedroom arts. Yerong was a fast learner and an apt pupil, but Wuguizhen was a small place, and the fighting in the vicinity prevented any merchants from getting through, so business was slack.

Lihuang had been there over a month before he managed, surreptitiously, to seduce her. "This isn't the sort of place you should settle down in, and we can't get through to Chaozhou," he advised her. "But you're so beautiful, and you have such marvelous talents that, if you were in Guangzhou, I don't doubt for a moment that you'd earn pots of money every day. I have a wife at home who looks rather like you. If you and I were to slip off quietly to Guangzhou and rent a bigger place there, I could be the manager, while you and she could entertain a few men whom you really like, fellows with money. Wouldn't that be more pleasant? Why bury yourself in a place like this?" This speech left Yerong more than eager to go with him.

One evening he spent thirty or forty cash on liquor and got old woman Fan helplessly drunk. Then he and Yerong bundled up some clothes and jewelry, hunted out a few silver dollars from the old woman's bed, and caught a boat going downstream. They had made a clean getaway; by the time Fan came to her senses, they were a long way off. After sailing directly to Guangzhou, they took a sedan chair to Lihuang's house, which they approached by the back door.

Mistress Ru heard a knocking at the door and told her maid to open it. She was astonished to see her husband walk in accompanied by an attractive girl. Lihuang noticed that his wife was dressed quite differently, which aroused his suspicions, but he was so keen to pursue the business he had in mind and so eager to have her join him, that he adopted an ingratiating tone, explaining everything in detail and asking Yerong to come forward and kowtow.

Mistress Ru failed to return the gesture. "I finally get to enjoy a quiet life, and you have to come along and stir up more trouble for me! Do me a favor and get out of this house! If you persist, I'll go to the prefect and file charges against you and let him settle the issue."

Lihuang hastily bowed. "My dear wife, please don't let this get out! You'll have the say in whatever we do from now on. I have a lot of other good ideas that I want to tell you about. The girl's only a money tree, you know. I never fancied her for myself, so there's no need to be jealous."

"Why should *I* be jealous? You couldn't even keep one wife, and now you're proposing to keep two! How much money do you think you can shake out of that money tree of yours? All I want to do is file charges and have a clean break from you. Don't you go besmirching my good name by involving me in an abduction!"

Lihuang was reduced to kneeling in front of her and pleading, and she stopped her denunciation long enough to tell Yerong to go and sleep in the maid's room. That evening Lihuang gradually introduced his idea of using the house to entertain guests, but she retorted, "I have a spotless reputation. Why would I do such a thing? If you want to do it, then go and find somewhere else— you're not allowed to come here. If you haven't got that girl out of this house by tomorrow, I'll file charges the next day."

Ever since the New Year's festival Lihuang had been exposed to hunger and cold and forced to a do good deal of hard work. He had also indulged in an inordinate amount of sex with Yerong. Highly nervous on returning home, he had inevitably had to lay bare his feelings and apologize to Mistress Ru, and after midnight that night he began to run a high fever. The next day he found himself unable to move, and Mistress Ru had to call in a doctor, who diagnosed his ailment as a seasonal fever. Lihuang took some medicine for it, but haphazardly, and in seven days he was dead.

Chapter XX
Yao Huowu rebuffs Mola
Wen Chuncai outdoes Bian Ruyu

⤏

Commander-in-Chief Ren had arranged with Governor-general Hu to join forces with Brigade General Zhong and put down the rebellion in Chaozhou. By early in the fourth month the troops had assembled from all quarters. Commander-in-Chief Ren set out wine and held a meeting with the other commanders. "My soldiers were too weak and my officers too few, and on several occasions I failed to make the most of my opportunities," he said. "Recently the rascally baldhead has sent troops out foraging along the roads. We've killed several hundred of his men, but we've not been able to stop them. Fortunately, you are here now, Governor-general, and naturally we'll soon launch a campaign to suppress the barbarians."

"I failed to take advantage of my opportunity at Goats Foot, and I've long been aware that I carry a heavy burden of guilt," said the governor-general. "I will definitely join forces with you, Commander-in-Chief, to clear them out and atone for my crime."

Commander-in-Chief Ren then proposed combining their camps, but the governor-general replied that the camps formed two wings of the same army, and if the enemy did appear, each could come to the other's aid. Intendant Qu of Huizhou and Chaozhou urged the governor-general to unite the Chaozhou garrison with his brigade, to halt the fighting for three days, and then advance in two columns. The brigade, which had contained the eight thousand elite troops who had reinforced the attack on

Goat's Foot, was now reduced to Colonel Teng Xian, Lieutenant-colonel Yu Liang, Major Ji Ce, and three thousand men. Combined with the garrison, it totaled four thousand five hundred troops.

Scouts brought in reports that Mola had ordered Hai Yuan and Hai Zhen to lead five thousand men to hold off the governor-general; they were to dig deep trenches and build high earthworks but not to engage in battle. Mola himself would lead Hai Li and Hai Heng with Gu Xin, Meng Feitian, Xia Chizha, and Li Fanjiang, four capable officers, at the head of a force of ten thousand elite troops that would face General Ren. Although the latter's troops numbered less than five thousand, they were under strict discipline, and when they saw in the distance the rebel troops advancing on a broad front, they waited for General Zhong to deploy his two wings. Hai Heng, grasping two iron maces, raced forward on his horse with Hai Li close behind him, and from the other side Zhong Yu and Teng Xian engaged them. Xia Chizha and Li Fanjiang galloped out together and vigorously attacked the main force. Mola then ordered his men to advance, and Ren ordered the two wings to close and surround them. Arrows filled the air like a swarm of locusts. Li Fanjiang took one in the arm and turned back. A furious Mola, his left hand gripping a sixty-catty Buddhist staff and his right hand wielding a fifty-four catty Buddhist sword, charged into the thick of the fray, while the troops under his command advanced in overwhelming force. However excellent Ren's tactics were, the disparity in numbers proved to be just too great. Moreover, he had no one among his officers who was a match for Mola. His men could not hold their ground, but broke ranks and fled. He withdrew six or seven miles and camped, but he had lost over eight hundred soldiers as well as Lieutenant-colonel Yu Liang, and he was plunged in gloom.

Having forced Ren to retreat, Mola ordered his four finest officers to take a thousand men each and set up ambushes all around,
while he established an empty camp in the middle. If Ren should
attack, they needed simply to sound the alarm on all sides and the
enemy would be frightened into fleeing. Mola himself led Hai
Heng and Hai Li in a secret foray in the other direction, having
covertly arranged with Hai Yuan and others that they should raid
the governor-general's camp in two columns that night. Absurdly,
although the governor-general had been defeated in the fighting at
Huizhou, he had taken no precautions and his forces were routed
by Mola's surprise attack. Fortunately, Ren had not gone to sleep
for fear of just such a raid and, hearing the noise of combat to the
southeast, he at once led his troops there to relieve the situation.
Fierce fighting ensued in the darkness, and Ren drove Mola off and
joined up with the other force. The two leaders tried to console
each other, but at dawn they were just about to make breakfast
when Mola attacked their troops with his combined force. How
could this hungry and defeated army repel the attack? Even before
the battle began they had resolved to flee. Ren could not restrain
them and was forced to retreat once more himself. Mola's troops
fought well, each man vying with his fellows to be first, and they
slaughtered their opponents. Intendant Qu's horse stumbled, and
he was captured. The two leaders were left with over five thousand
soldiers but no feasible strategy. They moved troops from elsewhere, and at the same time prepared a joint memorial requesting
the transfer of officers and men from other garrisons.

Roaring with laughter, Mola made a triumphant return to
Chaozhou. He cursed Qu Qiang and then threw him in jail. He
also sent a messenger to Lufeng to report on the victory and arrange a date for a concerted attack on Guangzhou. Yao Huowu
had the messenger's ears cut off and told him: "Go back and tell

that priest of yours to take good care of his bald head, because before very long I'm coming after it."

> Though each man is a bandit,
> In practice they deviate.
> This one misjudges that one—
> Perfectly appropriate!
> This priest has a vulgar mind,
> Ready to go half and half;
> Now that priest has lost his ears—
> At least it's good for a laugh!

Let us turn to Mistress Ru. After burying Lihuang, she felt that her own household was now safe and secure, and she had a word with Yerong: "There's no need for you anymore, now that my husband is dead. You'd better decide what you want to do with yourself."

Yerong began to sob. "I have no home, no family. If you could find it in your heart to let me stay, I'd gladly serve you as a maid." Mistress Ru knew that Yerong was homeless, and she no longer feared anything that the girl might do, so she consented. Yerong kowtowed in gratitude. Three days later Mistress Ru sent Jishi a secret message by Axi, the page of the Shr family, asking him to visit.

It was the middle of the fourth month. The last of spring was over, and the sweltering summer heat pressed in upon them. In Guangdong it was a time of drought as well as of armed conflict. Following the rice planting in the second month, when there was a solitary shower, not a single drop of rain had fallen. It seemed likely that the first crop could not be harvested, and the price soared. In Jiangxi, Huguang and other provinces they heard the bad news, and their merchants did not dare travel to Guangdong. With a peck of rice selling for two taels, the people were in terrible distress. Jishi told Su Bang to make a careful inventory of the surplus grain his family had accumulated over the years; the total came to a little over 130,000 piculs. He then set up shops at each of the four gates through which commerce flowed between town and country. To each shop he issued 20,000 piculs of grain and assigned six servants to sell it to customers. Officially price-controlled rice was sold for five silver dollars a picul, which was equivalent on the Sima scale to three taels, six qian.[1] Readers, let us explain: if at that time the price was ten taels a picul, was Jishi not losing six taels, four qian on every picul he sold? If he had stuck to what was a fair price in normal times, he would still have made one tael, six qian a picul more, and the 80,000 piculs would have brought in an extra 128,000 taels. Although this was an instance of the good things that he did, when looked at closely, it also proves to be the foundation of his wealth. I only wish that rich men throughout the land would follow his example! Jishi told Su Bang and Su Rong to supervise the operation separately, bringing back the takings each day. When Prefect Shangguan heard of Jishi's generous action, he invited him in and congratulated him. He also posted two seasoned runners at each shop to prevent hooligans from stirring up trouble and shopkeepers from employing such corrupt practices as reselling the rice at a profit.

After the sale had gone on for six or seven days and Jishi was sitting at home with nothing to do, he heard that the Shr family had sent him an invitation. In a summer chair, with Du Chong and Qinghe in attendance, he visited them. "There's a meal waiting for you over there," said Bangchen, "so I won't press you to stay." He continued in a whisper: "Although Lihuang is dead, she's taken on a real beauty. You should go over and feast your eyes on her."

Jishi went around and through the back door. Mistress Ru had the room spick and span and a fine incense burning. She no longer had a mourning head wrapper around her head, but wore an unlined gown of white tribute silk with a black gauze skirt. Welcoming him in with a smile, she invited him to sit down, then set out wine and dishes and kowtowed as she offered him a cup of wine. "My husband died, and I'm indebted to you for the funeral. I've specially prepared a cup of weak wine to thank you. Please drink up."

Jishi pulled her to her feet. "You shouldn't have gone to all that trouble!" He took a sip of the wine. She at once offered him food, but he declined. "There's no hurry. It's hot, and I think I'll take off my gown." He stood up to do so.

Yerong at once stretched out a hand from behind to loosen his sash. He turned his head and looked at her. "Who's this girl?" he asked. Mistress Ru noticed how intently he was eyeing Yerong.

"She's someone my late husband brought back from Chaozhou," she said. "I'm keeping her here to attend on you." She called out to Yerong. "Come on, kowtow to the master!" Yerong did so.

Mistress Ru whispered in Jishi's ear. "Not only is she gorgeous, I'm told she has a great many inner virtues as well." Smiling, Jishi raised the girl to her feet and told her to stand beside him and pour him some wine. He asked her how old she was and where she came from.

"I'm fifteen," she said, "and I come from up north. We had a silk shop in Chaozhou, but one of the assistants made off with the capital. My father had a fit and died, leaving me with nowhere to go." Jishi was greatly moved by her tissue of falsehoods.

Having received instruction from Mother Fan, Yerong knew all there was to know. Seeing that Jishi had taken a fancy to her, she made eyes at him and pressed herself against him as she offered him wine. Jishi also had her drink a few cups herself. Mistress Ru saw that the two of them were getting along famously and slipped out of the room, excusing herself on the ground that she needed to see to the food.

Jishi put his arm about Yerong and drank for a while, then pressed her down on the couch and had his way with her. She was well acquainted with how to yield and then rise to meet his thrusts, and Jishi was thrilled. He called Mistress Ru back in and had her do battle once more. She lay down beside them and Yerong reared herself in front of her, while Jishi hovered around them both for a good two hours with many different moves—an instance of sheer, unbridled license. When they had finished, they poured more wine and had Yerong drink with them. That night all three shared the same bed, taking turns in fierce combat. From this point on, Jishi had two mistresses for little money, which was all very satisfactory—except that Yerong happened to be at a critical age, and her sexual desires were on fire. Moreover, Jishi rarely visited. And so it was inevitable that she should get up to a little mischief behind Mistress Ru's back.

One day just before the Duanyang festival, Jishi sent Du Chong over with cosmetics, festival dumplings, and silks for the two women, and Mistress Ru asked him to stay and have some wine and food. She told Yerong to keep him company, never imagining that the girl would seduce him. Because Du Chong was employed by the Su household, Mistress Ru was eager to secure his friendship in the hope that he would put in a good word for her, and she pretended that she didn't know what the pair had been up to. Later, when seeing Du Chong out of the house, she told him privately, "The master has already had his way with Yerong. You mustn't breathe a word about what you've done." Blushing furiously, Du Chong promised not to tell. He was genuinely contrite and departed with his face still red.

Let us turn to Jishi who, because Ruyu had returned to Qin-gyuan for the festival, was celebrating the Duanyang festival with his women only. In Rippling Pond in the back garden he had two miniature dragon boats made, and the whole family leant over the rail watching them. He also spent 3,200 taels to hire a troupe of Su-zhou actresses, consisting of fourteen girls and four women coach-es, who were assigned to the various apartments. One evening they were all performing in Know Thyself Pavilion when black clouds formed in the southeast and faint rumblings of thunder could be heard. Jishi ordered the dragon boats brought in, and soon after-ward there came a torrential downpour that lasted a good two hours. Jishi said to his mother: "With this storm, there's still some hope for the early rice crop, and my selling grain cheaply won't have been so useless, after all. The other day the prefect called me in and praised me to the skies, and I was afraid that if later on I ran out of grain, all my previous efforts would be wasted. I was thoroughly embarrassed. Fortunately he prayed sincerely for rain, which is why the heavens have sent us this timely downpour."

"He really is a good official!" said Mistress Mao. "The other day I was upstairs when I saw in the distance a crowd forming in front of the Buddhist temple. The servants told me that the prefect goes there every day to pray for rain, setting out early in the morn-ing and not coming back until noon, walking all the way in the full sun with no parasol men to protect him. I suspected that he was just doing it to make a name for himself, but later I heard that he spends every night outside in the yard, and that all of his staff from the highest to the lowest have to keep to a Buddhist diet and wear white clothing. And it has worked—sincere prayers really do move Heaven, and bodhisattvas really do work miracles." She turned to Huiruo and the other young women: "I'm an old woman, but you young ones should pray to Buddha, chant the scriptures, and revere the bodhisattva in order to perfect yourselves and be born as men in the next life." They promised to do so.

Because the paths in the garden were slippery with rain, Jishi had a number of chairs brought out and selected the strongest servants to carry the women back into the house one by one. Mistress Mao, the two concubines, and Jishi's sisters went upstairs, while Jishi and the others enjoyed some wine in Xia's room. Afterward he went to Qiao's room to sleep.

The next day was the festival itself. An endless stream of visitors brought gifts; some were accepted, others returned. Naturally there were servants there to manage the process in the traditional manner. As Jishi sat in the outer study watching the engraver make a gold-plated name tablet for Prefect Shangguan, Bangchen's page Axi brought in the four presents.[2] Mistress Ru had entrusted them to Axi, and he came into the study to see Jishi and whispered: "Mistress Ru also told me to bring you this one." From his sleeve he took a paper package covered with red cotton cloth. When Jishi withdrew into the porch at the back and opened it, it proved to contain a stomacher of red satin embroidered with large blue interwoven lotus stems among which was a pair of sleeping mandarin ducks. The lining was of white crepe silk, and it was exquisitely made, a dazzling piece of work. Jishi was delighted with it and told Axi to convey his thanks. "I'll be over to see her the day after tomorrow."

Axi bowed and continued, "There's also something I'd like to report to you, sir. I received a favor from you, you looked after the family, and so if I hear anything, I feel it's my duty to report it to you. If I didn't report it, I'd be afraid that you'll find out eventually and blame me for being ungrateful."

"If you have something to tell me, go ahead."

"Yesterday Du Chong from your household brought over

some presents and stayed more than two hours. I wondered why, if Mistress Ru was wining and dining him, she didn't call me over to keep him company. Later on their maid told me that Yerong, the new arrival, had been fooling about with Du Chong and that Mistress Zhu took no notice. It makes you look bad, sir!"

Jishi felt angry. "Well, you've told me," he said. "Just don't go talking about it to anyone else." Axi promised not to do so.

Jishi pondered how to deal with the matter. It would be easy enough to send Du Chong packing, but what a poor response that would be for the two favors Du had done him! Then another thought struck him: That story about the girl with the red whisk is considered an exemplary tale, and even if Du Chong is no match for Li Jing, surely I can do what Yang Su did![3] Moreover, a wanton creature like Yerong is hardly worth worrying about. Having made his decision, he dismissed the problem from his mind and sent messengers to the Wens, the Wus and the Shys to invite their womenfolk to join his family in watching the dragon boats and the plays. A few days later he sent three hundred taels to Bangchen and asked him to tell Mistress Ru to sell Yerong to Du Chong as his wife. The new couple excelled, he in talent, she in beauty. Moreover, Du Chong had swallowed some pills from Mola's gourd and was a worthy adversary for her. That the pair were grateful to Jishi hardly needs to be said. Jishi also instructed Bangchen to persuade Mistress Ru to remarry as the second wife of a staff aide, and he also presented her with four sets of clothing and two hundred taels. The details need not concern us.

A special provincial examination was held that year, and Ruyu threw himself into his studies in preparation for it. Chuncai, too, recited texts all day long, although writing an essay was really beyond him. His father had insisted that he take the examination for the sake of the prestige it would confer on the family, and Ruyu was obliged to set a dozen topics and write an essay on each of them for Chuncai to memorize. No matter what the topic was in the examination, he was to copy out one of the essays rather than simply to hand in a blank sheet of paper. Chuncai, however, was just too obtuse. It took him three or four days to memorize one essay, and by the time he had memorized a second, he had already forgotten the first. But thanks to Ruyu's constant supervision and encouragement, after studying for two full months or more, he had managed to memorize nine essays, after which Ruyu had him revise them daily, making several copies and then writing them out from memory several times. Jishi urged Chuncai not to take the preparation so seriously, but Chuncai, in his willful, stubborn way, kept on writing out the essays that he had learned. In the director of studies' preliminary examination held early in the seventh month, he resorted to a little trickery, hiring someone to take the exam in his place, and passed first among a hundred candidates. He then gaily entered the provincial examination hall together with Ruyu and enrolled for the provincial examination.

The principal examiner was a man from Yulin in Shaanxi province. For this examination he had received a secret directive from the emperor to the effect that there was not very much text in *The Doctrine of the Mean* and every conceivable topic would already have been covered by candidates practicing at home; in order to put a stop to this deplorable situation, the topics in this examination were to be chosen from the *Analects* and *Mencius* only. That is how the three topics in this examination came to be the following:

> "He did not change both his father's officials" as well as the following two segments, "and his father's policies, and this was what was difficult to emulate."[4]
> "This is the meat of that honking creature" as well as the following segment.[5]

"The 'Kai feng' deals with a minor wrong committed by the parent" as well as the following segment.[6]

If your aspirations are good, Heaven will fulfill them. It so happened that all three topics in the examination had been treated in essays by Ruyu that Chuncai had memorized. In the first topic the words "did not" are seen as flexible, and the first and last parts form the opening and closure. The middle part is divided into three alternatives. One is that to change his father's officials and policies indiscriminately would naturally have been wrong; the second is that to cling adamantly to his father's officials and policies would have amounted to "holding the middle without the proper measure"[7] and would certainly not be difficult to emulate; and the third would be to appoint men after weighing their ability to act according to the circumstances but without changing his father's intention in appointing officials or his thinking in imitating the heavenly way and working hard for the people. This alternative makes changes, and yet it's as if no changes had been made, and that is what is difficult to emulate.

The second topic took the words "this is..." and looked at them as embodying the instructive tone that the brother took toward Zhongzi in order to persuade him to change his mind. The brother didn't imitate a village woman's sarcasm, nor did he mention "vomiting it up," and this gave his argument more strength. However, Zhongzi's perverse eccentricity did set him apart from ordinary people.

The third topic refuted the commentators' argument that the case in the "Kai feng" poem concerned only a single person and the wrong was therefore minor, whereas the disorder in the "Xiao pan" extended everywhere and the wrong was a major one. The essay contained this dictum: "A girl's loss of her virginity is no different than an emperor's loss of his country. To say of a widow's remarriage that it is a minor wrong means that women of the common people will never in their lives commit a major wrong." Let us put aside this argument and, in order to determine whether the wrong is a minor or a major one, consider whether it had actually been committed or not. We find that in the "Xiao pan" Empress Shen has been deposed, the Crown Prince has been exiled, and the danger has even spread to the ancestral shrine—of course it was a major wrong. The mother in the "Kai feng," by contrast, although she intended to remarry, had not yet done so, and her seven sons knew her secret and wrote the poem to take themselves to task, which is why the wrong was a minor one. The essay also contained the dictum: "'Exchange for thread' and 'you were escorted' inevitably show how habit and custom change our nature; 'mulberry leaves fallen' and 'O dove' show the feeling of shame from within the heart."[8]

Chuncai copied out the three essays and handed in his paper very early; he was the first out of the hall. For the second and third papers he merely spent a few taels and hired a substitute to take the papers for him, which the man did in a perfunctory way. However, the examiners were greatly impressed by the essays in the first paper and hailed Chuncai as a brilliant talent. When the results were posted, he had passed in twentieth place, while Ruyu himself had fallen below the cutoff point, which caused the Guangzhou candidates to protest the injustice but which left Wen Zhongweng beaming with delight. Jishi strongly recommended that Chuncai immediately submit a certificate of illness, so that he need not go out and meet his fellow graduates, bow to the examiners, and attend the celebration banquet. Both father and son were reluctant to agree, but fortunately Ruyu also urged them to follow Jishi's advice, and they finally dropped their opposition. Not until the chief examiner had left for the capital did the Wen family hold a banquet of their own.

To it they invited Lü Jue of the Salt Administration, Wu Bi-yuan of the River Police, Miao Qingju, registrar of Nanhai county, seven or eight wholesale and port merchants, as well as Ruyu, Jishi, Yannian, and so on, filling eight tables. Platters of assorted fruit were set out on a large buffet table. There were performances by actors from the north, the Honor and Glory troupe and the Good Fortune-Long Life troupe. Zhongweng and his son offered wine to the guests, and then after the actors had come forward and pre-sented their congratulations, everyone offered wine and flowers to Chuncai before going in to eat. After two hot courses had been served and four short plays performed, Biyuan and the others had the tops taken off the tables formed into two circles for the guests. The cooks brought elaborate fruit-filled delicacies with a "Plucking the Cassia in the Moon Palace" theme. Miao Qingju was the first to speak: "Well, Son-in-Law, with the support of all these gentle-men you have actually passed with high honors, which really is a matter for congratulation. However, the other day when the chief examiner was here, why didn't you go and call on him? If you'd sacrificed a few hundred taels and bowed before him as a 'wet' protégé, you'd have been assured of a metropolitan degree in the capital next spring."

"After all the grueling work he did on the three papers, my boy came down with a chill, and that's why he couldn't go out," said Zhongweng. "He'll make up for it next year by paying the exam-iner a visit."

"Before I became an official," continued Miao Qingju, "I took the preliminary examination several times, but that benighted magistrate couldn't appreciate my writing. He said you can't use exclamations in the exordium or write freely in the body of the essay—things like that. He also said that my essays were only a little over three hundred words in length, and that that was too short, and he refused to select me. This went on until a certain worthy named Hu came here as magistrate and chose me for the prefectural school. Although I never took the prefectural examination, I did prepare some elaborate presents and take them along to thank him. And this is what he told me: 'With a talent like yours at your age, why do you have to go looking for grief in the examination hall? You'd be far better off becoming a warden here with me and aiming for a nice, secure civil service post after the third triennial review. Wouldn't that be better than being one of those beggarly licentiates?' When he said that, I felt as if I were awakening from a dream, and I lost no time in buying myself a clerk's position. After a dozen or more years, having served out my term, I went to the capital, and it so happened that this same Hu Futai had been recommended for a position there and had risen to the rank of second-class secretary of one of the boards. Because we were old friends, I received strong support from him, which is why I've gotten as far as I have. You can see from my experience how important it was for you to pay your respects to that examiner."

Wu Biyuan and the others all agreed with him, but Jishi was so furious that he was rendered speechless and Ruyu succumbed to a fit of laughter.

"Don't you worry, Father-in-Law," said Chuncai. "In any case, I have six more good essays that I know by heart, and I'm sure that I'll be successful in the metropolitan examination. So long as you have true learning and genuine talent you don't need to go calling on people. Even if I should top the list of graduates, it still won't have cost more than a few hours' work on the part of Brother Ruyu. I just have to get through a couple more months of hardship."

At this point Jishi, afraid that Chuncai might go on further, intervened, "Now that Uncle Miao has told us what he was like as a young man, let's have a cup or two to liven things up."

The servants poured out more wine, Jishi handed a cup to each guest, and they all got up and bowed to thank him. The actresses Fengguan, Yuguan, and Sanxiu also came up and kowtowed, and asked if they could present another play and also if they could offer wine to the guests. Miao Qingju and the others had chosen the pieces previously performed. Now Ruyu chose the "Uproar at the Banquet"[9] scene, while Jishi chose "Falling Off a Horse,"[10] and Yannian "Monkey Seeks the Palm-leaf Fan for the Third Time."[11] They drank heartily and enjoyed themselves. Afterward Jishi returned home and spent the night with Huiruo. They talked about what had happened at the party and had a good laugh.

As Jishi got up the next morning, a servant came in to report, "The new governor will be here soon. It's that Master Shen who used to be the Guangzhou grain director."

"Quick! Go and find out when his boat's due at the dock," said Jishi. "I want to pay my respects."

Let us explain: After Master Shen was promoted to be lieutenant-governor of Jiangxi, the emperor began to view him with increasing favor. In the seventh month he was summoned to an audience and told to look into how the situation along the coast should be managed. His memorial strongly recommended Qing Xi as someone familiar with coastal defense who was capable of controlling both Guangxi and Guangdong. The emperor was pleased with the recommendation, and since the Guangdong governorship had long been vacant, he appointed Shen himself, and also instructed Qing Xi to take up the administration of the two provinces again as soon as possible. The order declared that Hu Cheng had made inappropriate decisions in trying to root out the bandits and was demoted to be intendant of Huizhou and

Chaozhou. He would continue to hold the office of governor-general until Qing Xi arrived.

Jiangshan and Shen Yinzhi had traveled together to the capital to take the provincial examinations. Yinzhi had graduated, but Jiangshan had failed once more and was living in his son's lodgings. Li Yuan told his father in confidence the story of Yao Huowu and the secret message Jishi had entrusted him with, and at that point Jiangshan gave up all thought of examinations. Instead he begged his son's fellow graduate, Censor Geng, to submit a memorial stating that he, Li Jiangshan, would be willing to accompany Governor Shen Jin in order to serve in the military and thus repay a small part of the debt of gratitude that he owed. The imperial rescript asked the board concerned as well as the Guangdong governor, Shen Jin, for their opinions, which they provided. By the terms of the imperial order, Li Jiangshan was to receive an honorary rank identical with his son's and to go with Shen Jin to serve as his counselor on military affairs. On receiving the imperial order, Jiangshan told his son to go back and marry, while he himself accompanied Master Shen. In the middle of the ninth month the two men set off.

Traveling together from post station to post station, they arrived in Guangzhou on the twenty-eighth of the eleventh month. All of the officials were there to welcome them. Master Shen entered the governor's yamen, where he received the seal of office, while Jiangshan looked for a residence.

Jishi had sent in his card at the dockside. After Master Shen had entered the governor's yamen and the civil and military officials had briefly presented themselves, he sent in his card again. Shen was delighted and called him in, served him tea, and said how distressed he had been to hear of his father's death, explaining that he had been unable to go into mourning because he was serving as an official. He went on to ask about other family matters. Jishi told him everything, and Shen was full of sympathy and praise. Jishi also congratulated Shen on his son's success in the examination, then took his leave and hurried over to Jiangshan's residence. The two men, suddenly reunited after a long separation, felt a joy that was tinged with sadness. They spoke for a while of everyday matters, and then Jiangshan sent his servants out of the room and said, "This journey of mine was forced upon me. Because of what you told my son last year, I asked the emperor's permission to come and serve here. But I don't know if what this Yao fellow says is sincere or whether it is simply an excuse to delay matters in the hope of putting off heavenly retribution."

"In my opinion what he says comes from his deeply held feelings," said Jishi. "If he receives a letter from you, he will surely surrender with his head bowed. Not only am I certain about this in my own mind, I could also take him a letter instructing him about the nature of good and bad fortune and persuading him to submit to punishment at the governor-general's hands."

"If you can do that," said Jiangshan, "Master Qing will surely put your plan into operation as soon as he gets here."

Chapter XXI
A friend's letter leads a hero to submit
A year's leave allows a censor to marry

After his defeat at Chaozhou, Governor-general Hu had given orders that the walls and moats of all the towns in the area should be rigorously guarded. He had also told several thousand soldiers of the Gaozhou garrison to advance and capture Mola that autumn. But Mola was crafty and an able tactician, and his four Defenders of the Faith were all exceptionally fearless warriors. Although Commander-in-Chief Ren had some extraordinary triumphs, to some extent throwing the enemy into confusion, in the end his achievements could not obscure the earlier failures. In the ninth month the governor-general received a stern reprimand from the emperor, and in the tenth month an imperial order demoted him to the position of intendant for Huizhou and Chaozhou. Withdrawing to the boundary of Chaozhou, he awaited the transfer of authority.

Early in the twelfth month the new governor-general, Qing Xi, arrived, and Hu Cheng had to return to Guangzhou to hand over his seal of office. Qing Xi faced in the direction of the imperial palace and kowtowed as he received the seal, to the applause of the numerous officials gathered there. Qing Xi told Hu Cheng to remain in the capital for the time being and accompany the army when it advanced in the spring.

Soon the old year was over. When Shen left the court, the emperor had told him as a matter of urgency to cooperate with Qing

Xi in rooting out the bandits in order to spare the people of Guangdong. Shen therefore invited Governor-general Qing, Commander-in-Chief Ren, Counselor Li, and Intendant Hu to a conference. By noon everyone had arrived. Officials served tea, after which Shen raised his hand and began, "I have received personal instructions from the emperor to cooperate with Governor-general Qing in capturing the Huizhou and Chaozhou bandits. I am embarrassed to say that I have only a modest knowledge of civil affairs and a limited capacity for military matters, and I am asking you gentlemen to enlighten me."

"Commander-in-Chief Ren has tried several times to stamp out the rebellion," said Governor-general Qing, "and he has been fighting continuously for a year now. I expect he has a thorough knowledge of the facts about the two bandits. I hope, Commander-in-Chief, that you will put forward plans for our consideration, after which Governor Shen and Counselor Li will decide the issue."

"I bear a heavy burden, having several times brought shame to the imperial army," said Ren. "By the emperor's grace I was not executed but allowed to continue serving humbly in the army. I would never dare do anything but present my ideas clearly to you in the hope of repaying his mercy. In general, the two bandits' crimes in rebelling are equal, but Mola's wickedness exceeds that of Huowu. Huowu is entrenched in an impregnable redoubt, and although he continues to defy the court, he has not taken human life lightly. The fact that he deliberately rebelled may well be due to some particular issue. Last year he released sub-prefect Hu and rebuffed Mola's emissary; when Cao Zhiren unintentionally encroached on Jiaying, he withdrew his troops; and when Lü Youkui got drunk and assaulted a common citizen, he had him flogged— all of which stands to his credit. As for Mola, his crimes of greed, cruelty, arrogance, and license are truly heinous, and the common people suffer greatly, so we should naturally destroy him first before turning our attention to Lufeng. However, Mola is a ferocious opponent, infinitely cunning, and we will be heavily dependent on the formidable qualities of you two gentlemen as well as on the counselor's brilliant planning."

"Counselor Li volunteered in court to attack the enemy by joining the army on the Guangdong coast," said Governor-general Qing. "He must surely have some extraordinary plan that will benefit the region. May I call on you to enlighten us, Counselor?"

"I have just one trivial point to make," said Li. "I'd prefer to leave the decision to you gentlemen. Throughout history there have been only two methods of suppressing bandits: negotiation and liquidation. I wonder if Intendant Hu has ever called upon these bandits to surrender?"

"The bald-headed bandit has been so wild and irresponsible that he might well not respond to an overture," said Intendant Hu. "The Yao bandit and his men conquered two counties in the space of just a few days, and so their morale is at its height. Moreover, because General He's whole army had been wiped out, I swore that I would destroy them without delay. That is why I never considered negotiation."

"I have listened with great respect to the Commander-in-'Chief's views," said Counselor Li. "They are indeed the perceptive views of a seasoned veteran. Mola's wickedness is so great that it rises to the very heavens, and in his case one must naturally advise liquidation. Yao Huowu rebuffed the messenger from the demon priest, and he may well not be ill-disposed toward the court. In my humble opinion, we ought first to negotiate with the Lufeng bandits and then proceed to liquidate Mola."

"My nephew's is a scholar's opinion, which is necessarily an armchair strategy," said Governor Shen. "Would Commander-in-Chief Ren and Intendant Hu agree with it, I wonder?"

"I would agree that what the counselor is suggesting is the correct policy," said Ren. "I had just returned from marine patrol when I fought at Chaozhou, which is why I didn't think of it."

"First negotiate, then liquidate," said Governor-general Qing, "that's standard military practice. If I may call on you again, Master Li, how would you suggest that we go about this negotiation?"

"I would ask each of you gentlemen to choose your finest troops and move them to Huizhou. Then I would draw up a document for the bandits describing the respective dangers and benefits of each course of action, offering them mercy but also issuing threats at the same time. The bandits will gain some idea of what it means either to surrender or to resist, and naturally they will choose to surrender to our army with their hands tied behind their backs."

"Since the governor-general and the general are in agreement on this," said Shen, "my nephew should quickly draw up such a document. But we have still to decide on a skilled and dependable person to deliver it."

Having settled the issue, they parted. Only Hu Cheng smiled to himself, believing that the plan would not work.

Next day Commander-in-Chief Ren took his leave and returned to Huizhou, and the governor-general and governor selected ten thousand elite troops and brought in Ba Bu and other experienced officers. They arranged to set out at the beginning of the second month. Li Jiangshan's draft of the document was now complete. He settled on the main thrust of his argument, in which he used his own name, and presented it to the governor-general and governor.

Li Jiangshan, by imperial assignment counselor on military affairs in Guangdong, recipient of an honorary rank identical with his son's as censor on the Henan circuit, directs this document to Yao Huowu, self-styled Commander of Fengle:

From ancient times to the present day, there has never been a heroic figure who has seized land by illegal means, and in this dynasty there has never been a bandit who was not eventually suppressed by force. Under our emperor, the one man does good,[1] and the five sacred mountains are free from strife; the people within the four seas lead frugal lives, and the farthest territories prostrate themselves in submission. The king of Yelang in the western regions once thought his kingdom great,[2] but his maps and population registers were returned to the east. Among the southern tribes, even before the Qiong bamboo cane was presented,[3] the ruler had bound himself to the north. Qi was full of apprehension,[4] and it took only a writing brush to chastise it; the king of Minyue[5] was like the mantis that tried to defy the chariot wheel, and it took merely a whip to subdue him. All of the meritorious deeds not recorded in the historical texts are to be heard on the lips of the people. Although the events took place far away, how can you not know about them? In your remote outpost on the Guangdong coast, you have begun an insurrection. You tell yourself that Yang Yao[6] put too much faith in the impregnable nature of Lake Dongting, where any attackers would have had to have wings, and that Zhigao[7] took refuge in a corner of Yongzhou, where no one could have fought his way in. Just as a feather dance is performed at court,[8] with your bows and nets you are deceiving our people and harassing our troops.

Alas! A wild beast about to enter a trap cannot be reprieved even if it wags its tail; a bird caught in a noose cannot be pardoned even if it throws itself on the hunter's mercy. The emperor has blazed forth his anger[9] and decided on a display of our military might.[10] He has ordered Governor-general Qing of Guangdong and Guangxi and Governor Shen of Guangdong to come before him and draw up plans for the provinces. The state of Shu employed a learned general, Ma Su,[11] but his army was forced to withdraw from Jieting; the ivory tally of command was bestowed in the palace, while the bronze ring was broken in the field. Now, wherever the sun bathes the earth with its rays, it melts the frost and snow; after a long drought the people long for a rainbow[12] and rush to give their allegiance. How dangerous, some of your men will say.[13] As a counselor, I claim a certain foreknowledge, an ability to see into the future. I think of you and your men as frogs at the bottom of a well; why are you not behaving like filial sons and obedient grandsons? When the sparrows fly up in the morning, surely they know they are in the emperor's domain! Therefore beg for your life from the commanding general, and he will save you. If you have no intention of rebelling again, you should ask for a decree sparing your life. But your word will have to be as firm as metal or stone, as lasting as mountains and rivers. If your old schemes are still alive, if your ambitions are not yet dead, then a mighty, fast-moving army in five columns, employing Sun Wu's[14] tactic of applying maximum force, will attack you with powerful bows and armor-piercing arrows; they will bring you in bonds before the palace gates, and heads will roll. The mountains will be uprooted, but not by reliance on the five titans; Heaven's net is finely woven, and there may well be no escape. Hang up your bows, destroy what you have, the good as well as the bad, and your exploits will be engraved on brass pillars, and the farthest corners of the land will be filled with song. But if you ignore this opportunity, you well come to regret it. Hence this document.

"The strong buildup makes a powerful impression," said Governor-general Qing. "It should serve to sap their courage." He turned to Shen, "And now we must choose a suitable delegate."

"My nephew tells me that there's a senior licentiate here in Panyu county named Su Fang who is young but experienced. He used to be a pupil of my nephew's. He'd be willing to go."

"This is a critical mission, not some routine task, but if you two agree on him, I daresay he's qualified," said the governor-general.

"He may be young, he's shown a good deal of ability," said Li. "Moreover, he has actively sought the task, but only out of a sense of public duty. He's outside right now, and I would urge you to test him."

The governor-general called Jishi in. He came forward and paid his respects and was told to take a seat. After he had been given a cup of tea, the governor-general remarked, "Counselor Li has strongly recommended you as the one to offer amnesty to Yao Huowu in return for his surrender. If you were to go, I wonder how you would put the case to him?"

"I'm just a licentiate and I lack debating skills, but if I you were to appoint me, I would simply have to announce the court's order and stress the commander's benevolence and awesome power. The objective would be to make him understand the cardinal principle of obedience as opposed to rebellion and lead him to lay down his arms and submit and then go on to render service by destroying the bald-headed bandit. I wonder what you think of that argument?"

"Excellent! You have the looks of a Zhang Xu[15] and the ambitions of a Zhong Jun,[16] and one day you'll surely be given national responsibility. If Yao Huowu really can recapture Chaozhou, Governor Shen and I will certainly beg the emperor to show him mercy, not only pardoning him for his earlier crimes but also giving him special treatment as a reward for reforming himself." He told Jishi to set out ahead of the army on the twenty-eighth. He also detached two lieutenants from his own brigade to escort him. Furthermore, if Jishi was successful, he would appeal to the emperor to bestow his favor on him.

Jishi thanked him and left. He was then taken by Jiangshan to his residence and invited to stay and share some wine. "This mission of yours is critical for restoring peace to Guangdong, and you'll need to be extremely careful," said Jiangshan. "In addition to the document, I also have a letter for you to take to Huowu. It seems that he himself will not be too hard to persuade, but I fear that his followers may not agree, in which case you'll need all your powers of persuasion."

"I found out some time ago that the people forced into rebelling were all militiamen previously recruited by Governor-general Qing. Later, because Governor-general Hu changed the regulations, the local officials resorted to trickery and extorted money from the militiamen, with the result that they became disaffected and turned to banditry. Provided we make known the generosity of Governor-general Qing, they will naturally submit. I am to set off five days before the army, and I expect Huowu to be here in Guangzhou before it reaches Huizhou."

"I hope you're right! Tomorrow morning I'll send someone over with the document and the letter. You don't need to take leave of the governor-general again. I'll speak to him for you."

Jishi went back home, to find the two lieutenants with upward of twenty troops waiting at his gate. He told some of his servants to play host to them, while he went in and ordered others to pack up for the journey. Du Chong, Aqing, Sheng Yong, and Awang would go with him. After receiving Jiangshan's document and letter, he drew the soldiers' wages, and embarked.

Because he was on a military mission, he was greeted by local officials all along the way. Arriving in Huizhou, he met the commander-in-chief, and then he and his escort of thirty or more set off on horseback for Goat's Foot Ridge.

From the top of the pass they saw a group of men approaching them on horseback. There was a shout of "Fire!" followed by a sound like that of a watchman's rattle as arrows filled the air like a swarm of locusts. One of Jishi's soldiers was wounded, and Jishi at once told his men to withdraw, while he sent Du Chong on alone to deliver the message. Du Chong spurred on his horse, shouting "Don't fire! Master Su has something he wants to talk to you about." Only after Wang Dahai and the others had received detailed information from him did they fire a cannon to open the checkpoint and draw up their troops to welcome Jishi. Generals Wang and Chu, who already knew him, arranged a feast. At the same time they called up five hundred troops. Wang Dahai himself would lead them in escorting Jishi and his party.

In less than two days they arrived in Lufeng. By now Yao Huowu and his men knew that a new governor-general had been appointed and that he was none other than the Qing Xi who had recruited them as militiamen. They all wished to surrender, their only fear being that their crimes might be too grave to be pardoned. On hearing that Jishi had come bearing a document, they realized that a favorable imperial order must have been issued, and they were overjoyed. Yao at once ordered Dun'an and Feng Gang to go out and meet him, while he himself waited in front of his headquarters.

Before long Jishi arrived, and Huowu welcomed him with a bow. Jishi told the soldiers to wait outside, while he went into the hall with Huowu and handed over the document as well as Jiangshan's letter. Huowu read them both and said, "I had no idea Brother Jiangshan was here. If I had known, I'd have laid down my arms and surrendered long ago."

Jishi then related how the year before last he had told the full story to Li Yuan and how on his return to the capital Li had told his father. This was what had caused the latter to request an imperial edict calling on Yao Huowu to surrender.

Huowu bowed again and thanked him: "I am indebted to Brother Jiangshan and his son for their support in a variety of circumstances, and I must think how I can repay their kindness. Please stay here a few days, while I gather my brothers together and go before the governor-general, where fate will decide whether we live or die." He sent messengers on horseback to withdraw the officers in charge of the Jieshi and Jiazi garrisons, and at the same time ordered Feng Gang to review the troops. Those originally garrisoned there were to stay, while the new additions and those who had pledged their allegiance later were to come with him. He also ordered Han Pu to calculate the surplus money and grain that they had in storage and to set up ledgers to turn over to the court. The local officials confined to jail were to be taken to Guangzhou and handed over to the governor-general and governor for punishment. He held a grand banquet, which was joyously celebrated. He also sent men to host the lieutenants and the Su family servants as well as the twenty-odd soldiers who had come with Jishi. Each man was paid for his expenses. That night he took Jishi back again to the former official residence to sleep.

Next morning Huowu led his men to visit Jishi at the residence, where they were invited to sit down. Their conversation went on for some time, but Dun'an had still not arrived. Huowu sent someone to hurry him along, but then one of the gatekeepers reported, "The strategist set off at midnight last night. I don't know where he went, but he left a message for you, sir, plus all of the money, clothes, and other items that you've given him. They're locked up in the building, untouched."

Huowu hastily pulled out the message and read it:

As a mere commoner, I received the favor of an appointment. We spoke together for a little while and had a meeting of minds. I was given responsibility for an important task, and I worked hard at it for a year or more without failing in my duty. But now the governor-general is offering you amnesty, and you will give your allegiance to the emperor. I performed a divination last night and found that when you, sir, as the great roc spread your wings, the little birds will soar upward too. My only regret is that my wretched self is not destined for higher office and that I cannot serve for long at your side and have the pleasure of observing your great achievements. I shall take my ease afloat on the sea—I wonder what the Master of Red Pine[17] is like! I only hope that you, dear sir, will forgive me.

As Huowu finished reading, the tears were streaming down his face. He heaved a sigh: "Only a tiny fraction of Dun'an's strategic talents have been displayed so far, and now he has suddenly left us. What a terrible blow!"

Jishi tried to console him: "Don't grieve, General. He has turned his back on success and fame. Each man seeks his own ideal."

"He joined us after the beginning, and now he's left us before the end," said Feng Gang. "Meetings and partings are all a matter of fate. Why take it so to heart?" They prepared a banquet, at which Jishi spoke of Mola's depravity and his vicious treatment of the people. If the general could get permission from the governor-general to attack and destroy this priest, he could certainly expect to receive high honors.

"Since I have dedicated my life to this country, I'd willingly go through fire and flood for it," said Huowu, "but I would never presume to hope for honors. I seek only to avoid punishment!" And there we shall leave the subject.

When Jishi had spent three days in the camp, the officers from Jieshi and Jiazi arrived and Huowu ordered his men to erect the flag of surrender and set forth together. At Goat's Foot Ridge they joined forces with their other troops, making a total of fifteen officers and twelve thousand cavalry and infantry, all bound for Huizhou. On learning that the governor-general and governor were already in Huizhou and encamped with Commander-in-Chief Ren about ten miles outside of town, Huowu ordered his men to set up camp at Pingshan while Jishi went ahead to give his report. After that Huowu and his men took off their armor and, with their hands bound behind their backs, waited at the entrance to the camp. When the governor-general, the governor, and the commander-in-chief learned that Yao Huowu's entire force was ready to offer its allegiance, they were overjoyed. They congratulated Jiangshan and Jishi and had cannon fired to open the camp. The whole army was arrayed in full battle dress, and the officers lined up on each side. Then the order was given for Huowu to enter.

Joining Han may be like joining Heaven,[18]
But surrender is like facing the foe.

Huowu and his men came forward on their knees and kow-towed to admit their guilt. The governor-general and the governor both stood up, and the commander-in-chief released the rebels from their bonds and allowed them to sit and drink tea, com-mending them repeatedly for their action. Huowu handed over the ledgers detailing the surpluses in the treasury and storehouses and also the local officials who had been arrested together with the people's accusations against them. The governor-general and governor received the books and ordered that the officials be sent to the prefect of Guangzhou for investigation. Huowu knelt down again and pleaded, "I am guilty of monstrous crimes, and it would be impossible for me to repay you for your magnanimous pardon, gentlemen. However, I am willing to lead my troops to Chaozhou and capture the demon priest in order to atone for my sins. I humbly await your decision."

"General, you righteously rebuffed the advances of the rebel priest, which augured well for your pledge of allegiance today," said the governor-general. "Since you wish to render service by eradicating the rebels, I myself, with the governor and the commander-in-chief will recommend that you be appointed to lead the troops in their advance. Let us go into Guangzhou together and quietly await the imperial response." Huowu bowed in gratitude once more. Then the governor-general rewarded them all with a feast. He ordered Major-general Ba and the prefect of Huizhou to accompany them and issued twelve thousand taels, five hundred jars of wine, and five hundred catties of meat as a reward for the troops who had surrendered. Although Lü Youkui, Ho Wu, and others had surrendered along with Huowu, they inevitably still harbored some disloyal thoughts, but when they saw the governor-general treating them with such consideration, their animosity was quietly dispelled.

After discussing the matter, the governor-general and governor divided the twelve thousand men up among the brigades. Yao Huowu and his officers were to join the governor's brigade, and Governor Shen wished to put Yao Huowu in temporary charge of the brigade's military affairs. He recommended as much in a memorial, at the same time choosing civil and military officials to take up office in Haifeng and other places. Li Jiangshan received Yao Huowu and ate with him by day and slept beside him at night.

They accompanied the governor-general and governor back to Guangzhou, and Jiangshan had much wisdom and encouragement to impart. Huowu also enlisted Jiangshan's help in requesting a favor of the governor-general: that he redress the injustice done to his brother. Jiangshan promised that after Huowu had distinguished himself at Chaozhou he would ask the governor-general to write a memorial to that effect.

Before long they arrived in Guangzhou, and that very day the three leaders sent a memorial to the emperor by express delivery and then waited to put his response into practice. Governor Shen told Huowu to take the rank of lieutenant-colonel, and naturally he lived with Feng Gang and the other officers. Meanwhile Jiangshan was left with little to do. Apart from idle conversation with the governor-general and governor, he spent his days in the company of Jishi and Ruyu, enjoying himself with wine and poetry.

One day as Jishi returned from dinner at Huowu's quarters, Du Chong came back with him and said: "I have something confidential to report, sir." Jishi took a seat in the study and dismissed the servants. Du Chong continued, "I did something very wrong last year, but with your great generosity you helped the two of us to marry. I've been regretting that I had no way of repaying you, but today I heard you discussing the Chaozhou situation with Masters Li and Yao, and I know only too well what a dangerous enemy this priest Mola is; he cannot be defeated in short order, and even if you do defeat him, the outer defenses of Chaozhou are so strong that you could not take that city with less than seventy or eighty thousand men. But I've thought of an idea that could serve both to repay your generosity and also provide me with the beginnings of a career. I'm wondering if it could be put into practice."

"If you have an idea, please tell me about it."

"I knew that priest when I worked at the Customs. When he made off with the stolen goods, he left a package behind in which a lama priest's ordination certificate was hidden—a prized possession of his. I retrieved it, and I have it with me. Moreover, I paid a visit to the Chaozhou area the year before last, and I got to know a few of the Customs clerks. I plan to use the fake surrender ploy with him. First, I'll go and pledge my allegiance. As soon as he sees the certificate, he's bound to employ me. When you and Master Yao lead your troops to Chaozhou, I'll find an opportunity to shoot an arrow with a message attached giving you the date and time when one of the city gates will be opened and you will be welcomed in. Wouldn't that be an easy way of capturing him?"

Jishi was thrilled. "That's brilliant! But you'll need to be very discreet about it."

"I know. Please don't tell the others, lest the news leak out. I'll set off tomorrow." Jishi approved the plan, and Du Chong slipped away in the early hours of the following morning.

It was now time for Jishi to shed his mourning clothes. He invited several dozen Buddhist and Daoist priests to hold services for the deceased. After the spirit tablet had been burned, Jishi realized it was almost time for Li Yuan to return and marry, so he told Su Xing to buy whatever was necessary. He himself chose a day to marry Qiao and to take Wuyun and Yeyun as concubines. Each was given her own room and allocated two personal maids. Everyone addressed Wuyun and Yeyun as "concubine," and they were ranked on the same level as Xia and Qiao.

> Despite an array of beauties to please the eye,
> He's distracted wherever he happens to go;
> For now his amorous desires are at an end,
> And he lets his horse trample the fruit the girls throw.[19]

Back in the capital Li Yuan had intended to wait while Shen Yinzhi took the metropolitan examinations and then travel south with him. During the last Lantern Festival, he had gone to wait on the emperor with a Censor Jiang, and the emperor had asked him whether he was married or not. On his knees Li had replied, "My father, Li Guodong, arranged a match for me with the sister of Su Fang, a senior licentiate of Panyu County in Guangdong, but we are not yet married." The next day a eunuch handed him an imperial decree:[20]

> To Li Yuan, serving as censor on the Henan circuit, who as a minor attended the banquet for successful metropolitan graduates: Now that you are about to participate in the capping ceremony,[21] this is the right time for you to take a wife. Your father, Guodong, enthusiastically volunteered in court for service, and has hastened to the Guangdong coast. You have the cap and accoutrements of a censor and serve at court. Now the ice is about to melt, and still you tarry during this most auspicious time. The peach trees have started to bloom, and you have not yet planned a meeting for the second month of spring. The wind is chill in the censorate, and the nights are long as measured by the water clock. Surprised at the Three Stars in the sky, you still wait for the dawn audience, and it concerns me greatly. I am now granting you special leave to return home and complete the splendor of the marriage ceremony. Even with the golden lotus-shaped lanterns removed, a light will shine in the heavens; palace brocade will be bestowed on you for your garments, and the fragrance will be sensed among the people. I shall appoint a senior minister as matchmaker to regulate the ceremony.
>
> Ah! Coins from the heavens will be scattered inside the boudoir,[22] and the warbling of luan-birds will be heard among the stars. Brushes will write their prothalamia, their silver handles glimmering like jeweled hairpins. The multicolored

silk coverlet will be splendid; the night attendants will have
scented the bed; and a sealed document will confer honors on
the bride.

On that day there will be spring along the river as you
present the goose[23]—a son will indeed be returning home in
triumph. But next year when at dawn I hear the cock crow, I,
too, shall be waiting anxiously for your return. Do not go on
enjoying your shared dreams, but bring them to an end.

On receiving the order, Li Yuan did not dare tarry but that
very day left the court after thanking the emperor for his kindness.
He sent a messenger ahead with a letter for Guangdong, while he
himself took leave of his colleagues and Yinzhi. In the capital this
incident circulated widely as a marvelous anecdote. We need not
go into detail about the people, at least three hundred of them,
who wrote poems for Li Yuan and offered him farewell meals.

He traveled first to Jiangsu and reported to his grandparents
and his mother. After staying with them for three days, he went by
way of Zhejiang and Jiangxi to Guangdong, arriving in the third
month of spring. Jishi had received his letter from the first post-sta-
tion, and everything was ready. When Li Yuan arrived, he greeted
his father, and then visited the governor-general, the governor, and
the other provincial, prefectural, and county officers as well as the
Wen and Su families. The wedding was arranged for the first of the
fourth month. Li Yuan was going to stay with the Su family, as Jishi
had proposed, but his father insisted that he stay at his residence,
and the son had to agree. On the wedding day, all the officials in
the province sent presents and offered congratulations. There was
a brilliant display of lanterns and much song and music, needless
to say. The bridal sedan chair entered the inner gate and the bride
was helped out. Li Yuan first faced in the direction of the court and
expressed his thanks to the emperor for his kindness, then bowed

before the wedding candles. Maids holding lanterns showed the couple to their wedding chamber, where naturally the dozen maids and serving women from the Su household surrounded the bride and attended on her. It was late at night before the guests departed. Exhilarated by the wine, the bridal couple entered the wedding chamber, and Pearl put down the fan she had been holding in front of her face, undressed, and joined her husband beneath the covers. Their wedding night was joyous, as may well be imagined. There is a "Remembering the Flute-playing on Phoenix Terrace" that shows just how joyous it was:

> The pillow is stitched with lovebirds, the bed inlaid with
>   ivory,
> The curtains are of the finest silk, the screen
>   embroidered—
> It's rightly called a bower of bliss.
> Flowers lean against the courtyard trees;
> Moonlight shines through the curtain hooks.
> She arose that morning, freshly made up,
> Her delicate complexion powdered and perfumed.
> She pulled her cloud puffs aside,
> Graceful as ever,
> With a special kind of charm.
> Far into the future
> A hundred-year marriage now begins.
> See the lotus burning in the censer,[24]
> Soft jade in a fairy palace.
> It's a pity the day was long and the people tired,
> It seemed to last for three autumns.
> Afraid that her beloved would mock her
> Alas, he mentioned how bashful she was,

But in the grip of passion,
A flush suffuses her cheeks
And spring seeps into her brows.

Chapter XXII

*After receiving high office, a civil official joins the army
While taking defensive measures,
a demon practices magic*

⤳

After routing the army led by Governor-general Hu and Commander-in-Chief Ren, Mola had been amusing himself with wine, women, and song. When he heard that Huowu had humiliated his emissary, he flew into a rage and determined to mobilize his forces and seize Huowu's territory, but Haiyuan and the other Defenders argued against such a course, urging him not to create another enemy for himself, and he finally let the matter drop. He had done a great deal of construction in the prefectural yamen, building an As You Like It Tower, an Enchantment Hall, and a Studio Escape and filling them with girls of good family selected during the Lantern Festival. He now indulged himself with a gargantuan appetite, venting his passions in the most appalling manner, relying on the secret use of his great asset—the ability to withhold his semen while ingesting his female partner's essence. However, there is a limit to any man's vital powers, while the supply of female beauty is inexhaustible, and gradually his mastery of muscular control began to fail; he would ejaculate without being able to ingest, and he could no longer prevent the women from absorbing his semen. As a consequence his thoughts turned to the past, when he possessed a large quantity of endowment pills, but unfortunately he had lost them in Guangzhou and could not make any more because he lacked the exotic ingredients found only in the islands. Later he heard from his scouts that Yao Huowu's entire force had surrendered, and he realized that he was isolated and would surely be locked in a life-and-death struggle. It occurred to him that "before an army marches, its food supply goes on ahead." Recently, the consumption of army provisions had been heavy, and there were no reserves left. He ordered Haiyuan and the other Defenders to lead two thousand troops each and attack the towns in the surrounding area to seize storehouses and also gain the support of some of the towns. However, each garrison had received secret instructions from Commander-in-Chief Ren to mount a strict guard on its walls and not go out and fight, and the Defenders returned with their mission unfulfilled. Mola was reduced to telling them to go into the countryside and ask rich landowners to lend him provisions so that he could mount a defense.

One day he was enjoying himself in As You Like It Tower when an attendant reported: "General Meng has brought in a man from the capital to see you. He says he used to be on Your Majesty's personal staff and is making a special visit here to offer his allegiance." Mola ordered the man taken to the Rear Palace for an audience. After dallying a bit longer, he strolled over and took a seat at the head of the hall. Along each side a hundred or more executioners were arrayed.

The man in question came forward and kowtowed. "Where are you from, and what is your name?" thundered Mola. "I suppose you've come from Guangzhou to spy on me?"

"My name is Du Chong. I used to be an attendant of Bao Jin-cai's in the Customs, but I don't suppose you remember me now that you've become a monarch. And all I know is how to serve my master, not how to be some sort of spy."

"That superintendent of yours has ruined everything! Well, what brings you here?"

"After His Honor's property was confiscated, I had nowhere to turn. I had picked up two prized possessions of Your Majesty's, and I wanted to bring them to you, but the army was blocking all the roads, so I made a detour through Huizhou, where I was captured by soldiers under the command of Yao Huowu and held for a year. Now Yao has surrendered and I've at last been able to come here." As he finished speaking, he took out a gold-lacquered gourd and a cloth wrapper, and presented them with both hands.

Mola was delighted to see the two familiar objects and told Du Chong to stand up. "Good lad!" he said. "It can't have been easy for you. But what position were you hoping to get?"

"I can't use a weapon and I don't know anything about writing, so I wouldn't presume to be an official. I'd prefer to serve Your Majesty. I'd like to be employed by you, sir."

"Very well. I do need someone to watch over the gate to my inner palace. Let me put you in charge. Since you were in service with the superintendent, it is fine for you to go into the women's palaces and convey messages, just so long as you don't go into places like As You Like It Tower or Enchantment Hall." Du Chong kowtowed in gratitude, and moved into quarters beside the palace entrance. A number of attendants came by to kowtow, addressing him as "sir," and many of the regime's civil and military officials also visited to offer their congratulations. It was a lively occasion.

The next day, after attending Mola's morning audience, Du Chong went with him into his private quarters and paid his respects to the four imperial concubines, who questioned him about the past. Then he visited the various civil and military officers, some of whom invited him to tea or dinner. He did not return until the evening, when Mola gave him a command arrow and sent him out to tell Zhou Yude to speed up the collecting of provisions in the area. Taking the arrow, Du Chong mounted a horse and rode to the residence of Chief Zhou to deliver the order. It was the first watch when he returned, and he went into the palace intending to give his report, only to find that Mola was having a nightcap in Studio Escape. He didn't dare go in himself, but told a girl attendant to relay the report for him. When she returned to say that His Majesty had received it, he began slowly walking out again past Pinwa and the other concubines' doors. Since Mola had discarded his old loves for new ones and had not visited his concubines in a full month, they were inevitably full of resentment, and on seeing Du Chong, they felt correspondingly warm toward him. In addition, Du Chong was quite captivating—an attractive young fellow with romantic looks and a graceful figure. Just as they were leaning against their doorways hoping that Mola would come by, Du Chong happened to walk past, and Pinwa called him in. "Where have you been?" she asked.

"I've been to report to His Majesty. I waited outside Studio Escape for some time before coming here."

"What's His Majesty doing in there?"

"I didn't go in, so I don't know. He appears to be having a drink with a number of ladies."

Pinwa heaved a sigh, and gave orders to the attendants. "See that all the doors are locked. This Master Du is an old friend of ours. And quickly go and ask the three other ladies to step over here. We're going to give him a party." The attendants went off.

"That's most kind of you, milady," said Du, "but I wouldn't dare accept your invitation."

"We're the ones giving the party, so what are you afraid of?" said Pinwa with a laugh. "It's not the way it used to be in the

Customs; no one here would dare to tell any tales. And even if His Majesty did learn of it, he couldn't stop us. Have a little gumption!" As she spoke, she went inside, and the attendants pulled Du Chong after her. Soon the other three concubines arrived, wine was set out, and delicacies were arrayed in front of them. The four women told Du to sit beside them, while the maids poured wine and they all enjoyed themselves. The wine had been made by Mola with the use of drugs, and it was extremely potent. Du had no head for wine, and he adamantly refused to drink, but he could not hold out against the women's repeated insistence, and before he knew it he had lost his balance, keeled over, and collapsed. Pinwa ordered the wine taken away, and then she and the other three stripped off Du Chong's clothes and laid him on the bed. Because he had been taking Mola's endowment pills, his instrument was long and slender, a dazzling sight. The four women all "opened the door to the intruder," taking turns to gorge themselves as they satisfied their ravenous desires.

This was not the first time they had played this kind of game, nor had the game been confined to any one man, and the attendants were quite accustomed to it. But when Du came to his senses, he could not suppress a feeling of sheer terror. The women tried to calm him, and he began to relax a little. Moreover, he still had an arrow fitted to his bow and felt he simply had to shoot it, so he did his utmost in dallying with the women, all of whom praised his youthful vigor. From this time on he and the four concubines formed a unit, and the attendants, who detested Mola for his cruelty, and who also appreciated the tips that Du Chong doled out, were hardly willing to betray him. Meanwhile Du attended on Mola every day, transmitting his orders and wielding a considerable amount of authority.

Let us leave him and turn to Ruyu. Although to all outward

appearances he was content with the quiet life he was leading, his mind was set on success in the examinations. When he learned that Li Yuan had received an imperial decree allowing him to marry—a glorious event—he determined to excel, too. This was the year of the regular triennial provincial examination, and in the Su household he devoted his whole attention to his studies; he did not so much as look at the garden, and he was never without a book in his hand. When he heard that Jiangshan was a famous scholar from Jiangsu, he asked his advice on the essays he had written. Jiangshan was unstinting in his praise, but warned him: "The structure ought not be too strict nor the line of thought too complex; for historical allusions you should use only those that are commonly met with; and you should on no account quote from such works as the *Xun Zi* or the *Lie Zi*. Your style needs merely to suit the current fashion; you certainly shouldn't imitate the school of Ouyang Xiu or Su Shi. Those are the techniques you need for success. No doubt the examiners qualified with that kind of thing themselves and now employ it in selecting others. I've been competing for upward of twenty years. I've failed so far, and I fully expect to go to my grave as a licentiate, but you should be warned by my experience." Ruyu took the point and modified his approach.

Li Yuan had now been married a full month, and Jiangshan told him to take his bride back to his native place and attend on his grandparents for six months, which would also qualify as a filial act since he would be taking his father's place. Having said goodbye to the officials as well as to friends and relatives, Li Yuan chose an auspicious day to set off. Pearl found it almost impossible to part from her mother, her birth mother, her sister-in-law, and her sister, but having married, she had to follow her husband, and she managed to overcome her distress. After the Duanyang Festival they set off accompanied by a bevy of servants.

Jishi returned from seeing them off, to find his mother's face still streaming with tears. He tried to calm her: "Pearl has gone with her husband to his native place. He's a distinguished official and she's a woman of rank—why, it's a matter for congratulations! In two or three years' time, she'll feel homesick, and she'll be able to come back and see you. Why do you have to be sad?"

"I know that after a woman marries she follows her husband, but when in all the years since I married have I ever felt homesick? Moreover, in her case, the distance is greater, and if for four or five years there's no communication between us, that will be the end. The little hussy goes a few hundred miles away simply bursting with enthusiasm! How can I bear to part with her? As for Belle, you must make it clear that her husband has to live with us; on no account must you let her go off to some distant place as well."

"That's simple enough. In any case Ruyu's family live quite close, and she could come home often. The only problem is that Ruyu may also become an official, in which case we can't be sure that she be able to come."

"I'm told that he's been studying day and night," she said. "Try and persuade him to accept his present situation. What's the good of being an official, anyway? Look at Master Qu; he rose to be governor, and yet he was captured by bandits and is suffering terribly."

Jishi laughed and was just about to reply when a maid reported, "There's a whole lot of people outside in the hall with good news. They say you've been made an official, sir, and they want you to go out and reward them."

Jishi laughed as he went out. "You were just saying how bad it was to be an official, and now here's another case of it! Who would want to be one?"

It was the imperial rescript to the joint memorial from the governor-general and governor, which ran as follows: "Yao Huowu is permitted to serve as lieutenant-colonel. As for his fourteen staff officers, the governor-general and governor are instructed to appoint the men at their discretion as captains or lieutenants; on an agreed date they are to lead the troops to attack and eradicate the Chaozhou rebels. Licentiate Li Guodong is to be employed as an intendant of the Court of State Ceremonial at the fifth rank, and Senior Licentiate Su Fang is appointed as a secretary of the grand secretariat; both will be attached to the army as counselors. Governor-general Qing Xi will be promoted the first rank and Governor Shen Jin the second." Jishi took a look at the *Beijing Gazette* and distributed money among the crowd. Then a messenger came with an order from the governor-general's and governor's offices to say that the next day everyone was to gather at the governor's residence to consider certain matters. Jishi acknowledged receipt of the message and ordered a chair to be made ready. He went first to the governor-general's and the governor's yamens to express his gratitude and then on to Jiangshan's residence and Lieutenant-colonel Yao's headquarters. On his return, he found that the governor-general, the governor, and the high provincial officials had all sent cards, and that the civil and military officials of the prefecture and the local counties were arriving in an endless stream to offer their congratulations. He sent servants with thank-you cards to each of them. The whole day was spent in hectic activity of this kind. Next morning he went to each yamen to pay his respects.

Although his position as secretary was only at the seventh grade, it carried considerable prestige. As secretary, you wrote a card in fist-size characters to present to people. If you met a grand secretary, you referred to yourself simply as his disciple; if you met the president of a board, you gave a deep bow only; and if you visited a governor-general or governor or some other high provincial official, you entered and left through the inner gate.

After Jishi had paid return visits to the various officials, he went to the governor's yamen for the conference on eradicating the rebels from Chaozhou. The decision arrived at was that for the time being Yao Huowu would be the commanding officer, and that Jiangshan and Jishi would be counselors. Colonel Ba Bu would command the left wing of the governor-general's brigade, and Zhong Yu, who had been in charge of the Chaozhou garrison, would command the right wing; both would be under the control of Yao Huowu. Four thousand troops would be transferred from the governor-general's brigade, two thousand from the commander-in-chief's brigade, and four thousand from the governor's brigade; those troops, together with the two thousand from the Chaozhou garrison, would make an army of twelve thousand. Feng Gang and the other officers, twenty in number, would take part together in the expedition. The emperor was notified, and an express message was sent to Zhong Yu urging him to join them before Chaozhou. The army would set forth on the twentieth of the fifth month.

Jishi called on friends and relatives on his way home, where his mother, wife, and concubines, hearing of the provision in the rescript that he should join the army, could not help trembling with fear. His mother set out wine in the inner hall to serve as a farewell celebration, but although Jishi felt quite calm, she was filled with a nameless dread, and Huiruo and the other women also looked extremely anxious. Naturally it was far from a happy occasion. A contemporary poet wrote a "Ballad on Joining the Army" that describes it precisely:

> Your life while away at war,
> Is always full of care.
> Once you've joined the army,

It's all a matter of chance.
And so you pity yourself,
Not daring to tell a soul;
Instead you steel your nerves,
And gaily order wine.
Your women already know
But cannot bear to probe.
When his women hear the news,
They at once expect the worst.
And flustered, change the topic,
While their hearts they are pounding.

That night he slept in Huiruo's room. The next day people were still besieging the house with their gifts. Jishi told his servants to accept them all, recording the donors' names, and when he came back from Chaozhou he would invite them to a banquet. He attended farewell parties at the various officials' houses and thanked them all. And every day he also received the loving attentions of his womenfolk.

After a few days Lieutenant-colonel Yao had made his troop selection and reported back to the governor-general and governor. Then, together with Jiangshan and Jishi, his counselors, he set off. The governor-general and governor together with the entire civil and military establishment came out of the city to see them on their way. Yao Huowu bowed in accepting the commanding officer's sword and seal. Before returning to the city, the senior officials offered him three cups of wine; they also offered wine to the two counselors, and all of the troops were rewarded with money.

Huowu went into his tent and sat down with his counselors. After each of the officers had paid his respects, he handed down orders: Qin Shuming, Lü Youkui, and Ho Wu would lead two thousand of their finest cavalry to spearhead the vanguard; Ba Bu as general of the left would have Wang Dahai and Chu Hu as his deputies; Zhong Yu as general of the right would have Jiang Xinyi and Gu Shen as his deputies; the deputy commanders of the central column would be Feng Gang, You Qi, Yang Dahe, and Cao Zhiren; Xu Zhen, Qi Guangzu, and Han Pu would be in charge of transporting provisions. The flag ceremony was held, cannon were fired, and the mighty force raced off in the direction of Chaozhou.

It was a time of sweltering summer heat, and the countryside was parched and bare—the world was like a furnace. The troops suffered—their bodies ran with sweat, and they were under a fearful strain. Fortunately, General Yao cared for his men and shared their hardships. They got up at dawn and did most of their marching in the evening, with a stop at noon. Jiangshan also wrote a "Midsummer Marching Song," which he taught the soldiers to sing. In fewer than ten days they reached Chaozhou.

Mola was avoiding the summer heat in the Jade Palace, whose gem-studded rooms brought cool air, when suddenly he received an urgent report and burst out laughing. "You don't go to war in the height of summer or the depths of winter! Yao Huowu doesn't deserve his reputation! That man knows nothing about the art of war! In less than a month's time those few troops of his will have turned into the ghosts of Flaming Mountain."[1] He sent out a command arrow instructing each of the Four Defenders to take the troops under his command and set up camp outside the city walls, mounting a strict guard over the entrance. They were not to engage in battle, merely to wait until Mola came and decided on a course of action.

When Qin Shuming learned there were troops coming out of the city, he camped a dozen miles away and waited for the main force. Huowu's army arrived the next morning, and Qin reported,

"The rebel forces are camped up ahead. We haven't tried to engage them, and they haven't challenged us. We're awaiting your decision."

Huowu ordered them to challenge the enemy. Responding with one voice, the three officers led the troops under their command right up to the enemy's camp, where they yelled and cursed for a long time without provoking any response. Returning despondently to their own camp, they reported as much to their commander. Huowu was completely baffled, but Jishi remarked, "I've heard that the baldheaded bandit is devilishly cunning and is apt to raid your camp just when you least expect it. That's how Governor-general Hu met defeat. If the bandit won't come out and fight during the day, I expect he will do so at night." Huowu nodded in agreement, and told You Qi to take a command arrow and order the men in each camp not to take off their armor or go to sleep. If one camp should be faced with an emergency, the other three were to come to its aid.

Let us turn now to Mola, who that evening was on the point of leaving the city. He ordered Du Chong to mount a close guard on the palace gate, and left the four chieftains, Zhou Yude, Zhou Yuli, Li Fanjiang, and Yin Haoyong, to guard the walls, while he took Xia Chizha, Meng Feitian, Kang An, and Gu Xin with him. He entered the camp at the first watch, and the Four Defenders received him and reported on the day's events.

"They've been slaving away all day," said Mola, "and they're bound to want to sleep in the cool of the evening. You four take your men out at once and make a raid on their camps. If they're prepared for you, all you need do is turn back. I will send troops in support." The four mounted their horses and led six thousand troops in a sneak attack on the forward camp. Fortunately, Qin Shuming and his men had not gone to sleep and promptly engaged them, but the Chaozhou troops attacked in such massive force that Qin's men could not hold their ground. Fighting desperately, however, the three officers managed to escape. By the time the other camps came to their aid, the Defenders' troops had withdrawn. Qin had lost over three hundred men and horses, and he went before the commander asking to be punished.

"It's because I didn't take adequate precautions," said Huowu. "It's not the vanguard's fault."

Next morning the four camps rose together and advanced on Mola's encampment. Mola, too, ordered his troops out to do battle. Because of his earlier defeat, Qin Shuming was fuming with rage, and he charged out in front of the battle line. Haiheng confronted him, and they fought. After thirty or more jousts, Haiheng began to weaken, and Haiyuan whipped his horse on to attack from the other side, but Lü Youkui was there to confront him. Haizhen and Haili charged forward together, and on the other side Zhong Yu and Ba Bu confronted them. Wang Dahai and Gu Shen and others also paired off with the four chieftains in fierce fighting. When Qin Shuming flailed with his sawtooth mace, Haiheng tumbled from his horse, and a single blow was sufficient to end his life. Enraged at the sight, Mola charged out wielding his priest's staff in a frontal attack, but Qin Shuming raised his mace in both hands to parry the blow, which felt heavy indeed. In his left hand Mola held a Buddhist sword with which he slashed Qin across the middle, but Qin ducked out of the way. A vicious battle ensued for a dozen jousts, until Feng Gang noticed that Qin Shuming's face and ears were turning red and realized that he was no match for Mola. He gave a meaningful glance at Cao Zhiren and the two men galloped out together. Mola defended himself against his three adversaries, parrying thrusts from front and rear and blocking blows from left and right, but his success was merely defensive—he had no ability to counterattack.[2] Ho Wu also raced forward with his iron staff, and Mola could hold out no longer, but used a feinting tactic to retreat, all the while uttering something in an unknown tongue. In a flash, a wild wind sprang up that toppled both men and horses, and Mola's troops took advantage of the confusion to charge ahead. Qin Shuming and the other officers knew that the wind had been produced by Mola's demonic magic and were thinking of retreating when suddenly the wind howled and the sand flew, and they could see nothing in front of their eyes. The wind's strength varied from moment to moment, and the men didn't fear it, but boldly advanced until they had surrounded the enemy. Mola turned to give battle but could no longer use his magic. Even the wind dropped, and once more there was a scorching sun overhead, but because of the wind the troops felt cooler and plucked up courage and vied with one other. Meng Feitian and Kang An were killed by Chu Hu and Wang Dahai. Mola's horse was struck by Ho Wu's club, and Mola was knocked off. The troops were about to seize him, when all of a sudden he vanished. Haiyuan and the other leaders quickly withdrew their troops in defeat. Huowu withdrew his own men for a moment and recognized the achievements of Qin Shuming, Chu Hu, Wang Dahai, and Ho Wu. Lü Youkui's left arm had been struck by an arrow from Haiyuan. Altogether over five hundred wounded men were sent back to base camp to recover.

That evening a celebration feast was held during which Huowu consulted his men. "Mola's demonic magic did not appear to be all-powerful. But just now he fell off his horse and escaped; I imagine he is skilled at the five techniques of invisibility,[3] and that's why it was impossible to capture him."

"Falling off your horse and vanishing—that's the earth technique, of course," said Jiangshan. "Nowadays nobody has a complete grasp of all five techniques, and he probably knows only one or two. When we do battle tomorrow, the officers should engage him in turn as before, while the commander takes cover behind the standard in front of the camp and shoots an arrow at him. Then we'll see if he's capable of the metal technique. If he is, he'll be invulnerable to swords and arrows, which will make him very difficult to deal with."

"Yes, let's follow your suggestion," said Huowu.

To their surprise, the next day Mola sent out his troops but did not engage in battle. Instead he used demonic magic to stir up a great wind and then ordered his men to set fires and use the wind to fan the flames. Huowu and his men were caught entirely by surprise. They lost a battle and withdrew some ten miles before setting up camp. Since the weather was excessively hot, both sides then stopped fighting for the moment.

Chapter XXIII

Commander Yao triumphs in a single night
Iron Mouth Lei reads faces and predicts lives

After Du Chong in Chaozhou heard that the daughter of Academy student Tao had died as a result of Mola's savage debauchery, he seethed with hatred. On the evening when he learned that Mola had been defeated and three of his generals killed, he gave out that he had to conduct a street inspection, then went alone and by a circuitous route to the assistant salt comptroller's office and called at Tao's house next door. Tao invited him in and asked his name.

"Don't be too shocked when I tell you. I'm Du Chong, on the staff of Prince Daguang, in charge of the palace gates. I've come here specially to talk to you about something."

Tao was quick to bow. "So you're Master Du. I didn't realize—please forgive me." He went on, "Master Du, what instructions do you have for me, coming here so late at night?"

"I'm under secret orders from His Majesty. Because the army's rations are running low, he has set seventy thousand as the contribution for each rich household and big property owner in the city, fifty thousand for each affluent household, and thirty thousand for each well-off one. You are on our list as affluent, so you will need to contribute fifty thousand. I know you're a good man, and I was afraid you might not be able to lay your hands on that much money at short notice. I've come to warn you in advance, so that you can get your contribution ready in good time and be sure to send it in."

Tao Zhuo was aghast. "But His Majesty has it all wrong, sir! I'm solely dependent for a living on the rent from some three thousand mu of barren land. These last few years there's been constant fighting, and my tenants haven't had a grain of rice to bring to town—all of it went in taxes. Not only do I not have fifty thousand in the house, my own life is not worth half that amount! I beseech you to plead poverty in my case. My whole family will be grateful."

"That would be a mistake. Once His Majesty has issued a military order, no one dares to try and get it revoked. If you're short by as little as a single cash, I'm afraid your whole family will be executed."

"But I've never had any feud with His Majesty," said Tao, shedding tears. "Why does he feel it necessary to take my life away bit by bit?"

"His Majesty has never forced you to pay any levies before. How can you say such a thing?"

"He may not have made me pay any levies, but he did take my daughter's life."

"How did that happen? Tell me the truth, and I'll try to help you."

"It's a tragic story." He proceeded to tell how his daughter had gone out to look at the lanterns and how she had then been brought to her death.

"In that case, I suppose the Second Defender's death in battle yesterday was retribution for what happened to your daughter."

"But he's not the one that I blame!"

"Who is, then?"

"I'm sorry, that was just a slip of the tongue. It *is* Defender Heng."

"Look, you needn't try to deceive me. I have the same enemy as you. Because he abducted four concubines, I pretended to offer him my allegiance in the hope of carrying out my own vengeance. If you have something in mind, you might as well tell me about it."

Tao still refused to trust him. Not until Du Chong had stabbed his own arm and sworn an oath did he finally say: "There's no evil that bald-headed bandit won't stoop to. The whole city is seething with hatred for him. We're planning to get a crowd together and then, when General Yao's army arrives, we'll throw open the gates and surrender. My only fear is that the bandit is so powerful that they won't be able to capture him."

"You mustn't be too hasty, though. Wait until he's beaten back inside the city, and then we'll send a message giving a date and a time for the gate to be opened. How many men do you have who are prepared to surrender?"

"Altogether four hundred five."

"That's plenty. We don't need any more, lest our secret leak out, which would be disastrous. When it's time, I'll come and tell you, and all you need do is open the gate. I still need to come up with a plan to kill him." That night Tao invited him to stay and drink with him, and the two men indulged themselves to the full.

Returning to the palace, Du conferred with the concubines: "His Majesty has been badly beaten day after day, and it doesn't look as if we'll be able to stay in this city much longer. What are we going to do?"

"What choice do we have?" asked Pinwa. "These days he doesn't take the slightest notice of us. If the government troops come into the city, we'll run away with you."

"But that's childish! We couldn't escape, but even if we could, sooner or later we'd be caught by the local officials and executed, anyway, as members of a rebel household."

"Well, what do you think we should do?" asked Pinxing.

"Let's take our time before deciding." They drank some wine

and went to bed, where Du paid court to each of them before remarking, "Let's wait until His Majesty is driven back into the city and then settle on a time to get him drunk. I'll open one of the city gates and welcome the government troops in. You should take your chance while he's drunk to stab him to death. That way, not only will we avoid the death sentence, we'll gain some merit and one day be favored by the court."

"But that man has a tremendous capacity for drink!" said Pinwa. "How are we going to get him drunk?"

"I've prepared some medicated wine. He'll need only one jug of it to get helplessly drunk. When he falls down, you'll just have to seize the chance and act." The women were persuaded.

> Four lotus thrones did he arrange;
> Buddha's body will die cross-legged.[1]

Lieutenant-colonel Yao ceased operations for ten days, during which he prepared a large quantity of cowhide, cotton mesh, and the like to prevent Mola from attacking them with fire. He also obtained a vast amount of dogs' blood and excrement to defeat Mola's demonic magic, and then advanced in four columns. Mola proved unable to come to the aid of his troops and suffered another defeat. After withdrawing to camp, Huowu consulted his officers. "We need to seize this moment while morale is high to find some way of destroying him. We mustn't let him build up his strength again."

"He's used to gaining his victories by raiding the enemy's camp," said Feng Gang. "Let's use the same tactic on him."

"But since he's so good at raiding others' camps," said Huowu, "surely he'll have taken his own precautions? I'm just afraid we'll have little to show for our efforts and will merely be wasting our men's lives."

"Let's divide our troops into eight detachments," suggested Jiangshan. "One detachment will raid his camp; two others will be there to back up the raid; four more will divide into two wings and search out his ambushes; and the last one will outflank him and cut off his retreat. Together we're bound to succeed."

Huowu approved the plan, and ordered Qin Shuming, Lü Youkui, and Ho Wu to form the vanguard in raiding the camp; Feng Gang, Yang Dahe, and Cao Zhiren would provide support; Zhong Yu, Jiang Xinyi, and Gu Shen would attack on the left; and Ba Bu, Wang Dahai, and Chu Hu on the right. If there was no ambush, they would join in the raid on the main camp. If there was an ambush and they managed to smash it, they would also turn back and attack the camp. Huowu himself together with You Qi would outflank the enemy and get to his rear, while the two counselors would guard the base camp. The men left to carry out their orders.

Despite his crushing defeat, Mola had in fact prepared for a raid on his camp. He ordered Haiyuan and Haili each to command one thousand five hundred troops and set up ambushes to right and left. If enemy troops came to raid the camp, as soon as his men heard the signal cannon, they were to attack from both sides. He himself with Haizhen, Gu Xin, and Xia Chizha kept cool inside the camp and drank together. After the second watch, soldiers reported that a large number of troops were on the road north with banners hidden and drums silent. Mola gave a laugh. "Just as I expected!" he said, and gave the order, "Put on your armor, mount your horses, and wait until they're here. When we fire the signal cannon, you're to come charging out. This time we're going to wipe them out to the last man!"

Qin Shuming and the other officers were leading two thousand men in secret to the front of the camp when they heard a thunderous cannon shot and Haizhen came out wielding a battle-axe with the whole force charging after him. Qin realized that the enemy was prepared, and he quickly retreated the distance of an arrow's flight. Lü Youkui had already engaged Haizhen. Mola came racing up on his horse, and Qin Shuming and Ho Wu engaged him. Xia Chizha and Gu Xin also rode up. On the other side Feng Gang and his men arrived, and Yang Dahe fought with Gu Xin and Cao Zhiren with Xia Chizha. Feng Gang raised his huge halberd and thrust at Mola from one side. Xia Chizha proved no match for Cao Zhiren and after a dozen jousts was killed by a thrust of Cao's spear. Gu Xin was stunned, the grip on his weapon slackened, and he was cut down by Yang Dahe beneath his horse. Then Feng Gang and the others made a concerted attack on Mola and Haizhen. Mola, relying on the ambush he had set, fought ever more fiercely, refusing to yield an inch. After two hours, Zhong Yu's and Ba Bu's detachments, having smashed the ambushes and beheaded Haiyuan and Haili, came charging into the main camp. Mola was unable to hold out any longer—how could he possibly withstand the addition of several more bold officers and two detachments of elite troops? Realizing that the situation had turned against him, he hastily fought his way out through a thicket of swords, spears, and maces. He shouted for Haizhen to withdraw his troops and return to the city to regroup, and the two men, with upward of a thousand beaten troops, fought their way out of encirclement and fled south with the combined forces in pursuit.

Mola had gone less than a mile when a cannon shot rang out and a large number of troops blocked his path. Leveling his broadsword, Yao Huowu roared at him, "Don't run away just yet, Mola! Leave your bald head behind!" Enraged, Haizhen whipped his horse forward, and You Qi, thrusting with his spear, engaged him. Mola also fought his way forward, viciously wielding his priest's staff. "You can stop showing off, you baldheaded bandit!" shouted Huowu. "I am here!" He slashed with his broadsword. Mola quickly blocked the blow, but noted the skill and the force behind it.

"You there, are you Yao Huowu?" he called.

"Since you know my great name, why don't you get down off your horse and submit?"

Quickly blocking the blow from the broadsword, Mola said, "Yao Huowu, let me give you a piece of advice. I've been in foreign countries as well as China, and I have never met anyone who is my equal. If that broadsword of yours is a match for my priest's staff, you qualify as a true hero. However, your brother spent over twenty years in Guangdong, and yet his head hangs in the marketplace. Why bother to put up such a desperate fight? Wouldn't it be better to join with me, dividing Guangdong evenly between us and enjoying riches and honors together? Think about it."

Huowu roared, "Vile bandit, stop trying to incite us. En garde!"

Mola roared back. "So you think I can't kill you, do you? Since we are both thought of as heroes, let no one come to our aid. We'll fight each other, just the two of us."

It was now broad daylight, and behind them the pursuit arrived, having beaten Haizhen and smashed the remaining troops. Huowu shouted to his officers, "Don't come to my aid. Watch me take him." The officers restrained their men, and none went forward. The two adversaries traded blow for blow, circling each other and fighting over fifty jousts. Mola, whose lower parts were much weakened, could not counter Huowu's marvelous strength. He would have used his demonic magic, but he was so hard-pressed by Huowu's broadsword that he never had the time. He turned his head and looked at his men, of whom only one, Haizhen, survived, and was forced to call out, "I can't kill you. I'm going." He suddenly rolled off his horse and disappeared. The officers raised their weapons and hacked Haizhen to pieces, then withdrew their troops to camp.

Using his invisibility technique, Mola alone managed to return to the city, where he told Zhou Yude and the other three chiefs to guard the four gates and get more cannon ready. He himself went into the yamen, where a number of officials of the regime greeted him with a bow. Du Chong followed him into the palace. He kowtowed and asked, "How did the battle go, Your Majesty?"

"I've never suffered such a bad defeat since I first raised an army in the islands. The defenders are all dead. A few of the chiefs are still left, but they can do no more than guard the city. If things should get any worse, I'll fall back on Mt. Fuyuan, then return at some later date to take my revenge."

"Chaozhou's walls are high and thick. How are they going to be able to break through with their ten or twenty thousand men? Put your mind at rest, Your Majesty. In scorching weather like this, with a stout wall in front of them and their food supply running low, the natural course would be to withdraw."

"You will have to take great care," said Mola. "If there's a military emergency, even if it comes in the middle of the night or the early hours of the morning, see that you report it to me at once. Take this command arrow and inspect the walls once every night and day, warning the troops and their officers. Those four chiefs are not to be compared with the four defenders. When Yao Huowu's troops withdraw, I'll reward you with a few dozen palace women."

Du Chong left with the command arrow. Accompanied by a dozen trusted soldiers, he carried out inspections night and day. In secret he wrote out a confidential message that he shot with an arrow, setting midnight on the twentieth of the seventh month as the time when he would covertly open the north gate and admit the government troops. He also told Tao Zhuo to wait inside the gate on that day and arranged with Pinwa and the palace women to put their plan into operation at the same time.

Let us turn to Yao Huowu who, after emerging victorious and withdrawing his troops, was considering how to attack the city. "Chaozhou is where I used to be stationed," said General Zhong Yu. "The wall is seventeen miles long, over sixty feet high and more than five feet thick. Even if we lay siege with all of our troops, we still won't be able to cover half of it. How can we take the city? Before we plan an attack, we'll need to request another thirty thousand troops from the governor-general and governor."

Huowu asked Jiangshan to prepare a detailed request and notify both yamens. That evening Jishi told Jiangshan and Huowu about Du Chong's feigned surrender. "Just make it appear that you're about to attack, taunting and cursing them every day, and see if we receive a message," he advised.

Huowu was delighted. "If this plan succeeds, the city won't be difficult to take. When it comes to allocating credit for restoring the peace, your name will certainly head the list." He issued a series of orders: Ba Bu, with a colonel on his staff, would attack the east gate; Zhong Yu, also with a colonel on his staff, would attack the west gate; Qin Shuming would attack the south gate; and he himself with Feng Gang and others would attack the north gate. He ordered all the troops to put up banners emblazoned with the words "Counselor Su." He also ordered Yang Dahe to lead five hundred troops and remove all the boats along the shore in order to prevent Mola from escaping by sea.

After attacking for three days, Huowu's men had taken several dozen casualties. On the evening of the fourth day a soldier under

You Qi's command found an arrow with a blob of wax attached to it and handed it to You Qi, who passed it along to Yao Huowu. Huowu opened it out and read it:

> I, Du Chong, humbly direct this report to my benefactor: I traveled from Guangzhou to Chaozhou and returned to the priest certain articles in a bundle that I had picked up. He trusted me implicitly and told me to keep watch over the palace gates. Now he has ordered me to inspect the city gates, giving me a great deal of responsibility. There are four concubines in his palace who come from Heh, my former master, and they have entered into a plot with me. On the night of the twentieth of this month they will put Mola to death. I have also secretly arranged with Tao Zhuo and four hundred other wealthy men who have suffered under Mola to open the north gate at midnight on the twentieth and welcome your army in. They will hang a glass lantern on the gate tower as a signal. I hope that you, sir, will inform General Yao and his men and that on that evening their combined force will attack the city. Respectfully, Du Chong.

The three men were elated. "We are indebted to Master Su for setting up this plan," said Huowu. "On that date we'd better attack at the other three gates during the day, so that they don't have time to take any precautions. In the evening we'll put the plan into operation." He then had his troops surround the city at a distance, not going near the walls, and to allay suspicion he spread the rumor that he didn't have enough troops and would need to go back to Guangzhou and raise another large contingent in order to attack the city.

Meanwhile Mola was in his palace. Addicted to wine and sex though he was, he actually stopped for a day or two and went out to inspect the defenses. When he observed that outside the walls the government troops were taking it easy, he thought of exploiting the situation with a sudden sortie but lacked the necessary support, and besides, he was afraid of Yao Huowu's extraordinary strength. So he simply ordered the chiefs to keep a careful watch and went back to lift his spirits with wine and women.

On the twentieth, returning from an inspection of the defenses, he noticed that the government forces were attacking at only three gates, and the idea of slipping out of the north gate and escaping to the islands crossed his mind. He discussed it with his concubines. "With your powers, Your Majesty, you can go anywhere you like," said Pinwa. "We're the only ones who'll suffer— all of us will be doomed. I once heard a storyteller say that Lü Bu was unable to fight while carrying just one woman.[2] How will you fare, with so many to carry? If you insist on going back, we shall have no choice but to take our own lives as soon as possible."

"Now, don't be upset—I was only asking you your opinion. How could I bear to part with you? In fact, if it wasn't for all of you, I'd have left here long ago." Eventually he did think of a plan and ordered wine to be served for a party. As they sought to enjoy themselves, some of the women flattered him while others complained.

After they had been drinking for some time, Mola sent for Du Chong and gave him an order: "Today the bandit troops are attacking at three gates only, and I'm afraid there'll be trouble tonight at the fourth. Here's my command arrow; see that they take even more precautions there."

Du Chong knelt down. "I have made up a tonic wine that will lift Your Majesty's spirits. You have been under a strain for some days now. Let me offer you a few pots of the wine as a token of my filial regard."

"Good lad. Bring me the wine, then go about your business."

Taking his trusted men with him, Du Chong galloped to the

north gate, where he told Li Fanjiang: "By His Majesty's orders, since the government troops are attacking today at only three gates, we must take great care in guarding the fourth. He told me to guard this north gate, while you make a round of inspection. We'll get no rest tonight." Li left with his troops.

At midnight a crowd of men approached the gate tower and put up a glass lantern. In the distance one could see the government troops approaching, and Du Chong joined the crowd in opening the gate and waiting for them. With Qin Shuming in the lead, the officers passed through the gate, and the common people knelt down on both sides of the street to greet them. Du Chong kowtowed in welcome to Yao Huowu, Jishi, and the others. Huowu took his hand and commended him, at the same time asking him for details. He then ordered Zhong Yu, Ba Bu, Feng Gang, and others to fight their way through the remaining three gates, but on no account to kill or harass any of the common people. He himself would take the other officers, with Du Chong as guide, and fight their way into the headquarters of Prince Daguang.

Mola was sprawled on his couch, hopelessly drunk. The four concubines were too weak to kill him, but Lü Youkui dispatched him with a single blow of his axe. How terrible!

> The warrior was not in battle taken;
> The hero was slain as he lay in bed.

Lieutenant-colonel Yao and his counselors took seats in the yamen hall. They put out a notice to reassure the public and at the same time sent troops to the other three gates to link up with the rest of the army. Lü Youkui presented Mola's head, and the other officers reported their achievements one after the other. Only

Zhou Yude was unaccounted for; he had fled when the north gate was opened, and no one knew where he had gone. The next morning Huowu told Jiang Xinyi and Han Pu to survey the contents of the warehouses and treasuries and take temporary control of the affairs of Haiyang and Jieyang counties; he had Zhong Yu lead his original force back to garrison Chaozhou; he ordered the release of all the women whom Mola had kept; he handsomely rewarded Tao Zhuo and the men who had assisted him; he gave the four concubines to Du Chong to take back; and he sent men to the prison to find out what had happened to Qu Qiang. (They returned to say that he had wasted away and died in the second month.) The victory feast lasted for three days, after which the army began its return journey. The captured officials of the Mola regime were loaded into prison carts and taken back to Guangzhou, where each was to be dealt with separately.

It was the middle of the eighth month when they reached Guangzhou. Governor-general Qing and Governor Shen had received continuous reports of Yao Huowu's victories, and they knew that success was at hand. Then they received the news that Mola was making a last stand in Chaozhou and that no attack on the city could succeed without additional support. They conferred and were about to send reinforcements when they heard the news of Jishi's feigned surrender stratagem and the fall of Chaozhou and canceled the order. On the day of the army's return, Governor Shen was supervising the examinations, and it was Governor-general Qing who led the civil and military officials outside the city walls to welcome them. All along the way pipes and drums sounded and brilliant banners fluttered in the breeze. Huowu and his officers dismounted and walked together into the city, after which the troops were sent back to the brigades they had come from. On Mount Yuexiu a feast had already been arranged and the governor-general raised a cup and congratulated them on their success. Huowu drank it on his knees. Next it was the turn of Jishi and Jiangshan, and the two men bowed, then stood as they drank. Huowu presented the list of officers who had acquitted themselves with distinction and also handed over the officials who had served the Mola regime. "I will join Governor Shen in composing a memorial to seek directions on how to proceed," said Governor general Qing.

Huowu knelt down once more as he reported on the injustice done to his brother and begged the governor-general to report the facts to higher authority. The governor-general undertook to do so.

That same day they dispersed. Jishi and Du Chong went back home where, needless to say, the whole household welcomed them with great joy.

Du Chong found another house in which to accommodate the four concubines. It so happened that at this same time Bian Ruyu finished his examination and a grand banquet was held in the Su residence. The following day numerous officials and friends and relatives paid visits. Jishi welcomed them and then returned their visits, all of which occupied several days. He then issued invitations to a party for the people who had previously given him presents. These activities occupied a dozen more days.

One day, as he was taking his ease at home, Wu Fu reported from the gate: "His Honor the prefect has sent a physiognomer to see you, a man by the name of Iron Mouth Lei." Jishi invited the man into his study.

> A strange countenance,
> Less than five feet tall,
> Pure white hair and whiskers,
> Seventy years and more.

Carefree and contented,
With an air of high integrity;
Reserved and aloof,
A character from before Fu Xi's time.
In a voice that is loud and clear,
No blandishment is heard.
In haste, quiet and composed,
Never taking a careless step.
Lofty and pure as a stork in the heavens;
Unsullied as a white colt in a deserted vale.[3]

Jishi received his visitor with respect and humbly begged him to take a seat. "Where is your home, sir?" he asked. "And how did you come to be a friend of His Honor the prefect?"

"I'm from Jiangyin in Jiangsu, and I depend on my fulsome flattery to arouse the gentry's interest. His Honor the prefect isn't an old friend of mine—I met him entirely by chance."

"Someone given to fulsome flattery certainly wouldn't go around proclaiming that fact. Aren't you being too modest? But let me ask you this, sir: Would you prefer vegetarian food?"

"I may look like a priest, but I'm actually a disciple of Confucius," said Iron Mouth. "In the time of great peace,[4] there were no Buddhists or Daoists, so why bother to be a vegetarian?"

Jishi laughed and ordered wine and food to be quickly prepared, then told a servant to invite Yannian and Ruyu to join them. Before long the two arrived, bowed, and took their seats. "The three of us beg you, sir, to give us the benefit of your teaching."

"Then please compose yourself."

After Jishi had taken a seat at the head of the room, Iron Mouth looked at him and said, "Your countenance is aqueous in nature, and you will obtain the aqueous advantages.[5] Your frontal aspect shows a yellow light,[6] which means that you will fulfill all your desires. Your seal court shows great happiness—all of your plans will succeed. Kindly show me your hand." Jishi held out one of his hands, and Iron Mouth continued: "It's as soft as cotton floss, which means that you lead a leisurely existence and enjoy considerable wealth. The palm is blood red, which signifies both wealth and official position. Unfortunately, your features are too perfect, your back is not well-endowed, and your figure is far from full—although you will receive government office, you will not rise to a high position, and although you will accumulate wealth, it will be easily dissipated. The good thing is that your fate lines run deep—you will have eight sons and grandsons and live to the age of seventy."

When he had told Jishi's fortune, Yannian came forward. Iron Mouth glanced at him and said, "You're very handsome, and you're certainly a clever young man, but you have a turbid expression, and you will inevitably become an impoverished scholar. A white, powder-like vapor signifies the judicial punishment of your parents, while the bluish tinge in your cheeks indicates a separation of brothers. The fortunate thing is that your earth treasury is smooth and glossy, and in your later years you will enjoy a little comfort and ease. Your hanging discs are bright—your family will be able to escape adversity."

After he had finished, Ruyu took the seat, and Iron Mouth said, "Your three lights are shining brightly and your six mansions are high. Your figure is remarkable, and you will certainly distinguish yourself. Your appearance is both elegant and refined—you will always be a man of virtue. Your waist is round and your back well-endowed, and you'll naturally wear a jade belt and court dress.[7]

With your soaring eyebrows and brilliant mind you are certain to attain power and prestige as well as to exhibit loyalty and integrity. However, there is a slight flaw in all this perfection; although you'll rise to become an official of the second rank, you are destined to be dismissed from office three times. In old age, however, your fate will be smooth, and you will enjoy the beauties of nature. You will have two sons and live almost as long as Jiang Taigong."[8]

Afterward wine was served, and Iron Mouth, as if oblivious to their presence, drank heartily. Jishi had one more question for him: "My brother-in-law was pleased with his performance in the provincial examinations. The results will be announced soon, and I am wondering if he'll be able to join in the celebrations. Please take a look at his face."

Iron Mouth raised his head. "Propitious clouds shine in the palace of destiny[9]—within ten days he will receive the top position. Yellow vapor issues from his high span—within a year he will attain official rank. Not only will he succeed in the metropolitan examinations, he will also be appointed to the court. Congratulations!"

As the party ended, Jishi told his servant to bring out thirty taels as compensation for the physiognomer. "Other men don't accept gifts," said Iron Mouth, "but I never refuse them. By reading faces you get money, which helps you to read more faces. Everything in the world ought to work like that!" And away he went without saying goodbye.

Chapter XXIV

His womenfolk compose beautiful lines
His brothers sing a song of court delight

⁓

To whom shall I open my heart?
Success was not in my destiny.
I meant to write an opera,
But feared the experts' scrutiny.
I've embellished past and present,
Shed the bonds of profit and fame,
And casually cast my youth away
In a different kind of game.

On the eighth of the ninth month the results of the examination were announced, and as expected, Ruyu passed, an event that kept Jishi busy for days on end. By this time Governor Shen had left the examination hall, and Jishi hurried over to report to him. He congratulated Shen, whose son had graduated in the metropolitan examination and been sent to study at one of the boards, while Shen in turn congratulated Jishi on his achievements. "I've talked it over with the governor-general," he added, "and we don't think it would be appropriate to submit a memorial about Heh Zhifu's concubines; instead we should just allocate them to the most deserving officers. According to General Yao, the only ones still unmarried are Lü Youkui and Ho Wu. The remaining two concubines we ought to send to you for your women's quarters."

Jishi quickly bowed. "To be frank with you, sir, I already have

a wife and four concubines, and I can't accommodate any more—
that would be to repeat Master Heh's mistake."

"In that case, we'll need to think of someone else to send them to."

"Du Chong was highly praised by you and the governor-general in your memorial, and he'll surely be receiving imperial favor.
While he was at Chaozhou, he worked on a scheme with two of
the concubines, and I have little doubt that he was intimate with
them. Could I ask a favor of you, sir? Award them both to him."

Shen readily agreed, and promptly transmitted the order to
Du Chong, who kowtowed his acceptance.

Jishi returned home, where before long Du Chong brought
the two women to visit him. He was living with Yerong at the time
and taking turns to come in and serve Jishi.

Now that Ruyu had passed the examination, Jishi's mother
insisted that he marry into the Su family before she would permit
him to go to the capital for the metropolitan examination. After
consulting with Bian Ming, Jishi arranged that Ruyu would join the
household on the third of the tenth month and set off for Beijing
the month after that.

No sooner was the banquet for the successful candidates over
than the imperial edict came down: "Qing Xi and Shen Jin are both
advanced one rank for their military achievements; Yao Huowu
is promoted to brigade general; he is to proceed to the capital for
an audience at which he will be assigned to a provincial post; Feng
Gang and the other officers are to be assigned by the governor-
general and the governor to be lieutenant-colonels, majors and
captains according to their ability; Li Guodong and Su Fang are to
come at once to the capital to take up office; Du Chong is to be
given a post at the ninth rank by the governor-general and governor; Yao Weiwu is to be restored by an act of clemency to his
original position; Hu Cheng is to be removed from his position

and proceed to the capital to await punishment. In a further act of clemency the next year's taxes in the Huizhou and Chaozhou prefectures are to be reduced by one half." On receiving the edict, Jishi consulted with Jiangshan, then asked Governor Shen to petition the court, stating that he would rather remain at home with the rank of secretary than take up office. Shen agreed. He later did so, and naturally the petition was granted. Jiangshan and Huowu made preparations to travel to Beijing with Ruyu.

Soon it was time for Ruyu's wedding. Jishi moved Huiruo upstairs in the main building, with Wuyun and Yeyun downstairs, and gave the six-room apartment in the east court to his sister, opening up a separate inner gate on the eastern side. In all the wedding expenditures he followed the example of Pearl's wedding. There is no need for us to repeat the clichés about weddings.

After the fifth day Jishi was busy all the time. It so happened that at this time Bangchen died and Wu Biyuan was appointed administrator of Lingtang township in Panyu county. Jishi sent someone to offer money to help with the costs of Bangchen's funeral, while he himself went to congratulate Wu Biyuan. Biyuan mentioned that he had received a letter from his son Daiyun: "He's opened a wine-rice store in his house with the capital you gave him.[1] And he's also taken another wife, who's borne him a son. The only problem is that I'm an official here now and have acquired a great many debts. I don't know how I'll be able to get back there."

"Those little debts of yours are nothing to worry about," said Jishi. "I've heard that Lingtang township is a three-thousand-tael position; once you're there, you'll naturally be able to turn things around. The only drawback is that it's a little far from here, and we won't be able to see each other quite so often. Your daughter also wants to visit her parents, and I've been the one standing in her way. She can congratulate you and hold a farewell party at our house, preparing food for a day or two."

After staying with Biyuan a while, he took his leave and went to console Bangchen's family. Bangchen had no son, just the one daughter, Shunjie. She had met Jishi before, and so she invited him in. Wearing deepest mourning, she thanked him with a curtsey. Yannian pressed him to stay, but Jishi noticed Mistress Ru inside and felt embarrassed. Getting hastily to his feet, he departed in his sedan chair.

Du Chong had been designated a temporary sub-magistrate of Jiazi county. Having received his appointment papers, he was about to travel to his seat of office and was waiting to take his leave. As Jishi entered the study, Du Chong came forward and kowtowed. "In two days' time I'll be setting off with my wives," he said. "I've already been inside and kowtowed to the old lady and the other ladies. I was just waiting for you, sir, to give me your instructions."

"Now that you're an official, you're no longer on my staff, so there's no need to kowtow. But do you have enough money for the journey?"

"Out of your concern for me, you spoke to the lieutenant-governor. As someone with meritorious military service, I need to spend less than twenty taels on the staff there. From here to Jiazi should take less than ten days. A mere hundred-odd taels should be enough."

"But you don't have any money at all! Tell Su Xing to pay you two hundred taels for your own use." Du Chong fell on one knee to thank him.

"Although your post is only a minor one," continued Jishi, "it has still been given to you by the emperor's grace, and you will have many people in your jurisdiction. Rule no. 1 is that you must never seek to enrich yourself, and rule no. 2 is that you mustn't simply do as you please. Jiazi is on the coast, and the foreign pirates have not yet been suppressed. The other day the governor-general and governor conferred and decided that when things return to normal we should start recruiting militiamen again. But we'll need to go out of our way to treat the men well whom we recruit, and when they capture pirates we must definitely not make things difficult for them. You must have seen how the officials who did just that—the prefect of Guangzhou has found out the facts—have all been sentenced. Sub-prefect Wu was the sole exception; no one lodged an accusation against him, and he has actually been appointed prefect of Gaozhou. Clearly, the good and bad deeds of officials always eventually come to light. You can't go on deceiving the people, and above all, you cannot escape the law." Du Chong accepted all of Jishi's strictures.

Jishi returned to the inner quarters to find that his mother had invited Yerong, Pinwa and Pinxing to lunch and told Wuyun and Yeyun to join them. When Du Chong's wives saw Jishi enter, they came forward and kowtowed, and Jishi told the maids to reward them with clothes as well as provisions for the journey. He then walked over to Ruyu's quarters and cheered himself up with a game of chess.

"I'll soon be setting off for the capital," Ruyu remarked. "Your sister will naturally stay at home and attend on Mother-in-Law, but I'd like to use these few free days to take her to visit my parents, after which we'd come back here. I wonder if you'd be kind enough to tell Mother-in-Law."

"It's only right—you should certainly go. Set a date, and I'll tell Mother. The trip there and back shouldn't take you more than ten days."

"Tomorrow your father-in-law has invited me, and I'll be accompanying Master Wu. The day after that is the anniversary of

Master Yang's death, so let's make it the eighteenth." They played another game of chess and drank some wine.

The next day Han Pu and Jiang Xinyi returned to Guangzhou and came to call, and Jishi made return visits before accompanying Ruyu to a banquet at the Wens'. Chuncai wanted to go with the others to the capital, but Jishi tried to dissuade him: "All you need do is to wait patiently for a couple of years and you'll land a magistrate's job. Why do you have to go and take the metropolitan exam?" Wen Zhongweng agreed with Jishi. It was not until evening that Jishi and Ruyu returned.

Two days later, on the seventeenth, Jishi told his staff to prepare a banquet and that evening held a farewell party for his sister before going to congratulate the prefect of Guangzhou on his promotion to grain intendant. Prefect Shangguan invited him to stay longer, and it was dusk before he returned home. He went first to the women's reception room with its blazing lanterns and jeweled curtains, its censers of orchid and musk, and its crimson carpets. Huiruo, Xia, and Qiao, their hairpins askew and their bracelets jangling, were playing guess-fingers and drinking wine with Belle. Jishi sat down opposite Belle and asked her, "And how was the old lady?"

"She had three or four cups of wine, watched two scenes of an opera, and then couldn't hold on any longer and went upstairs to bed. The girls didn't want to drink, so we dismissed the maids who were putting on the opera. We're playing 'Three Heroes Fight Lü Bu.'"[2]

"That's too warlike!" said Jishi. "Let's play wine games instead."

"We were also thinking of composing some farewell poems," said Xia.

"Let's play a wine game first, then write the poems," said Jishi. "It's all the same. The topic will be Belle's first visit back home. You need a line from the *Four Books*, then one from the *Poetry Classic*, then one from any philosophical or historical text, then one from a song in *The West Chamber*, and finally a tune title combined with a line from the *Thousand Character Classic*. For anyone who doesn't give a proper answer, the penalty will be a cup of wine."

"That's far too much bother!" interjected Belle.

"You can't overturn my rules when you've only just been told you what they are! You're penalized one cup."

After Belle had finished it, Jishi drank the master's cup and began,

> Without waiting for the orders of their parents[3]
> Till with her lord she can go home[4]
> The hour is late and the way is long[5]
> With autumn branches hold off the setting sun[6]
> Two Hearts United; the husband leads, the wife follows[7]

"You made a mistake in your first line!" said Belle. "You'll have to drink a cup yourself."[8]

Jishi thought for a moment, then said, "All right, I'll drink."

Then it was Huiruo's turn:

> If for some reason he leaves[9]
> It could not take you so much as a morning[10]
> Huang Pu wished to write a poem[11]
> But told me to offer him a gold cup with my own hands[12]
> In the Back Court, the repast is set out, the seating
>   arranged

Xia began laughing before she said a word. "I don't have much of an education, I'm afraid; all I can do is come out with a few flattering lines. You mustn't scold me, ladies!"

"The penalty for a vulgar line is ten large cups," said Belle.

"Quick, now," said Jishi. "I have to be fair."

She began,

Common men and women, however unworthy[13]
But she went all the way to Shanggong[14]
He stopped her and met her, and treated her
    disrespectfully[15]
I do not know what she will do with me[16]
The Flower's Heart Moves; it is hard to set limits on a man
    of impressive bearing

Belle's cheeks flushed as she stood up and poured out a large cup and then forced Xia to drink it. The others all laughed: "Serves her right!"

Xia drank up. Next it was Qiao's turn.

Accompanying her to the door[17]
Very pleasant, the land of Han[18]
Forgetting how far he had come[19]
May my carriage follow swiftly[20]
Suddenly escorted me Inside the Gate; vast fame knows no
    bounds

Then Belle gave hers:

I was about to take a long journey[21]
I will go to my nurse[22]
I asked a traveler about the road ahead[23]
He said the mistress would remain behind for the time
    being[24]
Making it "Hard to Forget" for me; those with common
    interests are closely bound.

Then each of them drained a cup, and the maids brought in fresh wine and food. "Separate lines aren't as good as one continuous poem," said Jishi. "If someone does well, we'll all drink a cup to congratulate her, but if someone does badly, she'll have to drink a penalty cup. We must all be on our best behavior. There's to be no squabbling, and you're not allowed to push in front of anyone else." He picked up a sheet of notepaper. "We'll begin with me and finish with Belle," he said. Then he took up his brush and wrote,

A brilliant talent, the cassia's scent;[25]

"Let's postpone the penalties until the end," he added.

Then it was Huiruo's turn. She chanted the following lines:

Jade flutes again sound in harmony with the loving pair.
A hundred-year marriage begins this day;

Xia quickly continued,

Ninety presents, baskets and baskets full.
He's so helpful he caused her to love Feng Qian;[26]

"She's done it again!" exclaimed Belle. "Fine her a cup to be drunk later!"

"I'll fine her a *cup*, too," said Qiao, before continuing,

How can anyone, suspicious though she be, blame him as
Master Wang?[27]
With his brilliant brush he etches her eyebrows;[28]

Belle chanted,

Raising the tray, Meng and Liang put me to shame with
my spring lethargy.[29]
She doesn't realize that cooking the hen will lead to a
lonely life;[30]

Jishi continued,

How can you shoot the wild goose?[31] Let it fly up and
away!
Now only just of age, she will follow her husband.

"We've been focusing on stringing fancy conceits together instead of introducing the subject," objected Huiruo. "We mustn't let our poem get too unbalanced, with the nonessential things crowding out the really important one."

"You're right," said Jishi. "It really is time to introduce the subject."

Huiruo then chanted,

> She'll pay respects to her in-laws and raise a cup in
> congratulation.

With drinking and wine games, the night will be too short;
Xia continued,

> Choosing the topics, writing the poems, raising their wine
> cups—it goes on and on,
> Until the new moon peeps through the bed curtains and
> shines on her jade pendants;

Qiao:

> Beneath the Dipper and the scattered stars the wine is
> decanted.
> How good to seize the chance of a boat back home!

Belle:

> I don't know Mother-in-Law's preference in broth on the
> third day.[32]
> This journey is not taken because I love the land of Han;[33]

"These lines are mediocre at best," said Jishi. "Let me finish
it off."

> Rubbing her eyes,[34] the mother is consoled by the thought
> of children.

After writing the last line, Jishi commented, "This whole se-
quence is too disjointed, and there aren't any really good lines in
it. Qiao's one about wine makes something new out of something
old, and Belle's about broth takes naturalness to an extreme. We
should all drink a cup to congratulate the two of them, but the rest
of us don't need to be penalized." Two cups were then filled and
set before each of them.

No sooner had they finished the wine than Wuyun came in
and said to Belle, "You're setting off tomorrow morning, and the
master mustn't hold you up any longer. Twice your husband has

sent people over asking after you. But you still have to do me a favor—I want you to drink a cup of wine." She poured out a cup and offered it to Belle, who stood up to take it.

"It's very kind of you," she said, "but I've drunk too much already!" She took a sip, then handed back the cup. Jishi had Wuyun sit beside him, and they drank some more before going back to her room to sleep.

The next day Ruyu and his wife departed for his home. They took with them only a manservant, two pages, three or four maids and serving women, and brought their personal luggage and clothes in six sedan chairs to the dock, where they embarked. All of their other belongings they left behind. Jishi saw them to the dock, then returned and told someone to take a card and invite Wu Biyuan. He planned to give a farewell party the next day and asked Wen Zhongweng and his son Chuncai, Li Jiangshan, and Miao Qingju to join them. The servant he had sent to the Wens' reported back: "The young master had a son this morning, which is why he didn't come to see Master Bian off. He can't come to the party tomorrow, either, but he invites you to attend the Bathing of the Baby ceremony the day after that. Today he's going to go and bring the mistress back." Jishi sent someone over with presents. Among other developments, Feng Gang had been appointed commander and Qin Shuming counselor of the governor-general's brigade; Lü Youkui and Ho Wu were commissioned as majors in the Jieshi garrison; and the prefect of Jiayingzhou, Shr Buqi, had been named prefect of Guangzhou. As a result, Jishi was kept busy with congratulations and farewells for the next ten days or more, while looking forward to Ruyu's return.

Jiangshan and Huowu had settled on the eighth of the tenth month for the start of their long journey. Ruyu returned on the fourth, and after he had been to pay his respects to everyone, he arranged to travel together with the others in two large boats. Huowu and his wife, Mistress Qin, would travel in one boat, while Li Jiangshan and Ruyu would share the other. They packed up their belongings and said their farewells.

First came a party hosted by the governor-general and the governor, then one by the other high civil officials of the province, and finally one by military officials such as Colonel Ba. Soon the day of departure arrived. Jishi arranged with Chuncai to hire a large pleasure boat and invite some actors to perform. He told Su Bang and Su Wang to bring the kitchen staff and prepare a banquet on board, then go to Huatian and wait there. He himself would join the civil and military officials at their farewell parties. Because Governor Shen had come out of town in person to see them off, the other officials attended in particularly large numbers. Huowu and Jiangshan thanked them all individually. They first asked Governor Shen to return to his yamen, then begged all the other officials to get into their sedan chairs, and finally sounded the drum to set off. Jishi and Chuncai were on Li's and Bian's boat at the time.

Soon they arrived at Huatian, and the actors on the pleasure boat saw them coming from a long way off and beat their drums in welcome. The five men all transferred to the other boat, where Jishi handed them wine, and they went into the cabin and sat down. "General Yao, I wonder where you will have the honor of holding office once this journey is over," said Jishi. "I hope that, when it's convenient, you will favor us with a letter."

"I have received so much affection from you, and I've not repaid even a tiny part of it. If I do receive a position, you may be sure that I'll send a special messenger with the news."

"When you arrive in the capital," said Jishi to Jiangshan, "I expect you'll be sharing lodgings with my brother-in-law Bian Ruyu.

Even my brother-in-law Li Yuan is due there as soon as his leave is over. If my application to resign from my official post should not meet with imperial approval, I beg you to do what you can to help."

"Of course I will. If by some chance I find myself in an official position, I shall certainly resign myself when the time is right."

"Brother-in-Law, you are certain to succeed in the metropolitan examinations," Jishi said to Ruyu. "But after receiving an appointment, you must ask for leave to come south. Your father will be anxious to see you, to say nothing of my mother and sister."

"After I've taken the examination," said Ruyu, "whether I'm successful or not, I shall want to come home. And as for my parents, I hope you will look after them."

"Of course I will."

"Partings and reunions are a fact of life—they're all a matter of chance," said Jiangshan. "Why are you so reluctant to part with us, Jishi? Just think; when I started teaching here only four years ago, Heh Zhifu's arrogance and lechery were at their height and Governor Qu was displaying that cranky, stubborn streak of his, and both men fell afoul of the law. I hardly need mention Daiyun's villainy. And as for Chuncai's success in the examinations, what an extraordinary thing that was! Yinzhi, my son, and you—all three of you have achieved something notable in a short space of time. Also, quite unexpectedly, you met Brother Huowu and enjoyed a great triumph. As for me, all I've ever done in my life is sew garments for other people's weddings."

"If you and Master Su hadn't come to my rescue, I'd have had a worse fate than either Heh or Qu," said Huowu.

"Rise and fall in the world—they're both impossible to predict," said Jiangshan. "Four years ago we had no idea what the situation would be like today, just as we have no idea today what it will be like in four years' time. The truth is that many people can see the danger of the Four Temptations, but few of us can get beyond them. Heh Zhifu embraced all four, Governor Qu only wrath. Dai-yun and his father both craved wealth and sex. Brother Yao in the past couldn't help being overly aggressive and hot-headed, while I couldn't help befuddling my senses with too much wine. Jishi is the only one who is fond of wine but doesn't go wild over it; who delights in sex without being lewd; who has a great deal of wealth but doesn't hoard it; and who can take criticism without losing his temper and yet at the same time throw himself into the thick of the fight. Among the young his like is rarely to be found! His learning isn't outstanding, it's true, just his essential kindness. If he were also full of learning, he could almost equal the ancients."

That day they drank until afternoon, when they separated and went back to their own boats. Jishi was still reluctant to part, but Jiangshan laughed out loud. "Why do you have to be like this?" he asked. "Let's see what things are like in a few years' time." And with a wave of his arm, the boats set off.

Notes

Introduction

1. For a comparative study of polygamy and sexual expression in this novel, see Keith McMahon, *Misers, Shrews, and Polygamists* (Durham, N.C.: Duke University Press, 1995), 251–64.
2. East India Company Factory Records, preserved in the British Library. See under "Canton Diary" and "Canton Consultations" for the eighteenth and early nineteenth centuries.
3. See his memorial to the Jiaqing Emperor on the seventh day of the second month of 1799. *Qingdai mimi jieshe dang'an jiyin* 清代秘密結社檔案輯印 (Beijing: Zhongguo yanshi chubanshe, 1999), 6:2152–53.
4. Confronted by his nemesis, the governor Hutuli 瑚圖禮, who had been ordered to report on him, he seized a snuff bottle and thrust it down his throat. That is the official account. For a different, more sympathetic account, see Zhaolian 昭槤, *Xiao ting zalu* 嘯亭雜錄 (Beijing: Zhonghua shuju, 1980), *juan* 4, 110.
5. Militiamen (*xiangyong*) hired by landowners play a large part in other novels set in Guangdong at about this time. See particularly *Honglou fu meng* 紅樓復夢, the preface of which is dated 1799.
6. For example, the character Lü Youkui is of exactly the same type as Li Kui in *Shuihu zhuan*, and his name even echoes Li Kui's. Note that the novel adds another evil rebellion that is not related to contemporary history: Mola, a former member of the White Lotus Society, seizes control of the city of Chaozhou and holds it until he is beaten by Yao Huowu in command of government forces.
7. On the Huizhou rebellions, see Dian H. Murray, in collaboration with Qin Baoqi, *The Origins of the Tiandihui: The Chinese Triads in Legend and History* (Stanford, Calif.: Stanford University Press, 1994), 61–69.
8. See chapter 17.
9. See chapter 4 of the novel, in which the narrator refers to Mount Yu.
10. See Shi Rujie 石汝傑 and Miyata Ichiro 宮田一郎, *Ming Qing Wuyu cidian* 明清吳語詞典 (Shanghai: Shanghai cishu chubanshe, 2005), 838.

Chapter I

1. The reference is to Xi Shi.
2. The superintendent of Guangzhou customs was known to the foreign traders as the *hoppo*.
3. The so-called Consoo Fund, it was a collective insurance fund.
4. The text gives his childhood name as Xiaoguan, only later switching to Jishi.
5. Hu Guang was a Han dynasty official who was respectful and even ingratiating; people called his attitude the "doctrine of the mean."

Chapter II

1. That is, acting in a supporting role.
2. The *Xuanhe pai pu* by Chü You of the early Ming may be the manual referred to. This combination has five 5-dot dominoes and one 4-dot domino, making 29 dots altogether. The sentence is evidently to be taken in two senses: "Lusting after flowers [dots], you won't get to thirty" and "Lust after flowers [sex], and you won't live till thirty."
3. The second month of the third year of Jiajing equates to 1524.
4. Emperors sacrificed at this temple, and in times of national disaster rich men were sometimes permitted to buy official positions in return for their contributions.
5. Read *mu*, "admire," as *cuan*, "seize."

Chapter III

1. From the *Yi jing* (*Classic of Changes*).
2. Act IV, scene 3, in the edition by Jin Shengtan, the one she would presumably be reading. It describes the first lovemaking between Zhang and Yingying.
3. *The Story of Jiao and Hong* (*Jiao Hong zhuan*) was probably a version of the Yuan dynasty romantic tale *Jiao Hong ji*, the most famous version of which is the Ming play of that name by Meng Chengshun; *The Lantern Festival Destiny* is the *Deng yue yuan*, a Qing dynasty novel; *A Captivating Tale* is the *Zhaoyang qushi*, a late-Ming novel set in the Han; and *A Merry Tale* is the *Nongqing kuaishi*, a Qing novel.
4. This is a line from the scene of the play she has been reading.
5. Wu Gang was a Han dynasty figure who studied immortality. Sent to the moon to get cassia, he cut down the cassia tree.
6. Confucius, as quoted in the *Li ji* (*Record of Ritual*).

7. A reference to the "Tale of Immortals," which tells how two young men meet and fall in love with two divine maidens. See the *Taiping guangji*, 61.

Chapter IV

1. The text contains a reference to the extremely tall Cao Jiao. See *Mencius* 6B.2.2.
2. This is a lame pun between his name and the word *wenxi* ("revise").
3. A reference to Tao Qian's "Tao hua yuan ji." The people of the Peach-blossom Stream urge the visitor not to tell anyone else about the paradise he has just seen.
4. Tao Zhu (i.e., Fan Li) and Yi Dun: iconic rich men.
5. Ehuang and her sister both became consorts of Emperor Shun.
6. Yuewang tai, the supposed site of the palace of Zhao Tuo, king of Southern Yue (approximately 230–137 BCE).
7. Presumably a reference to the paintings of the Guangzhou harbor made in the Western style for export, perhaps specifically to the work of Shi Beilin (known to the Westerners as Spoilum), who was active in Canton from 1774 to 1805. If so, it would show the closeness of the author to the China trade.
8. Zhao Tuo served the Qin emperor in Longchuan in Guangdong, which later became his own base of operations.
9. When he declared himself independent, the Five Mountains area was the extent of his kingdom.
10. Originally a Qin dynasty general, Ren Xiao became Zhao Tuo's strategist.
11. Lu Jia was sent by the Han emperor to persuade Zhao Tuo to accept a subordinate role in the Han empire.
12. Emperor Wen of the Han, trying to change the open hostility that had grown up under the influence of the Empress Lü, repaired the ancestral tombs that she had ordered destroyed.
13. The state of Changsha, with encouragement from the Han under the empress, had been at war with Southern Yue.
14. Lü Jia (d. 110 BCE), a longtime supporter of the Zhao house, finally led an abortive revolt against the Han.
15. The numbers of the songs in the Mao edition of the *Poetry Classic* in which the lines appear are as follows: 47, 161, 196, 52.
16. 1.
17. 152, 2, 164.

18. 6, 234, 224, 113, 164.
19. *Di*, "younger brother," is in the falling tone. When used verbally, meaning to show respect to an elder brother, it is pronounced *ti*, in the rising tone.
20. 159.
21. 265.
22. It means "Alas, alack!" It is a response to tragedy, especially death.
23. 76, 280, 241, 55.
24. This is not a line from the *Poetry Classic*, but four consecutive words occurring in *Mencius* and in the *Great Learning*. *Shi yun* means "as the *Poetry Classic* says."
25. I have not attempted to rhyme the translated versions.
26. An early form of the "wooden fish," a kind of drum beaten by monks or nuns as they chanted.
27. Wu Gang was a Han dynasty figure who was sent to get the cassia tree from the moon. The story signifies success in the examinations.
28. A cliché derived from the *Analects* 9.23.

Chapter V

1. "Riding the dragon" with "fiancé" forms a phrase meaning a fine son-in-law or fiancé. Here, of course, it has additional meaning.
2. The brother of Chen Tuan, a Daoist master who could sleep for long periods.
3. Attributed first to Ban Chao, the Han dynasty strategist and diplomat.
4. The cliché: "Nice as the Liang Garden is, it's no place to dwell."
5. It is a variation on a common metaphor in Chinese fiction for male sexual inadequacy.
6. *Analects*, 2.8.

Chapter VI

1. Zhong Zi famously vomited up the goose flesh he had eaten. See *Mencius*, 3B.10.
2. Emperor Wu of the Jin dynasty was in the habit of riding around his palace in a cart drawn by a goat, and wherever the goat chose to stop, the emperor would spend the night. Accordingly, the emperor's women spread salt on the ground to attract the animal to their quarters. See the *Jin History*, 31.
3. *Analects*, 16.7. In their youth, men are enjoined to guard against lust.

The other two prohibitions are of bellicosity and acquisitiveness.

4. The allusions are to Wu Zixu (see his biography in the *Shi ji*) and to the silk gown that Xu Jia gave Fan Sui (who was only pretending to be poor).
5. Zhongtang Township is a unit of Dongguan county, east of Guangzhou.
6. A reference to the story of the Han dynasty governor Zhang Chang, who painted his wife's eyebrows.

Chapter VII

1. When the state of Chen was about to fall in the sixth century, Princess Lechang and her husband, knowing that they would be forced to part, broke a mirror and each of them kept half of it. They planned to meet again at the Lantern Festival.
2. See the Tang dynasty tale of "Kunlun nu" and "Wushuang zhuan." Each man rescues a girl from a powerful figure and restores her to her lover.
3. See note 2 above.
4. A reference to the romantic encounter described in the "Gaotang Rhapsody."
5. The first edition says *Shanwei*, which is corrupted to "*Youwei*" in later editions.
6. His original name is used from this point on.

Chapter VIII

1. She was the sister of Wen Zhongweng's wife.
2. This clearly reflects the downfall of Heshen, the corrupt and tyrannical favorite of the Qianlong emperor. In 1799, only three or four years before the composition of this novel, the Qianlong emperor died, and the Jiaqing emperor promptly purged Heshen, permitting him to commit suicide.
3. Cf. *Analects*, 2.20.
4. From the *Shu Jing* (*Classic of Documents*).
5. From the *Analects*, 11.26.
6. The reference is to the Qing dynasty novel *Hou Xiyou ji* (*Sequel to the Journey to the West*), chapter 13, in which the Pilgrim fights the Dame. Here it is used to mean that Huiruo outlasted Jishi.

Chapter IX

1. The reference is to the scene in chapter 4 of the novel *Shuihu zhuan*, in which Lu Zhishen, in a monk's garb, beats on the temple gate to be let in.
2. The source of this image has not been identified.

Chapter X

1 Qian is heroine of the early southern play *Jingchai ji* (*The Thorn Hairpin*). She attempts to drown herself when under pressure to take another husband.
2 The author has conflated the stories of two women: Cao E, who threw herself into the river after keening for her drowned father, and the wife of Cao Wenshu, who deliberately disfigured herself when pressed to remarry.

Chapter XI

1. Niu, the surname of the official whom Ho Wu kills, also means an ox.
2. Number 165 in the Mao version.
3. *Yi jing*, hexagram 13.
4. Guan Zhong and Bao Shuya, a famous pair of friends, were ministers of Qi in Warring States times. When Guan was young and poor, Bao shared his money with him. The point here is that sharing one's money with a friend is trivial in comparison to laying down your life for him.

Chapter XII

1. Asking about a prisoner's illness was a coded message from the official to the jailers to murder the prisoner during the night and attribute his death to illness.
2. The expression comes from an old joke involving the poet Su Shi and his verbal sparring partner, the priest Fo Yin. The line, which is quite innocuous in the joke, is delivered by Su Shi's sister at Fo Yin's expense. The author plays on the expression to mean that Yerong's vaginal fluid moistened the head of the abbot's penis and so spared her pain.
3. "Bald head" is a derogatory term for a Buddhist priest; it also refers to the glans penis.

Chapter XIII

1. Much of this language is from the relevant parts of the *Yi jing*. See Richard John Lynn, trans., *The Classic of Changes: A New Translation of the* I Ching *as Interpreted by Wang Bi* (New York: Columbia University Press, 1994), 179.
2. The text has "months" rather than "days."
3. Qiu Fu imprudently led an army into Mongolia, where it was annihilated.
4. See his biography in the *Shi ji* (*Records of the Grand Historian*).

Chapter XIV

1. The text, which has previously referred to the hero as Su Xiaoguan, explains that from this point on he will be referred to as Su Jishi (Jishi is his style).
2. A common term in jokes. It usually means people concerned mainly with the superficial aspects of life rather than with things of substance.
3. She kissed the two men at once. The character is composed of three mouths.
4. The character shows a woman between two men.
5. The character can mean to be in the middle of two objects or forces.
6. The reference is to the *Poetry Classic* (Mao 87). A woman is calling to her lover to lift up his gown and wade across the river to join her. The translation is based on Arthur Waley, trans., *The Book of Songs* (New York: Grove Press, 1960), no. 39.

Chapter XV

1. Wankui's daughter is engaged to Jiangshan's son.
2. By the poet Su Shi, in one of two poems entitled "Song Shu ren Zhang Shihou fu dian shi."
3. *Poetry Classic* (Mao 23). Cf. Waley, *Book of Songs*, no. 63.
4. "Shujishi" was a rank in the Hanlin Academy that is usually translated as "bachelor."
5. From one of Zhu Xi's (1130–1200) poems entitled "Chun ri" ("A Spring Day").
6. The most famous seduction plot in Chinese history. (Fan Li used Xi Shi's beauty to ensnare the King of Wu.)
7. A common expression based on an early fable about a clam that was locked in a struggle with a snipe. An old fisherman who was passing by nabbed both of them.

Chapter XVI

1. Recognized as a heroic act of filial piety.
2. The expression comes originally from Sikong Tu's *Shi pin*, section 11 ("Implication").
3. The references are to the *Lizhi pu* (*A Guide to Lichees*) by Cai Xiang of the Song dynasty and *Lizhi tu xu* (*A Preface to Lychee Painting*) by Bai Juyi of the Tang dynasty.
4. Perhaps the seventeenth-century play *Changsheng dian*.
5. A type of lichee, as are the terms in the previous line.
6. From *Analects*, 20.2.
7. *Classic of Changes*, hexagram 2.
8. The so-called superficial scholarship is actually the earliest.
9. That is, the Mao preface, which does refer to this poem.
10. This argument, and much of the wording, comes originally from the Southern Song scholar Zhang Ruyu's *Shan tang kao suo*.
11. Mao 4. The translations here and below are those of Arthur Waley, *The Book of Songs*.
12. Mao 8.
13. Mao 106.
14. Mao 40.
15. Mao 48.
16. Writing a note or letter to officers indicates influence peddling.

Chapter XVII

1. A kind of drum beaten by monks and nuns as they chant the scriptures.
2. A quotation from the *Poetry Classic* (Mao 45).
3. A cliché to the effect that beauty is a curse.
4. A reference to the wife of Dou Xuan of the Later Han dynasty. The emperor married Dou to a princess, even though he was already married. His first wife, who wrote a poetic plaint to her husband, became a standard reference for an abandoned wife.
5. Part of a Buddhist exhortation: "The bitter sea is without limit, but turn your head (i.e., repent), and the shore is at hand."
6. On the analogy of the vulgar Wu dialect expression *yao luan*, "bite... balls," it presumably means "you have made me furious, you have got me mad."
7. This second line is incomprehensible, to the translator at least.

8 A service for the souls of the dead, but here it evidently refers to different sexual configurations.
9 Combining farming with study was a kind of rustic ideal for some Confucians.
10 Consisting merely of seats on a flat surface.
11 The plum is described as from Dayuling, a mountain on the border between Guangdong and Jiangxi. It was a favorite poetic reference, because the plum trees on different sides of the mountain blossomed at different times.

Chapter XVIII

1. The reference is to Han Xin; see his biography in the *Shi ji*.
2. Three kneelings, each of which involved three kowtows, were customary on receipt of orders from the emperor.
3. Ruyi was originally a Buddhist symbol.
4. Presumably by going to the magistrate's residence first rather than to see Jishi.
5. Silk flowers made in the palace.

Chapter XIX

1. That is, borrowing something from one person and giving it to another.
2. Associated, in fiction at least, with the sybaritic emperor Yangdi of the Sui dynasty.
3. "Die" meaning to have an orgasm.
4. *Mencius*, 5A.2. Cf. D. C. Lau, trans., *Mencius* (London: Penguin, 1970), 140.
5. The reference is to Liu Yuxi's (772–842) poems on visiting the Xuandu Temple in the capital. On his second stay in the capital, he noticed the peach trees that a priest had planted, and then ten years later he found that the trees had gone. The reference to Pingyang is to a poem by another Tang poet, Wang Changling, on the lonely plight of a Han princess. Oddly enough, both Liu's and Wang's poems are held to be satires about political conditions and only superficially about peach blossom.
6. The *Shi lei fu* (*Classified Allusions in the Form of Rhapsodies*) was compiled by Wu Shu (947–1002). Chuncai is actually referring to the expanded version, *Guang Shi lei fu*, of the early Qing dynasty; see *juan* 30.

7. Spring floods.
8. In fact it is not in the *Thousand Poems*.

Chapter XX

1. The small Sima scales were used for weighing silver, etc.
2. Traditional gifts of wine, etc. The stomacher, by contrast, is an intimate, personal gift.
3. In the famous Tang dynasty tale *Qiuran ke zhuan*, the red whisk girl elopes with Li Jing from the household of the powerful minister Yang Su.
4. See D. C. Lau, trans., *The Analects of Confucius* (London: Penguin, 1979), 155.
5. "He went out and vomited it all up." See Lau, *Mencius*, 116.
6. "[W]hile the 'Xiao pan' deals with a major wrong." See Lau, *Mencius*, 173.
7. From *Mencius*, 7A. 26. See Lau, *Mencius*, 188.
8. All four examples come from poem 58 in the Mao version.
9. *Mudan ting* (*The Peony Pavilion*), scene 50.
10. *Pipa ji* (*The Lute*), scene 10.
11. See the novel *Xiyou ji* (*Journey to the West*), chapter 61.

Chapter XXI

1. *Shu jing*, "Lü xing." This text makes frequent use of phrases from the *Shu jing*.
2. Yelang was a small kingdom whose ruler believed it to be great. See *Shi ji*, 116.
3. A special kind of bamboo, suitable for canes. See *Shi ji*, 123.
4. Probably a reference to the "Revolt of the Seven States" in the Han dynasty. The king of Qi hesitated, did not join the revolt, but killed himself. See *Shi ji*, 101.
5. This refers to the Minyue state, of which the king declared himself emperor. It was destroyed by Wudi in 110 BCE.
6. Yang Yao (1108–33) rebelled at the beginning of the Southern Song. After many unsuccessful attempts to suppress his insurrection, it finally crumbled.
7. Zhigao, a leader of the Zhuang people, set up own kingdom and in 1052 attacked the Song. He took Yongzhou in 1053, but was eventually beaten.
8. From *Shu jing*, "Da Yu mo."

9. From the *Poetry Classic*, Mao 241, in Waley's translation.
10. From *Shu jing*, "Qin shi."
11. In 228 Zhuge Liang's vanguard general Ma Su was defeated by the Wei general at the key location of Jieting.
12. From *Mencius*, 1B.11. Cf. Lau, *Mencius*, 69: "The people longed for his coming as they longed for a rainbow in a time of severe drought."
13 From *Shu jing*, "Tang shi."
14 *Bing fa* (*The Art of War*), chapter 4.
15 Zhang Xu (422–89) was noted for his good looks.
16 Zhong Jun as a young man was a strategist for Han Wudi.
17 Chisong Zi (The Master of Red Pine) was a legendary Daoist immortal.
18 A saying attributed to Ban Chao, the Han dynasty strategist and diplomat.
19 A reference to Pan Yue, who was so handsome that admiring women threw fruit at him as he passed.
20 The decree is derived from Yuan Mei's (1716–98) application in 1739 to the emperor for leave to marry. Here it has been turned around so as to come from the emperor. Much of the florid language is kept. For Yuan Mei's application, see his "Ni qi jia gui qu biao" in *Xiaocangshan waiji*, 1, in *Yuan Mei quanji* (Nanjing: Jiangsu guji chubanshe, 1993), vol. 2.
21 That is, he is turning twenty.
22 The scattering of coins in the bedchamber was a traditional part of the wedding ceremony.
23 Traditionally, the prospective son-in-law presented a goose to the bride's parents.
24 A reference to the bride's tribulations.

Chapter XXII

1. The reference is to the *Xiyou ji*, chapter 59.
2. *Huan bing* in the text is probably a mistake for *huan ji*.
3. These are magical techniques practiced by Daoist adepts using the "Five Elements" (metal, wood, water, fire, and earth).

Chapter XXIII

1. "Cross-legged" refers to the sitting posture adopted by Buddhist priests as they willed their own deaths.

2. A major figure in the Three Kingdoms saga.
3. From the *Poetry Classic* (Mao 186).
4. A reference to the reign of the sage kings.
5. Aqueous signifies honors and prosperity.
6. The frontal aspect is one of the 135 positions on the face according to physiog-nomy.
7. A jade belt was worn by high officials.
8. A famous statesman and strategist of the beginning of the Zhou dynasty who lived to a great age.
9. The spot between the eyebrows.

Chapter XXIV

1. The rice mentioned here was for use in winemaking.
2. A kind of chess named after an incident in the Three Kingdoms saga. See *San guo zhi tongsu yanyi*, chapter 5.
3. *Mencius*, 3B.3.6.
4. *Poetry Classic* (Mao 154; the translation is that of Waley, no. 159).
5. From the biography of Wu Zixu in the *Shi ji*.
6. *The West Chamber* (Jin Shengtan version), part 4, act 3.
7. In this and the succeeding answers, the first element is a tune title, and the second is a phrase from the *Thousand Character Text* (*Qian zi wen*).
8. The line is correctly quoted, but it is slanderous as applied to Belle and her husband. (Mencius is describing the behavior of immoral young people.)
9. *Mencius*, 4B.3.
10. *Poetry Classic* (Mao 61, in Waley's translation, no. 44.)
11. Source unidentified.
12. *West Chamber*, part 4, act 3.
13. *Doctrine of the Mean*, 12.
14. *Poetry Classic* (Mao 48, in Waley's translation, no. 23).
15. *Zuo zhuan*, Duke Zhuang, 10th year (slightly misquoted)
16. *West Chamber*, part 2, act 3.
17. *Mencius*, 3B.2.
18. *Poetry Classic* (Mao 261, in Waley's translation, no. 144).
19. Tao Qian, "Tao hua yuan ji."
20. *West Chamber*, part 4, act 3.
21. *Mencius*, 2B.3.
22. *Poetry Classic* (Mao 2, in Waley's translation, no. 112).

23. Tao Qian, "Gui qu lai ci."
24. *West Chamber*, part 4, act 2.
25. Legend has it that there is a cassia tree on the moon. Successful examination candidates are said to snatch a twig from the tree. The first line here sets the rhyme, which is followed by all the even-numbered lines. I have not tried to make the English rhyme.
26. Feng loved his wife so deeply that when she ran a fever he went outside until he was freezing, then came back and embraced her, thus bringing down her temperature.
27. Wang Kui was a classic ingrate. A village prostitute, Gui Ying, believed in him and encouraged him to persevere with his studies, and he swore an oath that he would be loyal to her. After taking first place in the next examination, he decided that it would not help his career to be allied with a prostitute and married someone else. Gui Ying then killed herself, and Wang Kui died soon after.
28. A reference to Zhang Chang, who painted his wife's eyebrows.
29. Meng Guang of the Han dynasty raised her tray to the level of her eyebrows to show her respect for her husband, Liang Hong.
30. Baili Xi had to leave home for lack of prospects. On the evening before he left, his wife cooked him a dinner, but there was no food in the house except a laying hen, which she killed for his farewell dinner. Later, he became a high official in the state of Qin, and she went there as a washerwoman and shamed him into taking her back as his wife.
31. Probably a reference to the *Poetry Classic* (Mao 82), an aubade in which the woman rouses the man and sends him forth to shoot a wild goose, promising him a lifetime together.
32. The reference is to a famous short poem by Wang Jian of the Tang dynasty. On the third day after arriving in her new household, the new bride had to go to the kitchen and cook the broth for her mother-in-law. It was an ordeal for her, since she did not know her mother-in-law's tastes.
33. The *Poetry Classic* (Mao 261) contains the line, in Waley's translation, "Very pleasant the land of Han" (see no. 144). A father is sending his daughter away to be married.
34. In expectation.